WHEN
ROCKS
DANCE

WHEN
ROCKS
DANCE

Elizabeth Nunez-Harrell

ONE WORLD

BALLANTINE BOOKS

New York

A One World Book
Published by Ballantine Books

This edition published by arrangement with G. P. Putnam's Sons, a division of
the Putnam Publishing Group, Inc.
Library of Congress Catalog Card Number: 92-73018

ISBN: 0-345-38068-1

Cover design by Kristine V. Mills
Cover painting by Paul Goodnight
Text design by Mary A. Wirth

Manufactured in the United States of America

First Ballantine Books Trade Edition: November 1992
10 9 8 7 6 5 4 3 2 1

For my grandparents,
Georgiana and Albert Nunez,
Florence and Charles Arneaud.

We need our own myths and legends to regain our lost self esteem, our regard for each other as a people capable of working together to move the mountains that stand before us.

—JOHN OLIVER KILLENS
Black Man's Burden

AFTER THE RAINY SEASON

1

The Hurricanes had long come and gone, and the land grew dry again. High up in the Central Mountain Range in Trinidad, the poui trees began to shed their leaves like the giant deciduous trees in the cold lands of Europe and North America. Yet there would be no winter here in the burning heat of the tropical sun. Life stirred restlessly at the tips of the naked branches of the poui. December, and already the pale outlines of buds, some orange, some yellow, some red, could easily be detected. By February the poui would set the hills on fire with their flaming colors. From the valleys, softly climbing between majestic immortelle and tonka bean trees, cocoa trees, the lifeblood of Trinidad, gently dropped their delicate white flowers to make room for the purple cocoa pods that would soon hang from the sides of their trunks. The earth smelled good—of worms turning the soil fresh as they delved deep to escape the blistering sun.

Emilia, sitting outside of Hrothgar's house, took no notice of the earth smells. Her mind was elsewhere, though her eyes anchored themselves to the cocoa trees. Slowly, she raised her hands from her thighs and, hesitating for a brief second, finally rested her fingers on her swollen stomach. Inch by inch, not removing her eyes from the cocoa, she let her fingers move tentatively, searching the sides of her belly, until she stopped them, froze them still, when she felt, as she hoped she would not, the firm roundness of two tiny heads pressing against her flesh. She sucked in her breath and looked away from the cocoa. Her eyes turned watery and the skin beneath them trembled and grew jet black. "Twins," she moaned. "Always twins." Her grief rose like the thick black smoke of a smothered fire and clouded the brilliant day. Emilia knew that it was time for her to see Taro, for she had already spoken to the Warao.

For eight years, at intervals of two years apart, she had watched her belly rise slowly like yeast-filled dough, its surface growing rounder and rounder, smoother and smoother, and then stretching paper-thin, inflated by an insatiable energy beneath it that cracked her skin along its dry spots, drawing white long creases where the moisture was sucked into the hungry swelling. Finally, at the end of nine months within each of these intervals of two years, her belly fell suddenly, collapsing like under-baked bread, spitting out the center soft and harmless, still and lifeless. Not just one son, but two boys who fought to free themselves from the umbilical cord wrapped around their necks, twisting their bloodied bodies in rage, their faces distorted, their wrinkled fists clenched, their blind eyes rolling in their dull sockets until the midwife released them and they lay stiff and cold and blue in their mother's arms.

The third pregnancy was more painful, and Hrothgar, her English lover, pitying her at last called in his English doctor. Emilia did not protest though she knew that the doctor could not help her. But then hope still dimmed the truth and made the illusion more real. She desperately wanted a child. Yet, once again, in spite of the doctor, she gave birth to twin boys who strangled themselves, or as the malicious whispered, whom she strangled to death with her cord. Now, the fourth time that her belly rose, she accepted the truth. Feeling the heads of her twins, she was certain that this pregnancy, like the others, would be futile.

When Hrothgar returned home from the cocoa estate that evening, he found her lying outstretched in his bed, staring vacantly at the ceiling. He did not ask her. He simply said, "Twins again," and laid his aging white body next to hers.

She knew that he had grown tired of her constant illness, but also that he would not ask her to leave. There were few English women on the island, none who would look at him. And he was obsessed with her body. Yet she lied. "No. One child," she told him.

"This'd better be the last time," he said gruffly.

She shut her eyes and shifted her body to the edge of the bed. After her mother died, she stayed with him because she had nowhere else to go. She was only ten years old then, and her mother had been his cook. He did not touch her until two months after her twelfth birthday, and then he promised if she would bear him a son, old man that he was, he would will his cocoa estate and his house to her upon his death. She was not too young to know that at sixty he would not have long to live. That promise made her endure long nights of his body pressing roughly into hers. Was that why she was punished with dead babies? She had wanted no more nor less than every Trinidadian woman—a home that was hers, land she could pass on to her sons and to generations thereafter. What right had Hrothgar to the land? He and his people had crossed the seas and claimed it from her people as though God had given them right. No, she stayed in Hrothgar's bed to reclaim that land. And then . . . and then the babies began to die. The first time she accepted it. It could happen to anyone. She was not specially marked. And the second time, she grieved for the loss of them and she began to love them as if they had lived. She would make others to replace them, she said, consoling herself. The third time she was more determined, for then she knew that they also wanted to live, that they fought against the strangling grip of the umbilical cord, accusing her with their anger. Then the land ceased to matter to her: She wanted her babies. She'd keep having them and having them until she could birth them alive or her womb could no longer hold them. She was not prepared to feel the despair she now felt, when she knew that all her babies would die if the Ibo would not help her.

She waited for the time Hrothgar would go to Port-of-Spain to sell his cocoa. It would be soon, she knew, and when he left three days later, she was certain it would be at least a week before he would return. For she too had heard the talk about things going bad between the Portuguese traders and the English planters, ever since the Portuguese found out the English thirst for chocolate. And when the dust from Hrothgar's horse finally settled back into the dirt trail that led from his house to the main road, Emilia did what she should have done years ago. She went to see the Ibo, Taro, the most powerful obeahman on the island.

The Ibo had sent for her many times before, but always she had closed her ears to his messages. This time fear made her drag her heavy body up the hill to his shiny tin hut.

When he saw her after her torturous climb, the African shut his eyes. Her hair was all matted with sweat. She had lost her face with the swelling, and her once pretty mouth sucked at the air like an old donkey, her lips trembling. With his eyes squeezed together in a frown, the old obeahman screamed at her to leave his place.

"Shoo! Get away! Go. Leave here I say. Shoo!"

But Emilia had reached his front door, and weak from exhaustion, her body collapsed onto one of his goatskin stools. The old Ibo danced around her with his knotted cane, still shouting. Closing his eyes. He did not want to see her again. "Get out I say. Shoo! Shoo!"

Her breathing still tortured and difficult, Emilia tugged at the cloth wrapped around his waist and dug her nails into his withered body. The old man's eyes shot open in pain and Emilia pulled him to her. With her eyes.

"Why didn't you come before?" The Ibo softened. He stopped dancing.

"Hrothgar . . ." She said the name of her English lover, slowly and softly. "He didn't—"

"You forget who you are." The Ibo would not let her finish.

"But the pain, Taro."

"You forget who you are!" the Ibo shouted, anger blazing from his eyes.

"The pain."

"You forget who you are." The Ibo lowered his voice to a harsh whisper.

"I came from Africa."

The Ibo put down his knotted cane and pulled a stool next to her. "Those two in your belly, they will die like the rest." His voice was toneless and flat. Final. "I can't help you now." He sat down.

"Please, Taro. The pain."

"Then stop it."

"Stop?"

"Stop making them. Stop the babies."

Emilia wiped the sweat off her top lip. The babies groaned in her belly and shifted their weight to her left side, contorting her body. The protrusion, momentarily throwing her off balance, made her look sadly comical. Defenseless. The Ibo leaned over and touched her where her navel was lying flat on the other side of her belly. Emilia cooled her hot face in his pity.

"Why Taro? Why me?"

The villagers in Princes Town say that Taro was one hundred and twenty years old then. He knew everything. As a young man, the son of an Ibo chief from Enugu in the eastern region of Nigeria taking instruction in Christianity from a white missionary on his father's insistence, he was betrayed into slavery and brought to Trinidad. And he remembered it all. Africa and freedom, slavery and colonialism.

"You lucky, woman," he said finally, bitterly as though regretting a moment of weakness. "You lucky you still living."

Emilia rested her head against the Ibo's polished tin wall, her eyes wandering across the ebony wood carvings that stood on a table in a corner of the room until they settled on a carving of a woman, her face serene, her legs bent at the knees, her arms drawn to her back, her body poised for flight. Quietly, as though speaking only to herself, she murmured, "I want children."

"You lie!"

"God owes me children. A woman must have children."

"You lie! Cocoa! Land! That's what you want."

Emilia hung her head. "Once before. No more."

"The gods owe you nothing. You sleep with that white man for land."

"Long ago. Not now. I sleep with him for children."

The Ibo snorted.

Emilia grasped his arm and brought her face close to his. "Help me Taro," she whispered. "Please help me. I can't take the pain no more. This time it's worse than ever before. I can't sleep. I can't work. It's their fingers. They claw at me and scratch me. I can feel their feet kicking, kicking. They know they going to die and they want to kill me first. I know it. And it's their brothers that died who are helping them. Stop them, Taro. You can help me."

"Too late." The Ibo pushed her away and crossed his arms. "You wait too late to see me."

"The Warahoon," began Emilia, pronouncing the last syllable of the name of the South American Indian tribe as though it rhymed with "moon."

"The Warahoon?" The old man's face wrinkled into a frown.

"Yes, I asked the Warahoon," replied Emilia, not denying her desperation when one market day she spoke to the Warao Indian chief who, it was rumored, was the only friend of a strange Portuguese—Vasco de Balboa, he was called—a white man who combed the beaches of Moruga like a stray dog defeated by vermin and disease. An educated man, they said he was, who once treated his son, Antonio de Balboa, like an outcast, a bastard spawned by accident from the womb of his black wife.

"He pitied me."

"Pitied you?" The Ibo wanted to laugh, but the frown etched on his face was too deep to alter.

"He said that the spirits of my dead babies want a resting

place." Emilia continued intensely. "He said that I must give birth to a live child so that they can live in that child. If I don't, they will torment me."

The Ibo grunted and Emilia grasped the corner of his robe, forcing him to look at her. "Help me, Taro. I beg you, help me."

Perhaps because he felt challenged by the Warao, perhaps because he felt pity for Emilia, the old man decided to help her.

"Take off your clothes," he commanded. "Do as I say."

Emilia felt no fear in the sudden terror of his voice. She felt no anxiety. Her soul responded to a comforting familiarity in the voice's awesomeness, a protective security in its forcefulness. Like a child, she obeyed. Like a child, she was grateful that he had found her at last. Like a child, she was glad that he would take her back to the point from which she had strayed.

She stripped her clothes off her swollen body with no restraint for a lost privacy. She exposed her heavy breasts, her bulging belly, the hairy triangle above her thighs with the swift impersonal detachment with which she had plucked feathers from dead chickens or had gutted the bowels of fish. She would expose herself. She would be ready for the Ibo to save her.

The Ibo did not look at her body. His eyes became glassy and they fastened themselves to her spirit. His hand reached for her elbow as he guided her, naked as she was, to a place behind his tin hut where a smaller tin shed stood hidden among the trees. Inside, he made her sit on a wooden stool next to a heavy metal tub full of leaves soaking in icy-cold rainwater. Then he undressed and slowly he began to cleanse himself. He was no longer an old man. A strange youthfulness now possessed his body.

They did not speak, and still the Ibo did not look at her. Emilia felt herself become a little girl again. She was watching the high priest cleanse himself while her dying mother stood at the doorway flushed with pride that her little daughter, her only child, was becoming a woman in the ways of her people. And when the Ibo touched Emilia to cleanse her too, she saw again her mother's joy as she remembered it was then, when she was only nine years old, and an Ibo priest in spite of slavery, in spite of the Christian God his master had forced him to worship in his church, had performed his rites, as her mother had asked him to do, and made her a woman that day.

After the Ibo bathed Emilia with the same icy rainwater with which he had cleansed himself, and after he rubbed her body with the sacred leaves he had blessed on the holy days of his gods, and after he anointed her nipples and her navel with his holy oils, he put on his robe and left her sitting there naked in the shed and went to his tin hut to pray. When he returned five hours later, he brought her clothes with him and helped her cover her trembling body, ashy and wrinkled from exposure.

The Ibo became himself again, and now he stood over her looking into her eyes, an old man.

"In my home where I come from," he began, pulling his robe across his right shoulder and holding his cane away from his body, "and where you came from, twins are a bad thing." He paused and his eyes gazed outside at the blue sky as though seeking affirmation from an invisible authority. When he looked again at Emilia, his head was held high like a king who had vanquished his enemies.

Emilia saw for the first time that the knots on his cane were really tiny carvings of men and women caught in various moments of activity: a carpenter, his hammer flung over his head; a jeweler, his fingers concentrated with exact precision on a gem beneath them; a weaver, her hands busy with the threads on her loom; a cloth dyer, a hunter, a farmer, a griot, a teacher, a singer, a judge, a warrior, and so on, and on, they descended his cane, the people he knew in Africa.

"A woman who has twins," the Ibo continued, "is *osu.* Outcast. In my clan, her children are left in the forest to die. Or to live, if their spirit is great. But the gods were kind to you. They let your children die. You are blessed. Your *chi* has smiled. I have prayed for you. But I can't help you now. You know in your body you carry twins again." The Ibo waited for Emilia to feel fear and despair. He watched her while the trembling began at the corners of her mouth, and before she could part her lips, he stopped her. "They won't die. The gods won't kill them. They want to test you. You have forgotten the old ways. You don't come to worship here. Your mother, she was loyal. She never forgot Africa. She brought you here when you was a child. She see you become a woman in the ways of our people. But you spit us out. Obeah no good for you no more. That, that is why trouble follow you. That is why you make twins. You spit us out! But you get a chance now." The Ibo watched her closely. "The Warao tells the truth. The spirits of your children will haunt you. But this time, if you prove yourself, you will have a new life. This time your sons will live, but two weeks after they are born you must do as your fathers before you did. Leave your twins in the forest at the mercy of our gods. At the mercy of their divine wisdom. Do that and you will conceive again. One child. You will have one child and in that child the spirits of all your children will live. They will find a resting place. Do that and don't forget the power that has helped you."

It happened as the Ibo said it would. One month later, Emilia gave birth to two boys. They were handsome babies, not pale and white like Hrothgar, but dark-skinned like herself, yet they had their father's straight hair and narrow nose bridge. Hrothgar was delighted and he boasted of the skill of his English doctor. He even said then that he was glad that the boys were black because they would be able to endure, better than he, the hot tropical climate to which he had exiled himself. He called them his cocoa planters. He made them his overseers. Emilia had done what no woman had ever been able to do for him. She had produced sons for him. In a burst of enthusiasm, Hrothgar penned his will, fulfilling his promise to Emilia. The boys would be his heirs. They would send the "Portogee" trader to the devil and make the Negroes till the soil.

So proud was Hrothgar of his accomplishment and his future achievements that he did not notice then that Emilia never cuddled nor kissed those babies doomed to death, nor that she refused to feed them. For those boys no longer belonged to her, and at night she could hear their brothers calling them, wailing for their death.

When the babies were two weeks old, Hrothgar visited the local chaplain, Father de Nieves, and persuaded him to baptize the children on the following weekend. The evening before the christening, Emilia dressed her sons for the first time. She told Hrothgar that she wanted to take them to her friends for their blessing before they went to the church the next day. Hrothgar refused at first, sensing that Emilia meant the obeahman, but then cowed by a sudden transformation in her, he became silent. Her face turned to stone, her eyes glazed with a determination that would brook no contradiction. Her softness vanished. She pushed past him, picking up her sons in her arms, and before he could call out to her, she disappeared into the neighboring forest.

That night Hrothgar waited for Emilia in the darkness of his room. He didn't hear her when she entered the door, and before his eyes caught the outline of her shape, she was already bending over him, kissing his forehead. He didn't feel her hand either as it slid under his pillow, but when the tiny pouch she had brought with her reached beneath his head, a hot burning sensation flowed through his body and he pulled her down on the bed toward him. In that tiny fraction of a second before his sperm entered her, he asked, "Where are my sons?"

"Sleeping," she said. "Sleeping with their brothers in the cocoa."

Afterward, Hrothgar hated her.

Nine months later when Emilia felt the head of her child drop toward the opening of her uterus, she went to the cocoa estate that Hrothgar had promised to his twin sons. There, under the dangling purple cocoa pods, she scooped out the rich, dark earth and made a shallow, soft basin beneath her. Spreading her legs across it, she placed her hands on her knees and, stooping low, she pushed her daughter safely out of her womb. And the earth cradled Marina.

2

Marina sat on the floor in the kitchen, her knees wide apart, her feet crossed at her ankles, her tiny hands tucked under her bare thighs. Positioned this way, she rocked herself slowly, back and forth, back and forth. Wisps of her curly light brown hair straggled into her face and clung to the corners of her mouth and on her smooth forehead just above her eyebrows where the thin layer of moisture that gathered all over her body was densest. One would have thought she would be uncomfortable, that she would want to push her hair off her face, but the little girl just sat there, rocking herself, back and forth, her mouth puckered into a childish pout, her eyes fixed in a vacant stare. She seemed only barely aware of her surroundings, as though her spirit had been transported elsewhere, leaving only the shell of her body responding mechanically to some hidden force. Yet the little girl was totally present in that kitchen, seeing and hearing distinctly every movement, each sound around her. The thin string of red ants, for instance, that began once more to scratch their way up the kitchen wall, their tiny legs moving feverishly to the eternal rhythm that urged them on to work even after her mother had just swept their home clean away with her cocoyea broom. And she heard her mother the first time that she called her name, her voice edged with tension and frustration.

"Marina!" Emilia shouted a third time. But the little girl continued to stare at nothing, her eyes seeing everything.

"Stop that Marina! Stop it! You make me nervous. And get off the floor and pull your dress down. I can see way up to your bloomers. Marina!" Her mother called again, "Marina, listen to me!"

The little girl could see her mother standing near the large wooden crate on the floor, one hand on her hip, the other suspending a saucepan in the air as though ready to fling it across the room. But she heard too the slight cracks and tremors in her mother's voice and her instinct told her instantly that the words carried no threats. Marina thus merely shifted her eyes downward across the floor when her mother spoke, but she did not stop rocking nor did she cover her bloomers. Her skirt remained where it was, rolled up over her slightly tanned thighs. She heard her mother sigh deeply and she tried to be unconcerned, but the stream of air that rushed out suddenly from her mother's collapsing lungs frightened her. She looked up quickly and saw the briefest shadow of worry cast wrinkles on her mother's fore-head. But in seconds, before the child could feel any pangs of conscience, her mother's face altered. Emilia had smoothed her brow, and abandoning her attempt to correct her daughter's behavior, she reached for a pile of plates on the open kitchen shelf, and continued to pack her most important possessions in the large wooden crate standing in the middle of the floor.

Freed from her mother's attention, Marina lapsed back into her vacant stare and let her mind drift to what occupied it most at that moment—the image of her dead father lying cold and still in his white satin-lined coffin on the front porch. That was how she saw him first when she was brought back from Mrs. Telser's house. It was an image directly connected to her mother's present activities in the kitchen, for she knew, though her mother did not explain the facts, that she and her mother were obliged to leave their home because her father was dead. Yet it was an image that she loved to dwell on because, as far back as she could stretch her young memory, that day was the first time that her craving for affection from her father had ever been satisfied.

She was not unhappy when her mother took her to stay with the Telsers after her father became ill. Still loving him, she was glad to be out of his reach. She was afraid of him then. Afraid of his steel-gray eyes consumed with the rage that burned his mind, of his gnashing teeth, of his blue-veined, wrinkled fingers tearing wildly at his disheveled hair and of the hatred that he always bore toward her which then became so intense that he screamed and cursed at the sight of her. But in his coffin, she kissed him and his face did not recoil in disgust. She laced her rosary beads through his still, snowy-white fingers and he did not push her away. She brushed her hand over his thin, graying, curly brown hair and he did not shudder at her touch. She remembered her mother's eyes on her then. How long she looked at her. Not at him. At her. Tears pouring down her cheeks, saying nothing. Crying, it seemed to the child, for her and not for the dead man.

The little girl's eyes flashed upward at that moment and they caught her mother's rounded back bent over the wooden crate on the kitchen floor, piles of dishes stacked in her hands. I look like my daddy, she thought. The thought carried no other meaning, no implicit comparisons with her mother. In fact it was on these grounds and these alone that the child assumed naturally that her father ought to love her. She had his same clear gray eyes, his same light curly brown hair, his same white skin, only slightly darker, his same freckles dusted lightly over her long nose bridge. It was natural that he should love her though he only showed that love to her that morning in his coffin.

It was when they lowered his body into the dark earth that the child finally seemed to understand the meaning of death and that her daddy had remained still in the coffin because he no longer had life. She cried then as though her heart would break until her mother promised her, crossed her heart and hoped to die, that she would see her daddy again soon. Very soon. Afterward the little girl could not understand why they had to leave their home.

"If Daddy is coming back, why shouldn't we wait for him?" she asked.

"I only promised that you will see him," her mother said, "but he can't stay."

"But why must we live with Mr. Telser?" the child whined, not satisfied.

"Because we have nowhere else to go."

Secretly Marina blamed her mother, but not with animosity or hatred, only with feelings as close to pity as an eight-year-old could get. As she felt sorry for her black short-haired kitten because it was not furry and fluffy. Not that she loved it less, but she knew that others shunned it because of the way it looked and so they shunned her. And she blamed her kitten when she knew that it could not change its color nor make itself furry. Perhaps if her mother's skin were not so black, they would not have to move from where they now lived. Again it was instinct that led Marina to this simple but hidden truth, though her sense of the cruel unfairness of that fact would not allow her to give it voice to her mother's ears. Or then it could have been the simple putting together of observations, like two and two, like dark clouds and rain, like sunshine and happiness, like black skin and laborer, like white skin and overseer, that brought her to this lucid understanding. Yet she thought her mother prettier than any white woman she had ever seen. She loved the smooth roundness of her skin and the way the sun changed her color from blue-black to oxblood black, so that at night she reminded the girl of the polished ebony mask that an old Ibo man had given to her mother before he died, and in the day of an overripe governor's plum, its red juices almost bursting through its black skin. Marina regretted too, that her hair was too fine to braid into the cornrows that looked dazzling on her mother's head. So, thus, while she was glad she resembled her father, she often wished she looked like her mother. For the only value she placed on her own English features was that they made her part of a father whom she loved. Yet she was not unaware that others thought her more beautiful because of that fact. More fortunate, even. That others thought her pale skin, clear eyes, and light curly brown hair were her most valuable assets, her most treasured possessions.

While part of her mind still drifted this way, Marina sensed her mother's eyes on her again and felt more than heard her move toward her. This time she saw instantly that her mother was not to be disobeyed. Immediately she stopped rocking and hurriedly pressed her fingers against the floor, pulling up her right buttock and bracing her body forward to get up. Her reactions were so swift and agile, like a puppy scampering to unfold itself into position to run, that her mother, meaning to be serious, burst out laughing. Marina, remorseful for her earlier obstinacy, ran to her and hugged her by the waist. At that very moment, as Marina pressed her head against her mother's soft belly, she saw from the corner of her eye, sliding across the kitchen floor, the dark shadow of a person in a long shapeless dress. Her muscles stiffened involuntarily and their hardness against her soft skin made her mother look down quickly at her. She pointed to the man at the door and felt her mother's body grow taut as hers had done as her eyes saw what she had seen.

"Go. Leave us!" Her mother's arms tightened across her shoulders. The shadow moved forward until it crept up on the wall and the man stood close to Marina.

"Emilia," the man pleaded. His voice was surprisingly gentle. "Please, Emilia, this won't take long."

Marina shuddered against her mother. The man was the priest who had read the last rites at her father's funeral. Her eyes riveted themselves to the object of her revulsion—his thin, long bony fingers that fiddled now, as they did then at her father's funeral, with the big black beads that hung from his waist down the middle of his stomach past his knees.

"Emilia," the priest repeated. "Forgive me."

"For they know not what they do," her mother mocked.

The priest smiled. A thin, saintly sliver of a smile that did not change the contours of his face nor the coldness in his eyes.

"You are too late," the child's mother said dryly.

The priest moved closer to them. "Is this Marina?" he asked.

The little girl felt her mother crush her tightly to her body, so tightly that she could hardly breathe. The priest took another step toward them, and the child saw his icy fingers leave his rosary beads and extend themselves toward her. Pure terror of those fingers made her duck her head roughly through her mother's close embrace. Her body squeezed itself into a tight, tense ball and slipped past her mother's skirts before the priest could touch her naked arm. Once escaped, the child did not look back. She bounded as if pursued through the open kitchen door, down the wooden steps, past the cleanswept dirt yard and through the thick hibiscus bushes that bordered the house.

Emilia made no effort to stop her daughter. She let her arms drop limply to her sides and her eyes follow the child's back until the rose-colored petals that had fallen off the shaken hibiscus flowers lay still on the ground and their yellow pollen no longer powdered the dirt.

After a while Father de Nieves removed his black hat and spoke: "She seemed afraid of me. I didn't—"

Emilia cut across his words. "You reminded her of her father's funeral," she said bluntly. Tearing her eyes away from the trembling bushes that were settling back into place in the spots where Marina had disturbed them, she turned her back to the priest and reached for some dishes.

If the priest thought her rude, he gave no indication. "She looks a lot like Hrothgar," he began again, placing his hat on the kitchen table.

"She is his child." Emilia pushed her iron coal pot toward the middle of the floor.

"A little like you though."

"Hmmm."

"Around the eyes—the cheekbones, I suppose."

Emilia did not answer.

"Yes, well, yes." The priest hesitated and then added

quickly, "What I came for won't take long. It won't take long." He paused, irritated that Emilia seemed to ignore him. When he spoke again, it was to beg for her attention. "Emilia, please. May I sit for a minute?"

Emilia reached for another pot on the shelf and then stopped her hands in midair as though she had changed her mind. Slowly she turned, looked at the priest and shook her head. "Sit." Her voice was harsh, and she pulled out another chair from under the kitchen table and sat down facing him.

"I have the will," the priest said, handing her a white paper rolled into a thin scroll and tied with blue ribbon.

"I know," said Emilia, not touching the paper. "Hrothgar gave it to you."

The priest let the paper fall on his lap. "You don't have to leave this house, you know."

"You are too late."

Father de Nieves touched his beads. "God will not make me late," he mumbled as though speaking to himself.

"You are too late," Emilia repeated in a tired voice.

"No!"

"Why didn't you come to the hearing?"

"It came so quickly, the day after they buried him. I—I—didn't know—"

Emilia let her head fall back on the top of her chair. She laughed, a bitter laugh rising from the pit of her belly. "You didn't know and you were in with them?" she asked.

"Emilia! Don't say that!"

"What should I say then?"

"If I were one of them, would I be giving you this?" Father de Nieves picked up the will again and pushed it toward Emilia. She took it from him this time and then dashed it to the floor.

"You are a hypocrite. You and your kind. A man of God!" she sneered.

The priest jumped to his feet in indignation, almost knocking down his chair. "And you—you—" he stuttered, pointing his thin fingers at her, his rosary beads clashing against each other. "I'll tell you—I'll tell you why I didn't come." His mouth opened wide to continue but the words remained frozen in his throat. He stood there with his face flaming, beads of sweat glistening on his forehead, the veins on his temples protruding blue and hard, but no words came from his mouth. After a while he calmed himself, mopped his face with his handkerchief and sat down again. His voice grew subdued and lifeless. "Do you remember the birth of your last twin sons?" he asked.

"Yes." Emilia met his eyes boldly, indifferent to the torment he seemed to be in. "Like my other twins before Marina, they were born dead."

"No. Not those," the priest said, lowering his voice. "The ones who lived." He was almost whispering.

Still meeting his eyes even when he tried to avoid hers, Emilia repeated in a loud voice, "None of my sons lived."

"Emilia, you know what I mean." The priest touched his beads. "Your sons who lived for two weeks."

"None of my sons lived." Emilia's voice was flat. Emotionless.

The priest got up and paced the room. "The week before your sons were to be christened, Hrothgar came to see me." The priest bent down and picked the rolled paper off the floor. "He gave me this. His last will and testament leaving his land, his house and all his worldly possessions to you."

"I know."

"So you admit that your sons lived?"

"I admit that Hrothgar willed me all his worldly possessions."

The priest stood in front of Emilia and bent his face close to hers. "Don't you see, Emilia? Don't you see? Hrothgar meant to give you a present for giving him two live sons. Don't you see?"

Emilia stretched out her hand and flattened it against the priest's chest, pushing him away from her and causing him to totter slightly. She offered no apology. She did not get off her chair. She looked at him directly and asked, "Why do you come now?"

Father de Nieves, barely recovering his balance, hardly heard her. His eyes were opened wide, shocked by her arrogance. Emilia had to repeat herself before her question could penetrate his mind. "Why did you wait so long to come here? Why do you come now?"

The priest grew pale and he sat down weakly on the chair. She could not have known his nights of torment, his agony. His sleepless nights, tossing and turning in his bed with his troubled conscience. He had come to give her the will. Shouldn't he get peace now?

"Why?" Emilia repeated again.

"Because—" the priest began. "Because I—"

"Because," Emilia interrupted, "because you are one of them. Because you believed I lived in sin with one of you. Because I'm colored."

"No. That's not true, Emilia. I just wasn't sure. Your sons did not live—I mean your sons died so soon after. I wasn't sure if Hrothgar meant to give you the land if his sons did not live."

"Father, my sons—" Emilia's eyes flashed.

"I—I mean, Hrothgar intended to give you a gift for his

live sons. He never spoke to me again about the will, but—but—I'm not sure."

"Why not, Father? Did he tell you so? Don't you think that he knew you had the will?"

Father de Nieves fought back the bitter bile that stung his throat. Emilia was right. He had no proof that at any time before his death, Hrothgar wished his will to be changed. In the nine years that Hrothgar lived after his twins had disappeared, he acted as strangely as the people. As though the boys never were. As though they had indeed been born dead. De Nieves went to him one day and pleaded with him to find the boys, to look for them, and Hrothgar threw him out of his house screaming that Emilia had buried the twins as she had buried her other dead sons. De Nieves saw then the seeds of his insanity. There, in the anger that rendered him silent about the death of his sons. He had seen others before Hrothgar grapple with the inexplicable and knew that men like him were too steeped in the world of matter, of dollars and cents, for the spirit to seduce them to peace. No, he saw then with dismal certainty that soon, very soon, Hrothgar would go mad with the truth. He wet his lower lip and begged for Emilia's understanding. "He was never the same after their death, Emilia. Surely you know that."

"I know nothing except that Hrothgar did not change his will," she replied stubbornly. "And," she added, "that you are too late."

"I'll tell them." The priest leaned forward.

"It's no use. Take your will and go. They have already sold the house and land."

"Surely you told them they are yours."

"I told them. And I told them that you had the will to prove it. But you did not come."

"I will make amends, Emilia, believe me."

"Why you want to stir up false hope in me? You believe I'm stupid? You think they would have sold the house and land if I was an Englishwoman? Even if I wasn't married to Hrothgar and had no will to show them?"

"Well, you have a will . . ."

"And what will that will do? They made up their minds. I know it. You too. They believed me all right when I told them you had the will. My friends came out to swear for me. But they said, No will, no land. I prayed you would come with the will, but even so I knew they would still find a way to take the land from me."

"Emilia," the priest pleaded.

"No. Go, Father, go. Just leave me be with my packing. Leave me be."

"Let me try at least, Emilia. They'll buy back the land for you. You'll see."

"Please go."

"And what will happen to Marina?"

"I'll take care of her."

"How?"

"Please!"

From the corner of her eye, Emilia saw the red edge of Marina's dress flicker against the white frame of the kitchen doorway. The blood drained from her face and her heart skipped a beat. She jumped to her feet like someone who had seen a ghost and stood there paralyzed, terrified to confirm her suspicions. How long? How long had the child been there? How much had she heard?

De Nieves stared at her, confused. "Emilia? Emilia? Is something wrong, Emilia?"

The red dress had disappeared. There were no sounds, no telltale footsteps, but Emilia knew she was still there. Marina had not gone. Emilia tried to compose herself. She had to get the priest to leave. She had to find out how much Marina knew. Clasping her hands to her head, her eyes on the doorway, she said, "Tomorrow, tomorrow. No more. My head. Please go."

But de Nieves followed her eyes and guessed the truth. "She just came, Emilia. Don't be alarmed. I saw her. She didn't hear you."

He meant to be kind but his tone was patronizing and he ignited the hatred for him that Emilia had kept at bay. Now she rushed toward him, her eyes blazing, her nostrils flaring.

"Get out! Get out! Get out, man of God!"

Startled, the priest jumped out of his chair and stumbled across the room. At the doorway he stopped, turned and faced her. Afraid, his lips trembling, but unable to run, as if threatened by a more awful anger. As if his Christian conscience that had haunted him since Hrothgar's funeral now stabbed piercing darts into his soul.

"I'll make up for this, Emilia. I'll see that the law gets this will. Believe me. Give me a chance. You'll have a legal right to the property—"

"Get out! Get out!"

"You'll have justice—"

"Get out!"

De Nieves backed away, his right foot searching for the top of the steps to the backyard as Emilia came closer to him. And at that moment, just as his toes touched the wooden step, he felt a hand grab his ankle, and spinning around suddenly, he lost his balance and toppled down the steps.

It was Marina who had pulled him, Marina who now coolly looked at him and said in a voice five times her age, "Now leave, Father de Nieves."

Emilia watched her daughter silently. She watched her

climb up the steps toward her and felt her tiny arms encircle her, and she shuddered.

"You should not have done that, Marina."

"You wanted him to leave."

"Yes, but you should not have hurt him."

"Didn't he hurt you?"

"You heard us?"

"No."

"Then how could you know what he did?"

"You looked angry."

"You're lying, Marina. I saw your dress."

"Where?"

"By the doorway."

"I just came."

"You didn't hear us?"

"Hear what, Mother?"

Emilia removed her daughter's arms from her waist. She sighed. Perhaps she had not heard her speak of her sons. "He could have helped us, but he didn't."

"What did he say?"

"Are you sure you just came?"

"Yes. Just as you were asking him to leave. You don't believe me?"

"It's not that, Marina. There are things you can know and things you're too young to know. Just yet."

"About why we must leave?"

"About why we must leave."

"But I know."

"Know what?"

"It's because of you."

"Because of me?"

"Father's friends won't let us stay here because they don't like you."

"How do you know that?" Emilia looked closely at her daughter.

"Father de Nieves said that Father left you his house."

Emilia tried to still the slight tremors in her fingers. "I thought you had not heard us."

"Father left you his house," Marina repeated.

"What else did Father de Nieves say?"

"Nothing. I didn't hear anything more."

For a second, mother and daughter looked at each other and no one spoke. No one needed to. They seemed to have arrived at a tacit agreement between themselves not to ask, not to say, and neither one dared name the subject. Finally, tearing her eyes away from Marina, Emilia said quietly, her voice betraying her effort to sound unconcerned, confident, "Anyway we'll do well at the Telsers'."

"No!"

It was the first of many times Emilia would see a hardness, a coldness in her daughter's eyes. The sort of expression that could come only from someone who had never loved, or someone who would not let loving, or feelings, stand in her way of getting what she wanted. There was a cold determination in Marina's voice, a tone that demanded an answer, and Emilia found herself speaking to her eight-year-old daughter as if she were already a woman, and she heard herself teaching her step by step a lesson she knew, she felt instinctively, would dominate her daughter's life, would determine all her decisions.

As if at that moment the world stood still for her, Emilia clasped her daughter's hand in hers, and looking deeply into her eyes, she beat out for her the silent rhythms of her forefathers' love for the land—their age-old kinship with the earth. The time had come for her to pass on the message of her people as each African mother in the Caribbean would do. Until each Caribbean child would lock its truth in his heart and take it with him wherever he went—in the cold, concrete lands of England's cities, America's New York, Chicago, San Francisco—giving it birth where he went. Yes, a man who owned land was a sort of god. He walked with gods. A man who owned land, owned a part of this earth. He was his own master. He belonged to no one. He could be no slave. He could grow his own food, make his own bed on his land. Yes, land was his most valuable possession.

Emilia taught her daughter this and more. A man, she said, owned land only if he owned the deed to it. But if a man had land, it did not mean that his woman had land. For if she, Emilia, owned the deed to Hrothgar's land, no law in the world, no person on earth could move them from where they lived. Nobody could force them to live with the Telsers. "You were born," she said finally to Marina, "on the land. Beneath the cocoa. The land took you from my womb. Before I touched you, the land embraced you. You belong to the land and you will own land one day. No, no one will force you to move from where you live. No, not like they did to me."

And indeed Emilia was forced to leave her house, though de Nieves was true to his word. He took Hrothgar's will to the colonial court and the judge acknowledged its validity. Hrothgar's house and land belonged to Emilia. But before the case was closed there were other settlements: funeral costs, land taxes, Hrothgar's debts, payment for which, since Emilia had no money, would be exacted from the house and land by Hrothgar's creditors, his friends. In time Emilia forgot her bitterness. In time she saw a sort of justice in the fact that she had lost the land that had cost her her babies. And she had Marina.

But Marina never forgot. The day she moved with her

mother to the Telsers' house, she swore that she would fulfill her mother's promise to her. No one, not even God, could stop her from one day owning the deed to land. And while she did not stop to consider why her father had not placed her mother's name on the deed to his house and land, she loved him more for willing his possessions to her, and she determined that she would make certain that any land she owned would have her name, Marina E. Heathrow, written clearly on the deed to it in large, black letters.

3

Ten years later, August 1901, a Warao chief crossed the silt-laden Orinoco River from his village on the north-eastern shores of Venezuela to penetrate the deep rain forest in Trinidad so that he could see the wife he had chosen for his friend's son. He had not hesitated the moment that he had heard the news of the tragedy that had befallen Antonio de Balboa. He knew then without doubt that one woman and one woman alone could save the young man.

He saw the woman's mother twice after that market day in Princes Town, when oblivious to the scandal she created, she clung to his arm, tears streaming down her face, and begged him to tell her why she could not give birth to babies that would live. It made him proud to see her respect for his people and his gods, and so the second time that she called on him, cradling two babies in her arms, he did as she asked.

For he too would honor the commands of her god. That was
the year before her daughter was born. The girl was eight
years old when he saw her mother again. Then she was a
broken woman, driven from her home as his people had
been driven off their island into Venezuela, and he swore to
her on the spirits of his dead fathers that her child would one
day own land far and wide in Trinidad, cocoa land that the
English sought to keep for themselves, land that they
hoarded for the thick, rich chocolate it gave them to warm
their nights in the frozen countries where they lived. It was
this oath that the Warao came to fulfill. For his friend's son
owned fifteen acres of this land. But first he had to see the
girl who, it was rumored, surpassed her mother's beauty, for
his friend's son loved beautiful women, and he had to be
sure.

The Warao made up his mind that he'd make the trip to
Trinidad alone although his men protested that no great
chief should travel without an escort. But the days of great
chiefs were almost over, and it wasn't worth it to bring an
entourage of followers and arouse to wakefulness past glo-
ries of days that would never return. When his pirogue
banked against the Moruga shore, the moon was still prince
of the darkness. He determined that it was good, for he
calculated that by the time he got to Princes Town the sun
would still have miles to travel before it would scorch the
earth, brazenly staring at the island from the middle of the
sky. If he were lucky and could see the girl and talk to her
mother before the village went to sleep, he should be back
in Moruga while it was yet daylight.

He knew the waters well between there and his village on
the coast of Venezuela. For the same silt from the Orinoco
River that covered the earth of his village was the very silt that
muddied the waters off the Moruga shore. This silt spread

itself outward from his village to the sea like a widening fan, and undaunted by swirling currents and fish it did not know in its saltless waters, it fondled the ocean floor until it washed itself onto the southern tips of Trinidad. So the Warao would not be troubled if darkness fell while he was still at sea, before he could be back in his village.

He pushed his two arms through the loops in the reed basket that his youngest wife had made for him, and, careful to avoid the row of gold bracelets tightly hugging both his upper arms, he hoisted the basket firmly on his back. It was heavy. Surely Emilia would feed him when she saw him. He removed the basket from his shoulders and took out the salted fish and bread and the bottle with the drink brewed from fermented ginger roots. He hesitated over the trousers. His men had thought it best that if he were going alone he should try to make himself unnoticed. But the Warao had not yet grown as soft as a woman. So he threw the trousers out of the basket. And the shirt and the shoes and the socks and the ribbon to tie back his hair to the nape of his neck so that he would not look uncontrolled. Uncivilized. Like a savage, the English would say.

By now the basket was almost empty. Except for the present he'd brought for the girl's mother and the stick and matches he carried in case he would only see the girl when the village woke up from its second sleep and he would have to return home in the dark.

The Warao decided on the present, the stick and the matches. But not on the basket. He pulled the present over his head and around his neck so it dropped until it reached the blue tattoo of a condor that opened its wings against the bronzed skin of his wrinkled, hairless chest. He stuck the stick next to the machete, between the waistband of his loincloth and his right hipbone, slanting it slightly so that it touched the sagging muscles of his once firm torso. Then he picked up the red ribbon that he had thrown away, and folding it into a thin, long band, he tied it across his forehead into a knot in the back of his head and let his silver-streaked black, coarse hair fall against the sides of his high cheekbones. He slipped the matches between the knot and his hair, his black deep-set eyes, shadowed by dark circles, surveying the land in front of him, his naked feet clutching the damp earth. He was ready.

He traveled by the same route he and his men always used. First through the coconut groves that hugged the Moruga shore. There he needed no machete; for the broad coconut palms jealously guarded the soft underbrush from the sun's stinging rays, and nothing grew tall there except the lecherous vines that preferred not to seek their own warmth. The Warao was cautious, though, when he walked under the coconut trees. He knew that at any time the trees, seeing the stranger, would set their sights upon their target, and when they had carefully measured distance and degree of impact, they would aim one of their nuts accurately upon his head. But the Warao lived among coconuts in his village in Venezuela, and so he searched the tops of the trees and chose his path under the clusters of young, green nuts, darting past the old, hard ones that pelted down from their trees for spite and in anger.

But between the coconut groves and the cocoa, the rain forest went wild. Here the green-feathered parrots disappeared unseen into the thick foliage, and only their deafening squawking and sudden, agitated bursts of flight distinguished them from the clutter of trees and leaves that grew indiscriminately everywhere. The Warao was glad that he had two things on his side. It was the end of the rainy season and the forest had been drowned by the last hurricane. Branches and clumps of broad-leaved plants lay limp and defeated on the ground, waterlogged, too sluggish to trap anyone. And he had his machete. Not that he needed it, for his men had cleared this path just two weeks ago when they had tracked through the forest near Princes Town to trade their goods. Yet in spite of the clearing, in spite of the fallen branches, the land was dark here, for vines and leeches and new shoots of greenery grew thick and rapidly in the spaces where the branches had broken off, and covered the tops of the trees before the sun could penetrate the earth. Still nothing troubled the Warao, and he was close to the end of the forest before he had cause to pull out his machete.

At first when he saw a thick log lying across the path, he thought no more than that it was another tree felled by the hurricane winds. It had not struck him then that no leaves or branches were strewn around the log. His mind was else-where, on the message he had come to bring for the woman's daughter. But as he approached the log, a sudden burst of sunlight grazed its surface and lit up an oily sub-stance that gleamed eerily on it. The Warao stopped in his tracks, confounded by this bright sheen. How did oil get on this log so close to the edge of the forest, so near to the cocoa? His abrupt change of movement stilled the vibrations his feet had sent under the earth, and the thing he took for a log felt it. It shuddered and long undulations traveled through its body.

"A macajuel snake," the Warao breathed, relieved. He reasoned that the snake had carried the oil on its body from the other side of the rain forest near the coconut groves. Yet he jumped off the path and held on tightly to his machete until he saw the snake contract its thick body forward and slither across the soft mud of the clearing through the twist-ing vines and branches of the rain forest.

It was then that the Warao became conscious of a slimy substance under his feet and around his legs and, looking rapidly downward, he saw that he had stepped into a shallow pool of murky black oil. His heart sinking, the Warao scanned the earth below him. A cold liquid ran down his spine. He shielded his eyes with his hand and peered into the forest. He sniffed the air. He knew now without doubt that the macajuel had not come from far. Stretched out before him, he saw patches of oil similar to the one he now stood in. It had not been like this when he walked this way last year. Not like this so close to the end of the forest. His eyes glued to the ground before him, the Warao prayed that the oil did not reach the cocoa. He had seen a field of corn devastated by oil near his village in Venezuela. But two miles south of where the forest merged into the cocoa lands that grew to the edge of Princes Town, the earth was brown again and no oil greased his feet. And the Warao thanked his gods, for he knew too that his friend's son's land, which lay fifteen miles east of where he now stood, was also spared this oil. He was grateful.

It was easier for the Warao to walk through the cocoa estates. In contrast to the rain forest, the atmosphere here was almost cathedral-like—still and peaceful, except for the occasional hummingbirds that buzzed their long, black, pointed beaks into rotting cocoa pods left behind by the farmers, who had to harvest the cocoa before the rains came. Bare of fruit and flowers, those trees stood still and graceful, protected from sun and rain by the majestic immortelle and the arrogant tonka bean trees that spread their branches high and wide over the cocoa pods, shielding them from the blazing sun in the dry season and from the rain that pelted down like bullets from the sky in the rainy season, and they made the path to Princes Town accessible to the Warao.

The Warao arrived, as he had calculated, hours before the sun had reached the center of the sky. He didn't want to be seen except by Emilia, the girl's mother. And he wanted to look at the girl who had become a woman to be sure that she was beautiful. So his friend's son would say yes. It didn't take much effort for him to find the Telsers' house, although he had never visited Emilia before. He had just to look for the highest of the brief hills in Princes Town. The English were like that. It reassured them of their superiority if they could look down on the people below, whom their king had chosen to benefit from his paternal care. It was frustrating for them in Princes Town because it was not a hilly village. But in time they found the hump on the town's back and they camped up there. Telser was the overseer. He'd have the second largest house, the one a decent distance from the warden's.

The Warao saw Telser first, in his khaki pants cut off at his knees, high socks sweaty under tall boots. He was talking to one of his servants, a young girl no more than fourteen, who went giddy with laughter when he passed his palm around her backside, sending her off to fetch something. Before the girl could get far, Emilia had choked her laughter down her throat and made the man pull up his socks.

"No need to talk to the servant girls, Telser. You tell me what you want, see. I'll get it done for you." The woman's voice was harsh with sweetness. The Englishman cowered under his mistress's anger.

"Must leave," he grumbled and picked up his riding stick and walked swiftly to the stables.

The Warao saw it all from behind the passionate balisier bush that hid him from their sight. He saw the man's lechery in the loose flesh that hung beneath his bloodshot eyes and he determined then that he must move swiftly. If the girl was beautiful, he had to get her now for his friend's son. He waited until the man had left and then he whistled softly like a kiskadee bird. One loud, long high shrill, followed by two short soft ones. Emilia heard it, but she couldn't be sure. The Warao repeated his whistle, *Ques que se?* Emilia stood still and listened. One loud, long high shrill, two short soft ones: *Ques que se?* Then she listened and remembered and her face broke into a deep worried frown, and in seconds she was at his side next to the orange and red balisier.

"What are you doing here? You never come here. You know you never come here. You know I never want you to come here. They can't see us together. Ever. You know that." Emilia's voice shook, her lips trembled, her hands grasped the Warao's bare shoulders. Ten years now, and her skin was still as smooth and black as a sea-washed pebble on the sand. The Warao's lips began to form a smile and then suddenly, arrested by a difference he now saw in her eyes, they dropped downward in confusion. She had acquired a cold hardness that he had not seen from behind the balisier. Instinctively he pulled away from her touch, and then ashamed of his actions and not knowing what to say, he gave her the necklace of red jumbie beads that he had brought for her. Still her eyes did not soften.

She asked him once more, "Why are you here? Why did you come here?" And she slipped the beads around her neck.

The Warao wondered whether he had made a mistake, but he thought again about the spirits that lived in Marina and knew that she and she alone could save Antonio de Balboa. Yet no sooner had he said the name of his friend's son than he saw deep frown lines gather on Emilia's forehead, and he understood that the news about Antonio de Balboa had reached her too. Quickly the Warao told her what he knew would make her change her mind and what he knew she had not known: that Antonio de Balboa owned fifteen acres of cocoa land. As he said this to her, the Warao was careful to allay her fears about the de Balboas. He reminded her that Marina was no ordinary woman and that no harm could come to a person who had the spirits of eight men in her.

By the time the Warao left Emilia her eyes had softened. Still she refused the Warao his last request—to see Marina, "to be sure Antonio would approve," as he explained.

"She does not know about you." That was all Emilia said, but it was reason enough for the Warao.

The Warao had to wait until the village was in its second sleep and the sun no longer stared from the center of the sky before he saw the girl, who had become a woman. And then he saw only her back, but the force of her beauty even from that position sucked the breath from his body, and he knew without question that, try as he may, Antonio de Balboa would not be able to resist her.

Indeed, the Warao could well have missed seeing Marina entirely when she came finally from a room in the rear of the house, so puzzled and preoccupied was he by the presence of three laborers who, unlike the others, did not sleep, but sat strangers to each other near the clumps of red and orange balisier. Not talking, not touching, but waiting too like he. It was their eyes that led the Warao to Marina, for he saw them turn in unison, riveted to an object in front of them. By then Marina no longer faced him, and the Warao saw only the back of her head, a heavy water bucket balanced gracefully on it, and her rounded, golden arms, and her slim, firm waist clearly outlined in spite of the shapeless sarong she wore, and her magnificent hips swaying under the weight of the bucket she carried. Marina did not turn her head nor stop, but walked directly to a galvanized bathing shed a few yards from the balisier where the men sat. It was then that the Warao unraveled the mystery of the laborers' presence. For moments after the door to the shed shut, and he heard the slop, splash, swish of water falling on naked skin, a low moan cut through the trees, and he saw a wet smirk mark itself across the face of each man. It was as though those sounds had sealed the distance between them, for they winked at each other, and laughing aloud, arms slung over each other's shoulders, they ran noisily back to the cocoa.

The Warao swore to himself that he would speak to Antonio about the girl before the dry season came.

4

Long after the Warao left, Emilia lay on her bed staring at the ceiling above her. She could not sleep. The relentless heat of the midday sun that usually sapped her strength until it bore her down into a listless, drowsy stupor had no such effect on her today. She was alert, awake. And when the Slop! Splash! Swish! of the water striking Marina's naked body reached the Warao's ears, she heard those sounds too.

She loves to punish me, Emilia thought, and she lifted her rounded body off the bed and walked across the room to the window that faced the galvanized bathing shed. She knew even before she parted the slats of the wooden jalousie that the three laborers would be sitting there in the yard as she had seen them every midday, crouched down by the balisier, waiting, she was certain, for Marina to take her bath. She fingered the red jumbie beads that the Warao had given her and sighed. "How she dislikes me. She does this to provoke me." She let go of the jalousie, shutting off the ray of light that had escaped through it, and stood still in the darkened room, tasting the familiar bitterness that had soured her mouth for eighteen years. Was it worth it? She swallowed hard and tried to drown the questions that began once more to ferment in her belly like a cancerous sore. Was it worth it for her? For Marina? Did it matter what he said, an old Ibo man who had dreamed to be chief of a tribe that had been ravaged by a people whose cruelty he never could comprehend?

She squeezed her eyes shut and forced back tears that welled up behind her eyelids. She could not, she would not cry for what she had no choice in doing. So many years—too many years—and yet the memory of her sons' deaths would not leave her. There was no way to tell Marina the price she had paid for her, the sacrifice she had made for her life. There was no way to explain to her the reason why, afterward, after Hrothgar's death, she slept with John Telser. She learned to live with the pain of Marina's scorn; she learned to live with the disgust she always saw in her eyes. But she hated her silence, though she feared more a direct confrontation with her. When it came finally, there was relief.

"You could have waited until she was cold in her grave," Marina spat out at her. Someone had told her that her mother now had Telser all to herself. "I always knew, but you could have kept it a secret. She liked you. You were her friend. She trusted you."

Should she have said then to her daughter that Telser demanded that she move into his bedroom? That she did it for her, for Marina?

"She paid you well, Mother, and she treated me as if I were

her daughter even after her children died."

Should she have said then, Emilia wondered bitterly: She paid me well because I relieved her of duties she hated to perform. Ann Telser hated to feel her husband's hairy hands on her. She could not bear the stink of his sweat nor his foul breath on her lily-white face. She hated the infernal sounds he made as he pumped himself into her, the vile words he used when he twisted and pressed deeper and deeper into her. She hated the weight of his body crushing down on her, and his reddened face and the white, sticky phlegm that spurted out of him. And the way he begged her, too. And when she found out that I was his mistress, she cried in my arms like a baby and kissed my hands, overflowing with gratitude. She paid me well to take her place in her bed, but more than that, she promised me that she would look after you like you were one of her own girls. That she would send you to school like her girls. She'd teach you manners like her girls if I protected her purity. Oh, she only began to fear me, perhaps to hate me, when her children died and you kept living, and she lay sick knowing that she would follow them. Yes, I continue to sleep with Telser, but for you, only for you.

"You will make yourself a common whore, Mother. Everyone will laugh at me."

Whore! Marina was too young then to know the meaning of the word. Too young and innocent, and yet she said it to her mother knowingly, her eyes flaming in rage. Is that why she wants to provoke me now? To flaunt her body for everyone's eyes, and for Telser's too? Emilia forced herself to stifle the questions. She listened again to the sounds in the yard. She heard the door of the galvanized bathing shed open and slam shut. She thought: I must tell her now what the Warao said. I must get her to marry Antonio de Balboa. She must not live as I have lived. Telser looks too hard at her.

Emilia opened the window and called out to Marina. The girl heard her and raised her hand. She wrapped her sarong more tightly around her firm, full body and casually put the empty bucket on the ground. Emilia called her again, and this time the urgency of her voice filled the girl with guilt and she hastened to her mother's room.

"Mother," she began before Emilia could say a word. "Mother, I swear I didn't think they would be there again today. I promise, Mother, I didn't."

Emilia pursed her lips and frowned. She had not expected an apology. "Sit down, Marina," she said.

"Mother, it's the truth—I didn't—"

"It's not that. Sit down. I have something important to tell you."

Marina brushed her wet curls from her face and sat on the wooden cane-backed chair near the window. She looked up at her mother, puzzled. "Is it something I did?"

Emilia thought: How the girl has learned to pretend innocence! No one would ever know how she dislikes me. She hides it well but her eyes never lie. They never stop accusing me.

"Marina, I think that it is time that you got married." Emilia said it bluntly, finding no other way to tell her. She knew her daughter well. She would see through any disguise that her mother could use to make her words more persuasive.

"Have you found someone?" Marina was equally blunt. She hardly batted an eye.

"Yes."

"Who?"

"Antonio de Balboa."

"De Balboa?" The name caught Marina off guard. "Mother, you are not serious."

"More serious than you think."

"But do you know what they say about Antonio de Balboa?"

"Yes."

Marina looked confused for a second and then her back relaxed and she smiled. "Well, of course, I don't believe what they say."

"And what is that you don't believe?" Emilia's eyes pierced her face.

"You know, Mother. What they say about him being cursed."

But Emilia heard the discomfort in her daughter's words and she pressed her again. "I think," Emilia began slowly, "you'd do well to believe what the people say."

Marina twisted her buttocks in her chair. "And you'd want me to marry him still?" she asked.

"It's more than that, Marina."

"But he has a wife, Mother."

"She's dead," Emilia said flatly.

Marina stared at her. "Dead?" she asked.

Emilia got up quickly from the bed where she was sitting and stood close over Marina. "Listen to me," she said firmly, "he has land. A lot of land. It won't happen to you. You are special. Special. You know it."

If Marina thought that there was anything peculiar in the way Emilia looked at her at that moment when she said, "You are special," she gave no indication of it. Her heart skipped a beat, her knees felt weak and her palms began to sweat, but these changes were imperceptible, imperceptible even to Marina who had long accepted the inexplicable fear she always felt when her mother looked at her in that penetrating way and called her special. It was the only compromise Emilia allowed herself with that silent pact they both made some ten years ago. Marina's mind clung to just one word that she had heard. Land. De Balboa had land. Her voice calm, she asked, "He has land?"

"A lot of it," her mother answered.

"How do you know?"

"I know."

"But no one has ever said—"

"They don't know," Emilia cut across her words. "He does not farm it."

"What kind of land?"

"Fifteen acres in Tabaquite. Cocoa land."

Marina looked doubtful and Emilia added quickly, "You are the only child I have. I won't lie to you."

"But who told you this?"

"Don't you worry."

"Not your—? Not your—?"

"No."

"Mother, are you sure your obeahman did not tell you this?"

Emilia walked to the window and looked outside. The Warao must be in the rain forest past the cocoa now, she thought. The people were waking up. She could almost hear their grunts and groans as they stretched out their limbs. A child impatient to get outside screamed and his mother yelled at him. Emilia put her hands to her ears and Marina misinterpreted her action.

"You don't want to hear me say that, but that's what you did. I know it."

Emilia turned to her. "Marina, it's not my obeahman who told me that, but I should have asked him."

"Then who?"

As much as she wanted to tell her, Emilia would not take the risk. She could not give Marina the slightest hint of her relationship with the Warao. She said quickly, "I think that this is your chance. You should take it now. It may not come again."

The quiet excitement in her voice infected Marina. She stood up, unable to sit still.

"This is your chance to own land," Emilia repeated. "Fifteen acres. You are a strong girl. No one knows this better than I. Nothing will happen to you. But the land, Marina? The land is what you always wanted. You were born for the land."

So intense was the excitement that Marina felt when her mother said those last words that she had to shut her eyes and close her lips firmly so that her mother would not see that she was smiling. She walked quickly toward the door, feeling a hot rush of blood mount her face. Without facing her mother she asked, "How can I meet him?"

Emilia sighed, relieved. "It will be arranged," she said. She saw that Marina was satisfied. But when the empty sound of the door closing behind Marina's back reached her ears, Emilia had to comfort herself again with the Warao's words. No, a woman with the spirits of eight men in her could not be harmed.

It was dark when the Warao reached the end of the rain forest just before the coconut trees, but he was not worried that he'd lose his way among the thick bushes. He had his stick and his matches. Extending his foot in front of him, he searched the ground with his broad toes until he felt the slimy grease that he had passed hours before. As he had done many times when darkness caught him here, he soaked his stick in the oil, struck a match to it and lighted his way through the rain forest and the coconut trees to his pirogue and the sandbanks of the Moruga shore.

5

The Warao chief's men were pushing and pulling their pirogues off the grassy sandbanks that bordered the Moruga beach, excited and exhilarated from the successful trading day in Princes Town, and drunk from the cheap distilled sugarcane rum they had bartered for, when the chief spotted his friend's son, sitting alone as his father had sat, staring hopelessly out to the sea, oblivious to the commotion a few yards from him.

It was the first time that the Warao had seen Antonio since he had heard the news of his tragedy. He was glad he had not seen him before, for now that he had spoken to Emilia, he had some hope to offer the young man. The Warao threw down the two squawking parrots that he had tied together and slung over his back, the remainder of the lot that he had traded in Princes Town, and signaled to one of his men to take over the supervision of their departure. He walked silently over to Antonio and touched his shoulder, but the young man did not look up. The Warao stretched out beside him.

Together they made a curious picture. Two stone figures seated. One, a short man whose chocolate-black skin seemed to mock the distinct Portuguese features of his face—the thin lips; the nose, long, narrow at the bridge, curving suddenly at the tip; the clear, coffee-brown eyes framed by soft, curly eyebrows. Only his high cheekbones gave credibility to the African origins of his skin color. He was dressed in a dark, baggy suit that seemed to swallow him and a gray felt hat that caused sweat to mat his thick, brown, straight hair. The other, a tall Warao Indian, about seventy years old, though only the sagging ripples of his olive-brown skin betrayed his age. Unlike the man next to him, he was almost naked, his body gleaming with shark oil. He wore thick gold bracelets on his upper arms, a spread-winged condor on his drooping chest, a tiny strip of loincloth barely covering his genitalia, a wide band of red cotton fabric across his forehead that tied in a knot at the back of his head and left his coarse, gray-streaked black hair to hang freely against the sides of his face.

One hundred feet or so from them, the other Waraos, as scantily dressed as their chief, whooped and hollered as they tugged at their canoes, from time to time pausing to take a swig of rum from the bottles that dangled from the reed baskets strapped to their backs. Their minds clouded by alcohol, they were indifferent to the masterpiece of oranges, reds and yellows that the sun had carelessly painted on the purple sky and was, as indifferently, beginning to erase.

The Warao cleared his throat, but still the young man did not look at him. By then the air around them was heavy with the scent of the stale shark oil that the Waraos rubbed over their bodies to protect themselves from the insects that bred typhoid, malaria and all sorts of infectious diseases on the islands. The young man wriggled his nose, but still he did not seem to notice that the Warao was sitting beside him. He continued to search the sea, bloodied by the sun that was slipping swiftly into it as she did every night on the coast of Moruga, dragging with her the last embers of her dying fires. In the tropics there is no twilight. Just blazing sunlight, minutes of a dazzling sunset, and then the pitch dark. In the rainy season when the rain played tricks with daylight, the night came more swiftly than ever.

"No second chance," his father, Vasco de Balboa, had been fond of saying, "to erase the errors of youth." Errors of youth? What errors of youth, Antonio thought, did he, Antonio, make that could cause his present misery? What errors of youth had his father made that caused his unhappiness? For years he had puzzled over this last question, hoping that in the answer, he could find the reason for his own misfortunes. "The sins of the father shall be visited on the son." Yet his father's sin was not so great. It was a sin of omission, not commission.

Antonio was twelve years old when he learned of it. It was a newspaper clipping that led him to it, a clipping his father kept between the pages of his sacred book. Curiosity about the clipping had maddened the young Antonio from the first moment that he realized that his father read only the book, nothing else, not even the newspaper. Only the book, over and over again. But Antonio's terror of Vasco de Balboa was so great that his fingers trembled every time he tried to touch the book, even to open its pages. Not that he should have had reason to fear his father. The man ignored him for years, as if he did not exist. But Antonio was afraid of his vacant eyes. A zombie he seemed, walking among the living, pausing only to read his book and talk to the Warao.

One day, however, Antonio could resist the clipping no longer. He had long since memorized the title of the book, *The History of Portugal,* under which his father had written in black ink, "by Herculano, a good man." Now he felt pulled to it like a moth to a candle, risking fire for the light. Cautiously he approached the table where the book lay. Feverishly, he stuck out his hand, stretched his thumb and index finger and, like a crab snapping its scissored claw, he clamped down on the fragile paper. Then, sticking his loot in the waistband of his pants, he ran as fast as he could, his heart thumping wildly in his shallow chest, his feet raising the sand. He ran until he reached the dark hollow in the trunk of a dead tamarind tree that lay discarded by the sea. There, he read the clipping and his opinion of his father changed forever.

The article had been torn out of *The Trinidad Spectator* of July 15, 1858. Antonio's eyes greedily devoured the first sentence, then the second, and he knew at last that he had found the mystery behind his father's presence here on the island. Hungrily he read

On the 16th instant, the William, *from Madeira, arrived in our port, having on board 188 immigrants from that island, 57 men, 67 women and 64 children. They seem a superior class of people to any that have yet visited our shores from the same quarter, or indeed from any other place. For cocoa plantations and domestic purposes we think they will answer well but, for cultivation, they are entirely unfit. No cruelty that was ever perpetrated in Trinidad could possibly be greater than to distribute them among the sugar plantations where so large a number of those who preceded them have been cut off.*

Many of them bear excellent testimonials from persons of respectability in Madeira, which commend them more strongly for confidential situations. It appears that these people have fled from their homes in consequence of a fierce religious persecution that was raised against them by the clergy of the Island. A large number of Portuguese scriptures had been distributed among them, which they gladly received and earnestly perused, the reading of which produced such a change in the minds of hundreds on religious matters, that the clergy soon observed it, and manifested their displeasure by indulging in a persecuting spirit little to their credit. We heartily welcome these strangers to Trinidad, where, we are happy to say, religious animosity is little known, and where persecution such as that from which they have fled, would not be tolerated.

His father was a runaway! An outlaw! A rebel against religious persecution! Antonio's chest swelled with pride. He forgot his fear. He rushed to Vasco de Balboa the moment that he saw him on the beach, returning from his walk with the Warao. The timing was right. Vasco de Balboa had decided a few days before to break his silence with his son. The Warao had convinced him that his life depended on his change of heart.

"Fools," Vasco de Balboa spat out after his son told him what he had read. "They were all fools who wrote this. Self-righteous heathens every last one."

"But the ones who came with you on the *William?* You were on the *William?* Yes, Father? Tell me about them. Tell me about you."

Life returned to de Balboa's zombie eyes. "I was talking

about them too," he shouted. "They were also self-righteous heathens."

Antonio quailed under his father's fury. Loving it. "But it says here that they were the good ones."

"We—they—I don't know if they were ever good. We boarded the *William* in Lisbon that day. They, the bad ones as you would put it, had come to throw stones at us. Rotten eggs. The entrails of pigs. And we bore it well. Their blows gave justice to our cause and made us more saintly and them more evil. Even in the eyes of the smallest child."

"Did you fight them back, Father?"

"Fight them? God no! We were martyrs for the cause of freedom and our belief in God. We took our licks with pleasure. We laughed to see our blood flow. Our dark, red blood. Our cuts and scratches . . ." De Balboa's dark eyes grew wild. The whites turned bloodshot. Antonio felt his old fear creeping up his spine. He cringed and his father pulled him up by his shoulders.

"You wanted to know, didn't you? I saw your eyes forever on my book. Don't you want to know?"

The boy nodded his head and tears brimmed at the corners of his eyes.

"No tears. Be a man. It's time you're a man. Your mother fills your head with dreams. I see it. I don't talk, but I see it. Listen to me. I'll tell you the truth. Those good men with me on the *William,* those dissenters fleeing religious persecution, were no better, no worse than the ones they fled from."

Antonio heard his voice tremble as he questioned, "Were you different, Father?"

De Balboa knitted his bushy eyebrows and let his thick, black straight hair fall on his forehead. His voice became infinitely sad. "I wanted to be different. I wanted to be good. But when the Bishop of Lisbon forbade me to read Herculano, called him impious, a traitor—when the Bishop ordered me—"

"The bishop ordered you?"

De Balboa looked past his son, his eyes skimming the metallic blue surface of the ocean, seeming to penetrate the vastness beyond. "Did I say *me?*" His voice faltered. "Did I say *me?*"

"You said the bishop ordered you not to read Herculano."

"Me. Yes, me. Yes, me. He ordered me." His voice drifted.

"Why you?"

De Balboa did not answer at once. His eyes remained riveted to the motionless horizon, but then in moments, as if he now heard the echo of Antonio's question, he tore his eyes away from the distance and stared at his son. "Why me? What are you talking about?"

"Why did the bishop pick on you?"

"Not me, stupid boy. He did not pick on me only. The whole lot of us good Catholics he forbade to read Herculano. All of us. That's when I decided to leave."

Antonio thought better of pressing him, of pointing out to him that he had contradicted himself. "Then?" he asked timidly. "What happened then?"

"Then we set sail for the Caribbean. It was a trading vessel, they said—we were to pick up cocoa in Trinidad and then go to Brazil—though they took us and those who ran from the cholera and yellow fever as passengers. The epidemics were not over. We were still dying like dogs in Lisbon and Madeira. We were not all rebels, you see. Some of us were simply afraid to die, so we carried our diseases with us to your world. In the end we were all cowards."

"Not you, Father."

"I? I am neither a coward nor a brave man. I am nothing. I was made nothing on that ship. We were running to freedom, you see. Freedom from persecution by the clergy. We wanted to be more worthy in the eyes of God and we believed that we had found a more perfect way to worship Him. How could I know that in the bowels of the *William* they hid their illegal cargo? At first I smelled the stench. The fetid vapor of decaying rats. The guts of fish left out to rot in sun. The stink stench of worms and maggots fattening themselves on the vermin of cesspools."

Antonio drew closer to his father. A perverse bonding grew between them, the son draping himself with the gloom of the father, wearing it as his birthright.

"Yes. Yes. I said to myself, something is rotting in the hold of the ship. Yet I would not ask. Was it because I heard those sounds too? Human cries, they were. *That,* I was sure of. Babies, women, men, little children. I wanted it to be a dream, a bad dream. Yet I could not sleep. Night after night those human groans tortured me. Finally I decided I would see for myself. I sneaked down at night like a common thief to the hold of the ship. Did I ask myself why didn't I bring others? Wouldn't the others be as anxious as I to rescue those humans? Stowaways, I told myself. The stench of human defecation almost drove me back to my room. Stinking! Putrid! Foul! I saw the shit oozing from the bottom of the door of the ship's hold. I knew the door would be locked even before I touched it. I grabbed for the keys. They hung on a peg not too far from the door. I turned the key. Click!" De Balboa was now crouched on the sand, his eyes round, his hands playing the part he remembered. "Click! Click! And then I saw them, Antonio. God, I saw them! Their hatred was so pure that I forgot the stench. They were fastened to each other by heavy iron chains. Body piled upon body. All eyes blazing with hatred. Africans all! Was I surprised to see them? Yes, I knew the ship had come from Mozambique, but the slave traffic was forbidden. Our good Portuguese King Pedro had seen to that. Not on the high seas! Not on his ships! Should I have known my holy compatriots would disobey our king, would deal in the trade of human flesh?" His eyes held Antonio. "Should I? Should I?"

The boy shook his head vigorously as if suddenly taken with ague.

"Ah, how well you lie for me. Good boy. Good boy. Then listen. Listen well. A soft thing rolled at my feet and touched my ankle," de Balboa continued hoarsely. "A dead rat? It was no rat. A child, no more than three years old. A boy just nine years younger than you, Antonio, naked and dead. Curled up like a fetus in his mother's womb. Then I felt a sharp pain in the back of my head and, mercifully, the world went black. They told me when I woke up that the man who had struck the blow to my head with his heavy iron chain was the champion wrestler of his clan. I believe them. You should have seen his strong arms. He picked me to fasten his eyes on the day he died. They hung him there, your rebels, your dissenters from religious persecution, your God-fearing martyrs seeking freedom. They hung him there from the mast until second by second, minute by minute, hour by hour, day by day by day, his body shriveled and he died, his skin stuck to his bones like dried parchment paper. Then came the vultures . . ."

Antonio's mouth felt dry, his tongue heavy. "But you were innocent, Father. You had done nothing."

"Ahhh. Nothing. I said nothing. I did nothing. I watched the vultures pick his bones dry and I didn't as much as ask them to bury him. I walked off the ship when it docked in Trinidad and asked no questions. What had they done to the other blacks? Where did they go, those ones who carried cholera and yellow fever? Where did they go, my comrades in freedom for the worship of God? I did nothing. I walked until I came to this beach, saying nothing."

"Were they Catholics like Mother and me? The ones who brought the blacks?"

"What?" the question caught de Balboa by surprise. "Catholics?"

"The ones who killed the man? Were they Catholics like me and Mother?"

"We were all Catholics running from other Catholics who tortured us in Portugal. We were Catholics torturing the new black underdog. They called themselves Presbyterians, but they were all Catholics."

"From this day, I'll no longer be a Catholic." The boy's voice sounded like a man's.

"I'll teach you. But like for me, it may be too late. Once a Catholic, always a Catholic."

Antonio did not know then what his father meant when he said that it was too late for him to stop being a Catholic. Later he would understand. But he often wondered on evenings like this one, as the sun died quickly, whether the errors of youth his father spoke of so dismally were those he made on that ship that brought him to Trinidad. Or was there something else that he had done way back in Portugal? Or was it the error he had made in Trinidad. Marrying an African, a freed slave girl? Was he too, like his son, punished by marriage? A grim smile crossed Antonio's face, and the Warao felt its pain.

"I know, Antonio," the Warao whispered, and rested his greased hand on the young man's arm. "I know, but you must talk to me."

"Know? Know what?"

"News travels fast even to the bushes in the Orinoco."

"Did he also tell you?"

"Antonio, my son."

"Am I to pay for his errors? He did nothing. Nothing."

The Warao did not understand him. "Your Sara," he asked, "did she die like the others? Your Sara?"

"Sara?" The sound of his dead wife's name catapulted Antonio into the present. As if he had unplugged balls of cotton from his ears, he heard for the first time the loud roar of the sea, the whooping and yelling of the drunken Waraos and the quiet voice of the chief. "Sara? Sara?"

"Yes. Did she die like the rest?"

"No. Not like the rest, but dead all the same."

"It was different this time then?"

Despair, like the relentless waves bathing the burning sand, washed over Antonio. This, he said to himself, was how his father felt when he saw the rotting carcass of the black slave. Nothing. Nothing. There was nothing but the facts. "She did not die like the rest. They wouldn't let her die like the rest. When the baby wouldn't come, my mother became afraid that Sara would die like Effie and Mildred. So she let the midwife do what she wanted to. Mother couldn't save my other wives, so I said, Why not? Then they came for Sara. She was burning up with fever by then. Delirious. Screaming and shouting. She didn't want to die. I tried to help her, but she wouldn't let me touch her. She kept shouting that I was trying to kill her, and just before she died, with her final breath and with her eyes, those eyes, she blamed me again."

The Warao remained quiet as Antonio stared blankly into the sea, waiting for his friend's son to continue.

"I had a daughter this time," said Antonio, breaking the silence, "but she died too, like my two sons. Perhaps Sara was right. I am to blame. I should not have let the doctor take her, burning with fever as she was, to the river. 'It's a cold river bath she needs,' he said. 'It will bring down the fever.' A pity the English have no cure for pneumonia," he added bitterly. "She died choking on her own spit."

The Warao put his slippery arm over Antonio's shoulder. "Many women die having sons and daughters."

"But the sons live. And the daughters live."

"You'll take another wife and have another child." The Warao's voice was gentle. Like a woman's.

"Never."

"Pray and it will happen." The Warao tightened his grasp on Antonio's shoulders.

"Pray? Me? Never."

"But your god," the Warao almost pleaded. "Have you asked your god or your priests for help?"

"They are fools," replied Antonio darkly. "Vipers sucking on the blood of the rich with hatred in their hearts for the poor and men with skins like ours. No. No, my god has no time for people like me, and his ministers are too busy making their profits. They cannot help me." Antonio's voice trailed off into a stubborn, bitter silence that the old chief tried to break.

"But your father," the Warao began, "he believed once." Then the Warao looked at the young man and realized his mistake. They didn't talk much, he and Vasco de Balboa, but he loved the sad Portuguese man from the day when he stretched out his hand to him and greeted him, like a chief, in the language of the Waraos. No white man before de Balboa had ever spoken to him in his language. They called his people savages, men without a culture, uncivilized barbarians who had no language, no words, but who grunted and growled at each other like animals. When these white

men needed his people's labor, they taught them language—their language, which alone they called language.
For ten years the Warao earned his family's freedom from
servitude by navigating the English trading vessels through
the coral reefs off the Caribbean islands, and so he learned
English well. Yet, the captains of those ships never knew, for
the Warao feigned ignorance of their orders, acknowledging
them only after they had stripped their language bare, had
reduced it to signs and gestures and monosyllabic words,
only after it was they, not the Warao, who grunted and
barked like animals. But Vasco de Balboa spoke the language of the Waraos, and so the Warao let the sad Portuguese know that he knew how to speak English flawlessly.
They were both chiefs who had lost their places. But they had
their pride. He asked de Balboa once why he left his son to
the care of his woman, and the man replied, "I have no son."

The Warao gave him no peace after that. "A son," he said,
"makes a man immortal. A son will keep his father's spirit
and pass it on to his son, and his son's son, and so on. So that
long after his final breath, the father will live."

Then one day de Balboa brought his son with him. That
was the year before he died. In those days the Portuguese
talked about his god, how fearsome he is, how his justice is
meted out in punishment that fits the crime, how the sinner
never escapes. He talked about his priests, how he hated
them.

The Warao now looked at his friend's son and shook his
head in pity. "I'll never understand your god. The gods of
my people can cure everything. Even the white man's curse.
And if the gods don't cure, they tell us why. Can't your
ministers tell you what to do?"

"Yes. Never to marry again." Antonio laughed without
mirth.

"And your mother?" The Warao removed his arm from Antonio's shoulders.

"She wants grandchildren. But for me? No more wives. No more children."

The old chief thought of Marina and calculated that it was time. He picked up a sun-dried stick that had washed up on the beach and began to scrawl on the sand. Bent over, his legs sprawled apart, measuring in his head the best way to put it.

"Your father and I," he began, "were cowards. But you. You must not give up. Because life fights you, do not tuck your tail between your legs like a sick dog and run."

"So? I should do what?"

"Marry again."

"I'm not a fool. I know when I am whipped."

"So if you are whipped, is that reason to surrender?"

"And why not?" Antonio asked bitterly, looking directly at the tattooed condor, its body strong and powerful, its pointed beak sharp and terrifying, an image incongruous on an old man's wrinkled chest.

The chief followed Antonio's eyes and argued for the beautiful woman who alone could help his friend's son. "Look at your father. What did he get from giving up? He was always unhappy. Look at me. You see my people there." He pointed to the other Amerindians stumbling against each other. Drunk. "We once called your island home. This was where we lived. Here. There. All over this island. We were great warriors then. The best. Not even the Caribs could chase us away. So they lived with us here. But we had your land. And the land where the great river meets the sea. We were strong. But that was before the white man came with his Africans and his guns. So we gave it all up, and now we sneak through your forest to beg for your rum. We didn't even fight back. Not once. We heard the first gunshots and we fled. We took our women and our children and we crossed back to the Orinoco. But maybe, maybe if we had fought back, we would not be where we are today. Now we give away our food for your rum. We have become weak. Like women.''

As if to illustrate his point, one of the Waraos, fighting with another for possession of a large mirror, tripped over a coral shell and fell, bringing the mirror crashing down with him on the sand. His opponent was about to jump upon him to renew the fight, when he saw his body reflected in the cracked mirror like a broken jigsaw puzzle. In an instant, a painful roar cut across the beach silencing the ocean, as the man, clutching his hair in fear, believed that his body, without his knowledge, had been slashed into pieces. The fallen man, taking advantage of the other's confusion, leaped up, and the fight continued to the accompanying shouts of the onlookers.

"Then you understand," Antonio said to the Warao. "I have nothing to fight with as your people had nothing to fight with against guns."

The old chief saw his friend's son consumed by a gloom that was as impenetrable as that which had destroyed his father. He would tell him now.

"I have a weapon for you stronger than guns," he said. "Not even your father—he could never understand why sometimes we must make sacrifice. Why sometimes we must return some spirits to our gods when they get angry. I made such a sacrifice many years ago when I helped a woman who had to give up her newborn boys to bring her some good."

"My god, you heathens!" Antonio shouted before he could stop himself, looking at the Warao in horror. "You murdered innocent babies?"

"I didn't say murder."

"God!" Antonio got up to leave.

"No, wait. Wait," said the chief, pulling Antonio down. "Wait and hear it all and you will understand." The chief told Antonio the story about Emilia and her suffering and the death of her eight babies. He explained that Emilia's babies would have continued to die if someone did not prevent their death. That he had told Emilia that the spirits of those babies would haunt her if they could not find rest in a child that would live. He explained to a startled Antonio how Emilia came to him one night and pleaded with him to take her newborn twin sons. She said that the obeahman had told her that if she gave up her babies to the forest, she would have the child who would have the power to consume all the spirits of her dead children.

"Emilia had that child," the Warao continued. "She is called Marina. Marry that woman. She will live. She has the strength of eight spirits. She will give you many children."

After the chief and his men had disappeared into the ocean. Magically. In a twinkling of an eye. Washing away the image of canoes plunging simultaneously into the crashing waves like a well-orchestrated military platoon, Antonio continued to sit pensively on the sand. In spite of the horror and disgust he felt for the story the chief had told him, there was a part of him that accepted the logic of events that mapped out his fate. That he should be rescued by the superhuman woman. He tried to tell himself that his father would have seen the wisdom in the old chief's advice. Vasco de Balboa would have explained the dead twins and the murder of the last pair as metaphors used by a primitive people to describe the courage and strength of Marina. He would have explained the Warao's logic: that his first two wives were too weak. Yes, marry that woman, Antonio. Marry her! But Antonio knew in his heart that his resolve to meet Marina had nothing to do with this cold, rational, emotionless approach so typical of the Europeans on the island, but rather his response to the not-so-distant rhythms of his mother's buried culture. It was not curiosity, not reason, not even an acceptance of fate, that drove Antonio to find Marina. It was a force within him stronger than himself. A will to live, an innate desire to reproduce, a muffled drumming from the world of his African ancestors that told him without logic or understanding that Marina would save him.

On September 2, 1901, Antonio set off on horseback to Princes Town to meet Marina, determined to speak to her and resolved, at least consciously, not to marry her, for though she might be able to help him, he refused to take the risk of remarriage.

On September 3, Antonio came face to face with a woman of incredible beauty, quite accidentally, or so it seemed.

It was the black woman, her head wrapped in a spotless white bandana, her large breasts and wide hips pressed against her long white dress, who asked him whether he knew if the Waraos would come to the jungle to trade their ground provisions the next day. But it was the younger woman whom he saw. Tall and arrogant, her face framed by light, almost golden hair—wild, unkempt, uncombed hair that at the same time seemed to be deliberately and artistically placed on her head strand by strand. The bridge of her nose was long, her nostrils wide and flaring. High cheekbones set off wild, gray eyes. Her full-lipped mouth was warm and generous. Tamed. And her skin was pale, almost white. She stood next to the black woman, looking shamelessly into his eyes, breasts projecting forward as though ready for argument, backside high and rigid, forcing her to lean slightly backward. And Antonio lost his voice.

On December 1, 1902, Antonio married the woman, Marina. Because she was beautiful, because he loved beautiful women, and because in the inner sanctum of his brain where his mind was free from the primitive grappling of the intellect, he knew passionately that this woman would save him.

BEFORE THE DRY SEASON

6

Virginia de Balboa braided the last row of her thick, coarse-grained black hair, putting the final touches on an intricate pattern of cornrows streaming from the center of the foremost part of her head down to her temples to touch concentric circles chiseled out with artistic precision on the back portion of her head. Over this incredible design, which she made easily from long practice as a child, she meticulously wrapped a large, bright red, cotton handkerchief. It was a hairstyle that unnerved Hilda Smith, her English adoptive mother. But Virginia liked it from the first moment that Mrs. Smith's African servant, Nean, had fashioned it on her head, saying that she was going to make her a princess. Of course, Nean meant African princess but Virginia heard only the word "princess" and, later when Mrs. Smith called it African, it was too late for her to discard the

71

style. She had already discovered that it made her beautiful. Nevertheless, Virginia covered her head in Mrs. Smith's presence, and so now, by force of habit, she automatically wrapped up her hair after she had painstakingly fixed it. Giving a final twist to her bandana, she slowly stripped down to her long, white, stiffly starched petticoat.

At fifty-two, her body still retained its sensuousness, though her skin was no longer as young and supple as it had been the first night when she obediently opened her thighs to Vasco de Balboa—her strange Portuguese husband. Then, at fifteen, her beauty was breathtaking. Yet Virginia wished it had not been so, for she saw her beauty as the cause of all her misery. She wished her legs were not long and slender, her breasts firm and round, her hips so seductive. She disliked the varied hues of reddish black that danced all over her skin. The ripe purple plum color of her face, the jet black of her eyes, like bottomless pits, the deeper purple of her thick, wide mouth, innocently sensuous. Overnight, it seemed to her, she had blossomed into a woman whose very skin suggested forbidden sexual pleasure.

It was her color, Nean had told her, that frightened Mrs. Smith. Her cocoa-black skin that could not hide her red blood pulsating beneath it. "The sun made your blood hot," Nean said. "Miz Smith, she 'fraid your hot blood. Watch, watch how she watching her husband watching you. You not pale and white like she. You watch out. Soon she put you out of here. Daughter or no adopted daughter, *oui.*" Virginia tried to laugh at Nean's words. Hilda Smith was her mother, even if she had not given birth to her. She had treated her like any English mother would have treated her English daughter. Given her the best education—music, literature, art—the best of everything. Yet Virginia knew that there was some truth in what Nean said. Harold Smith did keep his eyes on her. He found the oddest reasons to embrace her, to kiss her fully on the lips. He'd reach to give her something and his hairy arm would brush her breast. He'd lean over his chair to talk to her and his large hands would squeeze her thighs as if accidentally. She prayed that her mother would not see the desire burning in his eyes, but Virginia knew that Hilda Smith had found out her husband the day that she told her that it was time that she marry.

Virginia was not unhappy to leave her home and go to de Balboa. The Portuguese, it was rumored, was a quiet man. He had built a house by the beach and kept to himself, except for the Warao chief who was his only friend. No one knew where he got his money. They said he brought it with him from Portugal, but money couldn't last forever. He had to work one day. That's how they said Hilda Smith got her big idea. She'd give this Portuguese fifteen acres of diseased cocoa land that she owned in Tabaquite if he'd take her daughter. Not as his mistress, of course—Hilda Smith made that perfectly clear to everyone—but as his wife, his legitimate spouse. They also said that God rewarded Hilda Smith for her kindness and made obeah work for her, because she gave birth to a son, Philip Smith, not long after Virginia left.

De Balboa did not quarrel with the dowry Hilda Smith offered him for her daughter. "But I'll not sleep with you as man and wife. I won't share your bed," he told Virginia. "You may do as you please. I'll not have her sell you to me like a lump of coal. I'll have no hand in her slave traffic. Your color offends her," he scoffed. "I'll give you the land too. It's your right as her daughter." Yet de Balboa could keep only one of his promises. On the night of their marriage, harboring not lustful desires, but the dark, protective, guilt-ridden love he felt for all the natives of the island, and a self-righteous memory of the hypocrisy of his compatriots on the ship that brought him to Trinidad, he entered Virginia's bedroom, he discovered that side of him that he had long forgotten or thought had long ago died. Carnal desires that had plagued him as a teenage boy. Incidents with young girls and, tragically, with his first cousin, which left no question in his mother's mind that at sixteen he should leave her house. And no question in his mind, that a vow of chastity would be barely punishment enough for a sin that most surely destroyed his young cousin's chance of a suitable marriage partner.

De Balboa had long suppressed these feelings, but the sight of Virginia's incredible, voluptuous, brazen nakedness confronting him on his wedding night at the edge of their bed, rolled back forgotten days and aroused distant longings. Virginia lay still on the white sheet. Lips moistened and parted, her breasts a deep dark cocoa black, slightly lighter in color tone than her face, glaring tremblingly at him. Nipples rigid. Purple black. Flat belly. Narrow hips. A mound of wild, wiry black hair. Thighs the color of rich sun-ripened cocoa pods. Parted. De Balboa's eyes traveled rapidly down her body, his stoic detachment oozing swiftly out of his soul. He fell upon her ripping off only his pants. In a frenzy, de Balboa penetrated the innocent Virginia as though he had lost every ounce of his rational self, his Christian morality. At the end of his first climax, he lay back spent, and then the musky scent of her warm body, her dark skin, her purple-moistened mouth, indifferent, sensuous, forbidden, intoxicated him and he ravaged her again and again. And through it all Virginia did not have one orgasm though the mouth of her vagina remained wet, sticky and palpable all that night.

That was a long time ago and now Virginia waited, as she had waited every night for years since her husband's death, for the familiar sound of her son's knock on her bedroom door. Methodically, she shook out the pillows and placed them one atop the other, making a backrest for herself on the bed. Then she sat down with her legs stretched in front of her. Carefully she turned up the kerosene lamp on her bedside table and opened the prayer book that lay next to it. She stared at the opened page. Not reading. Distracted.

Perhaps, she thought, Marina could do what she had done to de Balboa, though God knows she did it unwittingly. Perhaps the girl could unmask her son as she had unmasked his father. Perhaps she would show him the shameful dark side of himself, and having seen it, he would be left an empty shell grieving for a self that never was. Perhaps Antonio would not come to see her tonight, though he had every night since his father had died—even on the wedding nights of his marriages to Effie, Mildred and Sara. Perhaps this girl had already charted for him the course that would lead him, as it had led his father, into the deep, dark abyss of his flesh, where nothing would matter to him but the shame of what he had done, or the hunger for the pleasures she had opened to him.

Yet she had not worried this way about Antonio's other wives. For Effie, Mildred and Sara were docile girls. Almost stupid. Indeed, it had been difficult to grieve for them, except for the loss of their beauty. For they were beautiful women. But Marina? Was it the strange story that Antonio confessed to her about Marina's birth that frightened her a little? Marina's mother, Antonio told her, had left her newborn twin sons in the forest to die so that Marina could be born. Marina was strong. She had the power of eight men. Nothing could hurt her. Not even childbirth, he whispered in her ear.

"Nonsense," Virginia told her son and closed her ears to

his story. "Nonsense. If you love her, marry her. The people in this village are superstitious. It's as if they hadn't left Africa. There's a story in everything. A jumbie hiding behind every bush."

But Virginia was uneasy. There was indeed something unusual about Marina. She seemed cold, detached. No, that was not it, Virginia corrected herself, she seemed confident, overly selfconfident and independent. As if she had chosen Antonio to be her husband and not the other way around. Was it Marina's cool indifference, her quiet detachment throughout the entire wedding ceremony that now irritated her? One hour before the wedding, she had seen Emilia pull Marina to where the mango trees stood clustered at the back of the house. She could not see nor hear them, but when they returned to the house, Emilia's face had crumbled as though she had been crying. Yet the girl had remained unmoved. When the wedding was all over at two in the afternoon, the champagne drunk, the dishes washed, the sad Emilia leaning on the arm of her paramour, the priest and some curious neighbors all gone, Marina surveyed the house from top to bottom as if it were all hers now and she were mistress of it.

So absorbed was Virginia in these reflections that she did not hear Antonio's knock on her door, nor his footsteps as he entered the room. His voice surprised her when it came at the exact moment when the idea dawned on her how she would save her son.

"Mother?" Antonio was touching her arm. "What are you thinking about? You look strange."

If Virginia was flustered or caught off guard, she didn't show it. With a mind adept at controlling her feelings and concealing her thoughts, she quickly pointed to the book in front of her.

"Othello," she answered closing the book. "I was thinking of Othello."

Antonio put his arm around her and kissed her briefly on the forehead. "You are always thinking of Othello," he said.

"And why not?" Virginia pulled herself more upright on the bed. "I feel sorry for him."

"And not for Desdemona?" Antonio teased carelessly, taking the book from his mother's hand and placing it on the night table. "She was an angel."

The comment was given casually. It was a point of view that Antonio had expressed before and Virginia had always ignored. Now it irked her, for no reason that she could completely discern except that in her mind's eye, as her son so generously complimented Desdemona, she saw the fleeting image of Marina, smiling sweetly.

"An angel? 'yet she wished/That heaven had made her such a man.' " Virginia mocked, "Well, she got such a man, didn't she? Didn't she know that he was black and therefore unsure of her? I mean why should she expect him to believe that she, a white woman, loved him when the entire society disapproved of miscegenation? An angel would have been more careful. She should never have given him occasion to distrust her."

The sudden outburst puzzled Antonio and he looked at his mother suspiciously. "But she didn't," he said cautiously.

"Oh, she did. She never should have supported any man, not even Cassio. And in her place I certainly would have guarded that handkerchief with my life."

"It was a mistake," said Antonio reluctantly.

"We pay for mistakes."

"She was innocent." Her point was beginning to annoy him.

"To risk losing her husband? She was the one who threw him away. Like a rare pearl."

"Come now, Mother."

"If I had a chance for such happiness—" The words slipped out before Virginia could hold them back and the room became uncomfortably quiet.

A familiar guilt nagged Antonio and he felt sorry for his mother. He sat down beside her on the bed and touched her hand. "Come on, Mother. What is it? What have you been thinking?"

"About your future."

"My future?" Antonio was relieved. He jumped off the bed and reached for the covers to pull them over her. "Well, my future can wait until tomorrow."

"No!" Virginia threw back the covers. "No! It's *she* who can wait."

"Mother!"

"Well, hasn't she waited before?"

Antonio's uneasiness returned. "It's my wedding night. I just came in to say good night." He hesitated and then added, "As usual."

Virginia tried to hide the frown that had gathered on her forehead. Was there anxiety in his voice? Anticipation of pleasure? "No, wait," she almost shouted. "It's important."

"On my wedding night?"

"I need you too," Virginia said quietly.

The guilt returned again and tightened around Antonio's chest. The old smells, the old sounds flooded his memory. Of a silent father walking on the beaches of Moruga, trailing behind him faint tinges of the stench of Warao shark oil. Of his mother, clean, pure, in starched cotton dress, teaching the village children in her one-room schoolhouse. Of squawking chickens and quacking ducks waddling across her polished floors when some unkind or jealous person let them out of their coops because the overseers and the ward officers bought their fowl from his mother and from her alone. She was the sole wage earner in the de Balboa household.

Antonio heard himself say, "I know, Mother. And you are important to me too. Always first in my life. And forever."

"Then you'll stay?"

Antonio nodded his head.

Virginia cleared her throat and tightened the bandana around her head. Within a blink of an eye her face changed its contours from the deep furrows of hardship that mark the face of a woman deserving pity to the soft lines of concern that a mother wears when she worries about her sons.

"You know, Antonio, the last few months have not been easy for either of us. People talk. They say all kinds of things. You know. About you and Sara, Effie and Mildred. I don't care. But I thought that if we moved. Lived somewhere else, you and Marina would have a better chance. A fresh start."

Antonio got up from the bed and walked toward the kerosene lamp. She was at it again, he thought, holding his guilt at bay. "I thought that you had something new to tell me," he said, suppressing his anger. "We've discussed this before."

"No. Don't turn out the light." Virginia stretched out her arm to stop him. "You haven't finished hearing what I have to say."

Antonio sat down on the rocking chair near the bed. "It's not that I mind, Mother. But you know the problem. We have gone over this. You can't stop people from talking. And, in any case, we don't have the money to move. You know that."

"Sell the land." Virginia kept her eyes steady on her son.

"What did you say?" Antonio stopped rocking in his chair. Years ago he had made the very same suggestion to Virginia and she had silenced him with her anger. Her mother, she said, had given her that land. The land was her link to her mother. She would not give it up.

"Sell the land," Virginia repeated.

"I never thought the day would come when you'd say that."

"We never got anything from it," Virginia said flatly.

"I know, but—"

"I've made up my mind. I've discussed it with a buyer."

"But who'd want that land now?" Antonio leaned forward toward her.

"Ranjit," Virginia whispered.

"Ranjit?" Antonio barely heard the name. His mother lowered her eyes.

"But he knows about our land?" Antonio shifted his body in the rocking chair. He felt uncomfortable.

"You mean that the crops are dying? Yes, he knows that. I told him."

"And he wants to buy it?" Antonio steadied his voice. He would show no emotion.

"Yes."

"Did you tell him why the cocoa is dying this time?" Antonio had to be sure.

Virginia did not answer.

"But Mother, not even Ranjit can do anything about this new disease on our land." He felt safer calling it a disease, but they both knew what he meant. The Warao had told them how far the oil had spread.

"How do you know what Ranjit can do?"

Antonio's lips began to form an answer, but the words

would not leave his throat. The discomfort he had felt a few seconds earlier, embarrassment in fact, had not dissipated. Virginia could always disarm him this way. Talking about Ranjit as though he were just another person. No one special. Daring him to suggest that he was anything more to her. Whatever he thought of the relationship between his mother and Ranjit, he said nothing to her about it. How could he?

Now she persisted again with her question, "How do you know, Antonio?"

He answered, flicking his fingers at a mosquito that had paused for a moment on his chin, "Come on, Mother. You know what the Warao said. Even our squatters have left the land." Then, unable to resist the temptation to needle her, he continued, "It was no good in the first place. That's probably why Mrs. Smith gave it to you and Father."

"Don't say that, Antonio." Virginia bristled. Her fingers clutched at the neckline of her nightgown.

"Why not? And why not, Mother? The cocoa was diseased from the moment you got it. Not this new thing with the soil, but the trees were dying all the same."

"Everyone's cocoa was diseased. Not only cocoa but sugarcane too. We could have saved ours if your father were not so stubborn. Many people did and made quite a living from the cocoa and sugarcane."

"You mean Ranjit?"

"Yes, Ranjit for example. Look what he did for his sugarcane. We could have done the same. But no, not your father!"

Antonio wanted to defend his father. "Father gave the land to you."

"Gave me? Gave me? You talk like a child, Antonio."

"Well didn't he give you the land? Don't you own it now?"

"And what did you expect me to do? Take a machete and pick fork and work the land like a dirt farmer? Is that what you wanted me to do?"

"No, but at least you could have understood Father."

Virginia bit her lower lip. She tried to control her anger. For one year, for just one single, solitary year that her husband had chosen to speak to his son, Antonio seemed to have forgiven him for twelve years of silence and rejection. Yet she would not lose her son now. "Tell me, what should I have understood? You talked to him. Tell me."

"That he didn't want people slaving on his land. Like the way the English take advantage of the people here. He didn't want that."

"I did what I could, but I couldn't control the squatters. I told them that I'd pay them if they harvested the cocoa. I'd give them a shilling for every bag of cocoa they brought me. But no, they began to cut down the cocoa. They said it was diseased. Everybody's cocoa was diseased but they did something about it. But not them. No, our workers—squatters—planted yams and cassava and dasheen! Who buys yams, cassava and dasheen? Not the English people! Not the English people! Why couldn't your father have at least helped me control the squatters?"

"He told you the land belonged to them."

"I thought he had given the land to me?"

"It was yours too, Mother, if you wanted to farm it."

"Oh. Then tell me, Antonio. Tell me." Virginia pressed the palms of her hands down on the bed and pushed her body more upright on her pillows, "Tell me, how do you think your father intended for us to live? To eat?"

Antonio lowered his head. "We managed," he said quietly.

"I managed. I sold chickens, ducks. I taught school. I managed."

"Yes, you managed." Antonio loosened his tie. Blood rushed to his throat so rapidly he could hardly breathe. God, he thought, she brandishes guilt like a weapon. Yet I helped her. I helped her manage. Wasn't she able to stop working when I began to teach?

"Then we'll sell the land?" Virginia kept her eyes on him.

"It's yours."

"Good. Good." Virginia lay back. She released him. "Good."

"Sell it if Ranjit's foolish enough to buy it," Antonio tried a final stab at her.

Virginia brushed the air with her hand. "He's a miracle worker with the land."

"He'd need miracles. The land is finished. Cocoa will never grow there again."

Virginia groaned. "You never say anything good about Ranjit."

"Let him buy it, then."

"So we'll move?"

Antonio shrugged his shoulders. It was getting harder for him to advance on his job. He had always thought of going to Port-of-Spain. "I'll talk to Marina," he said.

"Marina?" Virginia asked, her voice strained. "What does she have to do with this?"

"She's my wife. Have you forgotten?" Antonio got up to leave.

"No! Wait Antonio! I didn't mean it like that. It was your promise, remember? You said we'd move if we could get the money. And there's that new school in Port-of-Spain, Tranquility Boys School."

"If Ranjit buys the land, fine. We'll move if he buys the land." Antonio had already reached the door when he finished speaking.

It was not the victory Virginia wanted, but as she listened to Antonio's footsteps moving toward his room, she allowed herself to feel some pity for Marina. For if she did, as Virginia felt intuitively that she could, expose Antonio's carnal desires, she might have to pay the same price as she—Virginia—had been forced to pay. For Marina might reveal to Antonio the shameful force and urgency of his sexual needs, and as his father had done to Virginia, Antonio would exact from Marina, in the same measure, the cost to him of nights of nursing a sick conscience, lying uselessly in a narrow cot. He would make love to her only on those rare occasions when he could not control his passion, his desire to have her, and then there would be the shame that would make her hate her very body. But the pity was momentary, for in her heart Virginia knew that Marina was not the sort of person to accept defeat easily. No, indeed, she must move her son to Port-of-Spain where people read books and played the piano and the violin. She must take Antonio from this village where printed paper was useful only to wrap up fish or clean windows. Antonio would find distractions there—in that city Spain had once claimed as hers—and when Marina threatened to consume his waking hours, and his flesh made a mockery of his spirit, the city would be there.

Virginia drifted off to sleep with dreams of days she once knew. Days with Mrs. Hilda Smith, her mother. She saw herself all dressed up in lavender frills and white silk ribbons, holding a white alabaster doll with blond hair.

It was the governor's Easter tea party. In the garden the flowers bloomed, not common ones like bougainvillea, or hibiscus, or pink lady slippers—except, of course, for the more cultured anthurium—but exotic roses bred in green-houses in temperate climates, and blue-ribbon orchids coveted by the English horticulturist, and delicate lilies, straining to hide from the scorching sun under the shade of the wide saman trees. Across the lawn the ladies snickered under pastel-colored parasols and behind white gloves and they questioned each other about the one black face in their midst. Not the servants, of course, who were all black, nor the few colored guests whose pale skin made their blackness more acceptable, but the little black girl holding on tightly to the warden's wife. Virginia did not care, for her mother—the warden's wife, that is—pressed her hand and whispered in her ear, "Never mind, child. They can't see your whiteness but I can. You hold on to that wicked doll. She'll give back your whiteness to you and they'll see it too. So there."

The queen's royal band played a Strauss waltz in the covered round bandstand facing the wide, green savannah, and Trinidad's self-ordained English gentry smiled, and so did the doctors, the lawyers, the scholars, the clergymen. All the lovely ladies dressed in lace. Ah! Such was Port-of-Spain.

Antonio made one mistake on his wedding night. It was to cost him dearly throughout his marriage to his fourth wife. He related to Marina the conversation between his mother and himself. Casually. In the way of explaining why he took so long to return to their bedroom. He did not notice the change in her when he declared matter-of-factly that it wouldn't be a bad idea to sell his mother's useless land if he could get a good price for it. He was too consumed by the pleasure he took in their lovemaking, causing him, like his father before him, to lose all control of his passion. None of his three wives had been like Marina. None of them had the body, nor the power to distract him from his conviction that all human beings were part body and part soul and should be treated as such. For him, that night Marina was all body.

Lying on the bed in the frilly lace nightgown that Emilia insisted that she wear on her wedding night—probably, Marina thought, a present John Telser gave her mother after she had given herself to him—Marina waited for what seemed to her like hours before Antonio returned from his mother's bedroom. At first she was angry that she was forced to bear this humiliation of waiting. She was not accustomed to it. The men in her life waited. Not she. At eighteen she was still a virgin. Like most middle-class Catholic girls, she had done everything except allow a man to actually penetrate her. It was more because it was fashionable rather than because it was the ultimate mortal sin. It gave her power. Men breathing heavily down her neck, begging, pleading, as though their lives depended upon her. Some, it seemed, would die if they could not, if she would not let them, just a little, just the tiniest ever-so-brief second, enter her. And at the moment when they thought that they had conquered her, she remained always and finally in control, brushing them off with a laugh, leaving them to stumble and ejaculate in the empty air.

Antonio was different. If he wanted her sexually, she never knew. Perversely that was what made it easier for her to marry him, even though long before she met him she had decided that she would be his wife. She was challenged by this mild-mannered man who did not appear to want her as others had wanted her, who permitted himself only brief kisses on her hands and on her cheeks, who trailed behind him speculation about the death of his three wives and a devotion to his mother that could not be broken. It would be a challenge to expose this man's passion and to make him want her as he had never wanted or loved anything or anyone else in his life. But it was the fifteen acres of land in Taba-quite that drew her to him. The land, the land. That was why she married him. So she waited for him in the bedroom, bearing her humiliation. She would not treat him as she had treated others who had forced her to wait. When he came, finally, telling her of his mother's plans, she acted no differently. She opened her legs to him. Land. Land. She was born on the land. Land was her birthright. She would not lose it as her mother had.

Now, one hour later, she looked indifferently at Antonio's naked body sprawled across the bed next to her—spent, exhausted, in a comalike sleep—a smile of satisfied pleasure drawn across his face. Who would have guessed that this polite, respectful man had so much fire in him? Asking her mother, as if he were some English gentleman, "Mrs. Heath-row, may I have your daughter's hand in marriage?" Mrs. Heathrow? As though she were Mrs. Heathrow. Did the faintest smile cross his lips as he said those words, "Mrs. Heathrow?" Did his polite voice falter? Did he give the slightest hint that he knew that he had legitimized her? Did he even look at Telser?

And Mrs. Heathrow, playing with the beads with which she loved so much to decorate her neck, acknowledging the "Mrs.," ignoring Telser, sitting boldly in the very drawing room in which this man had called her Mrs., replied: "It would give me great pleasure if you did, Mr. de Balboa."

Marina thought: It was the land that made you so generous, wasn't it, Emilia? Yet you came dragging me into the bushes on my wedding day, my wedding day, to unburden yourself, to beg me to change my mind.

"He murdered those women, his wives," you whispered.

"If you thought so, Mother, why did you wait so long to tell me?"

"Because I was not sure—Alma—Alma said she saw it in the fire."

"Alma? Your obeahwoman, Alma? Mother, when will you learn to think as I do? I am strong, Emilia. Do you see me? Look at my breasts, Mother. Look at my hips. I can carry babies, Mother. I can carry babies and babies forever. I won't die like the others, just giving birth to babies."

How that shuts you up, Mother? How that makes you silent? Because you could have only me? Is that what makes you always so silent when I tell you that I can have babies? That I will have many children?

Marina fingered the lacy frills of her nightgown and sighed. *Telser gives you lace and my father gave you land. How different you were then, Mother, before you slept with Telser. Did you forget what you taught me? Could anyone make you give up land so easily? Even your obeahwoman? No. I've made my bed.* Marina looked at Antonio, snoring lightly next to her, and she shook her head. *Murder? The man looked incapable of murder.* Swinging her legs off the bed, she said aloud, "I'll make it right again for us, Mother, even if you won't try."

7

Not knowing what was on his wife's mind, Antonio woke to new feelings he had never imagined he would know. A warm joy in being alive flooded his whole body. The gloomy disposition of his father seemed a sickness to him now, a disease that he had participated in because life had shown him no reason to behave otherwise. Marina will end it all, he now convinced himself. Enchanted. The work of obeah. It didn't matter. The Warao chief was right. She could—perhaps she had the power—she could end the torment he had grown accustomed to and had accepted as his lot. A new smile lit up his face, and he reached over for his new bride, his hand playfully searching her side of the bed. Marina was not there.

He thought that perhaps she had gone to make her toilet outside at the rear end of the house, like his last wife, Sara.

Tiny Sara. Pretty Sara, whose body he never really saw, covered as it always was under mounds of starched cotton. At night when she thought it time to do her duty, she'd let him feel for her under the sheets and when it was over, she'd turn her back to him, draw up her knees and pull her starched nightgown over her feet. Before the sun rose, she would be out of her bed to wash away the smell of his sex, to purify her body. When he saw her again, she'd be sweating under the high laced collar of her long-sleeved blouse. Was he perhaps too rough on Marina? He trembled a little at the memory of the pleasure of plowing through warm, willing, tight, moist flesh. With his other wives it took him at least three nights spread over three weeks to break through, so fearful were they that he would hurt them. He was accustomed to tears, to shame, to pain. To the grating sensation of dry penetration. To the feelings of obligation and responsibility when it was finished. Not so with Marina. *She* moved his hand over her body. *She* let him touch her everywhere. *She* pressed his mouth to her breasts and wrapped her fleshy thighs around his buttocks. Her desire was boundless, her pleasure interminable. She gave her total self to him. Without limits.

Sara, Effie, Mildred were middle-class ladies. Colored Victorians. How the English colonists would have been pleased that they had fathered such mimics of themselves! All three had agreed to marry him because he was a schoolteacher, a professional. Because, as the district's schoolmaster, the house that the colonial government had loaned to him, deducting it from his salary, though not large, had all the requisites of colonial living—three bedrooms, a verandah, a living room, dining room and a kitchen. It was made of wood with some ornate pretensions to Victorian style and sat high on ten twelve-foot concrete pillars distributed evenly around the base of the house, the intention being that during the hurricane season—late July and August—the heavy rains would not flood the house. The Europeans, however, had a more urgent reason for this elevation. It was their protection from the snakes that casually crawled around the yard during the dry season in search of food and water. Simple as this house was, it commanded respect from the villagers, who had little more than caked-mud shacks covered with dry coconut palms, or sheds made of pieces of discarded tin, cardboard or wood.

When Antonio's wives came to Moruga, Virginia employed servants. For it was Virginia who persuaded the mothers of these women that their daughters would be in the upper class of the Moruga society. It didn't cost much, then, to hire a servant. A little more than twenty-five cents a month, an opportunity that any village mother would seize for her daughter since it always guaranteed her child food and shelter. But Virginia found servants a nuisance and only kept them to maintain her status in Moruga and to reassure the mothers of Antonio's wives. Not that a wife was expected to do nothing. It was her duty to plan the day's meals, but the servant girl would cook them. She would decorate the house, sew the curtains, the slipcovers for the Morris chairs, the tablecloths, but the servant girl would clean the house. Most of these servants, however, were too young and irresponsible, so supervision of them was left to Virginia. She liked it that way. It clearly established her as mistress of the house.

Perhaps in time Antonio's wives would have rebelled over the authoritative way in which Virginia ran their house had they not all, within months of their marriage, become pregnant and had sickly confinements. So perhaps it was because they were too weak to argue, and not because of their passion to imitate the ladies who roamed through the novels of Jane Austen and Emily Brontë that they occupied themselves with the prettier side of housekeeping.

It was the sounds of thin metal pans clanging against each other that drew Antonio at last from his bed, and a troubling concern that if Marina had gone to wash herself as Sara had done, she had taken far too long.

He found Marina in the kitchen, her back turned to him, bent over the iron stove, her long legs exposed by the upward slant of her backside provocatively hitching up her short cotton dress. For a second he stood there at the doorway, frozen between a tingling sensation in his groin and an unpleasant, annoying feeling grating against his brain. Unpleasant, because he could not locate its source, except that she should be there so soon in the kitchen, looking as though she belonged.

Before he could clear his throat, say a word, Marina had felt his presence and in that split second, caught in surprise by his sudden appearance, she jerked forward and spilled the kerosene from the can she was holding on the burning coals at the bottom of the stove. Immediately flames roared up past the cooking grill, surrounding a black covered long-handled saucepan on top of it. Instinctively Antonio lurched toward the fire, but Marina was too quick for him. Controlled, sure, swift, she had picked up the iron poker lying on the floor, and with Antonio foolishly hovering over her, she deftly stoked the coals back to a red glow.

"You shouldn't have done that, Marina," Antonio said, unsuccessfully trying to sound assertive.

Marina put down the poker and turned to her husband smiling. "No harm done. See."

"But what if . . ." Antonio's voice trailed.

Marina threw her arms around his neck and kissed him

fully on his mouth, her tongue brushing against his clenched teeth.

"Stop it, Marina!" Antonio pushed her off of him. Irritated. Aware of the swelling in his pants. He wiped his lips against the back of his hand, and Marina, seeing him do so, laughed and turned away to reach for a towel to lift the hot cover off the saucepan. "I thought you liked that," she said playfully, and stirred the cocoa in the saucepan.

Antonio watched her backside. God, he did not want to get angry. He moved toward the wooden kitchen table, painted white by pretty Sara. He pulled out a cane-backed chair, sat down and stared out of the window.

"Didn't you like it?" Marina was saying again. "Last night, I mean."

Antonio sighed. "Please, not here, Marina." It would be a good day, he could see. The sky was already a crystal-clear blue. He'd go to the beach. Perhaps he'd see the Warao.

"So where? In the bedroom?" Marina placed a blue china cup and saucer on the table in front of him.

He could smell her body. Musky sweet. God, how could he get angry! "You are lovely, Marina," he said, his voice heavy with the memory of the night before.

Marina smiled, hesitated, and then returned to the stove. "I made something for you," she said gaily, bringing the covered saucepan to the table.

Antonio was grateful that she had released him. Generously, he said, "Hmm, Marina. That smells good." And he lifted his cup to her, letting her pour the hot steaming cocoa into it. Pleasantly, it was exactly to his taste, rich and thick, a shallow circle of oil lazily floating on top, with just a hint of goat's milk to lighten its color.

"Where did you learn to make cocoa like this?"

Marina pulled out a chair from the table and sat opposite

to him, her back to the window, shutting off the dazzling early morning sunlight that had lit up the spotless kitchen. "Is it good?" she asked.

"Excellent."

"Mother—" she began and then waited as Antonio drank again. She took a deep breath and looked across the room intensely, as if searching for something among the rows of pots and pans hanging from hooks attached to a low beam in the ceiling. A strange place, she thought, to hang them so directly above the clay pots and china dishes neatly stacked on the open shelves. "Mother," she repeated, cautiously choosing her words, "she taught me how to make it. She taught me a lot of things."

For the briefest moment Antonio thought he heard a hint of provocation in her voice, and he looked away from his cocoa up to her. But her face was innocent, and he asked playfully, "Did she? What else do you know then, Marina?"

"About land."

"Well, I guess with Telser being an overseer, you probably do know something about land." Antonio drained the cup.

His casual reference to her mother's lover irritated her, and Marina got up and walked toward the kitchen door.

"Did I say something wrong?" Antonio asked. The uncanny pleasure he felt in seeing her face lose its calm control disturbed him, and confused, he raised his empty cup to his lips.

"You didn't tell me that we were going to sell the land."

"What did you say?"

"Why didn't you tell me that we were going to sell the land?"

"We?" Antonio heard himself ask.

Marina ignored the question. She returned from the doorway and sat down again opposite him, her back casting a shadow across the table, shutting out the sun. "I never thought that you would sell the land," she repeated.

"I didn't think it mattered."

"Why?" Marina looked deeply in his face.

"Please, Marina."

"Why didn't you think so?"

Antonio got up. She made him nervous. He wanted to go outside. Pretty Sara, she never asked questions. "I agree with Mother," he said, not wanting to seem indecisive. "We should sell the land if we can. It's no good."

Marina pulled her short skirt tightly over her knees and leaned forward in her chair. "Is it really your land? Ours? Really ours? Legally I mean."

Antonio looked at her. Her face was glowing like a little schoolgirl's. He wanted to be pleasant, but instead he was patronizing. "I suppose it is our land. Yours and mine. Though it's Mother's, really; but I can do what I want with it."

"And the deed? Does your mother have the deed?"

"I suppose so."

"Will she let you put your name on the deed?"

"Of course. It's on it already."

"And my name?"

"For God's sake, Marina, didn't you hear me last night? What does it matter about whose name is on the deed? Mother plans to sell the land. Don't you want to live in Port-of-Spain? City life?"

"Not if it means selling our land."

The "our" annoyed Antonio. "The land is totally useless," he said cruelly. "Or didn't I tell you? Oil has destroyed the cocoa. It's happening here just as it did in Venezuela. Our land is not worth a farthing."

"I don't care about the cocoa."

"What?"

"I don't care about the cocoa. It's land that's valuable."

"Valuable?"

"When we give up our land we become slaves again."

Antonio almost choked on his cocoa.

"We will be slaves if we sell our land," Marina repeated.

"My God, how foolish you are," Antonio cleared his throat. "On the contrary, it's those of us who remain working on the land for the English who are the slaves. Those ideas that you have, my dear, are the ones that chain down our poor people." He rolled up the sleeves of his white cotton shirt. "We are not hewers of wood nor drawers of water, Marina. We have minds. We should develop our minds. Do you see the Englishman tilling the soil? Does he chain himself to the earth?"

"No." Marina's voice was quiet. Soft with determination. "He doesn't have to. He owns the land. We give it to him and then he makes us work on it." She got up from her chair and walked toward the stove, exposing the dazzling sunlight that she had shaded with her back.

The sudden penetrating glare of the sun's rays blinded Antonio and he shifted his chair to avoid its force. He was irritated by Marina's answer, but not enough to engage her in further discussion. "But I'm not going to sell the land to the Englishman," he replied with finality, still shading his eyes with the palm of his hand. "There's an Indian man. Ranjit. Mother plans to sell to him."

Marina was reaching for the cocoa when Antonio said the name, Ranjit, and for a moment she just stood there by the stove, her hand on the saucepan, staring into space as though in a daze. "I had a teacher once," she said, "who explained it to me. He said that the Indians and Chinese flocked to our island like flies in search of food because there was sickness and poverty in their countries. He said that they were dying like flies from starvation and you could see them everywhere, lying in the gutters like dogs."

Antonio scratched his head. He was not sure what she meant by those words. "Maybe Ranjit's parents were starving," he said, finding nothing else to say.

"So that is why they love land," Marina continued as though Antonio had not interrupted her. "But the Negro hates it. That teacher said that the Negro hates land because it reminds him of slavery and the whips and chains they used to make him wear on the plantation. He said that for the Negro the earth is a dirty scourge that powders his face and stops up his nostrils."

Antonio scraped his chair against the floor. "I suppose he's right," he said.

Marina looked at him. "Is that why the men sign away acres of land like so much trash?" she asked quietly. She turned back to the stove and stirred the cocoa. "I've seen them enough times. Tall, strapping men they once were, and now their backs are bent with rum. The only use that they see for land is to exchange it for rum. The shopkeeper gives them rum and they give him land." She lifted the saucepan from the stove and brought it to the table. For a moment she watched Antonio pour his cocoa and then, when he finished, she spat out bitterly, "We are slaves by nature. Slaves."

Antonio wanted to end the discussion, to go outside, but the force of her insult struck him as though it were intended for him personally and he could not stop himself.

"If you want to talk about nature," he said tilting his chair on its back legs, "we can. I guess you can say that the Indians and Chinese are farmers by nature. What else can they be in countries where famine taught them the value of farming? If my life depended on tilling the soil, I'd know everything about growing crops. They have farming in their blood. It takes generations to get rid of that. I suppose that is what your teacher meant. Now the Negro . . . Why should he farm? He comes from a country where nothing stops growing. He'll throw out a seed willy-nilly and Pop! up grows a tree and another, and Pop! out comes a seed from that tree and another tree grows. He had nothing to do. Of course farming is not in the blood of Africans. But," he said, bringing his chair forward to stand on its four legs, "I doubt that slavery is."

Marina felt her face grow hot. He made her feel foolish. She had wanted to say that Negroes *act* as though they are slaves by nature. She hated his self-righteousness. "Then what is?" she retorted angrily.

Antonio answered, "Life. The love of life is in our blood."

"Rum, you mean."

Antonio laughed. "Rum, if that makes us happy."

"Is that what you tell your pupils?"

"They don't make statements like yours. But of course I tell them that we were not born to be farmers."

"I don't believe Ranjit was either, but he knows the value of land. Something we could learn from him."

The familiarity with which Marina seemed to speak of Ranjit unsettled Antonio. "Do you know Ranjit?" he asked.

"Not really. Except what they say."

"And what do they say?"

"That he's good with the land, and . . ."

"And what?" Antonio asked cautiously.

"And that he used to come to your house when your father was alive, so that your mother could teach him," Marina replied. Then, seeing the seriousness of his face, added quickly, "But I don't see anything wrong in that."

"In what, Marina?" Virginia had entered the kitchen to hear her daughter-in-law's final words.

"We were talking about Ranjit," Marina began.

"Yes," Antonio said quickly. He got up, walked to the large tin tub on the floor next to the door and put his cup and saucer in it, next to the other dirty dishes. No, he did not want to draw his mother into this conversation. "I told her that Ranjit may buy the land."

"I see him next week to settle it." Virginia frowned at her daughter-in-law. So soon. So soon she begins.

"Suppose he doesn't buy it?"

"He will, Marina."

"Did you tell him about the oil?" Marina looked at Virginia.

"Come," Antonio said, and tugged his wife's arm. "Come, there is something I want to show you."

The eyes of the two women locked briefly and then turned to Antonio. The time was not right for either of them. Marina let herself be led out of the kitchen, but Virginia stood there frozen, her heart trembling in her throat.

8

Of one thing Marina was sure: She did not love Antonio. Not as a woman loves a man or as women who love their men know that they love their men. No bittersweet anger stifled itself in her breast and cooled instantly when he decided to be nice. She felt no flutter in her stomach when someone called his name—another woman, whether she was pretty or not. She did not know the anguish of waiting, the prime occupation of women in love. Waiting for her husband to come home; waiting for him to eat the meal that she had spent all day preparing; waiting for him to admire the new dress, the new hairstyle; waiting for him to appreciate her. And since she knew that she was beautiful, it did not matter whether Antonio said so or not.

Unlike women who know that they are in love, Marina also did not know the gnawing anxiety of waiting for Antonio to be ready to make love to her, holding in check her own bursting passion so that he could feel that he was a man, so that she would not overwhelm, so that he could feel safe in knowing that he was the hunter, the fisherman, she the hunted, she the fished for. At times when she did not want to make love, she did not feel less of a woman when she said, no. Love did not make her think of him first and herself second. She was not in love with Antonio. It was the land, the land alone that had driven her to marry him. Fifteen acres, her mother had said, seducing her to the inevitable like the thirsty hummingbird to the glistening shell of the rotted hollow of a cocoa pod. She would not be like her mother. She would not be thrown out in the gutter like dirty wash water. She would not have her children's birthright snatched from her hands. She would not let herself be forced to make her way in the world by finding yet another man's bed. No, she would not let Virginia do that to her. She would not lose what was hers by right, a right she was entitled to by marriage.

For four weeks she talked to Antonio of all she remembered of that time when she was forced to leave her father's house. She told him what had happened to her mother after her father died, suggesting that the same could happen to her if he should die landless. Where would she go? What would she do? Antonio laughed, reminding her that his land was no good anyhow. She'd be better off with his pension from his schoolteacher's salary. Still she forced him to listen with her burning eyes. She made him choke down his arguments with her passion. The love of life, he had said, was in the black man's blood. Rum, he had told her flippantly, made the black man happy. Now she brought him to silence with her mother's words. A god!—she took him to the edge of awe with the possibility—a man who owned land was a

kind of god! His own man. No one else's. Skillfully she
played out the drumbeat of her mother's words. Yes, a man
who owned land owned a part of this earth. He was his own
master. From generation to generation the land would bind
his blood to the earth. His children and his children's children would have a place on the earth. But then soon she let
her ardor plunge her foolishly deep into the dangerous waters where always Antonio would challenge her: "We are not
hewers of wood nor drawers of water." No more slaves, she
had told him confidently. When we own our land we would
be free from the English. And Antonio, tottering on the
brink of surrendering to the spell she had begun to weave
around him, pounced upon her words. Education, he said,
would make them free. Yes, Marina was forced to admit,
Virginia's hold on her son was strong. Antonio would not
change his mind. He would sell the land as his mother had
asked him. And Ranjit would know better. He would buy the
land and she would be left like her mother, at the mercy of
a man's desire.

Yet Marina did not give up. Day after day, choosing her
time, measuring her words, she set out to fill Antonio with
her passion for land. But gradually, his stubbornness, his
cold inflexibility began to wear on her, and one night, unable to sleep well, she found herself fully awake and restless
at four in the morning. For the first time in her life she felt
lonely, and she let herself dream of an earlier time, a time
before she began to harbor the resentment that she now
nurtured toward her mother. She remembered that she used
to wake up with Emilia at this time, early in the morning
before the sun rose, when everything was still and quiet.
Pitch black. Emilia would tell her nancy stories of Br'er Fox
and Br'er Rabbit and then scare her to death with the evils
of the soucouyant, that old witch that lived under the silk

cotton tree by day and by night turned into a ball of fire. Or stories about la diablesse, the devil's bride, slinking in dark corners outside of dance halls, waiting to lure the unwitting with her beauty into the hell of her bridegroom. Marina remembered those days. Trembling with the pleasurable sensation of danger from which she was absolutely protected, she would creep stealthily with her mother to the donkey shed in back of the house. Together they would hitch the old donkey to the cart and ride him to the sea.

She knew then that they did not have to be so secretive. The Telsers were kind people, but it was their time together—hers and her mother's—and they shared it with no one. Shared not even the idea of it. All that ended with the death of the last of the Telser women, when Marina discovered that Emilia was Telser's mistress. But that morning, the memory of Emilia's disloyalty and immorality did not matter. Marina felt a strange longing for the warmth of those days, the secrecy of them and the sense of belonging and security she once had with her mother. That those hours with the warm seawater lapping over her chilly back were hers and Emilia's entirely. No one else's. So intense was this longing that she found herself unable to remain in her room, and leaving Antonio still snoring on the bed, she quietly left the house.

Marina walked briskly along the dirt road that led from her house to the main thoroughfare in Moruga, pulling the bright kerchief that covered her hair tightly under her chin. The dew that fell in the early morning in Trinidad was credited as the cause of a multitude of ailments, and Marina, like any other sensible Trinidadian, knew better than to walk with her head naked before the sun had chased away the last drop of moisture from the night. Once out of the dirt track, she walked about two miles down the main road past the open market, now empty, past the one-room post office, the moss-covered concrete police station, a scattering of broken-down rum shops that also sold groceries, past the brand-new Catholic church, and a few wooden houses that stood sheltered beneath enormous trees.

Streets like the crooked legs of a spider joined the main road. On either side of them Marina could see dirt shacks covered with coconut-palm leaves. In one or two spots, between some trees, a large house loomed. The ten-room brick house belonging to Harold Smith, the old warden who lived there with his grown-up son, Philip; the parsonage where the Irish Catholic priest lived shuttered behind lace curtains; the sprawling wooden house where the English overseer stayed to guard the cocoa for his country; and a few others slightly larger than de Balboa's that housed the more well-to-do— the village doctor, the cocoa estate owner, the English school principal. Close to the end of the main road, near the schoolhouse, where all the buildings stopped, Marina crossed the street and made her way through the tangle of bushes on the other side. A few yards away the soil turned sandy and the bushes thinned out giving in to the hundreds of coconut trees that cluttered the sky with their wide, green palms, but cleared the path beneath them. Marina sniffed the air and smelled the tangy fish scent of the sea, but still she could not see the water. Then abruptly the land sloped, and at its bottom, the sea rolled quietly against the well-worn sand.

When she reached the sandy shore, the sun had just risen from the sea. Across the silken-still water, five pirogues approached the beachfront rapidly, their occupants pulling vigorously at the paddles fastened to their hands. Curious, Marina sat on the beach waiting for their arrival, her short cotton dress which she used as a swimsuit flapping in the

quiet breeze that blew constantly off the sea, sending the sand tangled by seaweed, coral shells, and damp twigs into tiny mounds that quickly unraveled with the next breeze. Soon she found it totally impossible to keep her bandana fastened on her head, and then her pretty brown hair, naturally tangled, became matted. Impatiently she swiped away hair and sand from her eyes as the pirogues approached the shoreline, her heart racing as she saw that the men were the Waraos who came from the rain forest of Venezuela to trade their goods in Princes Town. Several times she had overheard Emilia talking with her friends about the Waraos, a Warao, but always the conversation ended when she appeared.

Excited now, Marina watched the Waraos bank their pirogues on the ridge a few feet from where the sand ended, strapping to their backs baskets that contained all sorts of ground provisions, like tania, yams and dasheen. Some balanced long hands of green bananas on their heads. Others held squawking parrots bound by their feet, and even monkeys destined for some cooking pots in Trinidad. Entranced somewhat by this sight, Marina did not notice that one of the Waraos, the oldest of the group, had left the others and was approaching her. But suddenly the crisp salty air around her turned thick with a stink like the smell of stale fish. Startled, Marina looked away from the canoes and spun around to see one of the Waraos—the chief no less, gleaming with shark oil, naked except for a tiny loincloth, a screeching condor twisted in the folds of his chest—looming over her.

She hugged her knees closer to her body not knowing what to do, staring at the man. The Warao locked her eyes with his, and for sixty seconds he stood there smiling without saying a word. Then he moved his hand toward her as if to caress her face, but Marina had recovered from her surprise

and she jumped to her feet and ran as fast as she could behind the wild almond trees that grew in a clearing where some coconut trees had died. She hid there and watched the Warao standing where she left him, his hand shading his eyes, searching the coastline.

He knows me. I know he knows me, she thought, her heart beating wildly. He's going to find me. But after a short while the Warao didn't seem to care. He simply shrugged his shoulders, and walked away to join his men. The indifference with which he did that, as if it were her loss not his that she didn't stay there on the beach, disturbed Marina and she felt a strong urge to seek him out. It was the sort of challenge she always liked. To approach him as he had approached her. It was the only honesty she would allow. But, later, as she tracked through the bushes on the far side of the village's main dirt road, following the Warao's path, she felt a nagging suspicion rise to her throat, her long-stifled questions about the rumors the villagers had spread about her mother.

She followed the Warao and his men for about three miles, careful to stay hidden, before she was forced to stop. In her haste to track the Amerindians, she had left her sandals swinging over her shoulders. But she was not like the other villagers, who lived their lives without shoes, whose feet had grown as thick as leather, who could be betrayed, even if their fortunes changed, by their feet. Flat and thick, the toes spread out forever. So while the thorns, sharp-pointed broken branches, the claws of dead crabs, sea-washed coral and insects not frightened by human smell, did not harm the naked, leathered feet of the Waraos, they tore at her soles. She was forced to stop. It was then that she knew that the Waraos were aware of her presence, for she heard their silence as she strapped her sandals to her feet. When she got up again to follow them, she heard their voices rise against

the squabbling monkeys, and their feet stomp fearlessly through the bushes.

After a mile or so, the forest gave way to a small clearing, cut, it seemed, by human hands. It stuck out incongruously, a clear round circle about ten yards in diameter, surrounded by thick trees that grew out tall from its edges. It was the Waraos' market. Marina realized with disappointment: He's not going to talk to me. She positioned herself closer to the clearing and watched the Waraos set out their goods. They rolled out their rice mats in a semicircle on the ground and neatly and carefully placed in the middle of each mat bundles of yams, tanias, dasheen, and edoes, the earth still clutched to them, and hands of bananas, and blackened sicia figs. They tied the parrots by their feet to each other and they too were put in heaps on the mat. The monkeys were not so willing to lie down, so the chief leashed them to a thick branch that he drove into the ground. When all the arranging was done, the Waraos retreated to the bush, careful, it seemed to Marina, to stay far from her.

It was about five-thirty now. The rising sun had turned the sky luminous, and Marina saw the first of the villagers peeping through the bush. It seemed that they knew where the Waraos were or they had agreed on a single entrance to the forest market, for they all took one path, coming in groups, men and women, no children, chatting noisily. They picked up the ground provisions, the bananas, figs, parrots and monkeys, each leaving something else. From time to time, one of the villagers would attempt to leave less than he should for a particular item, but his eyes would travel over the bushes to where he knew the Waraos sat, hidden but watchful, and he would add something else to the mat until he thought that his silent trader, seeing his every move, would be satisfied.

At about six-thirty, the sun had lit up the trees and the trading slowed down to a trickle. Finally no one was left but Marina and the Waraos. For a wild moment Marina thought of going around the clearing to where the Waraos sat. Perhaps if the chief saw her, he'd talk to her. But the Waraos had left their spot and were now rushing excitedly to pick up the things that they had bartered for. In spite of herself, Marina was relieved. Perhaps she had made a mistake. Perhaps the Warao had merely found her pretty. The thought of swimming in the salty sea returned to her, and in that instant, when she could actually feel the cool slap of the water against her back, now burning from the sun, she smelled again the stink, the stale odor of rotting fish, and she knew without looking that the Warao had come back. Her first impulse was to scream. He had come so silently upon her, having slipped away from his men. But the Warao's eyes looked softly at her and she remained still.

"Beautiful," he said at last. "Beautiful." He was looking at her with such tenderness that fear drained out of her. She lowered her eyes and remained crouched on the ground.

"Emilia's daughter. How beautiful," he said again with pride.

Some of them spoke English, that she knew, but this man spoke with such preciseness that if she shut her eyes he could be, for all she knew, a suitor, admiring her. That he knew her no longer alarmed her. She felt his familiarity then in the way his voice spoke her mother's name.

"You know me, don't you?" She found her voice.

"Your mother and your husband's father. Your husband too."

"Who are you?"

"I thought you knew."

"Why?"

"Weren't you following me? At the beach. I saw you. And then here."

Marina said nothing.

"You wish to speak to me?" the Warao asked again, still standing looking down at Marina.

"But you came to me at the beach," Marina insisted boldly.

"Because you wanted me to." The Warao smiled enigmatically.

Marina was disarmed. "How long did you know my mother?"

The Warao crouched on the damp earth, balancing on his toes.

"Before you were born," he said.

Marina felt the familiar sweat gather in the palms of her hands, and she knew why she had followed him. "It's true then?" she asked.

"Yes."

Her mind raced with fever in that simple single answer. Her head told her to run, but a kind of peace washed over her. Relief that at last someone had acknowledged what she had known all along. "Were you the one?"

"The one?"

"The one who took—"

The old chief smiled kindly. "Leave it. Let it go. You'll understand one day."

"But perhaps they could be alive?"

The Warao shook his head. "I took them deep in the rain forest."

"But, perhaps if you went back . . . ?"

"There were no villages there where I took them."

"But—"

The Warao drew close to her, not so that he could touch

her, but so that they now sat together like friends. "Shh," he said quietly, his finger across his lips. "Shhh! You are a charm child. Emilia's charm child. Her special child. Special . . . Special . . ."

Marina closed her eyes and allowed the illogic of those words to flow over her. The truth, naked and simple, unreasonable, was like the midday rain. Clear and crisp, washing off sticky sweat, soothing the hot body. One did not ask why it came at midday, at the hottest time of the day, in the dry season, the hottest time of the year. One only opened one's mouth and let the saltless water trickle down from forehead, nose and lips. She had heard the facts of her birth before, once when she was ten and unmistakably when she was fourteen, just four short years ago. But she had refused to believe.

First it was the whooping cough. In the schoolroom, the children in the front row started to cough up blood. Then, one by one, they disappeared from the class. Only she remained silent and healthy. They closed the four-room school and she still remained healthy. Then there was the mumps. The teacher didn't mind so much. There was no mess to clean up on the floor. So the children who could came to school, their necks and cheeks swollen, comical bandages tied around their chins and knotted on top of their heads. She was not the only one who didn't get mumps that year. The Telser girls were also immune, so no one looked at her in that special way as they had when whooping cough galloped through their village.

It was the chicken pox that made one of the girls spit out spitefully to Marina the story that her mother had told her about Mrs. Heathrow giving her twin sons to a "wild Indian" and going to the obeahman to put the spirits of those babies in Marina. "The devil's daughter," the little girl taunted, not knowing what she said, but burning with anger and envy because her skin, arms, legs, face and torso were covered with pussy blisters. The Telser children made Marina laugh. "She is jealous," they said twisting their faces in comic mockery of the girl. "Look how ugly she is." Yet, though Marina laughed, her knees weakened as the girl repeated the story. She felt an inexplicable urgency to hide the incident from her mother, to tell her nothing about what the girl had said, just as she had felt a time before when she overheard the priest, de Nieves, question her mother about her twin sons. Soon, within days, the Telser girls also became infected with chicken pox and in the mornings, as their mother tried to pull off their cotton nightdresses that had stuck to their bodies, they sent their screams of pain deep into Marina's heart, accusing her. That year, Marina asked her mother why her skin alone, in that class of twenty-five girls, had remained flawless, untouched. She got no answer, but from that day, her palms began to sweat.

When she was fourteen, consumption struck the island and Marina prayed that she would get it. Not to die. Just a little consumption. So she'd be normal. The whole school district was closed that year in August, in the rainy season. Everyone who could afford it wore shoes that season to keep dry. When her mother was not looking, Marina would take hers off and jump in the puddles of water, letting the rain soak her. Still she did not get consumption. She cut her lip once, to show Emilia the blood in her mouth. That was when the second Telser girl died and Mrs. Telser and the last Telser girl were burning up with fever. But her mother saw through her fraud and for once came close to telling her the truth. "You're special, Rosebud. You won't get it."

The third Telser girl died too, and Mrs. Telser, and Marina closed her ears to the gossip and went on living as though it were normal for her to be special. Teaching herself to perfection to pretend the tale she had heard had never happened, as though there could not be the remotest possibility that her brothers could be alive. And yet she had followed the Warao. Yet she had not quite succeeded in drowning the questions about the twins.

The Warao saw the furrows gathering on her brow. "No," he said firmly. "No! The past can never be returned to us. We live now. We make peace with now." Then he paused and smiled. "You'll be rich, my child."

It seemed normal, natural. The logical consequence of the twins' death. Yes, death. She must say death. They could not be alive. They could not have survived the rain forest. Alone. With no one to feed them. Rich. It would make sense that there would be some gain from the sacrifice of their lives.

The Warao felt her understanding. "It will bring you luck, Marina; your mother knows."

"How?" Marina asked, surrendering herself completely to the Warao.

"The land."

Marina drew herself into a tiny ball, clutching her knees to her bosom, and the Warao leaned forward to touch her hand, to seal their new intimacy. Instinctively, Marina pulled back, but not before, in that split second, the Warao's fingers had brushed the back of her hand greasing her pale knuckles with a smear of stale shark oil.

The Warao saw the corners of her mouth curl deep into her chin and her shoulders heave upward in disgust as she examined her hand, and he felt her revulsion. He started to his feet, to leave the girl. He was, after all, a chief, but Marina realized her mistake. She had just been washed clean of doubts and questions, and now she wanted to know. She could not let him leave.

"Please. I'm sorry. Please. Stay, please."

The Warao looked down at her, his brows grim, but his eyes still soft.

"Don't leave. Please. I want to know more. About the land. Please tell me."

The old chief crouched down on the wild grass. She was the wife of his friend's son. "Your mother knows," he said finally. "She should tell you. You'll get rich from this land."

Marina's head swam. "But Antonio wants to sell it. He says it's no good. The cocoa's dying. The squatters have left. It's worse than before. Nothing grows."

"I know," said the Warao slowly. "This disease comes from the center of the earth. It bubbles up everywhere. Even in my village. It happens to everyone's cocoa."

"Will it go away?"

"No."

"But—"

"Once I could only find it here at the edge of the forest between the stones. I used to light my stick with it. We were glad then to find it, for it grows dark quickly. But now it's everywhere. In the cocoa. Turning the soil slimy with oil. It's no good for the cocoa."

"Mrs. de Balboa knows," Marina muttered bitterly. "Yet she wants Ranjit to buy her land."

"No! Don't let Antonio sell it."

"But the cocoa?"

The Warao breathed deeply. "It's not the cocoa," he said, not believing his words. "It's the oil. There are people from North America who have come and they have put long poles in the earth. They want more of it they say."

"Why? What use could they have for this oil?"

The question puzzled the Warao. He really did not know why himself. It made no sense to him that the Americans would dig below this surface oil—pitch oil, his people called it, for it was black and dirty like the pitch they once possessed in La Brea. Yet he had taken the trouble to make sure that Marina would have land, to return to her what her mother had lost, so he'd make himself believe that the oil was valuable. Marina, after all, was a charm child. When she looked at him with expectation for an answer, he saw in her face the admiration his men once had for the wisdom of their chief, and he told himself that this pitch oil that they could see on the surface of the ground was really the top layer of a richer, more valuable oil. Pinching the folds of his chest near the belly of his tattooed condor, he replied, "Shark oil."

"Shark oil?" Marina repeated.

"Yes," said the Warao. "They have found shark oil left there by the great Indian tribes who once used to live on your land."

"My God," said Marina, now scornful of the Warao, sick that she had allowed herself to be sucked into his dreams. "God, we don't rub our bodies with oil like you. Shark oil! It is useless to us."

The Warao felt her scorn and became angry. He rose to his feet, drawing his body to his full height. "They said so once to us when my fathers used the pitch from La Brea to stop the water from coming into their canoes." This woman would not destroy the dream he had conjured of days long gone. "They thought the land was sick too. It was a curse, they said. From God. Your Christian god who loves to punish so much. It was a curse because they could not grow their sugar there. They could not understand it. All those pools of black tar appearing everywhere, and at midday the sun would soften it and shift the earth as he wished, moving huts from one side of the yard to the other. And if it rained you

could see the steam dance off that hot black pitch. It frightened your people too."

"My people?" Marina asked.

The Warao glared at her, irritated by the thin smile that
creased her eyes. He'd teach her about her past. "Your people," he repeated. "They told stories then of Br'er Rabbit
and Br'er Fox to keep their children away from the hot tar.
But the sea chief from England—Raleigh was his name, sent
by the English queen in the days when my people ruled this
land—he knew better." The Warao did not mind that Marina no longer looked at him. He remembered it all. "Raleigh," he continued, "he called it black gold. We showed
him and he learned. He used the pitch to close the holes in
his great ships. But then he went away. And after the white
men with guns had destroyed my people, they learned too
what we already knew. And now," the Warao's breathing got
heavier and the condor on his hairless chest heaved up and
down. "And now they pave their roads with it. Not here. Not
here. Except in places where they want to. But everywhere in
England they pave their roads with it. I hear them talking. I
see them taking the barrels of pitch. They will learn too that
this oil we put on our bodies kills the mosquitoes that breed
malaria. They will learn."

"Never!" Marina was unmoved.

The Warao snorted. He would not lose a battle before this
wispy-haired woman. He dug in his memory and tried again.
"El Dorado," he said.

"El Dorado?" Marina knelt upright. The Warao felt her
curiosity.

"The City of Gold left by our great people," he breathed.

Marina remained silent. Waiting.

The Warao summoned his gods. He had to find an explanation. "They buried their gold before the white man chased them out," he began, hoping that the old story of his forefathers would serve him now. "And covered the earth with oil to fool their murderers." He looked up at Marina and saw in her eyes that he had won.

"On my land?" Marina whispered, her lips trembling. "On my land?"

The Warao smiled and nodded his head. Marina got up on her feet and came close to him. Not touching him. The Warao stretched out his hand and placed his fingers on the upper part of her naked arm. Marina remained still. The Warao let his fingers slide down her arm, trailing behind them tracks of grease like snakes crawling down to her wrist. Still Marina did not move. The Warao lowered his eyes and muttered some words Marina could not understand, and before she could speak, he turned his back and disappeared into the bush, as quietly as he had come.

Two words—El Dorado. They seared her brain like molten lava, heating up the soles of her feet and the palms of her hands. Sweat dripped from between her breasts and cooled her belly, and the wind fanned her hair.

Charm child. El Dorado. To be rich. There were treasures to be found in the islands, the pirates had said. Gold and diamonds. Emeralds. All on my land. My land. Marina remained where she was. Transfixed. So intoxicated was she by dreams of buried treasure, that she did not feel the horror she would feel at another time when she realized again that her mother had so coldly abandoned her babies. Nor did she allow herself to wonder then if Emilia knew more than she said, when, at the last moment, she changed her mind and begged her not to marry Antonio. Indeed, for the time, Marina did not think about Emilia. But she nourished a sweet taste of self-righteousness in the results of Emilia's connivings. She was a charm child and it was her turn. It was her fate that she be both lucky and rich. She wanted to see this land, to touch this land in Tabaquite that was hers. She wanted to know it before Antonio would remind her that it belonged also to him and to Virginia.

Two days after she had met the Warao, Marina got her chance. Antonio lent her the donkey cart, but when she returned to Moruga the fire that she felt inside of her was the fire she herself caused. And it took every inch of her imagination to keep it burning.

9

Trinidad is so small that if you flew with the crows you could cross it from north to south in less than four hours, from east to west you could cross in less than three. But to the people who live there, the sea and land are varied and mysterious. So mysterious that when Columbus tasted the seawater off the southern coast of the island, he thought he was in the Waters of Paradise. And when he saw the three peaks of the Southern Mountain Range, he was certain that before him rose the symbol of the great mystery of the Roman Catholic Church, the Holy Trinity.

Unwilling to accept the possibility that he had made an error in his sextant reading, Columbus preferred to believe that he had discovered the Truth: The earth was not completely spherical but pear-shaped, and this land he had sighted was the top of the bulge of the pear. The Earthly

Paradise of which he had often read and yearned to discover!

How was Columbus to know that it was the Orinoco River, its tremendous energy unspent in its voyage through Venezuela, that gushed into the sea off Trinidad, diluting the salt of the water? Why should he doubt his discovery? "Ah," he must have said, "here is the place that God made for his Paradise on Earth. This land of sweet seawater. This land where God has laid before Man the truth of His Holy Trinity. As these three peaks are in one mountain so are God the Father, Jesus Christ His Son, The Holy Ghost the Spirit of God, all three persons of the one God. This island I will call Trinidad in the name of this divine mystery."

And though surely this island had another name, he was not too wrong to call it that, to see in this island elements of the fantastic, mysteries that could not be pierced by reason. For the island was populated then and was to be populated later by a people who approached life's mysteries not with an intellect disengaged from their oneness with nature, but with minds open to truths whispered to them from the sea, the earth, the animals, the birds, the fish.

To the people who lived on the seacoasts that bordered the island the sea was the most intelligent of beings and she was to be respected, feared and loved. She was not the same on all sides of the island. On one side she could be gentle, her force and strength already spent on the coral reefs a few miles off shore. On the other end she could be ferocious, leaving only the smallest border of sandy beach as she crashed into the rocks that faced her on the shoreline, eroding her way farther inland. Near Icacos Point, on the southwestern tip of Trinidad, where the hills of Venezuela are visible to the naked eye, where the great river Orinoco washes her silt in the brine of the Atlantic, she swirled her current deep, dark and treacherous beneath her surface waters, waiting for the foolish. The people knew about Calypso, who lived there among these currents. Tales of her power reached far inland to the towns in the south.

The story went that long, long ago, as the conquistadors who had plundered the great Indian civilizations of South America navigated their ships northward toward the calm waters of the Caribbean, their arms and necks weighted with the gold, silver, emeralds and rubies that they had ravaged from the Incas and the Aztecs, the holds of their ships loaded with more stolen treasure, Calypso lay there, under the sea, waiting and watching. And when the conquistadors, still hungry for the warmth of the tropical sun, had stretched their bodies on the decks of their ships, sprawled out like dough arranged on trays to be baked, the cunning Calypso rubbed her rounded buttocks against the hulls of their ships and pushed them gently into the waters off Icacos Point.

It was her steel-band music that the conquistadors first heard: "Ping-Pang Ping-Pang Pinkety-Ping-Pang." They raised their heads from the decks of their ships and looked across the sea and saw nothing. But Calypso beat her pans again: "Ping-Pang Ping-Pang Pinkety-Ping-Pang." And the conquistadors, lured by her music, tasting the promise of warm thighs and swollen breasts, followed her, plunging their ships through the waters between Icacos and Venezuela. When they sighted the land that Columbus had discovered for his people, lust had so etched its way into their souls, they forgot to look for the currents. Calypso, knowing that they were hers, raised her head above the water and shook her nappy hair, sending waves cascading to crash with fatal violence against the sides of the ships, churning the waters white, plummeting the sea through her tight curls. The conquistadors had no time for speech. They grabbed their stolen treasures and locked them in their arms. But then the current came swiftly up from the ocean floor, snapped against the prows of their ships and, in one precise, calculated move, pulled Calypso's prey silently down into the dark depths of the ocean floor.

The villagers tell that when the bodies of the conquistadors began to ferment in the bowels of the sea, the current vomited their skeletons, their arms still locked around their treasures, and pitched their bones against the rocks on the shore.

The Arawaks, the Caribs and the Waraos, who for a time were protected by these waters from the white men who came to plunder, then took the treasures from these skeletons and buried them inland near the mountain range, deep in the ground everywhere in the south of Trinidad. When the stories of El Dorado swept through the Caribbean, the villagers sat around fires on rainy nights and talked of dreams of finding buried treasure and living the life of Raleigh.

Such were the stories that Marina had heard, so when a descendant of one of these Amerindians had let slip his secret (for Marina knew that the Warao had not meant to betray his people), she was certain there was treasure to be found in Tabaquite. But when Marina arrived in Tabaquite, the villagers were grieving for their dying cocoa that was choked to inertia by the black, slimy oil that greased its roots, and they could not be brought to dream dreams of buried treasures.

Marina tried to explain. "He told me so. I got it from the Warao chief. His people put oil there to trick their enemies. Everywhere you see oil, there is treasure. That's why the white men are digging. They are trying to find the jewels. You know—the ones the Indians buried and covered up with shark oil."

The women sucked their teeth at her and turned their

backs. The men, easing the pain of the cocoa they had lost and the uncertainty of their futures, warmed their eyes on her body.

"Mr. George done find all dat gold already," one of them told her. "He gone to England. He a rich man. All de oil you see done uncovered already, *oui.*"

The children simply laughed. Mocking her. By the end of the day Marina felt the shame of her folly. He had tricked her, the Warao. He had made a fool of her. Yet she wanted to believe. Deep in her heart, she refused to relinquish the future that the Warao had held out to her. Yes, she was a charm child. Lucky. She would be rich. It was there on the land. Perhaps—she stretched her belief beyond her reason—perhaps the oil itself was valuable. The shark oil. That was it.

As she turned her donkey cart into the dirt track that led to her house in Moruga she stirred the fire at the soles of her feet. She would be rich. Antonio must not sell the land.

It was only six o'clock when Marina arrived at her house, but in a twilightless country the night drops suddenly like a heavy window shade pulled over a sun-drenched window. The darkness made Marina nervous. There was barely a moon, and the light it cast shaped shadows of vengeful conquistadors lurking among the trees and turned the shrieks of the cicadas into sinister cries. Marina was close to panic when she saw the bright light from the kerosene lamp on her front porch. Relieved and grateful that Antonio had left the lamp lit for her, she called out to him, but there was no answer. Yet she could see the flicker of light in his mother's room and as she entered the living room she could hear the soft droning of his voice and Virginia's.

"Antonio! Antonio!" she called again. "The donkey cart!

I need help with the donkey cart. What shall I do with the donkey cart?"

There was no answer. She thought for a second of knocking on the bedroom door, but she wanted no confrontation. It was difficult enough to keep up her spirits after her disappointment in Tabaquite and she did not need Antonio to call her a fool. Not just yet. She walked back outside and unhitched the donkey from the cart, letting the front of the cart fall noisily on the ground. Still there was no movement from the house. She patted the donkey, took off his bridle, and leaving him untied, she went to her bedroom and banged the door shut behind her.

Antonio did not sleep in her bed that night.

She saw Virginia first through her sheet in the orange haze of sunrise, white-bandana-wrapped head bent over a shelf in the open closet. But before Marina could find her voice, Virginia's piercing scream cut across the room, and in an instant the woman was gone as if chased by ten devils. Through the window Marina saw Antonio let go of the donkey, which he had finally roped, and race toward the house. By the time Marina reached the front porch, Antonio had caught his mother and had pinned her arms. Struggling to break free from Antonio, Virginia spat at Marina. "Devil! Devil! Go away from here! Get away from here! Get out of my house! Leave my son!"

Marina stood by the doorway and wrapped her nightgown tightly across her body. In spite of her confusion, her mind was lucid on one point: her mother-in-law had been searching her room. "What were you doing in my closet, Mrs. de Balboa?" she asked coldly.

"Devil! Devil!" Virginia repeated. "I told you so, Antonio. I told you why she left. To Tabaquite. Ha! Tabaquite! To her obeahman! Get out of my house!"

"Mother, please! Marina, do you know what this is about?"

"Know? She put it there. Go look for yourself, Antonio. See what a wife you have. Go! Like her mother. That's what she is!" Virginia strained against her son's tight embrace.

"Mother!"

"Go, I say, Antonio!" Virginia pushed Antonio from her and glared at Marina.

Coldly Marina turned and entered the house, Antonio following close behind her. Inside the bedroom near the closet door, they saw what Virginia had seen, what had made her run wildly out of the house. It was a little pouch made of pigskin, the bristles of the pig's hair still on it in places. It had fallen off the shelf and its contents, like omens of evil, lay scattered around it: tufts of human hair, the eyeball of a goat, clusters of herbs, a chicken leg with the foot attached and a small vial with an odious substance that stank up the whole room. Marina's eyes fastened on the hair, which looked familiarly like her own. She picked it up and confirmed her suspicions. It was hers. The same light-brown wavy hair. She knew then that she was implicated in whatever the intents were of the person who had placed those things there. Involuntarily she whispered her mother's name and looked swiftly over to Antonio to see if he had heard her. But Antonio was far too angry at the violation of his house to notice her. Quietly, before his unseeing eyes, she dressed herself and left the house.

10

I t wasn't difficult for Marina to find the most important
obeahwoman in Moruga. Alma. Her name would always
be Alma.

In Trinidad, Alma was as eternal as the sea washing every
morning upon the lazy beaches. The schoolchildren saw her
early, after they had gulped down their hot sugar water
flavored with tea leaves and goat's milk and had choked on
thick, warm johnny bake, which, if they were lucky, was dripping with salty red butter. They met her at the school gate
where she had already unfolded her wooden table and had
lined up her large glass jars crammed to the top with green
fruit swimming in water. No schoolchild in Trinidad in his
right mind ever ate ripe fruit. Mangoes, pomme cythere,
tamarind, guava, governor's plum were all best when they
were green, squirting pale sticky juices, and dipped into salt

made brick red by crushed peppers. Ripe fruit was for the end of the season when the trees got tired and would not bear any more. Then the children had to content themselves with sweetness. Yet even then they knew that Alma would find green fruit for breakfast.

At lunchtime Alma would sell chataigne from a large, old, tin can, its outsides blackened from the soot that came from the coal pot burning below it. No mother could explain why her child stole her farthings to buy Alma's chataigne. Almost everyone knew someone whose backyard was strewn with breadfruitlike balls splashed open, rotten, the chataigne peeping out of the whitish pulp, showing their dark brown pods. Free to anyone who cared to pick them up. But Alma's chataigne was sweetest. And so was her roasted corn. It was at night that the adults understood their children, when they too sought out Alma's pots, flickering away at a decent distance from the rum shop. On one coal pot, corn popping on the cob; on the other a large tin can filled with pig's tails and salt and pepper, fondling new corn on the cob to softness.

For each generation it was the same. Alma was there. Always there. They said it was obeah that made her food so sweet. Obeah that made her live so long. Eternal Alma. In her long, white, cotton dresses and crisp white bandanas, she presided over ceremonies on certain nights, and no one asked her then about her food or about her age. She was a different Alma then, but still the Alma who sold food and never aged. But Marina was new to Moruga, and so she had not yet met Alma. She asked the servant girl.

"I don't know no Alma, ma'am. I don't know nothing," the girl whimpered, biting frantically at what was left of her nails, staring wide-eyed at the house from which Virginia had just escaped.

"Listen, Jane," Marina said, shaking her roughly by the

shoulders. "Everyone here knows Alma. You better tell me. Or—you know what they say about me? My mother won't like it."

"Ma'am, I don't know no Alma. Please, Ma'am." Jane was now sniveling like a little puppy, tears pouring down her face.

"Jane—look I don't want to hurt you. If you don't know, tell me who knows."

"You could ask Miss Taylor, but I don't know. I don't know nothing." It was impossible for Marina to get any more information out of Jane. Anyhow, the girl was innocent and there was no reason to torment her. Miss Taylor probably knew more. Patting her gently on the head, Marina told Jane she could go.

At first when Marina asked Miss Taylor about the whereabouts of Alma, she got Jane's very repetitious response, "I don't know no Alma." In 1902, one did not give information about obeah to people with light skins, and Marina's pale face, dotted with freckles, was not above suspicion. Yet Marina was sure that Miss Taylor could tell her the way to Alma, and she asked her again. The woman narrowed her eyes at her. "Who you be, child?" she asked.

It was Emilia's past that gave Marina entry to the obeahwoman, for without realizing it, Marina replied, "Heathrow. Marina E. Heathrow." And Miss Taylor remembered the woman whose sacrifice of her twin sons was proof of her loyalty to obeah.

A dirt track led to Alma's house. It separated her wooden shack from the rest of the village. Indeed, surrounded by tall bushes on every side, Alma's house seemed to be in a different place altogether. A different country. Marina swallowed hard to chase away the slow fear that crept over her as she approached the house. She had seen places like this as a child when Emilia, having no one to leave her daughter with, was forced to take her along on her visits to the obeahman. Yet she had never grown accustomed to the bottles that hung ominously from dried branches planted in the soil in front of their houses. Alma's house was decorated in the same fashion. In one sweeping glance, Marina could see that the bottles were filled with liquids, some with roots, others with pieces of hair, cloth, fingernails, toenails—a multitude of items that warded off evil from the obeahman or woman and brought evil or good to others.

As Marina climbed the first step leading to the porch, she heard a woman's voice call out from under the house. "So you here. Come, chile. I is waiting for you."

Marina bent over the termite-ridden wooden stair rail and looked way past under the house, which, like many of the others in Moruga, stood on six stumps of tree trunks dug firmly into the earth. Clear across, to the back of the house, she could see Alma in a dirty brown-striped dress, a bright red bandana tied in a knot at the back of her head, sitting on a large, brightly polished tin can—probably a biscuit box— staring at her through clouds of smoke that billowed out of her pipe.

Marina approached her slowly, forcing back her fear with her determination to find out who placed the pouch containing a tuft of her hair in her closet. The obeahwoman sat still and called out to her again. "Come here, Emilia's chile. Don't mind what I doin'. Come on. You 'fraid, or what? I en't go' harm you."

Marina gathered up her courage and moved more quickly. Suddenly with horror she saw what the obeah woman was doing, but by that time Alma had pinned her arm down firmly with her bony hand.

"Never you mind what you seen' here, chile. Never you mind. Dis will help you."

Marina felt defiance, determination, courage, intelligence, reason sucked out of her like sap out of a rubber tree. She fell limp against Alma, her legs turning to jelly, and pointed a trembling finger. There, next to Alma, was an open grave. Marina had not seen it as she approached because there were no mounds of fresh earth bordering it. One had to be almost on top of the grave to notice it. A young black man of about twenty-four lay there. Naked except for a white loincloth like the one Jesus wore at the Crucifixion, wrapped loosely around him. On his eyes were bands of white cloth wound tightly around his head and sealed in spots with melted candle wax. A sickly odor emanated from him, not one of death, but of the herbs and oils that the obeahmen use.

"Is—is he dead?" Marina asked, trying to recover her composure.

"Nah. He here tree days now. He get up soon. Two, tree hours maybe, and tell you what you want to know." Alma shook the dust out of her dress and got up off the biscuit tin. Still holding tightly to Marina, she turned and walked toward her house.

"What's he doing there?" Marina asked stubbornly, recovered now since she could see by the rise and fall of the man's chest that he was still alive.

"Your mama never told you dis. Emilia en't playing she foolish, *oui!* She want to protect you. And is the very ting she want to protect you from dat will help you." Alma stopped walking, removed her pipe from her mouth with one hand, and still holding on to Marina with the other, she pushed her back at arm's length and looked her up and down, her curiosity traveling over Marina's body. Finally, clicking her teeth, she said, "But you white, eh? Let me look at you, chile. Just like you pappy. You white just like him. I see what Emilia mean."

Marina felt herself overpowered by this thin, bony woman who knew so much. She was a child in her hands. She didn't know where to begin. What question to ask first. She had come with one intention: to find out who had placed the pouch with the tuft of her hair in her closet. Now that question seemed insignificant next to answers to the questions about her mother and father. How could Alma help her? No words came to her lips. She allowed this woman to take her into her wooden house as if she lacked any will of her own or ability to move herself.

Once inside her shack, Alma talked rapidly, moving busily around her one-room house, pouring liquids and pieces of strange material into the many empty bottles that were lined on the shelves on the wall opposite to her bed mat. She began to talk to herself as though she had forgotten that Marina was in the room. "Yes, Lord, Emilia chile white like she father. You works in wonderous ways, Lord. Emilia can't have no live children and dere she have dis chile. Pretty as the queen sheself. White like she father. God rest his soul. Poor Emilia. She one child had to marry de Balboa son. I tole she not to let it happen. 'Emilia,' I says to her, de Balboa cursed. He a strange Portogee. He cursed and his son cursed. I tell she how de Balboa's son killed all his wives. One, two, tree woman. I tell Emilia. Well, dat how it happen sometime, *oui*. You give a child all you have. You work for yuh chile. You do everything. And yet dere be some children dat stubborn for so. You can't change them. Dat chile too stubborn. I will try, Emilia. I will do what I can for you, but I don't know what I can do." Alma kept muttering to herself between puffs on her pipe, keeping her back toward Marina. Finally, filling the last bottle on the row of bottles on the first shelf, she sat down on a stool, turned to Marina and asked, as though seeing her for the first time, "What you come to see me 'bout chile? Who send you here?"

Slightly taken aback, Marina answered quietly, "Well, my mother—Emilia Heathrow, that is—told me that I should come to see you if I was in trouble."

"And what kind of trouble are you in, chile?" Alma blew a puff of foul smelling tobacco in Marina's face.

"Someone put an obeah on me," Marina choked out.

"Oh! Emilia's chile? You Emilia and Heatrow chile?" Another puff of smoke. Alma seemed to have suddenly recognized Marina though only moments ago she had acted as though she knew her.

Marina felt as though she were in another world. The world of the insane. She made another stab at finding out what was going on. "You just said Emilia, my mother, told you—I mean, you just said that you promised my mother that you would help me. Who's that man outside? You just said he could help me."

"Listen," said Alma, her voice stilling Marina's. "Dere is tings dat take a lot of time. You can't push dem. Now tell me what happen."

"Somebody put a bag in my closet. It has an eye in it, some roots, and some herbs."

"Dat's all?"

"No, it had more things. A chicken leg, some medicine in a bottle."

"And?"

"A piece of my hair."

"You remember good chile. You a bright girl. I tole Emilia her chile be bright. I put dat medicine in your closet. And for your own good. Your mother tole me to do it. She pay a lot of money. Your mother pay for dis Mr. Harris out dere. Is Mr. Harris in that grave, you know. He doing a lot for you chile. He in mourning for you. His spirit come back soon and tell you everything."

Marina's suspicions were confirmed. Emilia had never given up on her conviction that Antonio could harm her! The promise of land might have made her agree to the marriage, but she would protect her child. The anger that Marina felt when she saw the pouch in her closet now flooded over her again. "She has that poor man out there in her madness?" she snapped at Alma.

"Careful, chile," Alma warned, making the sign of the Cross. "Careful wid your tongue. Harris's spirit could be hearing you and he could harm you. You don't know dese tings. I really surprise wid Emilia. She never tole you anything about obeah?"

"I know enough," said Marina shortly.

"But you don't know what Harris can do? Harris not Harris now you know. Is Harris's body lying in that grave. But dis not Harris. You see, chile, when someone wants to harm you, you can't always know how. You can know who sometimes. Like I know is de Balboa who pass it down to he son. De Balboa hated women, you know. Look at Mis de Balboa. A dried-up woman before she get fifty. She was nice, you know. A nice, beautiful woman. Dey all wanted Virginia. Dat's her name, Virginia. Why you tink de warden's wife gave her to de Balboa? Dese English women here 'fraid we black women. Well, I don't mean it that way," said Alma slyly, noticing again the whiteness of Marina's skin. "You know what I mean. When you have the hot blood in you. De women born here have hot blood. Not so, Marina?"

Marina smiled. There was no hurrying this woman for the

information she wanted. Yet there were things that she had seen between Antonio and Virginia that had made her wonder about Virginia's past.

"Well, like I was saying," Alma continued, "de Balboa hated women. He hardly used to talk to he wife. Nobody ever see him beat she or anything like dat. But nobody ever see him even smile at she. As a matter of fact, de Balboa never talk to nobody but de Warahoon."

At the mention of the Warao, Marina's heart skipped a beat. "Was he the same Warao who knew my mother?" she asked quietly.

"What, chile?" Alma's voice became stern and grave, her body rigid. "What, chile?" she asked again.

Marina repeated her question, bracing herself for Alma's response, but Alma's back had softened.

Putting her pipe to her mouth, Alma puffed slowly and grinned at Marina. "Trying to trap me, eh? Cockroach shouldn't walk in front of fowl."

"So it was the same Warao?" Marina made a question of the statement.

"Which same Warao?"

"The one who helped my mother."

Alma clicked her teeth and opened her mouth as if to answer Marina. Instead she shook her head, her youthful eyes revealing nothing. "Yes, de Balboa was a peculiar man, God rest he soul," she said, picking up from where she left off. "He dried de beauty out of Virginia. Is a good ting she had learning. At leas' she could teach. She a good teacher, you know."

Marina was sure now. Alma also knew about the Warao. She remained silent and let the obeahwoman continue.

"De Balboa son hate women too. Except he not like he father. He don't dry up he wives. He kill them. He kill tree already, you know." Alma clicked her teeth and sucked on her pipe for a while. "Yes, I know you don't believe dat. Emilia tole me. But you'll see. Mr. Harris here agree to find out how de Balboa son plan to kill you. You know the Bible, chile?"

"Yes, some of it."

"Some of it? Children dese days." Alma shook her head and paused. "While Jesus lay in he tomb for tree days dead, and on the tird day he got up and walked, where you tink he went?"

It sounded like the question a sphinx would ask. The answer must be simple, Marina thought, if she could understand the question. Alma looked at her with exasperation and dragged a wooden stool from under the table. She sat down and pulled her skirt between her legs, exposing two angular knees spread wide apart. Marina noticed with surprise how young her legs seemed to be. Almost as though they belonged to another person less than half her age. Only her feet seemed used. Flat, with no arches, caked with mud, long nails jutting menacingly from them.

Alma broke the silence. "Well, where you tink he went?"

Marina tried to understand the question. "Do you mean where did Jesus go on the third day after He rose from the dead? Or where did Jesus go when He lay in the tomb?"

"Dat's right, chile," Alma nodded in agreement. "Where you tink Jesus went on de tree days dat he lay in the tomb?"

"In the tomb."

"What you say?"

"I said that He was in the tomb."

"No, chile, you don't understand. Mr. Harris out dere, you tink he is in dat grave? Dat isn't Mr. Harris in de grave."

"Then who is it?"

"Mr. Harris, but not Mr. Harris. Just like it was Jesus in the

tomb, but not Jesus." Marina was beginning to understand
that Alma was talking about the difference between the body
and the soul. She tried again. "Do you mean the body of
Jesus was in the tomb, but not the soul of Jesus?"

"Well, I see Emilia must have taught you something."
Alma placed her pipe on the floor and began to clean her
toenails with one of the bristles from her broom, which she
had made from the dry stems of coconut leaves. A shiver of
disgust swept over Marina, and she looked away through the
window across the yard to where Mr. Harris lay still in his
grave. Alma, unconcerned about Marina's reactions, continued. "Jesus stayed in He tomb for tree days. His body, dat
is. But de real Jesus, in spirit form, He roam all over de earth.
He went all over de world searching and looking for what
people doing. During dat time He learn a lot about people.
All dey secrets, because dey didn't know He was dere. Dey
couldn't see him. So dey talk as if nobody was hearing dem.
When Jesus returned on de tird day, He was ready to enter
de body and take all the secrets of the world with him to He
father." Alma stopped cleaning her toenails and looked up
at Marina. "Now you know where Mr. Harris is now? Not
everybody can do dat, you know. And not everybody willing
to do it. Your mother paid Mr. Harris good. He don't do dis
for everybody. For some special people. Right now he spirit
seeing all de Balboa evil. You are a lucky chile dat your
mother love you so much."

Beads of sweat broke out on Marina's forehead and she
began to feel faint. She swallowed hard to steady herself.

Alma looked at her from deep, young eyes, incongruous
in a wrinkled face. She reached over and grabbed Marina's
wrist. Her voice changed to a hoarse intensity. "You understand me, chile? Harris could die for you today if he spirit
don't come back. Die for you. Die for you."

The room spun around at a terrific speed before Marina's eyes. Frantically she unclasped Alma's hand from her wrist as though her life depended on being free of her. Sounds, smells, colors swarmed over her, suffocating her. Drums from her past, her early childhood, flooded her memory in a mass of confusion. Desperately she tried to pull one coherent piece out. Some incident that could make sense. Aware that Alma still stared at her, she tried to turn her head away. Then the world went black.

Quickly Alma uncorked a bottle of a vile-looking liquid and stuck it under Marina's nose. Marina gasped, her arms flailing wildly about her, knocking the bottle on the ground. Alma picked it up and tried to return it to Marina's nose, but by then Marina had completely regained consciousness. "No. No. Get that stuff away from me. Get away from me."

"What happen, chile? You look white. What de matter? You see something? Is not time for Mr. Harris to come back. What you see?"

Marina stood up and leaned against the wall. She had to get out of that room, away from Alma and the past that had begun to make sense to her. She had seen Alma before, and she remembered when. Pulling herself together, she whispered hoarsely to Alma, "I must go now. I have to leave."

Alma threw her head back and laughed, a dry laughter without mirth, exposing her tobacco-stained teeth. The laughter stuck in her throat reverberating through her body, jerking her shoulders up and down in spasms. She reached over to touch Marina, but Marina was too swift for her. She bounded through the door, down the steps and across the narrow path, not turning back as Alma shouted, "Come back, Miss! Harris can help you! Come back!"

Marina did not stop running until she arrived at the beach. Finally there, she stretched out on the sand, feeling the afternoon sun on her face and drinking the clear, cool, salty air that swept across the sea. She had remembered! She knew where she had seen Alma before! Pieces of the jigsaw began to fit into place. Why Mr. Harris in the grave had scared her but not shocked her as it should have. Why the place had seemed somehow familiar. She could not have been more than eight years old. Her father had died not too long ago and they had moved into Mr. Telser's house. One night her mother told her that, as she had promised, she was going to take her to see her father again. Her child's intelligence required no logic. She wanted to see him again even if he hated her. Indeed, the more he had rejected her, the more she had sought his affection. It was as if her mind refused to believe that he could not love her, that he could despise her. Now, lying on the beach, watching the hot air dance off the blue ocean, a phenomenon that could be visibly seen with the naked eye on hot days, Marina remembered vividly where her mother had taken her that night. It was to Alma's house. Except that night the place did not look as it seemed to her a short time ago. There were people everywhere then. Dressed in white. And there was a lot of noise. Drumming. The women were shouting and dancing in a frenzy and the men were beating on drums. Alma was there. She sat on a stool as she had done earlier that day. But she was magnificent then. Dressed in a long, white dress with a large white headband on her head and rows of beads around her neck. At her feet was an open grave with a man in it. Dressed like Mr. Harris. From time to time Alma would get up and point a stick at the man and then the woman dancers would gather around the grave stomping, shaking, shouting. The pitch of their voices became higher as Alma shouted something in a foreign language, and then pointing her stick at the man, she commanded him in English to get up. The man remained motionless and the women joined Alma shouting, pleading, commanding the man to get up. Yet he stayed still. Then there were horses. Marina remembered them now. They were racing toward Alma's house bearing white men dressed in high, black boots, waving long whips through the air. Everyone ran wildly in all directions. Her mother lifted her from the ground by her waist and threw her in the donkey cart that brought them to that place and they sped home.

For the next few days her mother warned her never to tell anyone what she had seen. She told her that if she did, la diablesse would drag her into the rain forest and leave her there for the vampires to bite until she was black and blue and she turned into a ball of fire like a soucouyant. Emilia had so terrified her child that Marina had totally erased from her memory all the incidents of that night. When the police began questioning around the village about the strange murder of some man, Emilia did not have to warn Marina to be quiet. The child had no memory of that evening. Later, conversations among the women made no sense to her. That the man's spirit had forgotten his word and his name, and had drifted too far away so that it could not find his body, that his body died because his spirit could not hear them calling it back, seemed like gibberish to her. But at Alma's house, not long ago, she suddenly realized that the man the police had claimed was murdered was the same man she had seen that night, like Mr. Harris, lying in a grave in the backyard of Alma's house. Now her mind began to form the vague possibility that her father had not hated her, that he had feared her, and she felt in her heart that this fear was somehow connected to her mother and the visits that she made to her obeahman.

11

❖

When the sun with its customary swiftness plunged into the ocean, as it did each evening on the west side of the horizon facing the Moruga beach, the blue hard-shelled sea crabs scuttled out of their holes among the damp, matted bushes that grew beneath the coconut trees. The evening hours were their playtime. Foolishly they thought the dark would protect them from the men and boys whose dexterous hands could, in an instant, clamp down on their hard backs, leaving their vicious claws snapping impotently into the empty air. They never learned, these poor crabs, to accept the superiority of the human brain. And each evening, as they scuttled on the water's edge in search of any food that the salty waves had discarded, they were surprised by men with lighted kerosene bottles and burlap bags intent on capturing them.

Perhaps it was because he thought that he had waited long enough to avenge the murder of his dead brothers that one of these sea crabs, spying the sleeping Marina sprawled out on the sand, threw caution to the wind, and boldly scratched his way out of his hole toward her. He must have sensed in the calm rhythmic rise and fall of her chest that the moment belonged to him, for he did not hesitate, nor shuffle backward as it is in the nature of crabs to do, but hurried forward and began to mount her legs fearlessly and insolently.

But it is not the fate of crabs that they should win, and as he plunged his sharp claws deep into Marina's thigh, she woke up. In seconds she pinned him down with such force that his eyes pitched forward like two darts jutting out of his brow in powerless protest, and before he could struggle, she sent his body spinning into the air across the silver-edged beach.

The night surprised Marina, for her last conscious moments were in the dazzling afternoon sun. She wondered momentarily what she was doing there on the beach, but the sting of the cut that the crab had made on her skin recalled the pain of the long suppressed memories that Alma had awakened. Mercifully, she now realized that she had fallen asleep, and mercifully, sleep, like a salve, had dulled the raw ache of the open wound leaving a hard tough scab protecting its surface. She felt a coldness chill her heart now, and she wrapped her arms tightly across her chest. It was not the cool night air that caused her to shiver. Rather, it was the force of her calm determination there and then to feel nothing for her mother. Why? She didn't fully understand, but the reason, unclear, unraveled, lay vibrant and pulsating in the series of images cluttered in her mind. Images of dead twin boys, images of her dead father, of a dead man in an open grave, of horses thundering across the fields, of a living man a few hours ago sleeping in a freshly dug grave. She must go back home, she knew. Home to a marriage her mother had arranged and then too late had tried to prevent. Home to clean up the stage her mother had set with her obeah magic from Alma. It is too late now, Mother, she thought bitterly. Too late to change what you have started. And propelled by a desire to oppose her mother's designs, she decided then, in spite of the mocking laughter of the women in Tabaquite, that she would make a profit from the land. Yes, she would see to it that the de Balboas did not sell the land.

Yet the day's events had not ended for Marina, for Antonio's mother was not to be pacified simply because Marina had left the house. As Marina turned into the dirt track that led to her front door, she knew immediately from the wafted gray incense that thickened the damp air that the priest had been called. From where she was, she could see the house lit up with flickering candles that danced like fireflies imprisoned in a bottle. Some curious neighbors were huddled in small groups not far from the house, whispering excitedly, from time to time one or the other making the sign of the Cross. Quickly she left the dirt track and stepped quietly through the jungle of fiery bougainvillea that guarded the right side of the house, its red flowers, like clowns at a funeral, inappropriately giving color to the gloomy darkness. Raising her right hand cautiously over her face to avoid the thorns that stuck out menacingly from the bougainvillea, Marina searched for a passage to a clearing in the back of the house from which she could easily slip undetected to hide behind one of its supporting pillars. Blurring her vision in this way, she could not see her left hand reach for a knot of thorns. An involuntary cry of pain escaped her throat before she could stop it. In an instant, one of the spectators spied her, and a ponderous silence rippled through the small clumps of people, reverberating from clump to clump. All eyes were on her now and she could feel fearful respect for her in the way the people stood still, not moving, watching her run like a maneko escaping his snare. And she thought she heard one of them whisper, when their silence had ended and she was close to the pillars, "Emilia's chile. That's she daughter. Selfsame one. Emilia done do she do."

It was the sudden rise and fall of the priest's droning changes and accompanying new waves of thick, gray smoke from his censer that finally distracted the crowd's gaze from Marina. Hurriedly, Marina slipped into the dark shadows of the pillars and waited. She waited until the ceremony had ended, until the priest and the people had disappeared into the night, and, finally, until she heard the distant sound of Antonio's footsteps descending the back steps. Then, seeing Antonio signal to her to be quiet until he returned, she slumped to the dirt floor exhausted, and remained there hidden, her back against one of the pillars.

One hour later, Antonio was finally certain that his mother was asleep, and he returned to the back of the house to find his wife. At first, when he realized that Marina had left the house, he thought that it was appropriate, the only decent thing she could do. Like his mother, he saw a connection between Marina and the violation of his house, though unlike Virginia, he did not blame Marina. It was he who was at fault. It was he who had exposed his mother and their house to obeah by marrying a woman whose very existence was determined by the black magic of obeah. Why had he imagined that obeah would not follow him? Yet he did not believe in the efficacy of obeah, nor did he want to believe that his wife was foolish enough to try to work obeah on him. For what reason? Why? She had no cause for putting obeah

in his house. He had already married her. No, he began to
reason to himself later on, it was the villagers with their silly
superstitions, their constant whispering about his dead
wives. It was they who had done it, put that pouch in his
bedroom. They knew of Marina's past. They wanted to warn
him. The pouch was their way of telling him that trouble
would come to him if Marina was harmed. As the hours
passed, Antonio began to feel more and more guilty for the
way he treated Marina. She was blameless and yet he had not
gone after her nor sent someone to find her. He told himself
his mother needed him, that he could not leave her alone
with those people who had put obeah in his house, but his
guilt would not leave him. Now, when he returned to the
back of the house and saw Marina slumped to the ground
like a broken doll, her face innocent, the brown freckles on
her pale skin like alien spots of dust that could be brushed
away by a single flick of the hand, his remorse intensified. He
wanted to make up for his unkindness to her and his
mother's rudeness. She looked more beautiful than he remembered, and yet he could not forget she had a past that
linked her to obeah.

   " 'Beauty is truth, truth beauty'—that is all / Ye know on
earth, and all ye need to know." The words of the poet had
seduced him to her. Beauty, her beauty, had ensnared him.
How could she not also be good? The question haunted him
now as it had done ever since the day when Marina had left
his bed before sunrise and returned late in the evening, her
eyes glassy, her mind seemingly in another world, refusing to
say where she had been. In the days that followed, her obsession with going to Tabaquite was too intense for him to have
stopped her. Another man? No. He assumed she loved him.
It was her defiance that had irked him, her cold determination to do as she pleased. But did that make her evil, a devil

as his mother said she was? A bad wife, perhaps, but not evil. Bad, in the sense that she was not obedient—not as a child learns to be to his father, nor a slave is forced to be by his master, but as a wife should be. She lacked a sort of gratitude she owed to him, her husband, for marrying her—a sort of humility. For in his mind, only the ugly could not be trusted, and he saw infidelity, deceit, promiscuity, lasciviousness in the contours of a bony woman, her face swollen, with thick lips, bulging eyes and wide-spread nostrils mounted on a flat nose bridge. Not in the soft roundness of Marina's arms and legs, nor in the fragile paleness of her blue-veined skin, nor in the cool gray of her eyes, nor in the childlike innocence of her light-brown hair that fell naturally and artistically where it wanted. For though it was the suggestion of wild-ness, unrestraint, marked across her high cheekbones and generous mouth, and though it was the shock of her wide nostrils incongruous with a long, narrow nose bridge, and though it was her high buttocks, her rigid breasts that tempted him most, he permitted his soul to see only those parts of her that made her beauty convince him that she was also good.

If she could be called bad, then it was because she wanted her way in spite of his objections. He didn't like the way she did not stop arguing against his selling the land. Then there was the trip to Tabaquite so soon after their marriage. He could not prevent her from going, and she returned after dark, leaving the donkey loose all night. But looking down now on her quiet body, he felt his earlier anger toward her drain out of him. Whatever else she was, Marina was no devil. He dropped to his knees and touched her face, and she trembled slightly under the palm of his hand. Gently he placed his arm around her and cradled her against his chest.

Rocking her. He whispered her name and kissed her closed eyelids.

"Come, Marina," he said at last. "Come. Let's go to bed now. It's over." Marina leaned against him.

"Up," Antonio spoke without conviction, pulling her close to him. He regretted now that he had left her alone under the house, that he had made her wait while he read his mother to sleep. "Up," he repeated. "Up. I'll take you to bed now."

Marina stirred in his arms. She had seen him coming toward her and feigned sleep. She could not be sure if he had turned against her, if his mother had convinced him not to trust her. He had stayed there with Virginia. He had probably brought the priest to bless the house. Perhaps Virginia had made him believe that she, Marina, had put that pouch in his bedroom. It was not like him to make her wait. Nor would she have tolerated waiting before. But she couldn't have him against her when there was the land to gain. Now, determined to defeat Virginia, she asked petulantly, "You were so long, Antonio. Why did you leave me out here so long?"

"Mother—she couldn't sleep."

"She called me a devil, Antonio."

"Shh."

"She said I was evil," Marina tested him.

"She didn't mean it. Shh."

"But she said—"

"It's all over now, Marina. She was just frightened. Scared out of her wits."

"And you, Antonio? You didn't even come to find me."

"I couldn't leave her, Marina."

"After what she called me?"

"Forgive her, Marina. She was afraid."

"Devil. That's what she called me, Antonio. She said that I worked obeah—"

"No!" Antonio repeated, still holding her tightly.

"And what about you, Antonio? Do you believe that I work obeah?"

The question wormed itself into that uncertain portion of Antonio's soul. He dropped his arms, releasing her, and reached for a cigarette in his pocket. Before he could light it, he was seized by a bout of coughing that made him bend almost to the ground.

"You smoke too much," Marina said quietly, studying him.

The coughing fit ended and Antonio swallowed hard, wiped his face with the back of his hand and lit his cigarette.

Marina watched the red glow of the burning tobacco cast strange shadows on his face. "It's meant to frighten people," she said.

"What?"

"Obeah."

"It's not that simple."

"You mean you believe in obeah?"

"Believe? I don't believe in obeah, but I know it can do more than just frighten people."

"My God! So you believe in obeah!" Marina was now sitting upright facing Antonio. "I'd never have thought that. With all your education!"

"Marina!"

"No, you believe, Antonio."

Antonio pulled his cigarette from his lips. "I don't believe we have control over what we believe," he said seriously.

"My God, what foolishness! Admit it. You believe in obeah."

"I wouldn't dismiss the fact that obeah works for people who believe in it. Not me. I know intellectually it is nonsense, foolish." He paused. "But still I wouldn't dismiss it."

"You mean you're afraid that if you say you don't believe in obeah, somebody will work obeah on you," Marina said scornfully.

Antonio looked at her, on his face a sad expression bordering anger.

"It's like you're afraid to say there's no God because you're scared God will strike you dead with a bolt of lightning," Marina taunted.

"Jesus!" Antonio hissed, exasperated.

"Aha! So you believe in Jesus."

"Marina! For God's sake!"

"And in God too!"

"Marina, what is it you want? What is the matter with you?" Antonio forced himself to control his mounting anger. Even if it was not her fault, she, after all, was the reason why the villagers had put obeah in his house, making his mother sick. He stabbed his cigarette into the ground and twisted it into the dirt until the crushed tobacco spilled out of the paper wrapping and the burning embers faded into the darkness.

"I want to know why you called the priest, if you do not believe in obeah." Marina looked directly at him. "I want to know if you believe that I work obeah."

Antonio sighed and folded his arms across his chest.

"Well, do you believe I work obeah?"

"Let's go to bed, Marina."

"No! Tell me!"

"I believe what I have no choice in believing."

"Coward!"

Antonio pulled his hat over his forehead. He could not

ignore her. Woman that she was, still she managed to taunt him into giving her a response. For a fleeting moment he thought of Sara and the other women he had known. It would have been easy to have put his mouth on theirs and let them know what he wanted. They would have followed him to bed.

"Coward!" Marina repeated.

Antonio coughed. "I believe," he began slowly, "I believe that God is in heaven, the devil in hell, that Jesus Christ was crucified, died and was buried and rose again on the third day. I believe"—his voice grew harsh—"I believe because my mother gave me no choice but to believe. For twelve years, for twelve years before the last year when Father died, she fed me the tenets of the Catholic Church. Daily." His voice beat out his words automatically now, like that of a wound-up doll. "They were statements not to be questioned, but to be accepted, blindly. They were articles of faith woven into the very fabric of my existence. They were facts as indisputable as the rising sun in the morning, the falling darkness at night, the hurricanes in August . . ."

His voice trailed off but Marina pushed him to continue. He surprised her revealing so much and made her think of her own mother. Alma knew. Emilia had not taught her daughter obeah or even insisted that she participate in any obeah rite, yet obeah was present in their lives. Could she, Marina, have escaped it? Was it possible that she too believed in obeah without wanting to? Was it also an article of faith with her?

"Your mother forced you?" She questioned Antonio cautiously.

"Father was right when he made her stop, but the damage was already done. Twelve years is a long time to believe." He sighed and added bitterly, "Yes I have the great gift of the

Catholic Church. Faith. I have no choice in believing in God, Jesus, the devil and obeah. Yes, obeah. My beliefs are a prison I cannot escape from. They do not allow me the freedom to deny the existence of the supernatural world—of the other life which man must be ready to meet on the day of his death. Either God in heaven or the devil in hell. Nor to live my life as though the natural world, the world I know with my eyes, nose, tongue, and feeling is all there is. That when I die, I will no longer exist. Yet I cannot be comforted by a church that promises that if I obey her she will guarantee me a place in heaven. Nor by obeah that will take care of those who harm me and bring me happiness. So I suppose you could also say that I don't believe." Antonio's eyes stared deep into the night.

"You contradict yourself," said Marina.

"I suppose so."

"Yet you called the priest?"

"Yes."

"I knew it. Finally when all's said and done you believe in obeah. But not me," Marina said firmly. "Not me."

"No. For Mother. I called the priest for Mother." Antonio tried to dismiss her. "*She* wanted the house blessed."

Marina confronted him. "And you?"

"If the priest could make her feel better . . ."

"Feel better?"

Antonio pulled his knees to his chin and wrapped his arms around his legs. He wanted to withdraw, to stop her questions. He had said too much. He had discussed too much with her. He forced himself to laugh. "Well, Marina, perhaps the priest's medicine could be more powerful than the obeahman's," he said flippantly.

"So you agree with her?" Marina pressed him again.

Antonio bristled. "What does it matter?"

"It matters if you think as she thinks. That I worked obeah on you."

"No more, Marina. No more. Let's go to bed. No. No, you are too beautiful to be an obeahwoman, to work obeah on anyone." He reached for her.

Marina's body grew rigid, her eyes cold. She pushed him off her. "I know who did it," she said. "My mother. She did it."

Antonio sighed. "Don't be foolish."

"No! I'm not wrong. It's her way. She does such things."

"What things?"

"I know you've heard what they say about her.

"Marina, you are talking about your mother," Antonio pleaded.

"Yes, Emilia Heathrow is my mother." Marina said the words slowly and deliberately, pronouncing the name Heathrow carefully so as not to omit the second "h" in the name, reducing it to the villagers' pronunciation, Heatrow. She had never learned to ignore the taunts of "Heat Row, Heat Row. Your mudder is a heat row," that the children sang after her as she walked primly to church on Sunday mornings with the Telsers before consumption had left only Mr. Telser looking too much like her father. She never knew what the words meant, but she understood their intent as a sexual insult against her mother. Now, as usual, she wanted to make it clear that her name, which her mother had adopted easily from her first lover, was Heathrow.

"Yes," she repeated, "Emilia Heathrow is my mother, but she lives a life different from mine and she has other beliefs. It was she who placed those things in the closet."

Antonio grasped Marina firmly by her shoulders and looked steadily in her eyes. Slowly, without the least bit of passion he said to her, "We will get lost Marina if we keep searching for answers to questions that we don't understand. The whole thing should be dropped and finished. The priest was here, and my mother is satisfied that whatever was done is now undone. It was probably a foolish prank done by some silly person. That and no more. Don't give it any more significance than we have done already."

"So you don't believe the story of my birth?"

"Marina, please. No more."

Marina turned her head away from him. "No, Antonio! No! You are like all men. You hide behind our skirts. You explain all your actions by saying you did them for us. You remain always guiltless."

"What are you talking about?" Antonio searched his pocket until he found another cigarette.

"Why did you marry me?" Marina asked suddenly. "I want to know why you married me."

It was Antonio's turn to move away from his wife. He lit his cigarette and sucked in the smoke slowly, holding it in his lungs for a long moment. Finally he asked quietly, "What do you want from me, Marina?"

"The truth. Why did you marry me?"

"Because I loved you."

"The Warao said—"

"Who?" Antonio felt his body betray him. Fear, like a traitor snaked up his back.

"You know. The Warao. I met him some days ago." Marina measured her words.

"And?"

"He knows you and my mother. He knew your father too."

"So?" Antonio asked, careful to conceal his fear.

"So he must have told you."

"What?"

"You know." Marina now understood completely Alma's

silence at her question about the Warao. Her eyes opened wide in disbelief and she grasped Antonio's hand, saying nothing.

"Marina what? What is it?" Antonio asked, his heart pounding. Concern for her? Or was he afraid she had found him out?

"You married me because the Warao told you to." The words spilled out of Marina's mouth as her mind made the connection.

Antonio controlled his fear and answered her firmly, "No."

"Yes, that's what you did," Marina's lips trembled.

"Marina, please. You accuse your mother of putting a curse on us. And now you accuse me of asking a savage for advice, presumably to hurt you. I want to harm you, so your mother tries to harm us. Make sense."

"Not us! Not us! You! My mother did not want to harm me. No." In a flash, her mind took her to Alma's backyard and she shivered. Perhaps Emilia would go further this time to get what she wanted.

"Why would she want to hurt me?" Antonio was saying. "Why, Marina?"

As if she were in a trance, not aware of the meaning of her words, Marina answered, "She wants to protect me from you, Antonio."

"Protect you?"

"She thinks that you murdered your wives."

"And you believe her?" asked Antonio.

"I'm not too sure."

"What?"

"She can hurt you."

"She's your mother!"

"She knows. She always knew. She tried to stop me from

marrying you." Marina pressed her thumbs against the sides
of her head to stop it from throbbing. She felt an incredible
force, like a magnetic pull, dragging her consciousness up to
the surface, pulling it to a reality her conscious mind always
shunned. The muscles at her temples twitched nervously.
She resisted. She grappled for her hold on her habitual
scorn for her mother's ways. "There must be something
about you that kills women," she said slowly, struggling for
a rational solution, a sensible answer. "I don't think that you
murder them, but they die anyway. That's why you married
me. The Warao must have told you that I will survive. That
I have the spirits of my eight brothers in me, and I will
survive whatever there is about you that kills women." Her
temple muscles trembled. "She said that you were cursed,"
she added, finally.

"She?"

"Alma. She told my mother. She told me."

"I feel sorry for you, Marina."

"Why? Because, like you, I listen to what the common
people say?"

"Alma is not just the common people."

"So you know her?"

"No. I know about her. And I know that she can hurt
people."

"You mean she has powers. Like the Warao? Is that why
you followed the Warao's advice? You believed you were
cursed."

Antonio remained silent. He did not want her to probe
any further. She had discovered him. The one time he had
chosen to believe, and absurdly, it was in the irrational. Yes,
he thought to himself, yes I grasped the ray of hope that the
Warao offered me. Yes, I wanted to escape a fate that had
doomed me to dead wives and unborn children. But I am

innocent of the death of my wives. Perhaps I could have been more careful. Perhaps I should not have impregnated them. Still, it was not my fault.

"Women die every day here in childbirth," he said aloud. "What difference could it make what the Warao said? They bleed to death because they are too small to let their babies come out of their bellies. They burn up with fever because some midwife carelessly left the afterbirth in their wombs. Their hands, feet and faces become bloated because they hold too much water. Or perhaps they ate something that was not good for them. Even labor kills them. Their hearts stop pumping. Marina, there is not a town I know where some mother does not die every week. I don't think that you could find a family who could not name a mother, a sister, a cousin, a cousin-in-law who died in childbirth."

Marina moved closer to him. She waited until the beads of perspiration that had formed on his forehead began to drop slowly one by one on his heavy mustache. "But not many of them were married to the same man," she said quietly. "And not many of their babies died when they died."

Antonio's chest caved in, his body sagged. Yes, yes, yes. The Warao offered him hope and redemption. Hope that Marina's strength would let her survive, would let him over-come his dismal fate. Redemption, that he would be freed from guilt. "You should feel sorry for me, Marina," he said finally, hugging himself against the damp darkness that en-veloped them. He was now sitting as she, his back upright against the right side of the concrete pillar, his legs stretched stiffly out in front of him. Short and dark-complexioned, in the baggy dark-blue suit that he wore for special occasions, he was almost obscured by the night. "Maybe I am cursed. My three wives died. But you must know that I suffered. I blamed myself. God! Life! I had given up, Marina, until that day the Warao told me about you."

"So I was right."

"Yes, you guessed it."

"I didn't guess, Antonio," Marina insisted quietly.

"Well, you are right. I did seek you out. You were my hope. I had hoped to save my own neck. To put an end to whatever it was. A curse you say? To put an end to the curse that gives me bad luck. But when I saw you, Marina, all those reasons left me. You were more beautiful than I had ever dreamed. It may have started the wrong way, but you must believe me that I married you because I fell in love with you. Anyhow," he added wryly, "I have escaped nothing. Now I will lose you and so you see I am back to my unhappiness."

The superficial laceration that the crab's claw had made on her skin began to sting a little, and Marina drew her skirts tightly across her thighs to stop the burning, breaking the thin scab of clotted blood that had already formed over the wound. Antonio noticed the tiny spots of blood that blotted themselves on her skirts, but he chose not to remark on them. He waited for her response.

"So you don't believe the Warao?"

"What does it matter?"

"Do you think his story about me is true? Yes or no?"

"I don't know."

Marina watched the gloom on Antonio's face become more intense. Yes, he had believed the Warao, just as she had believed the old Amerindian chief when he said that she would be rich. But would Antonio believe the Warao now, or was his mother's influence on him so strong that he'd sell the land in Tabaquite?

"But you'd still marry me?" Marina asked.

"Yes."

"I mean, even if the Warao's story is a lie?"

"Oh, Marina," Antonio said hugging her tightly to him. "I have loved you from the first moment that I saw you."

Marina measured out her words. "More than you've loved anyone else?"

"More, Marina," Antonio whispered back.

Marina's teeth scratched his ear, and Antonio felt the hairs on the back of his neck rise.

"I want us to start a new life, Marina," he said hoarsely. "Away from here. From the Warao and his stories, from your mother and her tricks—all this."

"And from *your* mother?" Marina's voice came from deep within the creases of his neck.

Antonio groaned, responding to the erotic effect of her warm breath, wet with her moisture, fanning the thin strands of hair that grew oddly away from his hairline. His coffee-brown skin, cool from the night air, flushed oxblood red. His body tingled with pleasure. He pretended not to hear her question. His mind concentrated on the escape he had conjured. On another chance to start afresh. He fooled himself into believing that she was motivated by love, perhaps jealousy of his mother; that she wanted him alone, to be with him alone. "Ranjit will buy the land," he said. "We'll be together. I'll get a real school to teach in in Port-of-Spain. You'll like it, Marina."

Antonio did not feel Marina stiffen in his arms, the Warao's words of hidden treasure foremost on her mind. He did not see the furrows gather on her forehead as her feminine instinct wrestled with her impulse to oppose him. The time was not right. She had to possess him first. She had to wait until he was hers entirely, to wait until he would deny her nothing. She took his hand and slid it down the front of her bodice in the canal between her breasts. Then, as she felt sweat gather on his open palm, she rubbed his hand first over her right breast, then her left, until her nipples stood hard and rigid.

Antonio's body offered no resistance. He let his hand travel where she would and then, when he felt his passion mount uncontrollably, he stammered without conviction. "Not here—not here—Marina—not under the house—in the open . . . What if Mother—?"

Marina bit his lower lip and thrust her tongue deep into his mouth and when she pulled away, it was only to ask in a wickedly childish voice, "Do you love me?"

Antonio was totally disarmed. He could not answer, but his body, firm and strong, told Marina all she needed to know. And for the first time in his life Antonio felt the cool breeze of the night play upon his buttocks as he entered a woman. And for the first time, the heavens saw the son of that Portuguese religious dissenter, Vasco de Balboa, make love without restraint or caution, as though the very act and the woman he penetrated were all that gave his life meaning.

AN
EARLY
DRY
SEASON

12

The dry season in Trinidad can be very disquieting to the foreigner. Around midday the sun beats down relentlessly on brown grass, on some days igniting dried-up patches of the last season's crops and everywhere drinking up the sap out of those courageous leaves that take advantage of the early morning dew to unfold themselves before the sky. To the planters on the west coast of Trinidad, the burning sun is both a blessing and a curse. It puts the final touches of sweetness on the sugarcane but it can also start fires before the harvesters are ready. For though later they would set the cane fields on fire to make the stalks more accessible to them, the harvesters knew that they would have to work swiftly before the cane went rancid in the heat.

Virginia had never seen one of these large crop fires from close range, and so she never really appreciated the complaints of the villagers who lived near to the sugarcane estates. She did not feel the soot that fell indiscriminately everywhere—in the cooking post outside, on a person's best Sunday dress, on clean laundry hung out to dry, on windowpanes, not to mention on freshly washed hair. Hands. Feet. Darting impudently into nostrils. She could not know the acrid sweet-stink smell of that sugar as some of it got burned, or the stench from the factories fermenting the sugar into alcohol. She only saw from a distance, during her visits to Princes Town, the spectacular glow of the crop fires, which on clear days, common in the dry season, would light up the evening sky in a glowing dance of bright oranges, reds and yellows, extending the natural beauty of the late afternoon sunset way into the night.

The dry season for Virginia was a time of color. Incandescent, intense sparks that glowed stubbornly in a final effort to protest death. To her, the green leaves of the rainy season offered no challenge to nature. They persisted interminably to flourish on high branches, knotty weeds, lecherous vines, everywhere extending repetitious patterns on greens that grew like cancer, snaking up the pillars that supported the house and creeping through every slit or crack in its wooden frame. But in the dry season the flowers blazed out heroically. Barren of leaves, thirsty for water, marked for death, tall, brown trees were topped with the most delicate of flowers—reds, yellows, whites, oranges and purples. They were consoling reminders to Virginia that there was beauty even in the absence of fertility. The cicadas and frogs that screeched and croaked through the night, throats parched for want of water, also offered comfort to her. They took the pain out of the loneliness that was most intense for her in the early morning before daybreak, when, in spite of herself, her eyes would shoot open searching for companionship that she had long grown accustomed to knowing was not there. Then, at four in the morning, she would listen to the cicadas and the other insects that, unlike the treacherous mosquito in the rainy season silently thrusting its sting into an unsuspecting body, raised their voices boldly in protest to a creator who had determined their lot. They were her friends, these rebellious creatures. Neither she nor they deserved such suffering. Perversely, she took pleasure too in the shortage of water during the dry season. It gave her something to do when she woke up that early, when, in spite of herself, Ranjit would intrude on her thoughts, and she would think of her wasted life, the life with him that she could have had.

She was glad that the dry season came early that year. January was too soon, but the rains were stubborn. They had worked too hard in August and now they told the women to fetch water where they could. That morning, more than any other time, she needed to have a purpose, to be busy. She got out of bed quickly to fetch water from the common pump in the main street of Moruga where, by five in the morning, lines of women waiting for their daily ration would straggle on continuously until midday when the sun would force everyone to seek the cool shelters of their beds. Virginia pulled her long cotton dress over her head, covering her white petticoat that served as a nightdress. Then she sat down to roll over her legs the cotton stockings that were required of any lady of worth in the village. Of course the village women did not wear them, but the English ladies did—at least the older ones. And Virginia, a retired schoolteacher and mother of a district schoolteacher, was expected to have that part of her leg that was visible to the public covered in a similiar fashion. At that hour in the morning, and in the hottest time of the year, it was her unconscious compromise with the people for breaking the social code by fetching water herself and not sending her servant girl.

Tugging impatiently at the stocking, she tied the top of it into a knot that she tucked deftly against her leg just below her knee. She had not slept well that night. Off and on in intervals of half an hour she would awaken, tiptoe to her son's bedroom door and listen for the rhythmical sounds of his soft snores. Finally, around three in the morning, realizing that she could hear no sounds or movements, she crept cautiously into his room. He was not there, nor was Marina. She concluded that Antonio had gone in search of his wife. Not that she should not have guessed it. Antonio had stood by her like a dutiful son. He had calmed her out of her hysteria, made all the arrangements for the priest to bless the house, sat by her bed and read to her until she had fallen asleep. Not once during that time did he deny her accusations that Marina was responsible for placing the pouch in the closet. But she could perceive in his silence, his uncertainty. And she felt deep in her heart that Marina had taken a stronger hold of his affection than she herself had had. Antonio was all she had. Antonio and her books. Except Antonio was real. Until Marina, she alone had his affections. He made her feel lovable—desirable even. For to her, Antonio was a handsome man.

She should have done as he. Once, she could have said yes to life. That was twenty-nine years ago. De Balboa, as usual, wanted to have nothing to do with the crops that grew on their land. But it was an unusual year. For once there was no disease in the cocoa. For one whole season the cocoa trees blossomed with their fragile white flowers, and the farmers waited, and nothing happened. Except that the cocoa continued. For one whole season, their pods kept getting larger and larger and their green covering turned pink, then a rich, deep purple with no telltale signs of disease blackening their edges. The villagers of Moruga, Sangre Grande and Fyzabad held their breaths, for it had seemed that as soon as the Europeans thirsted for the taste of cocoa, the crops failed. As soon as their bodies craved the sticky goo that came from crushed cocoa beans and sugar, the cocoa refused to bear fruit. But not that year. So the villages celebrated. Cocoa was king again. De Balboa, in his habitual gesture of indifference, permitted his young wife to accept the invitation of his land tenants, his squatters, who were grateful for their landlord's generosity. Ranjit had come too, with the sugarcane farmers from Siparia. Virginia noticed him because he was the cleanest of the villagers, his black, straight hair slicked back, shining with coconut oil. He wore a clean white shirt, freshly starched brown trousers tucked into tall, black leather boots polished to a bright luster. And he was handsome. Perhaps few women would have agreed with her judgment, but it was the first time in Virginia's life that a man had aroused her awareness of the sexual difference between the male and female of the human species, a difference that suggested more than the simple means of distinguishing the sexes.

Ranjit was not tall, and his sapodilla-brown skin and angular facial features—sharp nose, pointed chin—were not arresting. He was of average height for an East Indian—about five feet three. He was slim without being thin, but he certainly was not muscular. Indeed, he had a small chest and a small waist, and one could call his body effeminate if it weren't for the fact that his chest was hairy and he did not have the wide hips so common among the women in Trinidad. No, it was in his eyes that Virginia saw his masculinity. In his clear, brown eyes that radiated gentleness, a sensitivity to all around him. And in the bushy eyebrows that guarded them and gave the impression that he was in control, that in spite of his kindness, he could not be used.

It had just begun to drizzle, as it sometimes did on a sunny day in the rainy season when the rain wanted to teach the sun a lesson. The villagers scattered madly about trying to cover the cocoa beans still wrapped in their damp white pulp and laid out on flat trays to dry in the sun. For some it meant merely pushing the drawerlike trays so that they would be covered by the sheds that housed them and their owners. But Virginia stayed where she was, waiting for the rain cloud to pass. And Ranjit saw her. Tall and graceful, with skin like ripe cocoa, her long skirts brushing softly over seductive thighs. She wore laced white shoes and carried a frilly parasol. Like the English ladies he knew. And the scarf that covered her head was fashioned like a turban, not the bandana of the common village women. She exuded superiority, and anger, like an unsheathed machete, stung his face.

"You have no cocoa in the sun, do you, Mrs. de Balboa?"

Virginia felt the man she had noticed burn her ear. She spun around, startled by the preciseness of his English, and their eyes met.

"Excuse me?" she murmured, tasting his insolence. A man with no cocoa in the sun is a man with no worries. A woman with no cocoa in the sun is a woman living the life of luxury through the labor of others.

Ranjit dropped his bold gaze before the black pools of her eyes. "I'm sorry. A bad joke . . ."

Before he could stammer out more, Virginia had recovered her self-assurance and coldly replied, "Then your bad joke has gone right by me. Good day." She opened her parasol, hitched up her skirts and hurried to the cocoa shed. When the drizzle had passed, she met the freshly dressed man again. He wanted to apologize.

"Will you forgive me, Mrs. de Balboa?" he said.

"Whatever for?"

"My rudeness about your cocoa." He looked sad. Comical. She felt sorry for him.

"Well, actually it's not mine," she said. "It's my husband's."

"I know," the man replied kindly, and then introduced himself. "Ranjit Ramloogan. I farm sugar." He said it with pride, as though he had an important job.

Virginia allowed him to grasp her hand in greeting. The man intrigued her. At twenty-one, she had seen no man of color act with such self-importance and arrogance. "What do you know about Mr. de Balboa?" she asked.

"What everyone else knows. That he doesn't care about his land. Do you?"

"I am here, aren't I?" Virginia replied.

Ranjit laughed, "But not like one of them," he said, pointing to the other villagers.

Again his insolence stung Virginia, and she was about to leave him when he confessed quietly, "Neither am I. That's why I noticed you and you noticed me."

That meeting was a long time ago. From then on they struck a deep friendship. For the East Indian found in Virginia the very alienation and loneliness that he too suffered. And he discovered that they shared the same desire to be more than what their conditions as colonized people living in a British colony had forced upon them.

A young woman, Virginia was then already an old maid condemned to a life of sexual frustration by a Portuguese man disenchanted with God and religion. Ranjit was thirty-one, burning for a life he could never have with his wife, Indira. An outsider in his community, he would hang around the yard facing his warden's drawing room when the warden's wife entertained, listening to music and chatter from another land, another culture. He felt different. Better even than the common East Indian laborer. When he discovered that Virginia was a schoolteacher, he made the trip twice a week to Moruga to sit with her in her tiny schoolhouse and learn what she knew. At first no one knew what he was doing on those afternoons when he washed the mud off his legs at the river near his shack, put on his Sunday-clean trousers, shirt and boots, hitched his donkey cart and disappeared until late evening. No one would believe it if they knew.

For on this one point, Trinidad's African people agreed with their English wardens: "Give a coolie land and you make him happy. That's all coolies live for." When Harold Smith said those words, he said them with admiration. For, failure that he was, he was truly in awe of the East Indian's uncanny ability to make the soil breed for him, to grow any fruit he wished, any vegetable in spite of the long months without rain, the hurricanes that drowned everything, the eternal bugs, the crippling diseases.

But Mrs. Smith, Virginia's adoptive mother, knew better. She prided herself on her knowledge of colored people. "A matter of time, Smithy," she'd say to her husband, forever mopping her brow with her lavender-scented lace handkerchief. It seemed, dry season or rainy season, her bony body was always wet, clammy with sweat, her red stringy hair clinging to her dough-white face. "A matter of time before the coolie does exactly what the Negro is doing now. You see, colored people are all the same, my dear. Coolie or Negro, they all have one desire and that is to be like us. The poor things imagine that if they could only change their skins"— at that point she would always look sympathetically at Virginia, her black daughter—"they would be white. It's more than skin, Smithy my dear. It's culture. Civilization. Intelligence. The Negro has left the land now, but soon it will be the coolie and he will give the same reason: he wants to uplift his race. The only thing that they will accomplish"—Mrs. Smith would laugh sarcastically—"is to prove their dependence on us. In the final analysis, they will come crawling back to us for food. Both will have abandoned their land for freedom and in a few years they will beg us again to enslave them. To save them before they starve like dogs in their well-furnished houses. Their land will be covered with houses and roads and they'll have nothing to eat. Then they'll plead with us. Then they'll beg for the whip. So we can show them again how to till the soil."

It was a dismal prediction. In 1872, it seemed to be bred from the malicious mind, so diseased by prejudice that it would disregard the simple reality that no East Indian seemed the least interested in leaving his land. Rather that they thrived on the land, that they loved the land. So when the people discovered Ranjit's secret, they thought that he was queer. Odd. Indira, Ranjit's wife, bore the pain of the gossip well. Her job was to bear children, something she also did well. She never spoke to her husband on any topic other than food, clothing and shelter. She didn't mind. None of the East Indian women around her thought that their husband's business was any of theirs. The women had their role and the men theirs. When she was told what her husband did on those afternoons, Indira burned some incense for him so that he would find his right mind. And that was all.

And the possibility of romance between Virginia and Ranjit was not ever a consideration. Certainly not one as far as the people who brought the gossip to Indira were concerned. A Negro woman and an Indian man just didn't see each other that way. But Indira didn't count on the longing for something more than a bed partner that festered in her husband's heart. Nor could she know the pain of loneliness that Virginia suffered because she, on the other hand, had no bed partner. It was one full year after their first meeting, seeing each other once a week, admitting to each other no hint of desire other than intellectual and spiritual stimulation, before Ranjit touched Virginia. For one short evening, with her husband wandering on the beach with the Warao, indifferent to his wife's activities, Virginia knew sexual fulfillment.

Ranjit meant only to kiss her cheek as he had done each time at their parting, but she turned her head at that moment. When their mouths met, nothing else mattered, not Virginia's husband or Ranjit's wife. They clung to each other like lost souls adrift on a raging sea. Unbridled passion, emotions pent up in marriages that they both thought had cooled desire, raged through them. She broke away first and led him to her bedroom, as if it were the natural and right thing to do. There, next to the bed where her husband let her lie untouched and unfulfilled, Ranjit undressed her. Tenderly, he removed each piece of her clothing one by one until she was naked. Then he kissed the body she was once ashamed of—her eyes, nose, throat, nipples, fingers, navel, toes, until she too admired the beauty he saw. Gently, his love for her making him restrain himself, pace himself, he entered her and waited. Waited until she too felt the flow, the burning fire, the sweet indescribable pleasure that let her fall against his chest exhausted when it was all over.

But the next week when Ranjit hurried to see her again, she had changed. She made it clear to him that they would not be together again, not that way. He did not question her. Not then. Not for a long time. But he asked her once again, long after, once his wife had died and de Balboa was long buried. He thought now, perhaps, she would say yes. He offered marriage then, but Virginia refused him.

The memory of her loss and her youthful days made Virginia think more kindly of her daughter-in-law. It was Emilia who worked obeah, not Marina. Marina was far too level-headed a woman to be involved in that. No, Virginia knew that it was her own fear of loss that made her search the girl's closet. It was fear of losing her son that made her react so passionately when she found those things. Did she expect that Antonio would ask Marina to leave if he found out that she worked obeah? And, if indeed she could make her son believe it was Marina who had put that pouch in the closet, would it make any difference to him? He said not one word against Marina. He did not defend her, but he did not accuse her. If, Virginia finally admitted, she were not to cause trouble between herself and her son, she had to drop the whole matter, or at least pretend to Antonio that she had forgotten what had happened. Now, as she picked up the empty bucket from the kitchen, Virginia decided that she would try. She would be nice to Marina.

From beneath the house where she and Antonio had stayed all night, Marina heard the clanking sound of the tin bucket upstairs and knew that Virginia was awake. She touched Antonio lightly on the shoulder and motioned him to be still. In a few minutes they could hear the creaking of the front stairs as the wooden boards gave way under the pressure of Virginia's footsteps. After Virginia turned the corner past the bushes of red bougainvillea, Marina and Antonio crept quietly upstairs. It was still dark, as it is in the early hours of the morning in Trinidad, and Antonio, still enjoying the immense sense of relief that he had experienced the night before, happily crawled into his bed.

But Marina had no thoughts of sleep.

When Virginia returned from the village water pump, she found Marina in the kitchen quietly stripping into tiny pieces the salted codfish which she had blanched a few minutes ago with boiling water to wash off the excess salt. Virginia grimaced. It was the kind of defiance in her daughter-in-law that she hated. She had tried everything she could to stop her from cooking, but finally accepted defeat when Antonio announced that he had never tasted sweeter food than that made by his wife. Virginia lifted the bucket of water off her head and placed it noisily on the kitchen table next to Marina's codfish. Slowly and methodically, she folded the white cotton cloth that she had used on her head to soften the impact of the hard tin bucket, her eyes concentrating on her hands. Finally clearing her throat, she said calmly, "Good morning, Marina. I'm glad you're back."

Marina was unprepared for Virginia's friendliness. Taken aback, she stammered nervously, "Mrs. de Balboa, I know nothing about what happened here yesterday morning. I was as surprised as you to see those—those things. I had nothing to do with it. You must believe me."

Virginia smoothed the folds of her skirt over her belly and heard herself ask what she had rehearsed she would not ask. "Where did you go, then? Where were you all yesterday?"

"I thought that you wanted me out of the way."

Virginia cast her eyes downward. "Yes." She paused, and still not looking at Marina, she added, "It was best."

"For whom? I didn't—"

"It does not matter now. I don't want to begin this all over again. The house is blessed."

"But I didn't have anything to do with what happened. And you threw me out of the house."

"Do you want me to apologize?" Virginia's voice was icy-cold.

"You asked me where I went as though you knew where."

Virginia looked at her directly. "I am surprised," she said, "that you knew where she was."

"Where who was?"

"The obeahwoman. With skin like yours, I'm surprised they didn't think you were white."

Marina laughed. "Do you think I look white?"

Virginia ignored her.

"I look English to you? They are only afraid of the English."

"Serves them right. They think every root and weed could cure any disease. The English people are right to stop all this nonsense. I'd burn their houses down too."

Marina stretched her hand and reached casually for one of the onions that were tied together in a bunch hanging from a string nailed to one of the wooden beams in the kitchen. "Well, it seems that when the English people have problems, they find their way to the same obeahman they want to destroy."

"Like whom?"

Marina shrugged her shoulders. "People talk."

"Whom do you mean? What English person have you ever seen go to an obeahman?"

"They say," Marina paused, slicing the onions into tiny cubes. Not once did she blink as the onion juice spurted in her face. "The governor's wife."

"Who?"

"The governor's wife. She went to the obeahman. And not once either. Several times."

"Poppycock!"

"It was for the lump in her breast."

"Nonsense!"

"Well, I heard that she drank the caraili tea and it cured the lump in her breast. It disappeared."

Virginia lowered her body down onto one of the cane-backed chairs placed around the table. Her voice was barely audible when she repeated, "Nonsense."

"Did you ever wonder, Mrs. de Balboa, why we don't get lumps in our breasts. At least not as often as they do?"

"English medicine is the best in the world," said Virginia, brushing her aside. "They don't need roots and all those—those dried-out leaves. They use science."

"Perhaps, but their women still come to the obeahman when their medicine can't work—"

"Nonsense!"

"Or when their lovers leave them and they want them back."

Virginia fidgeted with the collar of her dress.

"Or when they want wives for their sons." Marina gave a final slice to the onion.

"Never!"

"Then I suppose, Mrs. de Balboa, you did not go to the Warao to find a wife for your son," Marina said quietly, facing Virginia.

"To a Warao? My God, what next? He brings us our fish."

"Is that all?"

"Oh no, Marina, it's your mother who consults a Warao."

"So you admit it."

"Admit what?"

"You know."

"It's not I who believe that. It's the whole village. Everybody." Virginia spread out her hands.

"And you too," Marina sang, waving her finger at her.

Virginia got up from the table and walked toward the stove. "Where's Antonio?" she asked, refusing to let Marina confuse her, draw her down, as she felt, to her level.

"In his bed. Where else?"

"Well, I'm glad that he did not hear us."

"Antonio knows already," Marina said harshly. "He admits that he married me because the Warao told him what you said that the whole village believes."

Virginia poured herself a cup of hot cocoa and returned to the table. Distracted by Marina, she forgot to blow away the hot steam and she swallowed the cocoa before she could realize what she was doing. The hot cocoa burned the tender insides of her cheeks and blistered her tongue, but she suffered in silence. She let the pain harden the softness she felt toward Marina earlier that morning when she remembered her meetings with Ranjit. She narrowed her eyes. "Antonio should not have married your kind," she murmured. But at that instant, when she meant to be her cruelest, she knew that she would be defeated. For she realized too late that Marina would seize upon that lie.

Her eyes shining with revenge, Marina replied directly, "On the contrary, it is because I am my kind that you wanted Antonio to marry me."

"I didn't care one way or the other." Caught without defenses, Virginia tried to sound indifferent. Casual. "I had hoped that you would bring him some happiness—and he you."

"But you didn't try to stop him?"

"No."

"Not even though I'm a maid's daughter? I am illegitimate? My mother sleeps with her mistress's widower? My mother works obeah?" Marina sliced furiously down on the ripe tomatoes. Juice and tiny seeds splattered over the floor.

Virginia replied quietly, "My son wanted you."

"And so did you!" Marina had to force herself not to shout.

Virginia pushed her chair away from the table, the scraping sound of the chair against the unpolished wooden floor echoing her discomfort. "You were beautiful," she said simply.

Marina felt no pity. She pressed the palms of her hands on the table and leaned toward Virginia. "You wanted light-skinned babies," she lashed out at her. "Light-skinned with gray eyes. No more nappy hair for your black-skinned son. I know *your* kind. Nothing is good unless it's white. And nothing is bad if it's white." Marina saw Virginia's eyes get misty with hatred for her, and she added quietly, "Is that what your white mother told you, Mrs. de Balboa?"

"Stop it!"

"I know about the Smiths. Now Harold Smith acts as though you'd never lived in his house. And that Philip Smith, your white brother—does he even speak to you?"

Virginia grasped the edge of the table, the muscles in her arms grown rigid with her anger. Her eyes flashed red. "Hilda Smith is dead. Let her rest in peace. I want to hear nothing again from you about the Smiths. Nothing."

Her eyes frightened Marina. She realized that she had gone too far. She tried to look away, to get up from her chair and leave the table, but Virginia grasped her arm.

"Nothing," Virginia said again, her voice strained, "you say nothing about the Smiths from this day." She released Marina and leaned back in her chair.

"I'm sorry," said Marina.

Virginia glanced at her briefly and then got up slowly and walked away from the table.

"I'm sorry. Really I am," Marina repeated, afraid now that Virginia would tell Antonio and she would not be forgiven. Alma had told her about Harold Smith's desire for Virginia, but that seemed to be common knowledge in Moruga. Then two days ago the servant girl had said that there was a brother, Philip Smith. The red-headed Englishman who slept with every available woman in Moruga was actually Hilda Smith's natural-born son, the girl told her, glancing furtively around her as if afraid someone would overhear her. "He born after Miss Virginia left the house. Both of them making baby the same time. Miss Virginia, she having Mr. Antonio, and Miss Smith, she having Mr. Philip. But they never talk. Miss Smith she never talk again to Miss Virginia when Mr. Philip born. And nobody say nothing."

Whatever had caused the rift between Virginia and the woman who had adopted her appeared to be linked to Philip Smith, but Marina knew that she had trodden on taboo ground.

"I didn't mean what I said. I'm sorry."

Virginia stopped by the window and gazed outside, a faraway look on her face. "Yes," she said tonelessly. "Yes."

"I want to make it up to you."

Virginia turned toward Marina. "Make it up?"

"I didn't intend to hurt you."

"You want to make it up?" Virginia looked closely at Marina.

"Yes. What can I do?"

"Don't oppose me with Antonio," she said softly.

"Don't—"

"Yes. I want to sell the land. I want to leave this place. I'm tired of the ignorance of this place. I want to go where people read books and listen to real music. I want—"

"I can't do that, Mrs. de Balboa."

"You can't?"

"No, I can't let you sell the land." Marina had not intended to tell her about the Warao. Not just yet. She had counted on more time to bind Antonio to herself, so that he would do as she asked. But she felt pity for Virginia. She could not leave her with false hopes.

"Why?" The fire returned to Virginia's eyes.

"I'm sorry, Mrs. de Balboa. It would be a big mistake."

"Why?"

"It's for your own good."

"Why?"

"Your land is valuable."

Virginia wanted to laugh but Marina's seriousness stopped her. Still she asked cruelly, "And does your mother intend to cure the disease on the land with her obeah?"

Marina controlled herself. "The land is valuable," she repeated.

"Then Ranjit should give me a good price for it."

"No!" Marina sounded almost desperate. "The oil there hides something valuable. The Warao told me."

"The Warao? You saw the Warao?" Virginia's face tightened. Perhaps the Warao had also spoken to Ranjit. Perhaps Ranjit knew that the oil had spread to her land.

"He told me about the oil. It'll make you rich. It's shark oil, he said. The Americans are digging everywhere for it. In Fyzabad. Everywhere."

Virginia threw back her head and laughed. "My God! My God! Shark oil. My Lord! Shark oil! On my land!"

Antonio appeared at the doorway and looked first to his

mother, then to his wife. He had not hoped to find things patched up so soon between them.

"Antonio, come! Come hear your wife." The bitterness in Virginia's voice now worried him. "Come! She said sharks. Sharks! You know that Warao your father always used to talk to? Well, Marina met the Warao and he told her that there were some Americans digging for shark oil in Fyzabad, near your father's land. Shark oil! Can you believe it! Shark oil!"

"Mother!"

"The sharks! The sharks, Antonio, came out of the ocean and crawled on the land and then dug holes and buried themselves."

"Come now, Mother, I'm sure Marina did not say that." Antonio put his arm affectionately around Marina's waist.

"No. I didn't say that." Marina pushed Antonio away from her. The timing was wrong. She did not want to confront Antonio about the land. Not now. Not with his mother there, goading her.

"What did you say then, Marina?" Antonio touched her again and this time she let him fondle her waist.

"Can you imagine these people? They believe anything."

"Mother! Well, Marina?"

"El Dorado," Marina began, remembering her own scorn for the Warao when he told her of the shark oil. "The Arawaks and the Caribs put the shark oil there to hide their treasures. The Warao told me."

"And you believe him?" Antonio dropped his hand from Marina's waist, walked to the cupboard and reached for a cup.

"It comes from not reading. These people believe anything." Virginia poured his cocoa when he returned to the table.

"It's just a village story, Marina. The Indians did not bury treasure here," said Antonio.

"Then why are the Americans digging?" Marina did not want to look foolish.

"Marina, believe me, if there was treasure in that land, we would have found it long ago." Antonio sipped his cocoa.

"So what are the Americans looking for?" Marina insisted.

"For a way to stop the oil from coming into the cocoa, dear." Virginia said with exaggerated patience. "It's science, my dear. Something you obviously do not understand. They are looking for a way to channel off the oil so that the soil will be good again."

"Well, maybe it's not shark oil," said Marina. Like the Warao, she was groping for a more plausible possibility.

Virginia poured herself some cocoa and pulled her chair closer to her son.

"Perhaps it's the kind of oil that they have in England and America."

Virginia had grown tired of the girl. She put down her cup and looked at Marina with exasperation. "Then why would they want to ship it to their country when they have plenty of oil there? Why would they need more? It would be like bringing coals to Newcastle. For God's sake, Marina, how much kerosene could a person need?"

Suspecting that his mother and Marina were about to embark on an argument, Antonio said quickly, "Let's end all this. Whatever the Americans are looking for or not looking for it's in Fyzabad. Not on our land. We just have the grease that kills the cocoa."

Virginia laughed, and Antonio was sorry he had said those words. He tried to pacify his wife. "Come Marina, let me have some of that good food you cooked." And Marina, seeing that she had lost, gave her husband the marinated codfish that she had just garnished with slices of tomato and hard-boiled eggs, and said nothing more.

13

At six in the morning on a workday it was already too
late to get a ride from one of the villagers going into
Siparia to harvest the sugarcane crops. But Virginia was
lucky. One man had drunk too much rum the night before,
probably because, as he looked across the vast expanse of his
boss's cocoa estate, he knew with fateful certainty that the
roots of those trees had already snarled their way into
the cracks and crevices of the soil; that, thirsty for water in
the arid heat of the dry season, they had sucked into a pool
of oil that lay there languid and insipid, but treacherous.
Always treacherous. That oil would lick its slimy self around
those parched roots, then curl its way like liquid silk through
every vein and artery of the trees. Springing from ground
that was soggy with oil, these cocoa trees would never live to
bear fruit.

Probably this man, because he had already run the race from cocoa estate to estate in a futile effort to beat the oil—Fyzabad, Barrackpore, Tabaquite—was now exhausted and worn out. Probably because, as he arrived in each place that he had escaped to, he smelled the thick, slimy poison that he hated and saw the dreaded spots of white marring the bark of the cocoa trees, a sure sign of premature death. For though the smell of the oil camouflaged itself with the scents of the earth, he could detect its sinister odor reeking of the putrid guts of the underworld and he knew without question that the end had come.

Probably he was grieving because men like him would no more see days of sitting under the tall tonka trees, watching bean pods sprout like giant-sized purple teardrops from the bark of cocoa trees that grew under the tonka. No longer would men like him roll their naked feet over trays of moist-pulped beans until the beans, stripped of their protective skins, just withered dry in the scorching sun. No more would men like him know the taste, after those beans had been pounded to powder, after they had been seasoned with raw milk from the udders of goats, no more would men like him know that drink of the gods nor the days when they shared in the gods' creation. Probably because he knew all this, this man, in an effort to hide his grief, drowned his sorrows in a bottle of home-brewed rum.

It was probably Moruga that had killed the spirit in this man. Moruga, near the cocoa estates he had known as a child. Moruga not yet affected by this treacherous oil. And having at last arrived there and sniffed the earth, he smelled and saw in spite of her innocence, the lurid signs of that murky grease languishing underneath. Now he went with the sugarcane harvesters to Siparia, a grieving man, a defeated man, a man drunk on alcohol. So it was that this man was late and so it was that Virginia was lucky enough to be driven to the sugar estates where she would find Ranjit.

It was close to noon when Virginia arrived at Ranjit's yard. She knew that her old friend would be home soon, for the midday sun was merciless, and Ranjit would let his workers drop their machetes and return to their houses to sleep until the sun had moved from the center of the sky. Virginia shook out the old brown sheet that she had carried with her, spread it out on the cool, dark earth under a large breadfruit tree and sat down.

It was one week since her quarrel with Marina and there were no more arguments. Why then was she . . . ? Yes . . . afraid. That was the word. Why was she so afraid of her? She tightened the belt of her bright yellow dress around her slim waist and adjusted the tie she had made in her red bandana so that its ends fell to the right side of her neck, making her look girlish. Coquettish. How could Marina know how Virginia felt? What she thought? Could the girl know how Virginia's mother, Hilda Smith, felt to have her own child at last? To bear her own baby in her womb? She could forgive her. She had forgiven her years ago for abandoning her when Philip was born. Why must Marina open the wound again? Were the people in the village talking about her? They had remained silent so long. How much more had they told Marina? The dark pools of Virginia's eyes overflowed down her cheeks, and she reached into her pocket and pulled out a white cotton handkerchief and mopped her cocoa-colored face, already flushed with red undertones from the hot sun. "How much more?" she asked aloud. Hearing her own voice startled Virginia and brought her back to the present moment. She fastened her eyes on the comforting movement of the tattered flags that flapped lazily in the breeze from the top of four tall, weather-beaten, bamboo poles clumped together in front of Ranjit's house.

Yes, he would understand. Ranjit would know that she must leave Moruga. She would tell him about Marina, but not about what Marina said. She didn't have to tell him about the Smiths, even if he had heard the gossip. She dried her tears, and her eyes followed the frayed, tattered, home-made triangles of faded cotton cloth whose colors were once red, white, yellow, blue. She smiled. Ranjit was like her in spite of the Hindu prayer flags that he flew from the tops of bamboo poles, signaling the entrance of his house, and his past. He was no ordinary East Indian. No peasant. He would understand. He was different from the thousands of laborers who migrated from India around the late 1840's in search of food in Trinidad. Listening to the frayed flags slap against their weather-beaten poles, Virginia thought how lucky it was for her that Ranjit was born here in Trinidad, that he had not died in his mother's womb on that voyage from India across the rough seas, through the Indian Ocean around the bottom of Africa, up through the Atlantic. How lucky she was that his father had no love for him, that he had abandoned the son he was ashamed of. How lucky she was that Ranjit should know how to dream dreams and love the life she once had.

He was a strange boy from birth. Ranjit had come out of his mother legs first, almost killing the young woman who had carried him so safely in her womb in a cargo ship from Bombay to Port-of-Spain. He was always sickly, and his fa-ther despised him for it. He was a girlish baby and a girlish child. Even the features on his face were rounded and soft like a girl's. As a child of four, he was the size of a two-year-old. No one could interest him in boyish play. He preferred the kitchen with its pots and pans that made musical noises to his ear. And the river where the women beat clothes against the large stones, swaying their backsides rhythmically with each stroke, sending their youthful laughter pealing downstream, riding the crystal-clear waters that licked the gray boulders, cooling their sun-parched sides.

The boy loved it. Sometimes he'd strip naked and jump in the river, splashing the water all over his body, and the women would laugh at him, saying, "But look how little Ramloogan son is." And his mother would yell at him, threatening to beat him if he did not come out. But he wouldn't. He'd wait, for he loved to feel her two large, pendulous breasts pressed to his back as she would pull him up from the water by his waist, with one arm.

When he was five years old, his father, Ramloogan, was ready to return to India, the period of his indenture having at long last come to an end, but Ranjit was struck with a terrible case of malaria. His father, who could barely hide his disappointment in his girlish son, was now more scornful than ever that his boy, not his three girls whom he had brought with him from Bombay, caught the disease. Perhaps he would not have left Ranjit in Trinidad had he not feared missing the ship to India that would not wait for one East Indian passenger. Perhaps he would have tried to make this girl-child a man-child. Nonetheless, in spite of his wife's tears, Ramloogan left his son Ranjit in the care of a neighbor whose wife was barren and so didn't care that she had a son who was not a boy. Of course, Ramloogan promised to send for the boy. But he never did. For though he was poor, he was born a Brahmin, and no Brahmin ever sired a weak son.

The man who was not his father loved the boy, but he never told him. He was ashamed of this son who grew up to love the land as much as a man should love a woman.

One would see Ranjit, at fourteen, before the sun began its ascent from the east and long after it disappeared from the sky, hoeing and tilling and watering and planting. But his cabbages, tomatoes, lettuce, corn, dasheen, yams, carrots, eggplant were the best that could be found in Trinidad. The sugarcane he planted was the sweetest on the estate in Siparia, so much so that the other planters never put his cane stalks on the donkey carts headed for the sugar factories, but rather they stored them away to eat themselves at night after a hard day's work.

News of Ranjit's success with the land had reached the ears of the landlord, and the man offered Ranjit the same five acres of land that his father was promised, had he remained in Trinidad, if Ranjit would supervise the planting of the next season's crops. So by fifteen, already past the marrying age of his people, Ranjit was able to take a wife. He was now a landowner.

It was on this land that Virginia waited for Ranjit under the breadfruit tree near the flags in front of the modern house he had built to replace the mud shack he once lived in with his wife, dead now ten years, and his three sons, all of whom had left to work for the English on the sugarcane estates. He alone had stubbornly refused to work for anyone but himself.

At sixty, Ranjit had not given up on life. He had now accumulated quite a few acres of land, some by trading his labor, some by purchasing them from some Negro who either needed money for rum or wanted to move to the city to be a big shot. When Virginia offered to sell him her land, he was delighted. The thought of owning fifteen acres of cocoa land was more than he had hoped for. He was willing to give his entire lifetime savings and his children's inheritance for it. But that was in November before he had gone to Tabaquite.

Now, as he walked through the dry dirt track that led to his house with its galvanized roof, he had resigned himself to what he already had. He was satisfied with the land that was his. He had snuffed out the dream that for days had made him feel young again. When he saw Virginia, at first only her bright yellow dress spread out among the knotted roots of his old breadfruit tree, he had already washed away the last residue of bitterness that had soured his mouth, the gnawing suspicion that she had betrayed him. He was happy to see her.

"Ginny! Ginny!" he called, breaking into a slight run. For his age, in spite of the creases on his face, his body was still young. He threw the rope that was tied to his gray bisons into the hands of his yardboy. "Gi dem water. Dey tirsty." He spoke to the boy in the idiom he reserved for his help. "Ginny! What brings you here?"

Virginia reached for his hand and unfolded her legs from the ground. "You," she said, smiling, getting up.

"But twice since Christmas before the last? You want to see so much of me?" Ranjit almost giggled like a schoolboy as he leaned over to kiss Virginia on the cheek.

"Are you complaining or happy to see me?" Virginia tucked one arm in his and pulled up the folds of her yellow skirts with the other hand, exposing her skin and her white-cotton lace petticoats.

Ranjit saw her naked ankle and grinned broadly. "You know the day is always better when I see you."

"Come! Stop it! I'm here on business," she said, obviously enjoying Ranjit's open affection for her. But her words, though spoken fondly, broke Ranjit's gaiety. A frown lost its way in the wrinkles of his forehead.

"Is it ever otherwise?" he asked.

"Such as?"

"Well, you could come just to see me." Ranjit was cautious. Testing.

"I always do," Virginia said quickly, and then she laughed, making Ranjit feel foolish for his seriousness.

"Well, are we going to stay out here, or are you going to let me come in and sit on your Morris chair?"

"Of course. Come on in. Come on in." Ranjit's voice was warm with pleasure and he tightened his hold on her arm and led her up the front steps into his small drawing room. "Too much heat," he said, when they came inside, bustling around the room with his old man's energy. "I bet you could use a tall glass of lime juice. No?"

"No." Then seeing the disappointment on his face, Virginia caught his arm and added, "Not just yet. Let me sit down and relax a bit. That ground can be hard."

Ranjit laughed and pulled a chair closer to Virginia. "And your boy? How is he?"

"Oh, happy with his new wife."

Ranjit grinned. "He's a brave man to get married again. I doubt I would after three wives."

"I suppose so. You didn't after only one."

"That's because you wouldn't marry me."

"Don't tease, Ranjit," Virginia said, settling down more comfortably into the coconut-fiber stuffed chair that Ranjit had offered her. "I'm serious. I have business to discuss. I'm ready to sell that land you want so much."

Ranjit felt the sweat drip from the back of his neck. He fiddled with the belt on his waist. "That was in November." His voice was hardly audible.

"What did you say?"

"I said that that was in November." Ranjit sat down on the chair opposite Virginia.

"So? And now it's only January. You forget so soon?" Virginia loosened the red bandana that covered the corn-rows on her head.

"Wait a minute, Ginny," Ranjit's voice crackled slightly in agitation. "In November you didn't tell me everything."

Virginia smoothed the cornrows on her head and pulled the red bandana around her neck. "Like what, for example?"

"Like that your crops were dying." Ranjit sat at the edge of his chair.

"Oh, that! But I thought you knew that already, Ranjit. I thought you told me that you'd take the risk. Remember you said that for every disease there's a cure. Depends on the doctor, you said. Have you changed your mind?"

"Is not that, Ginny. Not that," Ranjit stood up. "This is no disease."

"What do you mean?" Virginia looked up at her friend, her heart sinking. "The cocoa on my land is dying of disease. Just like everybody's cocoa. I thought I told you this. I thought we discussed this."

"Ginny, Ginny—" Ranjit paced the room, knotting his graying eyebrows. "Ginny, you know how long I waited for cocoa land. How long! Sure, they say I'm an old man now and I should be finished with it all. Finished." He sat down again and swiped a fly that buzzed across his face. "But I'm not finished. Everybody wants cocoa. Why not me? I want to grow the sweetest cocoa they ever tasted. I want to make the best cocoa. It's sugarcane that is finished. You think they want to make molasses anymore, or sugar? It's rum. That's all they want. Rum. I can't grow sugar for rum. But for chocolate? Ginny, you don't think I wouldn't work your land day and night for chocolate?" Ranjit leaned back in his chair and sighed, and when he sat forward again it was to look sadly in Virginia's eyes. "But your soil," he said quietly. "It's no good. Why didn't you tell me?"

Had Virginia heard the pain in Ranjit's voice as he asked that question, she would perhaps have not had the courage to challenge him about her soil, or perhaps she would have remembered her feelings for him, and guilt would have forced her to leave his house. But it was Marina's face she saw at that moment, Marina taunting her about white grandchildren and Philip Smith. So she asked boldly, "Who says my soil is no good?"

Ranjit sighed. "Virginia," he began, looking down at the tips of his boots. In the rainy season, he couldn't wear them in the house. The land would have muddied them. Normally he couldn't even do so at this time of the year, but it was an early dry season and the fields were dry now. "You are one of my best friends, so I can't lie to you. Sure there is cocoa disease and sugarcane disease and bug disease, but on your land the soil is turning black and oily. That's what's killing your crops. You couldn't get a song for it now. Nobody wants it."

Virginia sat on the edge of her chair, her bottom lip twitching nervously. "You could put manure on it," she persisted.

"You don't understand, do you, Ginny?" Ranjit tried to control his agitation. Like her, he too sat on the edge of his chair. "I could put manure on it, yes. But nothing would happen. This stuff is coming from the middle of the earth and it won't stop. Didn't you know this, Ginny? Didn't you? Didn't your squatters tell you?"

Without moving, without indicating that she was at all crushed by anything Ranjit had said, Virginia began to cry. Not loud, hysterical sobs, which would have made looking at her less painful. Her eyes suddenly filled with tears that silently ran down the sides of her cheeks, some dripping onto her chin, some filtering into the corners of her mouth.

Ranjit got up immediately, his anger vanishing, and knelt beside his old friend, dabbing away her tears with his clean handkerchief.

"There's more to this, eh? Tell me."

"Don't, Ranjit. I don't deserve your sympathy." Virginia brushed away his hand in vain. "Do you see what I've come to? I'm ready to cheat a friend."

"No—don't say—" Ranjit dried her cheeks.

"Yes, it's true. I knew that my land was no good. But," she added quickly, grasping his hand, "you must believe me that when I spoke to you last, I thought that the crops were only dying of disease. Then I began to hear the rumors about the soil. And I hoped it was not true. I am desperate, Ranjit. I have to sell the land. I have to."

"Have to?" Ranjit touched her face. "Is there something you're not telling me, Ginny? We go back a long ways now. Ever since your boy was in short pants. If something is worrying you, I want to help."

"You can't help me, Ranjit."

"Let me try."

The red bandana at the base of her neck cast a youthful glow on Virginia's face. As if she knew that, Virginia pulled the bandana closer around her neck. She looked into Ranjit's leathery, worn face and saw the trembling in the corner of his mouth. Like a parasite leeched to the sap of an aging tree, she latched herself to his pity.

"It's my son's new wife," she murmured. "And perhaps it's me. You know how I've hated these people."

"Come now, Ginny."

"Yes. Even as you have hated yours."

Ranjit lowered his eyes.

"I've always wanted to leave this place, but now more than ever," Virginia said quietly, and she took the handkerchief from Ranjit's hand and blew her nose. "They have brought their ignorance into my house." Her voice was steady. "And she, my son's wife, is the cause of it all."

Ranjit, still kneeling next to Virginia, asked, "You couldn't mean the gossip about Marina? That's her name, isn't it?"

Virginia nodded.

"But you don't believe it, do you? Not that stupid tale they tell about her." He looked closely at Virginia. She shook her head. "Ah, I knew that! Then what is it? What did she do?"

Bending close to Ranjit, lowering her head so that her mouth touched his ear, whispering as though others could hear her, when in fact she alone was in the room with him, Virginia told her friend about the things she had found in Marina's clothes closet. And as she knew he would, Ranjit, whose hatred for obeah matched hers, immediately understood her urgency to move with Antonio to Port-of-Spain.

"They'll never stop," he said jumping to his feet, his body at sixty still agile from working in the fields. "Once they get started. They'll never stop. The fools. Soon your house will stink with every weed and foul-smelling stuff in bottles. They'll plant it under your mattress next, Ginny. Goat toes. Pig's ears." Ranjit shuddered. "No, Ginny. It's time you leave. It's time."

"I knew you'd understand."

"Come. I'll buy your land." Ranjit turned toward his bedroom where he kept his money in an iron safe under his bed, but before he could move, Virginia held his hand, stopping him.

Later on she wondered what had made her do that at that moment, but then as her hand instinctively reached to halt him, she heard her voice say, "I couldn't." She wanted to change her words even then. She wanted to say instead, Go ahead. You owe me something. You owe me. Didn't I make you what you are? Didn't I show you how to love their books, their music? She wanted to say, Buy it. If the land's no good, perhaps the oil is. Didn't Marina say so? Didn't Marina say that the Warao said so? And if not, perhaps the Americans could siphon off the oil. But her eyes caught Ranjit's, soft and loving, willing to give his life for her, and the words wouldn't come. Instead, she lowered her eyes and murmured, "No, I couldn't ask you to make such a sacrifice."

"Why?" Ranjit had made up his mind to help her.

"You love the land too much." Virginia folded her red bandana and tucked it away into the basket she had brought with her. Suddenly she looked older than her youthful fifty-two years. "No, Ranjit," she said with finality. "It would be a waste. My land can give you nothing. It grows only weeds and soon not even that."

"Come, Ginny, don't be so solemn. You are talking to me. Ranjit. The man who can make sugarcane so sweet that you can sweeten your tea with it." Ranjit smiled and squeezed Virginia's hand.

"Who are you fooling?" Virginia felt tired. "You just said that you were not the doctor for this disease."

"What shall I do in my old age, Ginny?" Ranjit persisted. "What? Sell it to me. I'll spend my last days working miracles."

"No, Ranjit. I couldn't do that to you." Virginia's voice was harsh.

Ranjit bent over her. "I owe you something," he said intensely. "Let me pay you now for all you've taught me."

"You did that already."

"Then take the money, Ginny. I'll take the land. They say

that I have magic fingers with the soil. I can grow anything. And who knows? This oil may go away just as suddenly as it came."

"No. I won't have you make this sacrifice for me," Virginia patted the folds of her skirts. His insistence grated against her nerves. She had made up her mind. "You know how I feel about charity."

"But—"

"That's final, Ranjit. As you said, even my squatters have left the land. I won't have you buy fool's gold."

"Then marry me and I'll take you to Port-of-Spain."

Ranjit said the words quickly and caught Virginia by surprise. For a moment her eyes sparkled and her lips quivered. A girlish softness swept over her face. Ranjit held his breath. But the moment passed. Hungry for love and companionship, yet having made a habit of dreams, these two people could no longer believe in the real possibility of fulfillment.

Virginia's face returned to its customary sadness and she said quietly to Ranjit, "Thank you. Thank you, my dear. I will always remember that you did ask."

She didn't need to say more. Ranjit knew that both his offers had been refused. She was a proud, arrogant, independent woman. Still he wanted to know her reason for saying no to him the first time, and so he asked, "But why, Ginny? Why did you refuse me before?"

"I was married."

"I know that. But afterward when your husband died. I didn't ask you until then. When he was gone. And Indira was gone."

"Yes, but I was married, when I—when we—"

"Just once."

"You don't understand, do you, Ranjit? We must pay for our sins either here or in eternal fires. It's a mortal sin for a married woman to make love to a man who is not her husband. I had to pay for that sin."

"Forever?"

"That's just the point. Not forever. Only here. In this world. If the punishment is enough."

And Ranjit could say no more. Christianity was the one aspect of European culture that he was glad that he had no part of. So he flew his Hindu prayer flags.

Virginia believed herself when she explained to Ranjit why she had not married him. Then, in the cool, galvanized house in Siparia, her reasons seemed truthful. For she was remembering her dying Portuguese husband, who screamed on his deathbed about retributions for sins. So it did seem possible, believable to her, that she had refused to marry Ranjit, because one evening she had permitted her passion to conquer her reason, and one evening only, she became an adulteress. But home alone in her bedroom in Moruga, wrapped in the darkness, listening to the dying cicadas scream through the night, her lonely body craved more comfort. And she knew that the life she had was the life she had chosen. For in spite of all she had taught Ranjit, in spite of his dreams, his love for music and books, he was still and finally a peasant, a dirt farmer, a coolie. She was, or she had been once, the daughter of Hilda Smith, the English warden's wife. And her blackness really belonged to the little alabaster doll that Mrs. Smith kept in her private box, the little doll that had sucked away Virginia's whiteness and left her black. For Marina was right. She had wanted little white babies and since her son's skin was black, she wanted, then, little white grandchildren.

Still, to be desired at fifty-two! For Ranjit to ask her to marry him! She could take the loneliness knowing that that was still possible. And her son would be kinder to her now, now that he knew that she couldn't sell the land. He'd feel sorry for her, trapped in a house with a woman whose mother worked obeah.

After Virginia returned from her visit to Ranjit, there was no more talk of moving to Port-of-Spain or selling the land in Tabaquite. Virginia seemed to have come to terms with her lot, to have accepted the fact that she would never leave Moruga. She avoided Marina, of course. She had not forgotten how Marina had insulted her. Yet she was polite to her and it appeared as if she had put the quarrel behind her with her hope for leaving Moruga. Or so it seemed to Antonio.

Nevertheless, Marina was not fooled. She saw now that Virginia was making a deliberate attempt to put a wedge between her and Antonio and to tighten her bond with her son. At mealtimes Virginia diverted the conversation from Marina toward herself and Antonio, whether the subject was trivial, such as the weather, or intentionally malicious, such as an amusing incident she remembered involving one of Antonio's former wives. In the evenings Virginia helped Antonio correct the children's work he brought home from school and discussed books with him—novels, plays and poetry that Marina had not read—excusing herself for excluding Marina, but clearly implying that Marina lacked the ability to understand.

At first Marina did not mind. It was a small price to pay, she thought, for keeping the land. Virginia, after all, had lost. Ranjit had refused her, she said. There was no way she could sell the land or get the money she needed to move. And since Marina was not in love with Antonio, she did not care that Antonio spent more time with his mother than with her. But after a while Marina began to be affected by her isolation. Lonely, she sought the companionship of the people in the village. Strangely, they too seemed to want to avoid her. She had not expected them to greet her warmly. It had only been six weeks since she had come to live in Moruga, and the people would be cautious. Yet they had treated her with courtesy before. Now they turned their backs on her, lowering their voices to a whisper when she approached them, not seeming to hear her when she spoke to them, or answering her only briefly, to the point. Even the children ran away from her.

Coincidental as it was that the villagers should ostracize her at the same time that Virginia and Antonio neglected her, Marina had no reason to believe that there was any connection between the two. Then one day as she was sitting alone near the village market on a bench that circled a large saman tree like a belt, she heard a voice behind her say loudly, "If I was you, Miss, I'd ask Alma what Mr. Harris say he see Miss Virginia and Mr. Antonio do." Marina slid around the bench to the other side of the tree to see who had spoken to her, but she was too late. There was nobody there, just the faint trace of a musky odor she recognized as the smell of Alma's hut. The other villagers who stood nearby must have seen the girl, or sent her with her message. Marina could tell by the way they looked furtively in her direction. When she asked them, however, they denied that anyone but she had been sitting on that bench for the past hour.

Marina was not afraid. At least she told herself she wasn't. She would not succumb to their silly, superstitious fears. She knew what the girl meant, but the idea was proposterous, that Virginia and Antonio would murder her as Alma suggested. There was nothing Harris knew that could affect her. There was nothing Harris could know. How could Harris possibly know what would happen in her life by lying half-naked and blindfolded in an open grave? But as the days passed, left to herself for long periods by Antonio and Virginia, Marina began to weaken. She told herself that she had accepted Antonio's explanation of the death of his wives. She reminded herself that she did not believe in obeah and would not believe that the de Balboas were cursed. Yet the girl's words stuck in her memory like a sore tooth until she spoke to Antonio, and his scornful response made her see another possibility in the girl's words, a more likely truth in her warning.

Antonio mocked her with her own words. She had said she didn't believe in obeah, hadn't she? Perhaps she was no different from her mother. Perhaps she too would let her life be directed by the words of someone who couldn't spell his name. He laughed and struck his final blow. Yes, hadn't she fallen for the Warao's fairy tale of El Dorado?

Marina could not defend herself. She was beginning to believe that the Warao had indeed tricked her with the story of El Dorado, though she had to admit he only mentioned the name El Dorado. He had said nothing else. Just that she would be rich. It was she who put the two together, his prediction of her wealth and the tales she heard of El Dorado. She had tried to find him, to get him to tell her more, for she had not stopped believing that the land in Tabaquite was valuable, but the Warao was nowhere to be found. For several mornings she had gone to the beach, searching the sea for signs of his pirogue, but each time there would be nothing. Someone would say she arrived too late. The Warao had left hours ago, or minutes, even seconds. She decided to go earlier to the beach.

Once, at four in the morning, she thought she saw a flicker of the Warao's lighted kerosene bottle dancing off the gray sea close to the beach on the other side of the bay, but she could not be sure, for many of the village fishermen brought in their pirogues at that hour. By the time she had crossed the beach, there were no more lights, only the red cork buoys bobbing in a semicircle in the gentle morning waves, marking the edge of the fishermen's nets submerged under the water. The fishermen, who by then had beached their shallow boats on the sand, shook their heads to her questions: No they had not seen any Waraos. Why would they? They never came in at this end of the bay. And they joined their strong, muscular women pulling at the seines, heavy with fish, seaweed, sand and salt water. Marina determined then to wake up earlier. To sleep on the beach if necessary so that she would meet the Warao, but those efforts too proved futile.

Now Marina concluded that Virginia had most likely paid the Warao to stay away from her and not fill her head with shark-oil treasure under the ground in Tabaquite. It occurred to her that that was another way to interpret what the girl had said. Yes, Antonio and Virginia would not kill her. They had not murdered Antonio's other wives. They would harm her in another way. Yes, Marina thought, Antonio was too quick to laugh at her when she told him that the girl had warned her about him and his mother. There was nervousness in his laughter. She had found him out and he knew it. Yes, he and Virginia were counting on the villagers' attitude toward her for their own purposes. Just as they hoped she would forget the Warao's promise if she did not see him

again, they hoped that she would find the villagers' avoid-
ance of her unbearable, and unable to tolerate her loneliness, she would be more than willing to agree with them to
move from Moruga to Port-of-Spain. Yes, Virginia still intended to sell the land.

Marina kept these suspicions to herself but now she
watched Antonio and Virginia closely. She found herself
keeping track of the minutes and then the hours that they
spent together. Eventually she realized that Antonio's habitual visits to his mother's bedroom before retiring to bed now
lasted longer than they had done in the early days of their
marriage. She casually mentioned this to Antonio, but he
deflected the implied criticism by saying it was a de Balboa
family tradition. None of his other wives had objected. Yet
Marina was now convinced that Virginia and Antonio were
using this time to make plans they did not wish her to know
about. Perhaps they had found a new buyer for the land.

One night she decided to spy on them. It was not easy.
Virginia's bedroom was squeezed between the kitchen and
the living room. It was a tiny room meant for the servant girl,
but Virginia, insisting that she was more comfortable in a
small room, gave her bedroom to the servant girl. Marina
had to wait until she was sure that Antonio was deep in
conversation with his mother before stealing across the living room to peep through a slit in the wooden panels that
separated it from Virginia's bedroom.

Squinting her eyes so that she could get an unhampered
view of Virginia's bedroom through the space between the
wooden panels, she was unprepared for what she saw, or
thought she saw. Or for what she heard, or thought she
heard. But she came to two conclusions that evening before
she slipped back to her room as she heard Antonio bid
Virginia good night—each conclusion almost the opposite

of the other: one, that Virginia was much more of an African, much more like her mother, Emilia, than she pretended to be; the other, that the relationship between mother and son was not what it would be in Africa. There was something unnatural about Virginia's love for Antonio. For she saw Virginia transformed into a vibrant woman of thirty, there, sitting on her bed, with Antonio on a chair next to her reading a book. She was more beautiful than she had ever seen her, looking not as a mother, or the schoolmistress she had been, but as an African princess—back erect, legs stretched out in front of her, her white lace petticoat flirting around her breasts and legs, her body round and warm.

Who would have believed that under those long, starched cotton dresses that she always wore, her body would be so supple? So wrinkle free? And who would believe that when she removed the bandana on her head that the dazzling patterns of cornrows that framed her face would make her more strikingly beautiful than any woman Marina had ever seen? And that her eyes and mouth would still have retained their innocent eroticism that, according to rumor, had frightened the warden's wife, changed de Balboa into a beast, set fire to Ranjit's passion, and now sent a stab of fear, not envy or jealousy, into her daughter-in-law's heart?

What did Marina actually see in Virginia's bedroom? Her husband sitting on a stool reading from a book and from time to time looking up at his mother to speak intently to her? This was hardly grounds for suspicion. Some minutes later though, Marina saw Antonio put down his book, and looking deeply into his mother's eyes, reach across the bed and clasp her hand in his. Yet she did not feel threatened by her husband's display of affection. To her, Antonio's actions were motivated by filial love, no more, no less. But Virginia's actions puzzled her.

Before her eyes, she saw Virginia become completely transformed by Antonio's touch. It was as though a bolt of electricity had passed from Antonio's hand to his mother's, and Virginia's body jerked forward from the bed to meet Antonio's. Under her cotton nightgown, her nipples hardened and formed a distinct outline against the thin cloth that hid them. Marina held her breath and pressed her eye against the hole in the partition, almost giving herself away in her excitement. Her alarm changed to disgust as she saw Virginia flick her tongue seductively across her lips and crane her neck toward her son. She watched Virginia's eyes glisten with passion, her lips aquiver and her body so consumed with desire that it seemed that she would pull Antonio down with her on the bed. Antonio turned away from his mother and Marina saw his face contorted by guilt and embarrassment. Yet Virginia did not release him. She leaned forward toward him and grasped his hand, forcing him to face her and then she whispered something to him. Her words seemed to relax him, for he laughed, stretched out his legs, turned a page in the book that he had let drop to his lap, and began to read once more.

If Virginia's actions assuaged Antonio's apprehensions, they confirmed Marina's. She knew instinctively that Virginia would try again, but she was surprised to see that it was Antonio who made the next move. He stopped reading, said some words to his mother that Marina could not hear, though she pressed her ear against the hole in the wooden partition, and then he once more clasped Virginia's hand in his. They were speaking softly now. Whispering. Her heart pumping fast for fear of discovery and disgust at what she had seen, Marina tiptoed down the narrow corridor that separated the kitchen from Virginia's bedroom. The partition on the left side was directly in back of Virginia's bed, and though there were no holes to peep through, Marina knew that she would hear more clearly the conversation between mother and son.

"Come now, your promise." She clearly identified Virginia's voice, coyly addressing Antonio.

"What promise, chuck?" Apart from her uncertainty about the significance of "chuck," which seemed a term of endearment, Marina's earlier suspicions were confirmed. Promises and plans had been made behind her back. They had found a new buyer for the land, she was certain. And Antonio had promised Virginia that he would keep his plans hidden from her, his wife! Marina listened closely and she heard Virginia's voice continue, speaking now about a Cassio. Antonio responded, but their voices seemed strange as though they were talking in another language or playing some game. Virginia called Antonio "my lord" and Antonio talked about his mother as though she were an Egyptian, as though Virginia were not right in front of him. If it was a game, it was a nasty sort of game for a mother and son to play, Marina thought, repulsed. Uncertain whether it would be better to see them at this game or hear them, she was about to leave the room, concluding that she needed to confirm with her eyes what she thought, when Antonio's words stopped her.

" 'Tis true: there's magic in the web of it," she heard him say. And using a strange form of English, he began to talk about prophesies, worms and mummies.

A shiver of fear ran down Marina's spine. For all his claim of innocence and for all Virginia's superior indignation, they both were as involved in obeah as her mother and Alma. She pressed her ear closer to the wall but she could hear nothing but Antonio's agitated laughter. At what? She couldn't tell.

Then hearing him get off the chair and bid his mother good night, Marina quickly pulled up the skirts of her cotton nightdress and ran softly back to her room.

Marina lay on the bed with her eyes closed, pretending sleep until her husband had changed into his nightshirt and slipped between the thin sheets that the villagers often used in the dry season, not for protection against any chilly weather (the nights were hottest at this time of the year), but for comfort, a feeling of coziness. She felt his hand move timidly across her upper thigh, as it often did when he wanted to make love, and she pressed her body close to his, encouraging him. She felt his hardness now against her hip and she waited. Paradoxically, soon he would be at his softest moment, his weakest. She nibbled at his ear and Antonio grew. She touched him and heard him groan, and when the blood left his head to center itself in the veins around his lower abdomen, she sensed that it was time.

"Antonio," she whispered, "do you love me?"

Antonio grunted and pulled her closer to him. He should have known then that something was wrong. He should have remembered the last time that she had asked that question. And perhaps he did. Perhaps it was the memory of the wind playing against his buttocks, of Marina's softness twisting and grinding beneath him that made him ignore the cunning behind her words. But if he did, Marina took no chances. She placed his hands on the wiry hair at the base of her stomach and asked again, "Do you love me?"

Antonio groaned.

"As much as you love your mother?" Marina whispered.

"As much—more—more."

"How much more?" Marina stroked his hand and shifted it to a warmer place.

"More. More than life," Antonio breathed heavily.

Marina waited for a few seconds before speaking again, pacing herself. "So you don't love her?"

"Whom?"

"Your mother."

Antonio mounted her. He pushed his knee against the softer side of her left thigh, preparing the way for himself.

"Do you love your mother?" Marina repeated, treachery tinkling on the edge of her voice.

The most infinitesimal shadow of a warning crossed Antonio's brain but the blood had left his head too long ago for his mind to take any heed of it. So he breathed, "Love her—love you."

Marina stiffened and Antonio felt her dryness with his fingers. Still he reached too far and he fondled her.

"You love her and you love me too?"

Antonio felt his legs go weak.

"Is that why you go to her room before you come to mine?"

"Marina!"

Marina placed the palms of her hands on his chest and with all her force, she pushed him off her. "Do you do this in your mother's room?" she hissed.

"My God!" Antonio grasped the edge of the bed desperately trying to prevent himself from falling to the floor, but he couldn't. His body hit the floor with a dull thud.

"My God!" His eyes widened in astonishment at the force of her anger. He had barely heard what she had said. "My God. What has got into you, Marina?"

Pulling her nightdress close to her body, Marina sat on her

heels on the bed. Looking down on Antonio, her eyes livid with rage, she spat out, "Do you think that I've liked it? Do you think that I've liked the way you and your mother and everyone here have been treating me lately? As though I was some leper."

"For God's sake!" Antonio got up from the floor and tried to compose himself. Foolishly he reached for his hat on the bedside table and put it on. He picked up his baggy trousers from the chair and pulled them on too. Then he found his tobacco box and opened it.

"Yes, act like you don't know what I mean. Go on! Say you don't know what I mean!" Antonio took out the brown paper from the box and began to sprinkle some tobacco in it, still trying to still the slight trembling in his hand.

"You're right. I don't know what you mean," he replied, rolling a cigarette.

"You and your mother, you have everybody keeping away from me. The Warao! The villagers! Everybody!"

Antonio lit the cigarette and sucked the smoke into his lungs. He looked masculine now in spite of the felt hat slouched ridiculously on his head. The cigarette drooped from his mouth. His hairy chest was bare and his trousers hung low below the hairline that started at his navel.

"Keeping away from you?" he asked.

"Yes. Keeping away from me. Don't think I haven't noticed? You and your mother. Family tradition!" she sneered.

"I don't know what you're talking about."

"You know exactly what I mean. Your mother has gotten you to avoid me. She has even made the Warao stay away from me."

Antonio looked surprised. "I believe Mother has been kinder to you than necessary."

"Than necessary?"

"She didn't have to be nice after the things you said to her."

"So this is her way of getting back at me."

"She doesn't want to get back at you."

"No? Then deny it if you dare. She told the villagers to shun me. I know it."

Antonio felt anger flood his neck. "She doesn't have to do that. Do you expect these people to talk to you when—"

"When? When what? Say it!" Marina's eyes burned, matching his.

"When there's all that talk about you possessing eight spirits—or whatever."

"Say it! Say it, Antonio! Get it over with! Me possessing eight spirits, and what else?"

"And your mother a murderer."

"So you say it, finally. All your denials! I knew you believed it. And now," Marina said coldly, "I'll tell you what I believe. My mother is not the only person who works obeah. Oh, don't look so innocent. You and your mother wanting to get the house blessed and all the time working obeah!"

"What?" Antonio had to control himself to keep from shouting.

"Yes, your mother, Mrs. Virginia de Balboa. You didn't think I would find out, did you? I thought that something was funny. The two of you always whispering together."

"What are you trying to say, Marina?"

"I saw you two tonight."

"Saw us?"

"Yes. Saw you and heard you. In your mother's room talking about plans and magic and dead people."

Antonio began to laugh. It was a mirthless laughter, but it felt good to him. She had made a fool of him, the silly girl, but also of herself. Perhaps she had peeped into the room and seen him reading to his mother. He thought that he had heard some movements outside his mother's room.

"Laugh if you want to. Laugh!" Marina swung her legs off the bed.

"Come, come, Marina—" Antonio moved toward her. "Don't be silly. Is that what all this is about? Was that you outside Mother's room? Why didn't you come in?"

"Why didn't you invite me in?" Marina was suspicious of his calm.

"You could have if you wanted to. Then you might have learned a thing or two."

"Such as?" she asked cautiously.

"Such as a play by Shakespeare." Antonio began to laugh again.

Marina almost hated him.

"Do you think I'm a fool?" she yelled. "Do you think I don't know what's going on?"

Antonio wiped away the tears from his eyes and walked toward the small bookcase in the corner of their room.

"No," he said, taking a book from the shelf. "Just ignorant. I mean it kindly. Here, I'll teach you. We were reading a passage from *Othello*. Look. Here. There." He opened the book.

At another time perhaps Marina would have admitted defeat, but fear of losing the land was still raw in her. She had not made a mistake. She had seen the look on Virginia's face as she had spoken to her son. She had seen the way she was dressed, like a bride, and there was no doubt in her mind that Virginia was not innocent. As Antonio read, Marina's mind brewed a clearer understanding of Virginia's plans, and before Antonio could finish, she was certain of what Virginia was doing.

"Antonio," she began, "Antonio, I know why your wives died."

Antonio stopped reading.

"It was her. That's why she never married again. It was her. She wants you, Antonio. You alone. No husband. You."

The slap that fell across Marina's face resounded throughout the house. Virginia jumped in her sleep as it reached her ears, but she did not awaken. Afterward, Antonio stood frozen where he stood, mortified as he realized what he had done, his hand impotently swinging at his side. Marina hugged her face and whimpered. In that one physical act, in that slap, Antonio knew that he had confessed his apprehension that his mother had grown too close to him. Too dependent on him. He sat down weakly on the rocking chair, and covered his face with his hands. Finally, finding his voice, he said, "I am sorry, Marina. I didn't mean to. I really didn't mean to. You see the power you have over me. You make me into some kind of animal. Savage."

Marina remained silent. If Virginia had heard her son's words, she would have grieved for him, fearing it was too late to take him away.

"Why, Marina?" Antonio asked. "Why did you say such a thing?"

"I was afraid," Marina murmured.

"Afraid of what?"

"Your mother," she answered.

"But why?" Antonio persisted.

"She controls you."

"You don't understand her." Antonio wanted to explain his mother to himself, to erase the specter that had caused him to slap his wife.

"It is she who is afraid of you. She has never had anyone but me." He needed confidence to see this through, to ex-

plain his mother to Marina. He reached again for his tobacco box.

"And your father," Marina said quietly.

"Yes, and my father." Antonio rolled a cigarette nervously. "But he was a strange man. He did not speak much
to Mother. He was no company to her. He would just walk
on the beach from sunup to sundown, talking to the Warao.
Or he just sat in his chair reading his book." Antonio
paused. "*The History of Portugal,* by Herculano, a good man.
He barely spoke to me when I was a child, except on that day
I found a newspaper clipping in his book. Then I understood him. But Mother never did. She—"

"And the land?" Marina interrupted him.

"The land?" Antonio frowned, baffled by her question.
His mind had drifted to another time years ago. "The land?"

"I mean," said Marina, as if she had only heard part of
what he had said, "your father could not have always walked
on the beach or stayed at home. He must have been kept
busy with the land."

"He did nothing with it. Nothing. I told you so once."

"Tell me again," Marina's voice was sweet.

And Antonio, needing to justify his mother's immense
love for him, responded, "I suppose that he should have
tried to make more use of the land. At least Mother thought
so. It made some money, but we didn't get it. The squatters
. . . Mother had to work to feed us. But Father was good—
deep in his heart . . ." Antonio stumbled over his words and
then steadied himself. "And he was right," he added with
forced conviction. "Mother—she didn't—well, she was no
farmer either. She wanted more."

"More?"

"She's a great woman, my mother," Antonio puffed his
cigarette and the smoke circled around his face making it

darker. Sad. His bushy eyebrows huddled together over his half-closed eyes.

"Yes. She wanted more for me. She wanted me to be like the English. Do you know that before I was twelve she had read me all of Chaucer's *Canterbury Tales* and all Shakespeare's plays? I even memorized the soliloquies in his tragedies. 'To be or not to be, that is the question. . . .' "

Antonio closed his eyes and when he opened them again, his face seemed sadder than it was before. He drew smoke from his cigarette deep into his lungs. "For one whole year I ignored my mother," he continued. "One year. Then my father died. I think it was during that year that she began teaching Ranjit. He probably saved her—gave her something to live for. But it was strange that in that year, in that year when my father talked to me, though I knew my mother was lonely, that she missed me, and probably my father, I did nothing. I had longed so much for the day when my father would talk to me that, though I once hated him for abandoning me, and loved her, I hardly spoke to her. I would not take the chance. Break the spell. You know what I mean?"

Marina remembered her visit to Alma and heard the horses thundering through the night and the women wailing. Yes, she knew what he meant. Once she had made herself believe that she would see her father again, though she knew he was dead and that he despised her touch. For a moment, she felt a sort of love for Antonio. A warmth, a connection, but the moment was brief.

"I consoled myself instead," Antonio was saying, "that my mother now had the friendship of Ranjit. But when my father died, I knew better. I knew what she had sacrificed and my only goal was to please her. I owe her a lot. And I mean to pay her," he added with determination.

The forcefulness of Antonio's voice as he said that last

sentence surprised Marina. "Pay her?" she questioned.

"I love my mother, Marina. And she needs me. I am all she has."

"She has Ranjit," Marina said quietly and firmly.

"He refused to buy the land. He has let her down."

"Your father did that years ago. He let her down. Why is it that you owe her?"

"Marina. No more. Father cared for Mother in his own way. There were things that happened to him that made him not believe in people. But he married her and treated her the best way he could. He—" Antonio hesitated. His father had called himself nothing. "He was afraid to show love, affection. He didn't even believe in himself."

Marina's lips began to form the question why, but before she could utter the sound, Antonio added quickly, "But I, I knew what I was doing. I saw Mother's pain. I could have done something. And now I will do all I can to make her happy."

Knowing what was in his mind, and wanting to get it out in the open, Marina asked bluntly, "Does that mean moving to Port-of-Spain?"

"Yes." Antonio was equally blunt.

"I see. So you are selling the land?" Marina wanted it stated. No whisperings behind closed doors.

"If we can." Antonio looked directly at her.

"Why didn't you tell me this?" Marina asked him. There *was* a plot, is what she thought.

"It didn't seem to matter," Antonio answered. "Nobody wants the land."

"And if you don't sell it?"

"I will sell it one day."

"And what if I want it?"

"You are my wife. The land is yours."

"Yes, but I can't stop you from selling it."

"No."

The finality of that word was searing.

"Fool," she said bitterly. "Your mother has used Ranjit's refusal to make you guilty. She sits there sniveling and begging for your attention. She wants you to feel sorry for her. She wants you to try harder."

Marina got to her feet, her eyes flaming with anger. And Antonio, not wishing to resume a quarrel with her, did not answer. He rose from his chair and walked out of the room, wondering for the first time whether Marina really ever loved him.

14

T he rain came as it should in the middle of February: lightly. Not in gushes with thunder and lightning as it would have come in August, but softly, shimmering down from the white clouds drifting lazily across a blue sky. Sliding down the rays of the morning sun, polishing everything, reflecting everything. It made the leaves on the trees look greener. It cleaned off the dust from the flower petals and wiped off their delicate stems. It made the asphalt on the road look brighter. It put a new shine on a galvanized roof and broken glass windows. It was the sort of rain that no one finds shelter from in Trinidad. It dances with the sun, splashing here, splashing there, everywhere spraying fine droplets sparkling with sunlight. And when it came, the people took out their tin buckets and lined them up on the ground directly below the edges of their roofs, hoping to catch the last trickles of water wrung from the final lingering clouds of the now vanquished rainy season. They would not see this rain soon again, for by March the sun would no longer be so generous and she would claim her rights to this season and suck dry the vaguest traces of dampness exposed to her rays.

January had frightened the villagers with its absence of rain. The dry season had come too soon, much too soon. Still, Virginia welcomed it, empathizing with its fated sterility. But Emilia, watching the flawless sky from her house in Princes Town, trembled a little, and when the rains came in February, she breathed more easily. There was still time. Time to warn Marina. How foolish Marina was not to wait at Alma's for Harris's spirit to return! Emilia controlled her anger. Harris had told her that she would get a sign. She'd know when to tell Marina. If it were right to tell Marina.

"It will get dry, dry sudden-like," he said rolling his eyes in their sockets as though looking at everything and nothing. "It will come before this dis time. Early. Before de dry season should really come. Seem like de rain never comin' back. Seem like de sun want to take over even de rain time. Den sudden-like de rain come again. Den. Den is time to warn you chile. Den is time."

Emilia didn't want to travel alone to Moruga, not that the trip was a long one from Princes Town, but she was, after all, a lady and she would not bear once more the scornful eyes of Virginia de Balboa, looking down her nose at her, a woman living in sin. As if Virginia herself did not once—sold to a Portuguese for fifteen acres of land, even if he did marry her. So Emilia spoke to Telser and regretted it, for try as this man might, he could not hide his excitement and anxiety to see Marina again. Then Emilia feared, not for what Marina might do, or might have done, for she knew that her daughter was a virgin when she married de Balboa, but she worried that Virginia might detect the lust in Telser's eyes and jump to the wrong conclusion about her daughter. She wanted to make an impression, to let that woman and her son know that her daughter had a proper background. She would not be caught off guard looking like a peasant, as she had on the day of Marina's wedding.

She had worn her finest creole clothes then. Her full, elastic-topped, white cotton bodice pulled over her shoulders, a rainbow colored shawl draped across her wide, white-eyelet skirts that lay on top of layers of petticoats, her head tied in a bandana whose colors matched the shawl. She had thought that she looked beautiful until she saw the scorn in Virginia's eyes and the shame in her daughter's. Until she saw Marina's face contorted with embarrassment as she looked from her mother's creole clothes to Virginia's high-collared lace dress, feathered hat and white gloves. Now Emilia knew that she had seemed a peasant to the de Balboas. This time she was determined there would be no mistakes. She selected her dress carefully from among the outfits that still hung in Mrs. Telser's closet. She dug deep in the wooden trunk that Telser had packed to be shipped to England after his wife had died, but which now gathered cobwebs in the room where he stored her things. Carefully, she retrieved the rouges and powders and lipsticks that Mrs. Telser once wore, and she prepared herself to meet her daughter, her new son-in-law and his mother.

Marina was expecting her mother. From the day the girl told her that Harris had reported to Alma what he had seen, Marina knew that it would only be a matter of time before Emilia would come to Moruga. She figured one week, two weeks at most, but when a month passed and Emilia did not come, Marina became nervous. She realized that she was anxious to see her mother, and although she had not heard from her either by letter or by message from a friend, she still expected to hear something soon. The truth was, though, Marina did not miss her mother. What residue of affection she had remaining for her after she discovered that her mother was Telser's mistress evaporated once she'd learned for sure what Emilia had done to her twin sons.

But Marina wanted to see her mother. That she could not deny, no more than she could sustain the veneer of indifference she wore on her face when the villagers reminded her with their hushed voices and turned heads of the warnings Alma had given her. Each day that her mother did not come Marina found it more difficult to resist her superstitious fears. Each day it became more and more difficult for her to renew her determination not to return to Alma or to go to her mother in Princes Town. She kept telling herself that she was a modern woman, an intelligent woman. Obeah might be the answer for some people, but not for her. She would not resort to it. She would not pay the price of abandoning herself to that superstitious belief. She would retain control of herself. She would not surrender herself to the dictates of some obeahman.

But Marina wanted to find out what Harris had told Alma. Finally, when Jane, the servant girl, brought her the news that her mother's horse-drawn buggy had just turned off the Moruga main road and was coming up the path to the de Balboa house, Marina could barely contain her excitement. She rushed out of the house to meet Emilia, not pausing to change her dress or fix her hair. But when the buggy stopped at the front steps and she saw Emilia, she regretted with all her heart that even for one second she had allowed herself to feel the slightest need for her. For there in the buggy, sitting next to her white lover, was a comic character. A true golliwog. Emilia's coal-black face was smeared with rouges and powders meant to put peaches and cream on an Englishwoman's cheeks. She looked like a Warao ready for war. Tufts of her nappy hair, like nervous wires, stuck out from her hat in the oddest places and were tangled among the ribbons and wax fruits that Englishwomen loved to wear on their heads. Marina's first impulse was to run away from it all, run back inside the house, but Emilia, who had not seen the disgust and shame on her daughter's face, who could not imagine that her daughter would be anything but pleased by her appearance, had jumped off the buggy and thrown her arms around Marina before she could move.

"Elegant, isn't it?" Emilia twirled after she had released Marina, and her lime-green organza dress shimmered in the sun. Elegant? On peaches and cream it would have been elegant. For it was a beautiful dress, something appropriate for the governor's tea party, perhaps along with a frilly parasol and long, slender gloves. The dipping neckline should have embraced firm breasts, not Emilia's heavy bosom. The two-tiered skirt and the ruffled train were meant for slimmer hips.

Marina would have hurled a stream of insults at her mother had her eyes not caught the mocking grin on Antonio's face as he came down the steps to meet his mother-in-law. Then pride, greater than her shame, made her say instead, "You look lovely, Mother."

"The best of London. The latest fashion. Not so, Telser?" Emilia winked at her lover. "And Antonio, how have you been treating my daughter?" She embraced Antonio.

"I'm a fortunate man," Antonio replied, smirking.

"And your mother? Where is Virginia?"

"It's the second Sunday, Mrs. Heathrow. She goes to Greyfriar's Church in Port-of-Spain every second Sunday."

Emilia looked mildly disappointed.

"I thought that was the Portuguese Presbyterian Church," said Telser, clearing his throat. He gave the reins of the horses to the yardboy.

"Yes—but Father. You know—"

"Yes—yes. Portuguese, wasn't he? But your mother? Surely—"

"No, Mother is not Portuguese."

Telser frowned, squinted his eyes. "But isn't Philip Smith related to her in some way? That red-headed chap. English, isn't he? Smith's son I mean?"

"The Smiths had adopted my mother when she was a child."

Telser looked genuinely puzzled. "It's all so complicated, isn't it?"

Antonio tried to change the subject. "Please, Mr. Telser, Mrs. Heathrow, come inside."

"Then, I say, you must be good friends of the Smiths. Haven't seen that old man since Hilda Smith died. Perhaps we could ride over there while the women talk."

"No!"

All eyes turned on Antonio. His lips, which had shut tightly together in a narrow line after he had shouted, now twitched slightly at the corners.

"Sorry, sorry, old boy. Didn't mean to stir up old skeletons. Didn't mean—"

"No old skeletons, Mr. Telser. Just we don't keep in touch with the Smiths."

"But surely with Philip. He's your age."

In spite of the sweet taste of justice Marina felt in Antonio's discomfort, her dislike for Telser was too great for her to permit him to continue.

"Perhaps, Telser, I can take you there if you're so anxious to see the Smiths." She looked directly at Telser and he winked at her.

Emilia's heart sank and she pulled Telser away from Marina before Antonio could see the wide smile on her lover's face.

"Come, Telly." She led him up the steps. "Come, let's go inside." Then in the living room, after the lime juice and the tea biscuits, and after she had shimmered and shimmied, and after she had distracted Telser from Marina and reduced the conversation to the dull, monotonous give-and-take of small talk—the strange weather, the diseased cocoa—Emilia made a frivolous excuse of wanting to have a girl-talk with her daughter and pulled Marina with her into the bedroom.

Once safely away from Telser and Antonio, Emilia somehow became her old self again, her rouges and lipstick no longer as comic.

"You are a fool, Marina." She flounced her body onto the bed, spitting out her words from behind clenched teeth. "You have always been a fool. Why didn't you go back and see Alma?" Her eyes flared at Marina, but the girl had not recovered from her humiliation and she saw no reality but her mother's disguise.

"You call me a fool." She had to control herself to keep from shouting. "You look like—like—Mother, did you see yourself before you left your house? Did you see your dress? That paint on your face?" Marina hovered over Emilia.

The words that had been brimming on Emilia's lips all afternoon were strangled in that instant. She looked confused, distracted. She touched her cheeks, pressed her fingers against her lipsticked mouth and shifted her body on the bed.

"Why? Mother, why?" Marina hissed above her.

Emilia patted the frills of the organza on her shoulders. "You—you don't like it, Marina?" she asked nervously.

"Like it?" Marina plucked the frills of the skirt that had embarrassed her, tossing them around Emilia's large hips. "Why did you, Mother? Why did you put this on?"

Emilia tried to smooth the ruffled frills. She searched for something to say. "It was the latest in fashion," she murmured almost apologetically. She felt as though some cruel joke was being played on her. "I thought you'd like it. At the wedding—"

"Don't mention the wedding, Mother. Look at you . . ."

"But isn't it the fashion?" Emilia's eyes widened in confusion.

Marina turned her back on her and walked toward the window. "Was, Mother," she said quietly, "was. And in England."

Emilia, mistaking Marina's quiet voice for an indication of forgiveness, tried to explain. "I just wanted to show them, Marina. I wanted to show the de Balboas that you come from people."

"But did you have to touch Mrs. Telser's clothes?"

Emilia recovered the anger that she had carried safely hidden with her to Moruga. "Well, they are mine now," she snapped, throwing the waxed fruit hat on the floor.

Marina watched the purple grapes bounce off their stems and roll around the floor. She has no shame. She has no shame left. She picked up the hat and turned it around in her hand, staring at the wax apple. "Never," she said to her mother. "They will never be yours."

Emilia felt the insult and drew herself upright on the bed.

"I am what I am for you. I did this for you."

Marina picked up a grape and stuck it back in its place on the hat. "Like you sent Alma to work obeah on me?" she mocked coldly.

"Yes. Like I sent Alma to work obeah on you," Emilia repeated boldly.

"So you admit it?" Marina looked steadily at Emilia.

Emilia met her eyes. "You should thank God that you have a mother like me."

Marina turned away from her and sat down on the rocking chair near the window. She stared at the land, now dry after the morning's drizzle. She'd make herself dry too. She'd let no love escape, no memories. It was finished. Done. Bile was bitter in her throat. A mother like her! Marina thought. She made Telser take her away from her own daughter. Nothing mattered now. She wished Emilia would leave.

"Mother, why don't you leave me alone. Just go away from here and mind your own business."

"If I did," Emilia was still indignant, "you wouldn't be now the owner of fifteen acres of land in Tabaquite."

Marina wanted to hurt her. "It's Mrs. Virginia de Balboa and her son who own fifteen acres of land," she said.

"You are his wife." Emilia stated the facts.

"Oh yes? Well, it's Mrs. Virginia de Balboa and her son who are going to sell their fifteen acres of land."

"They can't do that." Emilia seemed unperturbed.

"Yes. And there's nothing I can do—nor can you."

"I wouldn't say that, Marina." Emilia leaned against the headboard of the bed.

"You wouldn't?" Marina stopped her rocking, agitated. "What would you do, Mother? More obeah? You know only one way out of things. You say that you want to help me, but do you care? Do you care that I've been suffering here?"

Emilia got off the bed and walked toward her daughter. "I know, Rosebud, I know," she said patting Marina's head.

"No you don't." Marina jumped out of the chair. "It's you," she flared at Emilia, "you who have been causing it. You. Getting Alma to put all those things in my closet! No one will talk to me, Mother. No one!"

"Marina?" Emilia pleaded.

"Everyone looks at me as if I am a sort of witch. And the de Balboas, whom you are trying to impress—what did you expect them to think, Mother?" Marina faced her mother. "Imagine all that stuff in my closet! Chicken legs and eye-balls! Some of my hair! My hair! Mother, how could you?"

Emilia moved closer to Marina and took both her hands in her own and forced the girl to stay still. She looked intently into her eyes and, with a steady voice weighted with seriousness, she said, "They mean to harm you, Marina. I should not have let you marry him." She pushed aside a wisp of hair that crossed Marina's eyes. "I'm sorry that I let you marry him. I am sorry. Forgive me."

Marina tried to release her hand from her mother's, but Emilia held on tightly to her.

"You must believe me, Marina. I didn't think they could harm you. That anyone could harm you."

"Because you threw away your twin sons for me? Is that why, Mother? Is that why no one can harm me?" Marina snatched her hand away from her mother's grasp.

"Yes." Emilia looked steadily at her daughter.

For some seconds both women searched each other's faces. The room became strangely still. Nothing seemed to move. Not even the frills on Emilia's dress. A parrot screeched outside and his mate returned the call. Then the air was filled with the shrill screams of fertility rites. From above in the trees, green feathers fluttered down as the male parrot mounted his lover.

"Yes." Emilia repeated at last. "Yes. Yes. Yes." Her face drained of emotion.

Marina was not finished. "And you murdered that man for me too, Mother?"

Emilia sat down on the bed and put her hands on her knees to steady their trembling. She wanted to be calm. "Which man?" she whispered hoarsely.

Marina stood over her. "I have not forgotten, Mother, that night you took me to that place after Father died. I know why the police were there. I know what you do . . ."

Staring at her knees, Emilia said quietly, "You know, but you don't understand."

Marina walked back to the window and looked at the parrots. They had flown down to a bare branch on the tree. It was all over now, all their crying and screaming. The male parrot was affectionately nipping at its lover's neck, but the female bird, indifferent and unconcerned, rolled her black, beady pupils around in her red-rimmed eyes. You can't hold her with that, Marina thought vaguely and felt an uncanny empathy with the female parrot, who seemed to her as if she wished her lover would fly away and leave her alone to carry the burden, the seed of generations that he had surely deposited in her body.

"You never went back. You never looked for them," she said to her mother, pulling herself away from the parrots.

"What?"

"Didn't you ever wonder, Mother, if they survived?"

Emilia stepped toward her daughter, her hand held over her mouth in amazement, her eyes open wide. "My God! I never knew. How long have you hoped?"

"No! Don't come any closer." Marina blocked with out-stretched arms. "I don't want your pity now."

"I would have told you. I would have told you if I knew you hoped. My God, Marina, they're dead. Dead!"

"Then you killed them?"

Emilia turned away. "No," she said quietly. "I asked the Warao to do it."

"God! I want no part of you. I want no part of your life."

"I could not have him leave them there. For the wild animals—"

"God! God!"

"They would not have lasted. They would be torn to shreds in minutes. Maybe the quenk or the ocelot. Jesus, if the macajuel got them." She covered her face with her hands. "How could I do that? How could I, Marina? The torture. I didn't want them to suffer—"

"I want no part in this."

"I didn't want them to be tortured—"

"God! How could you be my mother?"

Emilia felt Marina's rejection as if a cobra had stung her in the very center of her heart. The sympathy she'd felt for her moments ago froze into a tiny, hard stone that lay in the bottom of her belly. She dropped her hands and raised her head high. "You are a part of it," she said with quiet intensity. "You cannot escape. You wouldn't be here if you weren't a part of it."

Surprised, Marina asked, "You mean alive?"

"And that too."

"What do you mean, 'and that too'?"

"Sit down." Emilia's voice was sharp.

"What?"

"Sit down. I know why you haven't left the room. You want

to know what Harris said, don't you? Don't you? Sit down, I say."

"Mother, stop while you can."

"No, *you* stop. Sit down, Marina." Emilia grabbed her daughter's arm and forced her to sit in the rocking chair near the bed. "You will listen to me now and then you may do whatever you wish. But I will wash this blood clean from my hands. You think it is easy? You think it is easy to make a child and see it die?"

"Mother, stop." Marina shifted her body to get up from the chair.

"Sit down!" Emilia hissed and the girl sat back on the chair like an obedient child.

"What do you know about making babies? Did you ever have one? Do you know what it is to love a child you make? Do you know what it is to watch that swelling in your belly, to watch it get bigger and bigger with your child? And to make yourself hate it even though you love it, more even, Marina, more than you love yourself? Do you know what it is?"

"Mother, I never asked you," Marina whispered.

"No, you never asked me, but I wanted you. I wanted you so much that I would have done anything to get you."

"Not me. It wasn't me you wanted. You didn't want me. You wanted to prove something to yourself. I gave you your womanhood. You should thank me, Mother. I made you a woman. You were barren, Mother. Oh, you could get pregnant, but you were barren. I made you feel good. But I would not have done as you did, Mother. I would not have murdered."

"There are laws," Emilia said weakly. "Laws we must obey."

"Whose laws? What laws are you talking about? Laws of the devil?"

"Laws of your people. Your ancestors."

"But we are no longer savages, Mother, running in the bush with grass skirts."

"Marina! Don't say that. Stop it!"

"You call that a law of civilized people that tells you to murder your own children—and—an innocent, foolish man?"

"We don't question our laws, Marina. We follow them."

"How could you let your children be killed?"

"God did it." Emilia's voice was flat. Blunt.

"God?"

"He could have stopped it. But he let them kill his son. At least I did not stay there to see it. At least I didn't let them torture my sons. I did not watch them beat my son for hours and put a crown of thorns on his head and drive long, cold nails through his hands and feet. At least I didn't do that."

"It isn't the same thing," Marina muttered.

"Not the same? Then all I heard was wrong then? Eh? Wrong, eh? The priests say that God did it to let you and me live. Your civilized priests said that God let his son be murdered and tortured to let us live. You and me."

"It's not the same," Marina repeated quietly.

"Well, I wanted you to live. And those were our laws."

"Father must have hated you." Marina's voice hissed through clenched teeth.

The room grew quiet again. Outside, the male parrot nipped his lover's neck once more, this time sinking his beak deep into her flesh. The lady parrot bled, the red stream of blood dazzling against her green neck, but she kept quiet. Still. Her lover spread his wings and beat the leaves of the tree with his feathers. He screeched and cawed and still the lady parrot was quiet. He rolled his black beady eyes. Blinked. Nipped his lady friend again. And then flew away. And the lady parrot kept still, her green feathers lost in the green leaves, her womb carrying her lover's seed.

"He was no better," Emilia's voice broke into the quiet of the room. "He was a common criminal, your father. Maybe a murderer." She smiled grimly.

"Go on, Mother, take it out on Father."

"How did you think he came here? Half the English people here are criminals, doing some of their time here in the colonies. They take on airs when they come here. We call them 'sir' this and 'sir' that and they get it in their heads that they are better."

"Stop it, Mother."

"Yes they do. We make them think they are better. And then they believe it and they act like they are better and they make us treat them like they were gods and we are dirt."

"He treated you as a wife. Father gave you his house and land as if you were his wife—"

"He did not marry me—"

"Neither did Telser."

"He did not love you."

"You made him hate me. You."

"Marina, they are all the same, Marina."

"He gave you his house and land," Marina repeated.

"No!" Emilia shut her eyes against the image that rose before her, of Hrothgar standing as clear as daylight in the doorway, she seated on the wicker rocking chair with Marina wrapped in cotton blankets, tucked next to her right breast. Nothing, she thought then, no one could ever dim the incredible joy she felt. Her daughter! Her daughter alive! Hrothgar came close to her and drew his fingers hard and cold across her face. She flinched and he locked her jaw between his thumb and forefinger. "When you are healed," he said, his voice sliding like a block of ice melting down her spine, "I want you back in my bed. Keep this child away from me. Always. Make no mistakes. I never want to touch it." He had not forgotten his twin baby boys.

"You made Father hate me," Marina was saying again.

"He hated you a long time before you were born," Emilia said. She had wanted revenge then, on the day Hrothgar spoke to her as if she were a common whore. Revenge for making her accept her role as a plaything, an object, a body without a mind, without a thought. She wanted revenge but she was patient. He had given her land when her boys were alive. But later, when he changed his mind, she knew what to do.

People said that it was his refusal to stop mourning the death of his sons that had driven him to madness. It was not natural, they said. There was a time for living, a time for sacrificing, a time for picking up the pieces, a time for forgiving. Yet it was his singleness of purpose, his obsession with twisting his total life's meaning, the sum of all he did and would do, toward that solitary purpose of grieving that caused the one lucid moment that Hrothgar would have on his deathbed.

Emilia heard him. She heard him reach through the fog of his insanity and grasp that memory that destroyed him.

"She murdered my boys." For the first time he gave words to the knowledge he kept to himself and let fester in his soul. "She'll never have this house. I'll punish her for killing my boys. I'll punish her. Take this to Father de Nieves." Emilia saw him give a piece of paper to his yardman. "Quickly! Take it. He'll understand."

It was easy for Emilia to bribe the yardman with the gold

the Warao had once brought for her. She took the letter from him, the note Hrothgar had signed changing his will. So Father de Nieves never knew he was right when he had guessed that Hrothgar Heathrow had never meant for Emilia to have his house and land, that those were gifts for his live sons, not for dead babies. For all she did then, Emilia still lost the house and land, but now she would not lose Marina.

"Listen, Marina. Listen to me," Emilia pleaded. "I wanted you to live. Not your father. I paid for you to live. See—see— the Telser girls? They died. Did you die, Marina? Did you? No, you were powerful. You were stronger. That's why I did it. That's why I let you marry de Balboa's son."

"Let me?" Marina's voice was cold.

"I could have stopped you."

"But you didn't."

"No, I didn't. I wanted you to have the land I could not have."

"You did it for yourself. You do everything for yourself. You murdered your sons so you would not be barren. You pushed me into marrying Antonio because you wanted to get back the dream you'd lost."

"Dream?"

"Yes, you didn't stop me from marrying him because it was your chance to own land. Through me! Through me!"

"It was your dream too."

"Yes."

"But I wanted to be sure that the de Balboas would not hurt you, so I asked Alma, to make certain, to be sure that the de Balboas' curse would not come to you. I asked Alma to say some prayers for you."

"Prayers?"

"Yes, prayers," continued Emilia. "Our way of praying. I raised you wrong, Marina. I should have taught you my way of life. Instead I showed you your father's."

"Thank God for that."

"Alma prayed for you, Marina. Why didn't you wait to hear what Harris found out? Why didn't you?"

"I don't want to know, Mother."

"But you will know. As sure as you will know that your father hated you."

"Stop it!"

"No. Harris said you will die."

"Stop it!"

"He told Alma how you will die."

"Stop it! I don't care. I don't care."

"And that before you die you will lose a lot of money."

Marina grew quiet, and her mother studied her face.

"A lot of money, he said," Emilia repeated.

"But—I have no—the Warao? Yes, the Warao. He told me—"

"Told you? He was here? The Warahoon?"

"No. I followed him."

"Followed him?"

"In the Warao market. He told me I'd be rich."

"And you believe him?"

"Well, you did. Once."

Emilia lowered her eyes and remained silent.

"Is that what Harris meant? That I'd be rich, as the Warao said?" For the first time since her mother arrived Marina's eyes sparkled. Twice, twice they said she would be rich.

"And then you'll die," said Emilia.

Marina laughed.

"Don't you want to know how you'll die?" Emilia asked.

"Tell me, Mother," Marina mocked.

Ignoring her daughter's sarcasm, Emilia replied, "Mr. Harris says that just as Antonio killed his first three wives, he means to kill you."

A buzzing sound traveled through Marina's head, and she clasped her hands over her ears. She tried to resist the pull of that force in her that would not deny the truths of her people's beliefs, but try as she did, she could not.

"How did Harris say I will die?" she heard herself ask as though another person had spoken.

"You will swell, Marina. Swell up like a frog—Harris says you will get pregnant like all the rest of Antonio's wives, but that your body will swell. He said he saw you when his spirit roamed. Your hands and your feet and your neck and face were all swollen. Your belly was swollen too. But it was as if you were pregnant all over. He said that you were shaking and sweating as if you had malaria. Except it wasn't malaria. He said you were talking as if you had gone crazy. Lost your mind. It is the de Balboa curse handed down from the Portogee father to his half-white son. The son gets the women pregnant and de Balboa's spirit does the rest. Listen to me, child. If you don't believe me. Listen to me."

A cloud of fear lifted off Marina with her mother's words. Had she said anything but that she would die in childbirth, anything else, she would have believed. Perhaps. But she felt good now. Free. How simple they were! Alma, her mother and Harris. She laughed. "That's all that Harris said? Mother, don't you see? Don't you see how foolish this is? All Antonio's wives died in childbirth. All! What else would Harris say? Ignorant superstition, that's what it is."

"Your death will be different."

Marina responded sarcastically, "How? I shall go mad?"

"I've seen greater cocks than you crow," said Emilia, slouched on the bed.

"But not as good as me." Perhaps it was the way that Marina sang those words while wriggling her shoulders that infuriated Emilia, or perhaps she could not bear to be ridiculed one minute more, or perhaps she could no longer tolerate her daughter's ingratitude, for she had taken pains to make the journey to Moruga. Whichever, Emilia decided there and then to do her duty, nothing more, as the mother of the child who, it was predicted, would die. She got up from the bed, reached under her dress and loosened the strings of her bloomers. There, stuck between her waistband and her skin was a tiny bottle half filled with purple liquid. She pushed the bottle toward Marina and the young woman flinched away as though a snake had darted toward her.

"Take it." Emilia gritted her teeth, again shoving the bottle toward Marina.

"Get that away from me." Marina backed away, slightly shaken by the intensity of Emilia's face.

"You take a little of it, just a drop." Emilia's voice was steady. "Just a drop. Every night. You put it in Antonio's tea. You hear me? You kill his nature. Every night. One drop." She moved in closer to Marina, pinning the girl's back against the wall. From the corner of her eye, Marina could see her husband and Telser through the window, walking past the sapodilla tree. She thought of calling to Antonio, but her mother was too quick for her.

"If you call Antonio you will regret it." And that was all Emilia said, but her eyes blazing with determination told Marina to be quiet.

"Now," continued Emilia. "Now that's better. Take the bottle. Hold it in your hand. There." She shoved the bottle into Marina's palm and forced the girl's fingers to clench it tightly. "Good, good," she said. "It took the obeahman nine days of fasting and prayers to make this for you. That's right.

Hold it tightly. Hold on to it and do as I say. You cut Antonio's nature, you hear me? He must not want to sleep with you. You have no children with him. Ever."

Marina began to laugh, a wild crazy laugh that made Emilia back away from her. She fell on the bed kicking up her legs in the air, rolling on the mattress, laughing. "Cut Antonio's nature? Mother, cut Antonio's nature?" She gasped.

"You will do as I say." Emilia's voice remained firm.

Marina sat up. "And how shall I get my children, Mother?"

"You'll be alive."

"Not that I'd do anything for children," Marina laughed grimly.

"Stop it!"

"No, Mother. You have had your lovers and you expect me to stop making love to my husband?"

"I have slept with two men. Your father and Telser."

"And I suppose you did that for me?"

"Yes." Emilia looked steadily into her daughter's eyes. "I did it for you."

"Then leave him now."

"What?"

"Leave Telser now. I don't live with you anymore. You don't need me for your excuse."

"I—I—"

"Why don't you, Mother? Why don't you?"

Emilia sucked in her breath and looked away from Marina. How many times had she asked herself that very question? How many times had seen that question brimming in Alma's eyes, the unspoken question lashing out at her from the eyes of the others who prayed with her at their obeah rituals. "In Trinidad," she began, searching for the right words to explain herself, "there is no other way for a woman to eat."

"You could work."

"And what do you think I do?"

"In other people's kitchens. You don't have to work for him."

"That time has passed." Was it really too late for her to start all over again? Had she grown accustomed to the life of relative ease she had now? Yet she had not deserted her African ancestors. Not even the old Ibo, if he were alive today, would accuse her of that. She was faithful to obeah. And Telser didn't interfere. Perhaps if he did, she would see reason to leave him.

"Never!" Marina confronted her again. "You never did it for me!" She clenched her teeth and spat out, "There's a name for a woman who takes a lover for money."

This time Emilia could not remain still. This time she would not let her daughter call her a whore as she had done once before. She raised her hand and sent it crashing into Marina's cheek.

Marina did not see her mother lift her hand. She did not even hear the sound of the slap against her cheek. She felt only a burning sensation on her face and she tasted the bitter venom of hatred that she had nurtured for her mother's way of life.

"Hit me, Mother. Hit me! But you are too late." Marina's voice was hard. Acid. She wanted to hurt her mother. "I'm already pregnant."

Emilia dropped her hands to her sides, and her body drooped. "When? When?" she asked weakly, "Harris said—"

"That's your trouble. Harris said. Well, Harris is wrong. I have not had my period this month." Marina looked boldly into her mother's face.

"But—"

"No buts, Mother. I always have my period on time. Not a day late. And I missed it."

"You're saying this to hurt me."

"You would wish I were, but I'm not. I am pregnant. I'm going to have a baby." Marina smiled, shaking the bottle in Emilia's face.

"Does Antonio know?"

"What difference does it make?"

Emilia moved toward her daughter to comfort her, but Marina threw off her arms saying, "I won't die, Mother. Remember? I have eight spirits in me. Here," she pushed the bottle toward Emilia. "Here, take your precious obeah medicine and give it to Harris. Tell the Warao to go slaughter some innocent children instead."

Emilia's hand involuntarily reached out to grab the bottle, but in that same instant she had an overwhelming feeling that her daughter was lying to spite her, that Marina was not pregnant. She withdrew her hand and in that split second the bottle left Marina's fingers and fell irretrievably to the floor breaking into smithereens, its purple contents splattering in all directions, splinters of glass scattering across the room.

Instinctively, Marina lifted her skirts to kneel and wipe up the mess, and, as if propelled by its own power, a tiny drop of the liquid, no more than a single spray of an exploding dewdrop, touched that part of her skin that had refused to heal when the crab on the beach dug its claw into her thigh, and she dropped her skirts quickly from the pain of its sting. Was it the vision of the crab struggling powerlessly against her firm grasp, wriggling in a futile effort to escape his fate that chilled her heart? A hard-backed scavenger that was no match for human strength? Was it the look on her mother's face, grown old in that single accident? She pressed her finger on her skirt against the spot where her skin was broken and saw with her mind's eye, the crab leering at her. Bent there at her mother's feet she knew how he felt, that arrogant, avenging crab. She felt as he had, overpowered by a force greater than her will. She was unsure. Uncertain. She looked up toward Emilia, a question forming on her lips, fear quivering at her temples—true fear that made sweat pop out through the pores in the back of her neck—fear of obeah, fear of Harris's words, fear of Alma's power. But Emilia's eyes showed no pity. She was finished. Exhausted. It was all over. She had done everything, all she could do. Her eyes swept past the purple liquid on the floor and her daughter's tortured face and she was indifferent.

"Perhaps," she conceded quickly, "I am too late." And, then, as though nothing had happened, as though she had left her old self there on the floor next to the broken bottle, Emilia picked up her skirts, adjusted her hat on her head and went out the door, yelling good naturedly to Telser.

"Come on, Telly. It's late. We have to go now. Come on. Let's say goodbye. Yoo hoo! Where are you, Antonio?"

But before Telser left, before Emilia could bustle him into the buggy, the Englishman found time to do what he had taken this long trip for. Seeing Marina emerge from the bedroom, not noticing the gloom that had settled over her, but knowing that Emilia was now in the front part of the house saying goodbye to Antonio, he hurried to the young woman. Like a schoolboy sneaking to steal his mother's last chocolate bar, Telser wrapped his arms around Marina and kissed her firmly on the mouth. And before Marina could recover, his hand reached deeply into her blouse and left a velvet bag with coins between her breasts.

15

Eating sapodillas in June. The old buzzard. Just like him to find sapodillas in this heat with nothing getting enough water to grow ripe. The dry season. Endless. Interminable. When would the rains come? Dust circling everywhere, trailing behind the squawking chickens screaming in fear as the red-necked cock, his feathers plucked out of his neck at birth to expose his lechery, thought it was time to make the hens lay eggs again. God, thought Philip Smith, I hate this place. And the children kept on chanting in their singsong voices: "June too soon / July stand by / August come it must / September remember / October all over." And their fat mothers chuckled and said, "Philip, why you doe go back to de modder country if you hate here so." Then they'd slap their thighs and throw back their heads and laugh among themselves. "But you is a born Trinidadian.

239

You belong wid us. You doe have no modder country to go back to."

Ah, but the old buzzard loves the place with its two seasons, thought Philip. Two that's all. One that leaves you drenched from July to October, sucking for air through the dense humidity. The other that dries the moisture off the hair of your nostrils, forcing you to spend days with a wet handkerchief over your nose to stop the dust. And this year the dry season seemed as though it would never end. The tall, spreading poui trees dropped their orange and red flowers, and their petals curled brown in the heat and mingled with the dust. They got ready for leaves, those trees, but still the rains did not know it was time to come. "June too soon," the children taunted again. So it was hot, dry, dusty and barren. And the cicadas no longer had voices to shriek. Still, Philip observed, the old man was wet. His face was covered with the succulent, plump pulp of ripe sapodillas. His mouth squirted their brown juice into the dry air, squeezing out the moist, black, hardshelled sapodilla seeds that danced off the dirt parched white by the blazing sun.

"He must be at least eighty-four, the old buzzard," Philip gnashed his teeth, "but he refuses to die."

Most of his father's friends had already returned to England when their bones had got tired and they had longed for their final sleep. His mother had long ago gone to England, taking Philip with her on that journey back. And he saw his first glimpse of heaven then. In England. It was in June too. Like now. Except there were four seasons there and in June the daffodils bloom. What irony! To be made to sing with the poet in school all those years about daffodils beside the lake, beneath the trees, fluttering and dancing in the breeze while the sun poured down hot and sweltering on an island that could never get cool enough to grow a daffodil!

He saw lilacs and jasmines, violets, and geraniums and roses then. There in England. And the air was so clean and clear. How quickly lies spread that in the islands there are flowers. There are no flowers here. Except in some fool's garden. Unless you call chaconia flowers, and bougainvillea, hibiscus and balisier, flowers, but there are no real flowers as there are in England. No place, nowhere else had he seen such beauty growing in the wild or sculptured as by the English landscape artist. There are blue flowers there and flowers the colors of which are never seen in the islands. And when his mother died and was buried among the lilacs that she loved so much, the old buzzard called him back home. Home to this godforsaken island with its lazy Negroes and its coconut-oil-greased coolies. He was only twenty then, with nowhere to go, and the old man promised, promised him that in ten years, by the time he was thirty, he could return to England a rich man.

From the shade of a dying mango tree Philip watched his father swinging stupidly in the brown burlap hammock strung between two poles under the house, his old East Indian servant squatting on the ground beside him. Soon, Philip thought, soon he'll fall asleep. But the man liked the fleshy brown fruit and it amused him to have his servant squash a sapodilla in his mouth when the hammock swung forward, ducking back just in the nick of time so that he would not be bowled over by a dry flesh-covered sack of bones. But in time the game ceased to amuse Harold Smith, and as the Indian lurched forward with yet another sapodilla, Philip saw that the old man's face, white in spite of the sun, had crumpled into a deep sleep. Philip watched as the Indian rolled out his straw mat and then stretched himself on the hot, dry ground next to his master. When he was sure that they were both asleep, Philip left his mango tree and tiptoed cautiously into the house.

He went directly to his mother's bedroom. The old man had locked it up since her death, but Philip always had the key to the door, and sometimes when he longed for that clean daffodil place and cool sweet-smelling meadowland, he sat in there and dreamed of their time together. But now there were papers that he had to find. Ronald Nest and Lee Lai had come to see him the day before, offering to buy his land in Tabaquite, all fifteen acres of it. They were willing to pay more money than he had ever dreamed of—money to return to the daffodil land. They were drilling for oil, they said, and they were sure that they would find some on his property. Philip hid his surprise. It was not so much that they wanted the land in Tabaquite for the oil it bore that surprised him, but that they called it *his* land. The only land he knew of that his father owned was sugarcane land in Siparia. He had been a fool to buy it. Philip had warned him: The days for making money on sugarcane were gone forever. The Europeans had seen to that with their beet sugar. Soon, very soon there would be no preferential tariffs on sugar from Trinidad, Philip told his father with fatalistic foresight. Cocoa would be king. And before that year ended, the sugar trade began to decline. Then disease destroyed the sugarcane crops the following year and the year after that. Then the laborers demanded more wages and burned down estate after estate when their demands were not met. By the seventh year, Harold Smith put his land in the hands of an East Indian manager and returned to his job as warden of Moruga, abandoning the very source of the wealth he promised Philip for his journey to England.

But land in Tabaquite? There was local gossip that his

father once owned land in Tabaquite, but that was all it was—gossip. The only people he knew who farmed in Tabaquite were some East Indians and a few Negroes. Some said that most of the land around there belonged to the half-Portuguese Negro, de Balboa, and they also said that he was related to this Antonio de Balboa. As Philip remembered, the gossip was that his mother once adopted an African girl who was so beautiful that his father desired her, and so his mother gave the girl to a crazy Portuguese man, Vasco de Balboa, so the girl could escape his father's lust. They said that his mother paid the Portuguese well with the land that his father once owned in Tabaquite. Antonio was the son of the African woman and the Portuguese. It was a foolish story common in this island. As if those sulky black women with their thick lips and big round eyes; their nappy hair; their hard, round breasts; their firm, long thighs; their round, soft buttocks; their undulating, smooth hips; their silky smooth arms—as if their musky smell; their inner thighs; their wiry hair; their long, long endurance; their sweet, sweet loving— as if—as if—Philip wet his lips and leaned back against the doorframe. The land meant nothing to him then, as it did now. Except if it could give him passage to England and money to live there. How Nest and Lee Lai could make money with oil was a mystery to him. But the daffodil land for the deed of ownership for the Tabaquite land? He would not tell them the story of the African girl and her Portuguese husband.

It would have been simple to ask the withered white man if they owned land in Tabaquite or if he had given away land that they owned in Tabaquite, but he didn't trust the colored-woman-loving man. If they did own the land, his mother would have the deed. She kept everything in that box under her bed. She loved papers, and records and mementos. She was a pack rat. She saved everything. She'd give away land, that he could believe, but she'd save the paper, the deed, the record.

He dusted the cobwebs off the box and placed it next to him on the bed. He had never opened it before. Out of respect for her? Keeping her secrets too from the old man who caused her death? Philip never really knew. The box was sacred to his mother and it was sacrilegious to break its lock once she was gone. A violation of her much-treasured privacy. The lock gave way easily, rusted and dried out in the two-season weather. Gingerly, Philip removed the cover, and a white lace handkerchief, as though buoyed by its own power, floated past his fingers and fluttered down to the floor. The movement caught Philip by surprise and chilled his heart. It was like a warning, it seemed to his overwrought imagination at the time, a warning from his mother not to go further. And he would have snapped the cover on the box had not a tiny foot, no longer than his small toe, caught his eye as the handkerchief fell, smelling of the perfumed dead.

Boldy he looked in the box. It was nothing. He sighed with relief. A little alabaster doll about six inches tall, with matted blond hair. Probably a childhood toy. Yes, that's what it was, a toy. Strangely though, he thought, knowing his mother's sense of propriety, the doll was naked. And oddly the smile on its face had none of the innocent sweetness of the dolls he had seen. But Philip gave these observations no serious consideration, though he hesitated a little to remove the little doll from the two bundles of papers lying neatly under it, one tied with bright red satin ribbon, the other with blue. It was the red-ribboned bundle that he reached for. The papers were longer in it. Official looking. The other was obviously a bunch of old letters. Carefully he untied the ribbon and opened the papers. It was a deed for land. For land in Tabaquite. Philip's eyes raced down the first page. Yes! Yes! It was for Tabaquite! England for Tabaquite! Feverishly his fingers turned the first page, and in that instant they touched a tiny white paper stuck between the first and second sheets of the deed. Philip would have disregarded the paper. Crumpled it and thrown it to the floor, so anxious was he to get to the final pages of the deed where signatures and seal gave it validity, had he not recognized his father's hand scrawled across the page. It was a letter.

My dearest Hilda,

I have done as you have asked. Mr. Vasco de Balboa has agreed to take Virginia, to marry her in fact. I have duly registered our land in Tabaquite in his name. I pressed him to keep the land out of your gratitude to him and the affection and high regard in which we hold Virginia.

I have rendered our deed now null and void, which I enclose for you for your safekeeping.

Your loving and faithful husband,
Harold Smith

In despair Philip turned to the last page of the deed. It was true. The words null and void had been boldly printed across the original signatures and new seals and signatures added to confirm the uselessness of the paper that he held in his hands.

For five minutes Philip sat there on his mother's old bed, staring at nothing, his mind made a vacuum by the sudden loss of hope, hope snatched away in the moment that he had savored it most. And as sometimes happens when a person has hoped and waited, and hoped for as many years as he could remember, despair finds it difficult to occupy the blank mind. No, Philip could not, would not now despair. When the stupor that had enveloped him finally subsided, a new hope crawled its way back inside. Hope, born it was true of desperation, but hope nonetheless, familiar and exhilarating.

Philip bounced off the bed, and not stopping to replace his mother's box nor to close her bedroom door, he rushed out of the room toward his father's office. There, he pulled open file drawer after file drawer, his fingers trembling nervously as he flipped through the files of copies of land deeds that his father kept as the ward officer for the southwestern part of Trinidad below San Fernando. D—D—de Balboa. Finally he found it. De Balboa! The deed, duly registered, as his father had written, to Vasco de Balboa, Esq. Behind the deed was the official government tax record for the land. A wide grin expanded over Philip's face as he read the contents, and at that moment, before he could close the files, he heard his father clear his throat at the doorway.

"Did you find what you were looking for?" gurgled Harold Smith, leaning against his East Indian.

"Go back to sleep, old man," replied his son, slamming the wooden file drawer shut.

"And what, may I ask, is in your hand? Ali go! Get it from him!" The old man's legs were wobbly, yet he pushed his servant with the vigor of a man in his prime.

"Watch it, coolie!" Philip walked boldly over to the old Indian man.

"Ali, take it!" shrilled the withered white man.

Philip stretched out one hand toward the East Indian and pulled him off the ground by the scruff of his neck, dangling his wiry, wrinkled legs comically in the air.

"Out you go, Ali. I'll call for you when we are ready." He

shut the door behind him and led his father spluttering in rage to the white, coconut-fiber-filled Morris chair near the desk. The cushions swallowed the old man.

"You are a fool, old man," said Philip in a strained, soft voice, "but you won't make me a fool."

The old man struggled to wriggle himself to the edge of the chair. Finally, craning his neck as far as he could, he looked over to the papers on his desk and recognized the de Balboa name.

"Why are you interested in the de Balboa land?"

"Because it is mine." Philip folded the papers and stuck them in the belt of his pants, next to his skin.

"It is not. Your mother gave it to the de Balboas years ago."

"You mean, you gave it to them."

"No, your mother." The old man scratched at some dried sapodilla pulp that still clung to his chin.

Philip stared brazenly at him.

Harold Smith cleared his throat. "Well," he began, "I expect you know it all by now. Saw you in your mother's room. You shouldn't have done that."

Philip grinned cruelly.

"Didn't make sense to me," the old man continued. "It was your mother's fault. Blameless. Couldn't see why we had to pay the Portuguese for the African girl. But she was like that, your mother."

"Like what?" Philip loomed over his father.

"Sentimental."

"As you were faithful."

"Look here, Philip—" Harold Smith was tired. "I'm an old man and I want no quarrel with you. The land no longer belongs to us. Why do you want it anyhow?"

"Because it's valuable, old man. Valuable!"

"Who says?" Harold Smith fanned his clammy, dough-white face with his straw hat.

"Nest and Lee Lai, that's who says. And they will pay too. Fifty pounds sterling, my passage to England."

The old man dropped his hands, threw back his head and laughed as if he would die. He slapped his knees, curled his legs and laughed. Finally, with one deep intake of breath, it seemed he would die indeed, choked by his laughter, and Ali came shuffling back into the room in time to dislodge the acrid mirth from his throat.

"You belong here, you fool. You belong here," the old man gurgled. "There's no England for you to go home to. You belong here. This is your home."

Philip stood still, quieting the rage that mounted to his head. Murder. No. Not murder on the brink of his departure to daffodil land. He brushed his red hair off his face, a face that refused to get brown in spite of thirty-five years exposed to unrelenting sunshine. Proof of his legitimate claim to England.

"You can stay here, Father," he said at last, "but I shall go where I belong."

In spite of himself the old man felt pity crawl up to his heart. After all, Philip was his son. And he didn't belong here. "Why would Nest and Lee Lai want to give so much money for that land?" he asked kindly. "They can find land anywhere."

"Oil, my dear father."

"Pipe dreams," the old man grumbled.

"Because they are not your dreams?" Philip questioned acidly.

"Oil will never be worth much," the old man responded.

"But I don't care what it's worth. Don't you see? They are paying me for the land."

"But I hear that in London they are trying to build a small carriage that runs on oil," Smith took pleasure in contradicting his earlier statement.

"I don't care, Father. I don't care." Philip was nettled.

"But the English horse breeders, horse dealers, blacksmiths, saddlers, stagecoach drivers, not to mention the railroad men, eh Ali?" The old man nodded toward his servant. "They won't go for it. Eh?"

"Father, I don't care."

"Well, the land is not yours," Smith said finally.

Philip looked as though he would explode. "Oh, but it shall be mine. See here. Look, Father, look. See?" Philip shoved under his father's nose the government tax records from the de Balboa land that he had found behind the deed. "See? You should be more careful, Father. You should see that your landowners pay their taxes."

Harold Smith placed a heavy hand on the shoulder of the East Indian squatting by his feet and braced himself forward on the chair.

"You cannot," he whispered.

"But I can, Father. Thirty-two shillings, that's all it takes and the land is mine."

"There is due process under the law," the old man insisted.

"What law?"

"The owners must be warned first that their taxes are owing. And there must be an auction if they refuse to pay."

"Okay," said Philip, "let's have an auction, Father. How much do you bid? Twenty shillings? Twenty-four? Forty? Ten pounds? Going, going, gone. Gone to Mr. Philip Smith for twenty-three shillings. Fifteen acres of land in Tabaquite. Out of my way, Father."

"I forbid you to purchase it." The East Indian helped Harold Smith to his feet.

"Forbid me?" Philip laughed. "Who do you think you are?"

"The warden here of the southwestern district of Trinidad." The old man leaned heavily on the East Indian, glaring at his son. "No deed is registered here unless it has my signature."

"You will refuse me, won't you? You are an old man. You can hardly pee or shit on your own without Ali. You slop your food all over you like a pig and yet you won't give it up. You must be warden here. You promised me if I worked for you—but you treat me like a boy. Fetch this. Fetch that. See that that's done. See that this is done. And it is you who are warden. Not me. God, I wish you'd strangle in your own shit."

The old man motioned to Ali to help him back into the chair. "When I die, Philip"—his breathing was slow now— "you can have my post." Then he added softly, "I've kept it for you, son. All these years, I've kept this post for you."

"Kept it for me? I don't want it. I never did. You promised me." Philip began to whine like a child. "You promised to give me money to return to England."

"That was a long time ago, Philip. Your place is here."

"Your place, old man. Not mine. Sell me the land now. I want out. Here. Here." Philip dug into his pockets and pulled out coins and notes and flung them in his father's lap. "Here. Here's pen and paper. Sign here on the bottom. I'll fill out the rest. It's my land. I want it now."

"Philip, I cannot." The old man pushed the money on the floor and Ali dropped to his knees to pick it up. "I promised your mother."

"Promised her? You owed her for your infidelity. And you

owe me now. Sign." Philip waved the pen and paper in his father's face.

"I cannot, Philip."

Philip felt the murderous rage boil with his blood and he quieted it. Murder. Not murder now of an old man who will soon die. Not murder on the eve of his own departure.

"There are others who will," said Philip at last. "You have always hated me. And now you have your last laugh. There are others who will."

"Which others?" asked his father. "Here, I am the law, Philip. I register deeds. No one else. You need my signature."

"I shall go to Port-of-Spain."

"You cannot, Philip." There was something in the quiet tone with which his father said "cannot" that made Philip stop at the door and turn back. "Cannot." The old man said it with such finality.

"You cannot do this," Harold Smith was repeating.

"And who will stop me?" asked Philip. "Not you, old man."

"No, not me. You and your mother, that's who."

For a brief second Philip thought he was going to laugh and then he recognized the trembling that fluttered across his lips. His old fear. His old terror of the people who lived on this island that was not his. His fear of their power to lure white people into their mysterious, dark, underworld doings. And his fear that his mother, for all her love of daffodils and lilacs, sparkled a little when the drums pulsated on certain nights around bright fires. When women dressed in white, heads tied with white bandanas, danced themselves into a frenzy and spoke in languages few white men ever understood.

"I don't know what you are saying, old man," Philip whispered hoarsely to his father.

Harold Smith closed his eyes and leaned back in his chair. The old East Indian servant mopped his face with a white handkerchief until Smith knocked his hands away so that the East Indian went back to squatting at his master's feet.

"We thought we could have no children, Hilda and I. That's why we took the girl," the old man began. "It seemed strange. English people adopting an African. But we didn't adopt her at first. At first she was just the baby girl of a freed slave. The woman died in childbirth. They all do around here. So we couldn't let the baby die. Then Hilda began to feed her. 'No,' I said to Hilda. 'Let the servants do it.' But I could see that Hilda's arms were greedy for a baby, and I could not refuse her."

The old man's voice grew still and Philip thought that he had drifted off to sleep, but in a few seconds he began to dream again. "She hugged that baby and kissed it and loved it. More than she loved me, I dare say. It wasn't jealousy. I wanted her to have a baby girl. But not a black baby girl. I told her that we would send to England for an English baby, but by then your mother really thought that that baby was hers. She had a little white doll with blond hair. A present from one of our friends. Your mother used to say that the little white doll took her baby's whiteness and left her all black. Then Hilda taught Virginia to read and to write. Your mother was not a peasant like me. But I suppose you know that, Philip. She had aristocratic airs. She loved her classical music—Mozart, Beethoven, Bach—and she and Virginia would play the phonograph all day and dance the minuet and talk Shakespeare. They despised me."

His father stopped talking again, but Philip was intrigued. It had been just a story, malicious gossip about Virginia and his father. His mother had never spoken about her and he had never seen this side of her. He coaxed the old man into talking some more.

"Can I get you some lime juice, Father?"

"No," Smith brushed his son off and started again. "Then, when the girl became a woman, your mother made me give her to de Balboa. Hilda said that he was a cultured man. Not like the rest of the Portuguese around here. She told me to give him the land in Tabaquite so he'd know the girl was not a commonplace servant. I didn't see why we should do that. I kept the land. Why pay a white man for taking your servant? So I told Hilda that I'd given the land to de Balboa. But the next day, she knew that I hadn't done so. She had gone to visit a woman they call Alma. Your mother could not resist the drums."

Philip lowered his eyes.

The old man breathed more heavily now, and Ali, watching him closely, fetched a cold glass of lime juice and placed it to his lips. Smith sucked at the glass for a while and then continued. "Yes, your mother loved the drums. Peculiar. She never let on to Virginia. She protected Virginia from the drums, but she loved them. Well, the next day, as I was saying, she came crying to me. She said that she'd lose the baby if I didn't give de Balboa the Tabaquite land. I didn't know what baby she was talking about. She said that she was pregnant. At forty-six! A forty-six-year-old woman pregnant! I didn't believe her. Thought that she'd lost her mind. But the Tabaquite land meant nothing to me. So I gave it to de Balboa. And she didn't believe me until she had the deed all null and void and saw a copy of the new deed." The old man sipped some more lime juice from the glass held by the attentive Ali. "Ah, but she was pregnant indeed. Forty-six and pregnant with you, Philip. I never asked why. I don't know how, but I do know that somehow you are alive today because I gave the de Balboas the Tabaquite land."

His father had finished. The sapodilla-eating man had drained his voice. He closed his eyes and fell asleep again. Philip watched him and did not move. His mind was frozen by the ugly smirch upon his mother's whiteness.

16

Take the dry cocoa bean. Put it in the heavy, black iron pan. Place the frying pan on the coal pot. Shake the frying pan until the cocoa beans dance. They are parched now. Take off the shell. Put the shelled beans in the heavy wooden mortar bowl. Take the mallet. Pound the beans. Pound the beans hard. Harder. Harder. Wipe the sweat from your face. No one will see you, and if they did? What if they did? You're only making cocoa for supper tonight. Yes, but do they know what you have in your pocket? Can they feel the bristles of the manumust twigs scratching your cotton dress? Pound the beans. Harder. Harder. But not too hard. They may suspect. You don't want them to suspect.

Mr. Smith looked ready for death, didn't he though? Did you see the wrinkles on his face? And how did he stay so white in all this heat? And his hair. He had all of it. Every strand. But it was silver white. Not flour white like his face. I didn't want to touch him.

Would you? His skin looked so clammy. An old wrinkled sack of bleached flour, he was. And who'd wear a suit in all this heat? The English are so peculiar. Even if it was a white suit. Linen, they say, breathes. Can you see cloth breathing? In and out and up and down. Ha—Ha!

Pound the cocoa now. Don't forget. Raise that mallet high. It will grind the cocoa. Don't you worry.

He had that coolie with him too. Can't go nowhere without Ali. Coolies never get old. Ever see an old coolie? I think they burn them by the river before they get old, and let their ashes wash downstream.

But keep it in your pocket. Grind the cocoa. You'll see.

The old man had to have Ali drive his donkey cart. And I bet Ali is the same age as he is. But then coolies never get old. "Good morning, Mrs. de Balboa," he says. And then he looks at my belly. And I know what he thinks. Those colored people. They never say Negroes or niggers or anything like that. Not to your face. Colored people. We are the colored people. They are the uncolored people. White is not a color.

I know when he looked at my belly he said, "Those colored people, they're always making babies." Mother, even while I lied to you, I told the truth. Did you know that I was telling the truth even though I thought I lied? Did you, Mother? Is that why you left me, Mother? I'm afraid—no, I'm not afraid. I'm not afraid— I'm not afraid.

Pound the cocoa beans. Good. They are ready. Now roll the grinds into a ball. Use your knuckles, Marina. Some more strength. Come on. You can do it. You are strong as eight men. Remember?

I guess that old Mr. Smith wanted to help me. You can never tell about these people. But he seemed so afraid. His son will kill him for sure. Could you imagine that Mr. de Balboa never paid the taxes on his land? Just one shilling a year. That's all, and he never paid it. Yes, but you could excuse him. He didn't want the land anyway. But she?—Virginia—she should have paid the taxes.

Why did the old man wait so long? He said he forgot somehow. Thirty-two years. That's thirty-two shillings. Thirty-two shillings from the fifty shillings Telser gave me. That leaves me. Let me see now. Two from ten is eight. Carry one. Add it to the three. Make that four. Four from five. That leaves one. One. Eight. Only eighteen shillings left. But it's worth it.

If I pay the taxes, the old man said, everything will be all right. If not, we lose the land. We? They lose the land. Not me. It's not mine. Can you believe Virginia? Trying to sell land that was almost not hers. And Antonio was planning to sell it to the old man? Funny, isn't it. The old man could have taken the land, if he wanted to. Why didn't he? Said he was taking a chance. His son had gone to Port-of-Spain to pay the taxes so the land would be his. I wonder why he wants the land so bad? The old man wouldn't say. Can you imagine Philip Smith with black, dirty land soiling his lily-white hands? He has something on his mind, for sure. Oil? No! Oil? But, perhaps—no!

I didn't have time to fetch Antonio from the schoolhouse. Mr. Smith wanted the money right away. Why tell Mrs. de Balboa? So I gave him most of what Telser gave me. Only eighteen shillings left. But I'm not taking any chances.

These cocoa balls look good now.

Make sure no one sees you. Take out the manumust from your pocket. Grind it in the mortar with the pestle.

I'll put it in his cocoa tonight. He'll never know. Virginia, she'll guess. But he'll never know. You'd like to see this, wouldn't you, Mother? The almighty Marina using manumust on her husband. But you're wrong, Mother. I won't die. I'll be rich.

It isn't that I believe in all this. It's just a little insurance. I can't take a chance. Antonio must give the land to me.

I want it now. I want it in my name now.

Scoop up the ground manumust. Put it in a piece of brown paper, then into my pocket. It'll be time soon.

Mother, did he really hate me—my father? Did he really hate me?

"Marina, you look tired. Move from the stove. Let me pour the cocoa."

"Oh no, Mrs. de Balboa. I'm fine."

"But isn't she perspiring, Antonio?"

"It's the heat."

"It'll rain soon."

"Come, Marina, let me pour the cocoa. You're carrying two now, you know. That baby's growing in there."

Why doesn't she stop all this friendliness? She hates me, for God's sake. I saw you dressed as a bride trying to lure your son into your bed. Pour your own cocoa, but I must pour your son's. Leave me with my husband.

"At least bring the cocoa pot over here to the table."

"Please, Mrs. de Balboa."

"Leave her, Mother. Do you need help, Marina?"

"No."

Turn my back to him and pour their cocoa at the stove. It's not a good idea to put the manumust in the goat milk. It'll float on top. One teaspoon in Antonio's cocoa. Good. The blue cup for him. The yellow for her. The red for me. Bring the cups to them.

"My, but you do make good cocoa, Marina. Doesn't she, Antonio?"

"Good, but—"

"But what? Always complaining, isn't he, Marina? But what, Antonio?"

"Oh, nothing. It just tastes—"

"Come give me yours."

"No." *I must take the cup from her. She'll taste it. Her tongue is sharp. She'll know.* "Give it to me. Here, Antonio. Did I make it too sweet? I put honey in yours."

"I suppose that's it."

"Well, I hate sweet cocoa."

"That's you, Mother. I love mine sweet. I told that to Marina last week. You remembered the honey. Thank you, dear."

Well, he drank it all. Let's see now, Emilia Heathrow. Let's see your manumust at work.

I'*ll put on my wedding nightgown. It won't look foolish. My belly is not all that big. Is it? He'll be finished brushing his teeth soon. Good. It looks fine. I'll pull down the neckline a little further. That's it. He loves my breasts. The Mammy's boy. I'll turn down the lamp. Not too low. Get into bed before he comes.*

"Marina, are you asleep?"

"No."

He can't resist me. I'll make him love it. Humble and sweet. That's how I'll be. That's what he wants and then—

"Will it hurt?"

"Oh no, I'll turn my back to you."

"I don't want to hurt you or the baby."

You couldn't stop if you wanted to. Hurt me? You wouldn't care if you ripped me apart.

"You won't, really."

"Just a little bit then. Do your breasts hurt? They are so big."

"Just for you, Antonio."

"Can I squeeze them? Good. You feel good. All warm inside. Can I go a little further? It hurts?"

Come on, get it over with and then I'll have you. Too late, Virginia.

"No, Antonio."

"Just a little more then. Oh good, you are good. A little more. Your backside feels good. Good. Can I put it there too?"

"If you want."

Men are such fools. They'll sell their souls for a little . . . Take it, Antonio, it's your turn now. Soon it'll be mine.

"Can I? Oh good, it's good. It's good, good, good. Ahhh!"

"A ntonio, the land, will you let me have it?"

"You can have what you want, Marina. You were so good. Did I hurt you? Just a little? Just a teeny little?"

"No, silly, I told you no. Can I really have it?"

"Yes, of course."

"Legally?"

"Well, it's yours now. Legally."

"I know, but legally with my name on it."

"But my mother owns part."

"Yes, but you would have lost it if I didn't give Mr. Smith the money."

"I'll pay you back, Marina."

Mustn't let him get serious. Can't lose the mood. "But could I have just five acres? Mine alone. With no other name on it but mine."

"Okay, if that's what you want."

The old man had never seen this before. Not in the eighty-four years that he had lived, and in the fifty years that he had been warden in southwest Trinidad. He had never seen a man come to him to give his land to his wife. True it was only five acres, but he had never seen this before. The young man demanded that no other name, no other name should be on the deed of ownership of those five acres of land, but his wife's, Marina E. Heathrow—Heathrow not de Balboa. All the while, the wife stood by smiling innocently. But Harold Smith would not question the young man. He did as he was asked. It was the last payment on the debt he owed Virginia de Balboa. But Antonio should have wondered why, when the deed was signed, the old man asked Ali to fetch him a bowl of water and a towel. He should have been curious when Harold Smith washed his hands and said, "Like Pontius Pilate, I wash my hands of this family."

THE
RAINS
COME

17

As the dry season ended and the rains came, first in heavy showers at midday that stopped as suddenly as they started and then in drizzles that began in the morning and trickled down relentlessly from the sky all day and into the evening, Marina's belly began to rise as it had not done before. She watched it helplessly, unable to stop the spreading, the thickening of her hips, the pulsating pressure that stretched her flesh thin and tight everywhere except for the small, soft, pink basin in the middle of her belly from where her navel jutted out hard and erect.

Every day, every hour it seemed to Marina, her belly grew larger and her breasts fuller. Then one day she felt a dampness on her chest and saw where her bulging breasts had released tiny trickles of a colorless, sticky liquid. She reached to touch her nipples, to stop the flow, and her mind took in for the first time how far the swelling had spread. She flinched as though her hands had touched burning coals and remained fixed to the spot where she was, her eyes staring in shock before her, refusing to look again at what she had seen. By and by her body relaxed, and hot, flowing perspiration poured down her face. She dared herself to look. Wasn't she the brave Marina who called her mother a fool? She raised her hands to her chest. Yes, yes, they had grown larger. She tried to bend her fingers, but the thickness around her joints was too dense for them to reach far. All around the tips of her fingers down to her palms and her wrists, her skin was smooth and rounded like the glassy swells on the sea before a storm. Yes, and on her ankles too! Her feet! Every one of her toes!

She rushed to the mirror. Around her eyes, her cheeks, her mouth, her skin had billowed out, transforming her delicate features. She could barely recognize herself for the swelling. It was true. God, it was true! Her mother was right! Swell up like a frog, Harris had said. Like a frog he had told her. God, how calm she had been when she had pounded the manu-must for Antonio's cocoa. How calm! How certain! The land had blinded her eyes. Yet it was not a game she played then. It was real. She believed that the manumust could force Antonio to give her the land. And didn't he? Like a man with no other purpose but to please her. But now another possi-bility tormented her. If the manumust worked, why not Alma's obeah? Why not Harris's voyage into the spirit world? They could be right. Wasn't she rich now? No, not rich, but she had five acres of land, five acres with her name—Marina E. Heathrow—on the deed, not de Balboa, not Marina de Balboa, but Heathrow.

She had returned to Tabaquite to see the land again after those five acres were legally hers. Then, not even the taunting laughter of the villagers, nor the oil that snaked relentlessly around the bottoms of the cocoa trees, that turned the air foul with the metallic odors of the underworld, nothing could take away from her the joy of owning the land. She took off her shoes and let her toes sink into the greasy earth. She scooped the dirt up in her hands. The black soil caught in her fingernails. This was hers. Her piece of the earth. She dreamed then of the time when the land would be greaseless again, when the oil would be removed from her land.

Yes, obeah had served her. The manumust had worked its magic. Obeah could work for her again. Marina considered her swollen reflection in the mirror before her. If she came to believe in obeah, must she also believe the prediction of the obeah woman? Would she die?

She turned away from the mirror, trembling. No, she didn't believe in obeah. Not like her mother. Not like Emilia. She wouldn't murder for it. Greed, desire, passion for land had driven her to the manumust. She couldn't lose all that she had married Antonio for. But it was happening to her as Harris had predicted. The swelling, the thickness around her limbs. Marina stifled the scream that began in her throat. With every ounce of strength she had, she fought off the hysteria. No. No, she would not die. Had she not seen others swell like this in their ninth month? Had she not seen the faces of some women bloated and puffed out into unrecognizable shapes as the time drew near for their delivery? She was the same. Her pregnancy was the same. It was water. She was retaining too much water. She would not drink so much. She would stop drinking. Eating too. It would bring down the swelling. It would be good for the baby. She touched her cheeks and forced her lips to smile. That's what she would do.

Antonio noticed the swelling too, but he said nothing. He didn't talk about the baby. He pretended it did not exist, that he didn't see that Marina's belly had grown larger than any woman's he had ever seen, or that her limbs had become abnormally thick, her face distorted. He bristled at the slightest mention of her "condition" and treated her as if she had no right to special attention.

Virginia knew that her son was afraid. She tried to console him. When the rains came and Marina's belly had completely overshadowed her feet, Virginia tried to dull the cold chill of her son's memory of the deaths of his first three wives. "She's stronger, Antonio. Don't you see. She'll live. Don't worry. She'll live."

But it was not worry that had chilled Antonio, it was his determination to hate Marina. When he left Mr. Smith's office, he knew what he had done. Indeed, as he signed the papers giving Marina sole possession of the five acres of Tabaquite land, he was gripped by the strange sensation that that, more than anything else in the world, was what he wanted to do. As if his life depended on it, he begged and pleaded with Harold Smith to draw up the papers there and then. "No, tomorrow would be too late." Why? Antonio did not know, but he felt the same urgency to complete the contract, to consummate the deal, as he had felt the night before to take Marina as he had never done before. The shame of the night still clouded his memory. In her backside? In her backside? How could he? Sodom and Gomorrah. But when it was all done, a bitterness toward Marina crept into his heart. He could find no reason to blame her. He had done it all willingly.

Yet—

Soon the bitterness turned to indifference. But Marina's belly mocked him with the proof of his desire for her, and in the depths of his soul he wished he could hate her instead. Yet he had not lived long enough to learn how to cultivate hate, how to let it seep into his bones, course through every vein in his body, mingle with his every breath, how to make it his first waking thought, his last dream at night, how to direct his every action toward that hate, to obliterate himself for the sake of nurturing that hate, to sell his soul so that hate could live. So soon he was to lose the will to hate Marina, and soon he was to love her once more, though he now doubted more than ever before that she ever loved him.

18

The people on the island have a saying:

> June too soon
> July stand by
> August come it must
> September remember
> October all over.

And in August that year, the rains came with more fury than they had done for as many Augusts as the villagers could remember. They brought the winds with them and lightning that split the sky into jagged parts and thunder that roared viciously out toward the land from the blackening sea. By the first week in August, the snakes had begun to crawl out of their watery holes and slide up the concrete pillars under the houses, slinking across any dry wooden plank that they could find. The wild weeds and plants that had knotted their way lazily and leisurely up to the sky, shooting their greenery everywhere and thirstily drinking the water they had been denied all the long months of the dry season, were now suffocating from excess. Their swollen branches gave way and fell limp, heavy with water that their roots had greedily absorbed. Flowers, defeated by the gushes of water that poured from the sky, fell to the ground forming a slippery carpet at the feet of their trees, stinking the air with their rotting perfume. This was not the time for delicacy. It was the time for treacherous vines, common weeds and desperate leeches, overripe fruit, watery mangoes, swollen citrus, decaying avocado. By the second week in August the rainwater had begun to destroy even these—everything except those tall trees that in dry season or rainy season refused to succumb to sun or water.

At first the villagers merely shut their houses and shacks tightly and put large rocks on top of their roofs to hold down the galvanized metal in the strong winds, but by the end of the second week, they began to panic. The water had seeped under doors bringing with it dirt, silt, slimy green leaves, dead branches. Those who had not taken the precaution to do as the affluent English had done, or who were not as fortunate as the de Balboas to have had built for them houses elevated on tall concrete pillars, packed their belongings on their donkey carts and moved farther inland to higher ground. By the third week of August, it looked as though the hurricanes would come before Marina would deliver her baby. Antonio watched dismally as his wife's body continued to transform horribly before his eyes. After each rainstorm her entire body, her hands, arms, legs, ankles, neck and face became more and more swollen, and she seemed to sink into a deeper and deeper depression that left her staring in the mirror for hours at the reflection of her bloated body.

In spite of himself, Antonio began to worry about his wife. He felt that it was his duty as husband to the woman and father to the unborn child that he should get help for her. But it was pity and love that he had put to sleep that stirred within him as he looked at her thick body. And he began to fear for her life.

As the days passed—August 12, 13, 14—Marina's condition worsened. Her fingers became so swollen that she could no longer move them. Her legs ached and her ankles grew so thick that she could barely shuffle across the room. She fought despair like a warrior until her mind grew weary and it no longer mattered to her whether it was obeah that had made her so, or it was merely the unborn child. She began to wish, as she had not before, that Antonio would talk to her. Before, his cold indifference had not troubled her. To her own sense of justice it was just retribution for the trick she had played on him—the manumust that she had stirred into his cocoa. But then the violent headaches began, the stomach-wrenching vomiting, all that Emilia had warned her would happen and she needed Antonio. She needed him to bring Emilia to her.

Once she caught Antonio staring at her, the fear so naked in his eyes that tears welled around the corners of his eyeballs. She could have asked for his help then, but the fear she saw was directed inward. It appeared to her that Antonio was afraid for himself, not for her. She saw in his eyes his fear of his own power to cause the death of his wives, and so she steeled herself against asking for his help. But when one night the red spots came dancing before her eyes in the middle of the darkness as she lay in the bed, she reached for him and begged him, forgetting her pride, her courage, her obstinacy. She begged him to fetch Emilia.

Antonio could not refuse her, though he had little faith that Emilia could help. By then his fear had brought him close to the edge of desperation. He was convinced that Marina was going to die like the rest of his wives, that he was cursed indeed. But outside the thick black clouds began to shoot bolts of lightning down to the earth, and the horses, afraid of the electric sky, refused to budge for him. Furiously he beat them but when at last they moved, their legs sank powerlessly into the mud of the rain-softened dirt street.

The next day Marina's screams made the thunder seem quiet, and Virginia began to feel as her son had felt. Afraid that Marina would die, she sent for the midwife, whose house like theirs stood upon pillars.

The English would not call Miss Victoria a midwife, though she admired and loved them enough to take their queen's name when her mother had given her the African name of Nefertiti. But to the people of Moruga she alone could deliver babies. If she was busy or at the market, they would wait for her, holding their babies in their bellies until she could come. No one remembered anyone who ever delivered any babies in Moruga except Miss Victoria.

When Marina saw the midwife's large body framed in the bedroom door, she sprang from her bed with the swiftness of someone who carried no weight and locked her swollen arms around the woman's neck. Hoarsely she whispered in her ear, her eyes darting darkly from Antonio to Virginia. "He's cursed. They're cursed. Take me away, Miss Victoria. Take me away from here."

Miss Victoria clasped the trembling Marina to her bosom. "Shh. Shh, dou dou." She rocked her.

Antonio reached for Marina's arm to guide her back to the bed, but the moment his fingers brushed her skin, Marina screamed with such terror that she sent him reeling backward into his mother's arms. "Get him out of here!" she shouted. "Get him out of the room!"

Virginia, who all this time had been standing quietly near Marina's bed, grasped her son's arm. "I'll keep him outside," she said to Miss Victoria. And she took Antonio out of the room.

After they left, Miss Victoria led Marina back to the bed, and gently pushing back the damp curls that were stuck to her forehead, waited until her breathing grew quiet and even. Then quietly she said, "You musn't fret yourself so. It not good for the baby."

Marina brushed Miss Victoria's hand away from her forehead and moaned, "Send for my mother. Ask my mother to come."

"Is not time yet."

"I need her now."

"You treat your mother bad, Marina."

"I need her. I'm dying."

Miss Victoria clicked her tongue and began once more to push back the curls off Marina's forehead. Slowly she said, "Obeah not to play wid, dou dou."

Marina ignored her. "I'm sick. Send for her," she repeated.

"You can't make obeah your playing and den trow it 'way, dou dou."

Marina groaned. "I'm going to die."

"No. Is not your time to die, dou dou. You en't go die. You have a lot of living to do yet."

"My mother—send for her."

"You did wrong, Marina."

"I'll tell her I'm sorry."

"Not dat. Tink I don't know? Tink people don't talk?"

"The pain. Miss Victoria, the pain—"

"Dat white man tell he son and he son tell all the women."

So what? Marina thought vaguely. So what? The old man told his son that I paid the taxes on the land. "So what?" she mumbled aloud to Miss Victoria.

"Is how you do it. Tink we don't know? Tink you hide from us?"

Marina's eyes widened. They could not—no one saw her—

"You put obeah in your husband cocoa."

"No!"

"Don't lie to me now, Marina."

"I'm sick. Can't you see how sick I am?" She was frightened now. How much could they see? How much power did they have?

"You not too sick to hear me out. You listen to me good if you want to live and see that baby you bearing. Obeah is holy. We a spiritual people, dou dou. We a loving set ah people, dou dou. Obeah punish we enemies, it bring us happiness. We don't use obeah for we selfish self. You use obeah to get land. Tink we don't know dat? Why you tink you suffering so, dou dou? You had a right, you had a right, dou dou, to use obeah to punish de Balboa. His father curse him and you. But you didn't use obeah for dat, dou dou. No, you use obeah for youself, you selfish self."

"No!"

"You can't hide from us. Obeah here long before you born and before we born. It tell us everything."

Marina felt the walls of her chest pressing in on her lungs.

She flung her arms in the air, fighting to catch her breath. "I'm dying. I'm dying," she gasped.

"You die only if you want to. Is your choosing. You the one who choose if you live or die. You the one." Miss Victoria placed her hand on Marina's swollen belly. "You the one." Her voice became infinitely gentle. "Shh! Stay calm. Stay calm."

Marina felt her muscles turn liquid.

"Shh! Shh! Good. Good. You breathe deep. In, out. Shh! Dat's it. You breathe good. Your mother make you strong."

"I'm dying."

"No. You strong, Marina, but not even all your strength can help you now if you don't believe in the spirit. Dat's how your mother make you. She believe in the spirit. You believe too, chile."

"In the spirit?"

"In the goodness of God and the power he work through obeah."

"And my mother?"

"Shh! You believe. She come soon to help you. Shh! Shh!"

Later Miss Victoria found Virginia in the kitchen placing a pot of water on the kerosene stove. Her heart softened when she saw her, sweat dripping down the sides of her face, her muscles straining to lift the pot. It was not her fault that her husband was cursed. She was not responsible for Marina's illness. Miss Victoria touched her shoulders. "Is no need, Miss de Balboa," she said. "Is not her time now. She had bellyache, but is not the baby."

Virginia put down the pot. Her eyes gazed sadly over the rings of flesh that now grew darker beneath them.

"Don't worry," said Miss Victoria. "I'll give you something to make her pee so she lose some of the swelling. There's nothing more we can do."

"Nothing?"

"Her water didn't break yet. Three days, maybe a week more." Miss Victoria's voice was soft, reassuring.

"But she's in pain. She has headaches."

"It'll pass. The headaches will go when she lose some water. Give her some orange-peel tea. Good for the belly-ache."

"Miss Victoria—" Virginia pleaded.

"You don't need me here now, Miss de Balboa. In truth."

"Will you come back?"

The midwife shook her head and walked toward the door. "You get her mother or Alma." She opened the door.

"Please stay." Virginia grasped her arm.

"No. I can't do nothing here," Miss Victoria said firmly and removed Virginia's hand from her arm.

"Please—"

Miss Victoria felt sorry for Virginia. She was a woman too.

"In about a week," she said, "maybe less, you get Alma or Emilia. It'll be her time then."

Virginia returned to the drawing room after Miss Victoria left. She felt helpless, useless. She saw Antonio sitting huddled on the stuffed Morris chair, brooding as she had many times seen her Portuguese husband do on his bed in their room, and she walked softly by him, brushed the back of her palm briefly against his cheek and then lowered her body into the chair opposite to him. She sat still for a few minutes, bending over, her elbows on her knees, her chin cupped into her hands, looking at her son silently and listening to Marina's groans and the roar of the thunder.

"Why, Mother? Tell me why? You must know." Antonio broke the silence, not looking at her.

"What do I know, Son?"

"Why do they all die?"

"She won't die, Antonio," Virginia said firmly.

"Oh, she will. Like all the rest."

"Perhaps if—" Virginia heard herself say. And Antonio, reaching desperately for the possibility of an answer, seized on the "if."

"If, what?" he asked.

"Oh, nothing." Virginia sat back and forced away the thought that crossed her mind. Perhaps if she sent for Alma or Emilia? Perhaps they could help Marina? No, she would not let herself think that way.

"Mother, please tell me. Do you know something? Are we cursed like they say?"

"Perhaps, your father." It was not the thought that came to her seconds before, but it was what she had wanted to say for a long time.

"Father?"

"You didn't know him, Antonio. Not as I did."

"I knew him."

"For one year."

"It was enough."

"Not enough to know him. Not as I did."

Antonio dared not look at her. "Does he have something to do with Marina?" he asked cautiously.

"The sins of the father, they say, are visited on the son."

Antonio's heartbeat quickened. "What are you talking about, Mother?"

"Your father. Didn't you wonder why he stayed away from people? Why he was so strange?" Virginia leaned toward her son.

"I—I—he could barely speak English," Antonio said at last.

"Is that reason enough for a man to abandon his wife and child?"

"Mother, I—"

"No, you didn't know. You couldn't know. We were like two strangers, your father and I. Sleeping in the same room, but in different beds. There was a time once. But then never again." Virginia rocked her body forward, backward. "He married me. He didn't have to, but he did. He planned just to give me a name. Save me from the warden and give me the land we now have. He thought that he was too good a man, too holy a man to desire a woman."

"Too holy?" Antonio tried to steady his voice.

"Then he touched me and he wanted me. On our wedding night it was me he wanted. No God. No Church. Me. And not because he wanted to help me, but because there was nothing on earth, nothing in the world he wanted more than my body. He would sell his soul for it. And he sold his soul."

"No. No, you're wrong."

"Wrong? I told you you did not know him. He was a priest, Antonio, a Jesuit priest!"

"No! He was just a Catholic! Like the others who came with him. He was running away—"

"What?"

"The Bishop of Lisbon—the bishop, he said, forbade him to read—forbade him—" Antonio's voice lingered over his last two words. Forbade *him*? That's what his father had said to him that day on the beach when he had found the clipping in his book. Forbade him, not them. Not forbade them.

"He was a priest," Virginia repeated. "Do you remember when he got sick? He told me then."

"I was with him."

"Not when he died. You weren't there when he died. He talked then."

"He was delirious. Malaria made him delirious."

"Hear me out, Antonio. He was delirious, but he said

things that make me wonder if the people in the village know the truth better than we can ever know."

"What truth?"

"He cursed you, Antonio. First he said that God had given him malaria because he had stopped you from going to church."

"I wanted to stop."

"Then he started to talk about his homeland. He told me that I had to call him Father de Balboa. 'I am a Jesuit priest,' he said. 'A man of God, and you are the serpent sent to destroy me.' For hours he talked about his days as a priest. He blamed me for making him desire flesh, he said. He said that God was punishing him for desiring flesh. My flesh. It was painful, Antonio. Humiliating."

Antonio bowed his head and looked at his hands.

His mother continued, knowing that he heard every word she said. "He screamed and cried for hours, and when he finally died, his last words were, 'The sins of the father will be visited on the sons. I give my sins to my son.' He gave his sins to you. Do you hear me, Antonio? That's what he said. I looked after you, took care of you. But then those women— your wives. At first I told myself that there was nothing unnatural about their deaths. Young women die in childbirth. But perhaps this time, Antonio, this time it is not the woman. It is you."

"He said once a Catholic, always a Catholic."

"What?"

"I asked him to teach me how to stop being a Catholic. He said he would try, but it would be hard. He never stopped being a Catholic."

Virginia nodded her head. "Until the day he died."

Everything fell in place for Antonio. His father's brooding. His contradictory statements about God, religion and priests. His mother's loneliness. No, it was not only that tortured African swinging on the mast of the *William* that had destroyed his father's soul, his sin of complicity with other Portuguese. No, he had done much worse. He had made others pay for his sins. The hypocrite!

"I had done nothing to him, but he made me suffer because he desired me. A priest! A priest desired me!" Virginia's words echoed his thoughts.

Antonio could not look at his mother. He wished he could say aloud to her the words that flooded his mind. He wished he could tell her, yes, his father was a he-goat, a ram-goat, a hypocritical, self-righteous ram-goat, but he could not. Was it because he too understood how the flesh, the human condition, could so mercilessly remind a man that he is a man, not a god who can control his passion, whose spirit was not imprisoned in clay? Was it that he understood that his father was a man, although a priest? Antonio's long weeks of abstinence, self-denial, his refusal to make love to Marina had taught him that the body could betray the mind and desire what the mind had decided it would not choose. Yet his father had also lied to him. Lied? No, he had not denied being a priest. Was it then a sin of omission? And was his last sin a sin of commission? He had cursed his son. He had willed him his sins. That was his inheritance. And for that, would Marina die? No. Antonio's face became rigid. He reached for his mother's hand.

"No," he said to her. "He won't have power over us. No more. Marina will not die. Not like Sara."

Virginia pressed his hand.

"I'll go to Port-of-Spain," he said. "I'll get the government doctor. We have time."

Marina's groans cut across the room and Antonio tightened his lips. "No," he repeated. "We have time. Miss Vic-

282 WHEN ROCKS DANCE

toria said that the baby is not due for a week. We'll beat him."

"The doctor won't come," Virginia said dismally.

"He must."

"Not in a hurricane, not to deliver our babies."

"He must."

"But if—"

"If what?"

"If, Father—Mr. Smith—asks him . . . I'll make Mr. Smith ask him."

"Mother!"

"He owes me. Get me a pen and some paper, Antonio."

"Mother, you don't have to beg—"

"No!"

"You have not said a word to Harold Smith for years."

"Give me the pen, Antonio."

Antonio did not move. Virginia got up and walked to the desk. She picked up a pen and scribbled a note on a piece of paper, folded it, put it in an envelope and then sealed it and returned to where Antonio sat.

"Give this to my father," she said, her tongue lingering on her last two words. She put her finger on Antonio's lips. "No questions."

19

If Antonio was curious about the contents of the note that he held, close to his chest, protected from the rain under his shirt and rubber cape, he did not appear so. Perhaps it was because his mind was obsessed by a consuming determination to save Marina. Perhaps it was because he was seized by an indomitable will to break his father—even in the grave. To punish him for lying to his son, for never letting him know who he was. "I am the son of a hypocrite! The seed of a priest! The son of God's bridegroom!" he shouted to the wind as he stomped through the mud and driving rain toward Harold Smith's house. "Liar! Woman hater! Curse bearer! You won't have her! You won't get Marina!" Then no sooner would he end this litany than he would remember his father's story of the horrors on the ship that brought him from Portugal to Trinidad and his mood would change abruptly and he would cry out instead, "My poor father! My poor, poor father! They wronged you. The Church wronged you!" After a while he would begin all over again, repeating his determination to save Marina, accusing his father and then pitying him. By the time he arrived at the top of the hill where Harold Smith lived, a single, solitary thought remained: He would save Marina in spite of his father.

Harold Smith had grown older in the weeks since his son had forced him to remember Virginia. His loose, white skin, already wrinkled and withered by eighty-four years of uselessness, now sank in toward his bones. If Marina could see him now she would not call him an old, wrinkled sack of bleached flour. There was no looseness about him now. No softness, no clamminess. He was bone. White, hard, jagged. A skeleton held together by crumpled parchment paper.

It was Ali who opened the door for Antonio and announced him to his master. At first the old man whined irritably, "Antonio? Antonio, who? Send him away, Ali—that's a good boy. Send him away." But when Ali whispered to him who Antonio was, Smith struggled from the chair and, pushing away Ali's solicitous hand, he shuffled toward Antonio shaking his cane, his blue-veined neck swelling red with anger. "Go away, de Balboa. Go away! I have done enough. Go away!"

The skeletal frame startled Antonio. In the dry season he had not seemed so old. In his mind's eye Antonio saw him as he had been, a Pontius Pilate washing his hands, a white old man who had witnessed Antonio's humiliation, then his defeat by a cunning woman who now lay dying on his bed. He braced himself for Smith's attack.

"No sah! No sah! Stop sah! Sit down, sah! Your heart, sah!" Ali held Smith away from Antonio.

"I've done enough for the de Balboas. Enough!" Smith broke away from Ali and began to strike Antonio with his balled fists, Ali behind him pleading with him to stop. "Go! Go! I've done enough." Then as though the energy that had brought him alive was suddenly sucked out of him, he crumpled in a heap in Ali's withered arms.

"Take him to his chair, Ali," said Antonio dryly. "I won't stay. I have a letter for him from my mother."

Ali lifted Smith into his armchair and Smith collapsed into it, his face ashy. It took him a full minute to unfold his body but finally he gurgled, "Letter? Letter? A letter from your mother?"

Antonio reached under his shirt, pulled out the letter and pushed it in Smith's hand. The old man made him uneasy. He wanted to finish his business now. Done enough for the de Balboas? What had he done, foolish old man? But for no good reason, the question worried Antonio.

Smith had let the letter fall from his hand. Now he leaned back in his chair and pouted. "What does it say? I don't want to read it."

More nervous than angry, Antonio picked up the letter and waved it in his face. "Read it, old man! Read it! It says that you must get the doctor to come here to save my wife. Read it!"

"I don't want to read it," Smith repeated and set his lips in a thin line that disappeared between the bones of his jaw.

"Read it!" Antonio shouted, grabbing Smith by the shoulders.

Ali darted behind his master and wrapped his arms around his chest pinning him down to the chair. The pitiful scene of this wiry, brown-skinned East Indian, his face leathered by age, as old as the white man, his master whom he was defending, momentarily shamed Antonio. He dropped his arms and backed away.

Smith was quick to take advantage of Antonio's weakness. "*You* read it," he taunted. "*You* read it."

Antonio's fingers clutched the letter to tear it apart, but his hands grew cold and his fingers remained still, frozen on the unopened envelope. He could not read the letter. He could not. He did not want to. He did not want to know what his mother had written. He would not allow himself to want to know. This irrationality bred of his long loyalty to his mother and love for her drove him to such anger that the old man, seeing the fire in his eyes, became afraid. Before Antonio could move or speak, he pushed Ali forward to fetch the letter for him.

Ali took the letter out of the envelope and gave it to Smith. Then he reached for the round magnifying glass that lay on the small table next to the chair. While Smith held the open letter, Ali moved the magnifying glass over Virginia's handwriting, pacing himself to the speed of Smith's reading. When Smith was done, Ali knew, and without being asked, he replaced the magnifying glass on the table.

Antonio waited. At first Smith made no sound. He sat there staring at something in front of him. And then a mournful rattle began to rise within him as though his bones knocked and clanged against each other in his empty frame. The ever-attentive Ali rushed to him, and in a futile attempt to help, grabbed his hands. Smith seemed to feel Ali's concern. His eyes moved feebly over to him, his lips twitched and then with a desperate effort to clutch on to life, he pushed his servant's hands from his and his head fell against the arm of the chair, throwing his mouth open in a wide, empty gape.

Philip entered the room at that moment. It seemed almost

by design. It was as if he had stood there nearby, perhaps behind the door. As if he had stood there for years, waiting. And when the final gurgle came from his father's throat, it was as if at long last, his silent vigil ended. Without a word, Philip closed the old man's eyes and took the letter from his rigid hands.

Antonio watched in silence as Philip read his mother's words. No emotion came from that man, no tears for his father, no grief. Antonio propped Harold Smith in his chair and was folding his dangling arms out of respect for the dead, when a wild laughter stopped him. He spun around and saw Philip, his head thrown back against the wall, laughing. "So you did it, old man," Philip said shaking the letter at his father. Then he turned to Antonio. "Come. Follow me."

On his knees, Ali began his dirge for the dead, tearing at his hair. Philip knocked him over as he passed by on the way to his room.

"Come, Antonio. I'll give you the letter you want. I have a friend, a Dr. Glentower. He'll do it for you." Philip crumpled the letter in a ball and tossed it on the ground. Antonio picked it up and read it.

When Philip gave him the letter for Dr. Glentower, Antonio wondered briefly why he would want to help him, but that thought was insignificant beside the one that now tortured his soul. Harold Smith had deserved his death. The letter was proof enough. He had deserved his son's cold dismissal of him. Looking at the dead man twisted on the chair, Antonio regretted that Ali still mourned for him.

The problem was to get to Port-of-Spain and back before Marina worsened. The rains flooded all the roads, and the hurricane with its high winds was threatening to come. For miles around there was not a person to be seen. Everyone who remained in Moruga had shut himself in his house and nailed down his doors and windows. The animals sensed the coming winds. The horses that Philip Smith had given to Antonio refused to be tied to the buggy, and when the broken streaks of silver lightning whipped across the sky, they reared up their forelegs and neighed as though their lungs would explode.

Philip was anxious for Antonio to reach the doctor, so he gave him his own racing horse. But no sooner did the horse descend the hill from Smith's house and gallop a few feet on the Moruga road than it turned around and raced back to its stall. Nothing could persuade the horse to go farther. Antonio was left with one option—to go by sea.

Philip Smith warned him that no fisherman would take out his boat in a hurricane. It was his duty to warn him, but he was glad when Antonio remained resolute. He would borrow a boat, Antonio told him between clenched teeth— steal one if he must, and go alone if he must. He would deliver the letter and bring the doctor back with him to save Marina's life. Philip smiled once Antonio was gone.

The winds now began to blow off the sea toward the land, and huge green palm leaves and ripe coconuts that had become slightly unhinged from the tops of the trees when the rain first started, whizzed through the air like flying cannonballs. Antonio did not fear them. He ran through the coconut grove to the sea, ducking and darting, narrowly escaping their paths. Nothing would stop him now, not the terrifying sound of the thunder roaring above him or the sudden crashes of tree trunks smashing to the ground. Not even the possibility that Dr. Glentower might refuse to return with him in a pirogue through the hurricane. He ran steadily on and on toward the sea. It was not until he was in sight of the edge of the coconut grove, where normally the sandy beach would begin, that he began to fear that his voyage was hopeless. The huge waves that had begun to swell in the early morning from far out in the ocean now moved inward toward the land and crashed into the coconut trees, throwing jets of water into the air, spraying white foam into the black sky. The beach had disappeared beneath the frothy, swirling currents, and there was no trace of sand anywhere. Whichever boats had been docked there were destroyed. In front of him Antonio could see the wind tossing and churning the surface waters at a terrifying speed. Broken trees, branches, and coconuts and pieces of boats were dragged out by the currents and then thrown back against the land. Behind him the wind bayed dismally through the trees, pushing the tall, slim trunked coconut trees with such force that they bent forward, almost doubling to the ground. For the first time since he had left Harold Smith's house Antonio stopped running. The despair that washed over him was so intense that he slumped down to the soggy ground, his head on his chest, his legs sunk into the matted debris around him.

That was where the Warao saw him when he came to find him. "Come! We go now, my friend's son." Those were the only words that the Warao said. And Antonio grabbed on to his extended arm like a drowning man clutching a rope thrown out to him.

On a calm day the waters from Moruga to Port-of-Spain could be treacherous. Just before a hurricane only a madman would journey along that route. But the Warao was an old sea warrior and he had conquered many seas before. He had come prepared for this battle. He would help his friend's son. He had heard of Marina's suffering.

The night before, he had knelt by the fire in the cave where he had hidden his pirogue and prayed to his gods and his dead fathers that they would protect him from the hurricane. After he had prayed, he had taken the ashes from his burnt offerings and smeared them around his eyes. In the corners where his eyelids met, he had made large white circles that made him look like the most fearsome of warlords. Across his cheeks he had painted his war signs in red, white, black and purple. He had stuck red feathers on the wings of the condor on his chest and blackened his torso. He had made anklets for his legs from the dried skin of dead warring sharks and had decorated them with beads and white feathers. He had put the same beads and feathers on the loincloth that covered his genitalia and on the headband that crossed his forehead. He was a young warrior again when he approached Antonio.

Out on the sea, the Warao stood at the helm of his pirogue, navigating the boat through the rough waters while Antonio rowed, his eyes fastened to Icacos Point where Calypso danced. There, the Warao knew his battle would begin. There, he knew that if he could turn the bend around the tip of Trinidad, he could head his boat safely northward through the Gulf of Paria to Port-of-Spain. Nothing seemed to daunt him. Not the darkening waters, not the mountainous waves, not the wind-whipped rain, not the blackening clouds. He guided the boat forward standing at the helm, the condor spread out on his chest, his warrior legs firmly planted apart. He was ready to meet Calypso. And when he sighted the rocks that protruded menacingly from the southwest, he knew that Calypso was close.

The waves began to swell higher and higher then, and the

pirogue mounted them, propelled by the incredible force of the currents. Antonio, who, without question, had done as the Warao had commanded, could no longer row the boat. It did not need him. Each wave carried the pirogue forward on its swell to the rock, dashing it down with powerful force against the surface of the sea as the wave crashed down from its peak, and a new wave, higher than the last one, picked up the pirogue again and pulled it forward. As if on command, the dark clouds spread out in the sky began to move into each other with terrifying speed toward Icacos. Out of their centers they whipped dazzling bolts of lightning into the rocks, and the thunder roared against them.

For the first time since the Warao came to save him, Antonio felt fear. He had followed him then because there was nothing else he could do. The Warao was his hope. When he'd appeared to Antonio, as if out of nothingness from among the coconut trees, he was a savior, a superhuman creature, a beacon come to lead the way. Antonio had tracked behind him then, climbing over boulders that separated one end of the bay from the other and had gone with him to his cave to get the pirogue.

On the sea, the Warao became someone Antonio had not known before, and Antonio wished that he had not gone with him. The rain poured harder now, the rain that had fallen before being merely a herald for the hurricane, a precursor, a warning of the tremendous power of the blackening clouds. Frantically, Antonio tried to bail out the water that flooded the bottom of the pirogue, but still the Warao remained where he was, standing at the helm.

As they approached the rocks off Icacos Point, the thunder circled them, grumbling in a low ominous pitch, and the clouds descended upon them enclosing the boat, the sky, the sea and the air in pitch-black darkness. Suddenly, without warning, the Warao began his war dance to his dead fathers. He threw his head back, lifted his face into the rain and danced. He spread his arms out wide in front of him and hopped, first on one foot and then the other. Dancing this way, he began to howl, a long piercing howl that tore against the roar of the wind: "Ah Wooha! Ah Wooha! Ah Wooha!"

Calypso heard him and she circled the pirogue.

"Ah Wooha! Ah Wooha! Ah Wooha!"

Calypso raised her nappy curls.

"Ah Wooha! Ah Wooha!" the Warao called.

Calypso dipped her head down to the ocean floor and then reared up abruptly, crashing into the front of the pirogue.

"Ah Wooha!" called the Warao again, reminding Calypso of his dead fathers, the sacking of his villages by the conquistadors.

Calypso churned the waters with her nappy curls and pelted the sea into the pirogue. Antonio curled up into a ball, his legs clasped in his arms, and he trembled.

The Warao grew still. He bowed his head. He knew what he had to do. He had navigated the Englishman's trading vessels through these waters. He himself, for twelve years, had taught the Englishman the secrets of Icacos Point, the position of every rock, every reef. Calypso had not forgotten. Now he began to beg for her forgiveness; he sang a dirge of remorse and Calypso heard him. She ducked beneath his pirogue, circled it twice and then she lay still. Frightened, the Warao opened his mouth to plead with her again, but she stopped him with her pans. "Ping-Pang Ping-Pang Pinkety-Ping-Pang." The Warao knew that he was forgiven. He spoke gently to her now in a language that Antonio could not understand. He sang again of his dead fathers and the plundering of his people, and Calypso listened. She played her steel-band pans to him and then she took his pirogue on her back and swam toward the rocks. The winds suddenly grew quiet; the waves became calm again; the rain ceased.

Calypso took her Warao on her back. All day and into the night she reared up and down, in and out between the rocks, and then, as the sun slid out between the edge of the sea and the sky, she left him there on the open sea, on the calm waters of the Gulf of Paria.

20

Emilia Heathrow had not abandoned her daughter. Indeed, she had enough reason to do so. But Emilia was not one to give up. She would not let the de Balboas win. They would not take the one child who had consumed all the babies she had not stopped loving. It was not pride that had kept her away from Marina. The girl could no longer hurt her. But her babies? She would do anything for her babies, her dead twin sons. They had not died for Marina for nothing.

It was Alma who told her to bide her time—to stay away from the de Balboas, to strengthen herself, to fortify herself until the hurricanes came. Then, just as the first torrent began to sweep through the southern coast of Trinidad, she must go quickly to her daughter's bedside and do exactly what Alma said.

Emilia took no chances. She did not have much money, but what she had, she gave to the parish priest in Princes Town to say a novena for Marina—nine days of masses in Marina's name. Now she would have both the Church and obeah on her side.

It was easier than Antonio thought it would be to persuade Dr. Glentower to return with him and a savage (as the doctor called the Warao) in a pirogue through perilous seas to a colored woman's house to deliver a colored baby. For one thing, the hurricane off the southern coast of Trinidad had not shown itself in the north. There were rains as there must be in August, but not the wind, lightning and thunder that warned that the eye of the storm was yet to pass. For another, Glentower had good reason for wanting to go to Moruga to deliver Marina's baby.

By this time the doctor had heard about the oil that was devastating the cocoa estates in the south of Trinidad, but he had also heard that the Americans were drilling the land for more of the oil. Fortunately for Glentower, he had inherited his father's peculiar attitude toward Americans. Though, like him, he thought of Americans as inferior, the mongrels of England or Europe, he nevertheless believed that they had an uncanny sense of knowing how to make money—"sniffing out wealth," as his father had put it. When Philip Smith wrote to him saying he owned such land that he wished to sell, Glentower saw his opportunity. The doctor, as sharp as ever, sensed desperation the moment Smith, not waiting for a written reply, came to see him in Port-of-Spain, and Glentower knew that he could bargain with him. He convinced Smith that it would take years, many pounds sterling to drain the oil from his land before he could farm it again with cocoa. Smith believed him, but to Glentower's surprise, he refused an offer of twenty pounds. He needed one hundred pounds to take him back to England, Smith said. Nest and Lee Lai had offered him fifty. Glentower realized that he had overestimated Smith's desperation, and a week later he wrote to him agreeing to meet his price, but Smith did not answer. Then one day the doctor received a strange letter from Smith saying that there were complications with the land, involving a colored family, the de Balboas, and promising that Glentower would hear from him again as soon as he had straightened out things. Now, when his servant announced that there was one Mr. de Balboa to see him with a letter from Philip Smith, Glentower was relieved. He hoped that at long last his answer had come.

"Well, come in. Come in, my good man," the doctor greeted Antonio, his voice warm and expansive with anticipation of his changing luck. "Come in. I hear you have news for me from Philip Smith. Come in." Then Glentower saw the Warao in his war paint. "Not the savage! Send the savage to the back!" he shouted, his face contorted in rage.

"He stays with me," said Antonio firmly. His wet clothes were soggy and stuck against his skin. He was still shaken from his sea voyage.

"Blimey! He smells!" Glentower held his nose and waved his arm in the direction of the back of his house. "Send him to the back," he repeated, ignoring Antonio.

"No!" Antonio stood closer to the Warao. Both men looked exhausted. Spent. Antonio had traveled too far to be subservient.

"Give me the letter from Smith," Glentower said angrily and then regretted his anger: The man had something he wanted. "I mean, come in. Leave the savage in the back."

"Not if the Warao chief cannot come in." Antonio's voice was soft, but firm.

"I'll call the sergeant . . ." Glentower threatened.

The Warao touched Antonio's arm. "No, my friend's son," he said, "I'll go."

Antonio turned to the Warao, confused. He wanted to finish his business with Glentower. He needed Glentower, yet it was the Warao who had brought him there. He wouldn't have the Englishman insult him.

"No," the Warao repeated, and he pushed Antonio ahead. "There'll be another time. For now, I will go."

Antonio felt uneasy, but he did not stop the Warao when he turned and walked toward the sprawling saman tree that stood in front of Glentower's colonial-style home.

"No! Not there. In the back!" Glentower shouted, flailing his short arms.

The Warao continued to walk across the front lawn, his war feathers damp against his skin, his war paint smeared from his battle with the sea. He didn't stop until he came to the ancient tree. Then he sat down under it, crossed his legs and folded his arms across his chest.

Glentower fumed and cursed under his breath. "I say, not there. In the back! Tell him go to the back, de Balboa."

The Warao did not move and Antonio remained silent.

Finally, clearing his throat, Glentower said gruffly, "Stubborn fool! Savages! We'll rid our island of them yet. Bloody savages! Well, come in, de Balboa."

Antonio kept looking at the Warao.

"Come in, I say. Don't just stand there. God, you look a sight! You stink of fish too. Ha-ha!" He laughed good-naturedly.

Antonio turned away from the Warao. His face showed no emotion. He had come to save Marina. Or was it himself?

Had he come to remove the curse his father had placed on him? He clenched his fists and dug his fingernails deep into the palms of his hands. Both purposes were the same. To save Marina was to save himself. They were the same. "I'll wait here," he said.

Glentower shrugged his shoulders and walked toward his front door, calling his wife. "Mildred! I say, Mildred, are you there?" He paused and turned to Antonio. "Wait a minute, old man. I'll be back."

Behind the lace curtain that shaded the glass front door, Antonio could see flashes of a bright yellow dress, of some-one pacing the floor inside. Before Glentower entered the room the dress paused, and a pale white hand shifted the curtain. Antonio saw cold, steel-gray eyes look scornfully over his tattered, wet clothes before the hand dropped the curtain, and before Glentower opened the door and shut it again behind him. From where he stood on the verandah, Antonio heard their heated whispers.

"Not in my home!" Mrs. Glentower hissed, "Not in my home. I won't be the laughingstock of the town."

"Mildred—Mildred," Dr. Glentower cooed.

"In the kitchen. Let him go to the back. To the servant's entrance."

"Shh—Mildred. He'll hear. He's a schoolteacher, not a laborer."

"I don't care." Mrs. Glentower stamped her foot. Antonio saw the yellow dress, saw the hand shift back the curtain again and the same cold gray eyes peer at him. Glentower tugged her away from the door. He was a carbuncular man, a solid square mass from neck to hips, a boxy man. The arms and legs that grew out from the sides of his torso were surprisingly short and thin. Ugly, Antonio thought disdain-fully. He could hear Mrs. Glentower's muffled squeals of protest as her husband apparently pulled her toward him. Then Antonio clearly heard Glentower mention Philip Smith's name. There were some more squeals from Mrs. Glentower and then silence. Whatever the doctor told his wife, worked, and she retreated quietly from the room.

Glentower returned to the verandah, his face flushed red, his shirt disheveled. He offered no apologies to Antonio, but he certainly seemed more restrained than he was before, more subdued.

It had begun to drizzle lightly, and way out in the distance to the south a few dark clouds were visible to the eye. "Looks like rain," said Glentower to Antonio. "Come in."

"No, thank you," Antonio replied. "I'll stay out here with the Warao."

Dr. Glentower opened his mouth to say something about the drizzle which was becoming more intense, but changed his mind when he saw Antonio's resoluteness and the Warao's eyes fastened firmly on him.

"Let's have it, then. The letter," he said.

Antonio reached inside the oilskin bag that the Warao had given to him before they left Moruga and handed Dr. Glentower an unopened, crumpled but dry, envelope.

Glentower almost snatched it from his hands. With the drizzle now soaking his hair and clothes, Glentower opened the letter and read.

Moruga
August 15, 1902

Dear Glentower,

A touch of good luck. Sorry I took so long. Complications. Seems my father gave away our land in Taba-quite to a Portuguese named de Balboa. That's his

son in front of you. Antonio de Balboa. Don't be
shocked, old man. His mother is as black as coals. But
the old man, my father, had a deep affection for her.
You know what I mean? The old bloke's dead now, no
fear. Anyhow it was all legal and the land belongs to
de Balboa. But now he's in trouble. He needs a doctor
and so I thought of you. Nice of me, isn't it? But for
a percentage, if you will. Two hundred pounds. De
Balboa has fifteen acres of the land you want. Five
acres belong strictly to his wife, but we can work it out.
You scratch my back and I'll scratch yours. De Balboa
will do anything for you to get his wife well again. But
you won't forget who your broker is, will you?

> Very truly yours,
> Philip I. Smith

Glentower grimaced. Vulgar sot, he thought, and then
said aloud to Antonio: "Says here in this letter that I'm to do
you a favor, old boy. What!"

"Yes. My wife is close to labor. She's pregnant and it's near
her time, but the baby won't come."

"Yes, yes," said Glentower impatiently, the rainwater trick-
ling down his collar. "But not out here. Let's get out of the
rain."

Antonio turned toward the Warao.

"Okay, him too." Glentower was desperate.

Antonio called to the Warao but the Warao would not
budge.

"He doesn't want to come in, don't you see?" Glentower
said irritably.

Antonio did not want to betray the Warao. He knew that

the Warao, having been insulted, would never enter Glentower's house. Yet he had to save Marina's life, so he followed the doctor into his drawing room.

"Well now, there's a matter of payment." Glentower began as soon as he was sheltered from the drizzle. He sat down, not offering Antonio a chair. "Says in this letter, you have some land. Right old chap?"

"Yes. Some land in Tabaquite." So Philip Smith had had his own plans, Antonio thought. The doctor will pay him for this, no doubt. As Marina had said, some of these Englishmen loved land, no matter how useless. He should have known that he would have to give the doctor something.

"I understand that the land is quite useless." Glentower studied his fingers. "All the cocoa is dying."

"It's all I have," said Antonio.

"Then why should I come with you?"

Antonio looked out of the window toward the Warao, and Glentower followed his eyes.

"Well, I suppose it's our duty, old boy." Glentower continued.

"Duty?" Antonio kept looking at the Warao.

"Old England never let her natives down." Glentower tapped the torn envelope against his right hand, looked out of the window at the Warao sitting in the rain and mumbled, "All that paint will be washed off him soon . . ."

Antonio held his tongue.

"Tell you what, chappie. Smith here has asked me to do you a favor. Seems that your father and his were old friends. Or was it your mother and his father?" Glentower winked his small black eyes at Antonio, and the young man gritted his teeth.

"My mother lived with Mr. and Mrs. Smith when she was

a child," said Antonio dryly. "I believe Mr. Smith, Mr. Harold Smith, that is, gave the land that we have to my father as a wedding present."

"So they say. So they say," Glentower conceded.

"Ten acres. You can have it all if you come to Moruga and treat my wife."

"Wait a minute here, old chap," Dr. Glentower moved to the edge of his chair. "Smith here says you inherited fifteen acres."

"Five of it belongs to my wife."

"And to you too, I believe. It's all legal. Husband and wife and all that."

"My wife won't give it up."

"But if you agree—with the warden's help—don't be so bashful. They say all you people control your women."

Dammit, Antonio thought, Dammit. All their damn civility and they are common thieves. The scum of England. Her trash that she got rid of in her island colonies. Smith yes, but one would have thought better of Glentower. Doctor and all that. Damn them.

"What's the matter, old boy. Afraid of your wife?" Glentower taunted. He stood up and slapped Antonio on the back. His short legs appeared dwarfed by his massive frame. "Why, Mrs. Glentower couldn't tell *me* what to do."

"I'll give you the ten acres if you come with me." Antonio offered cautiously.

"And the other five?"

Marina flashed before Antonio. He saw her wildness the last night that they made love, he felt the strange compulsion he had had afterward to give her sole ownership of five acres of land, and he hesitated. Miss Victoria had said a week, seven days before Marina would deliver. Perhaps he could find another doctor, perhaps the minister at Grey-friar's Church would help him. The Portuguese were loyal to each other, at least the Presbyterians. The baby, after all, would be his father's grandchild.

Glentower saw him faltering. "You don't want her to die, do you?"

Antonio mopped the sweat that had begun to collect on his forehead. She had said maybe less than a week; he remembered the midwife's warning.

"The land belongs to you too," Glentower egged him on.

Antonio took a deep breath. "You can have all fifteen acres if you save her," he said finally.

"Good! Good!" Glentower slapped him on the back once more.

"But only if you save her and she lives and the baby lives." Antonio repeated.

"Good! Good!" said Glentower. "Now let's get this all legal. You'll put it in writing." It was both a question and a command.

"And in writing that you get the five acres however you can. If and only if you save Marina and the baby."

"Don't worry, old boy. I will. And as to the five acres, Smith will make it as though you never gave your wife anything."

Across the lawn the Warao stood up under the saman tree. He seemed to know that the deal had been consummated.

Glentower left his house without speaking to his wife, and the Warao led him and Antonio to the pirogue.

The crossing by sea to Moruga was easy. The first wave of the hurricane in the south had ended by the time they approached Icacos Point, and Calypso, knowing that the Warao would return, had waited for him, and she buoyed his pirogue on her back and led him through the rocks and swam with him to the Moruga shoreline.

By the next morning, the rains in Moruga had stopped completely, but the people knew that it was merely a respite from the hurricane. Outside the de Balboa house, near the half-drowned green bougainvillea bushes, three men sat on low stools, beating a mournful rhythm on goatskin drums lodged securely between their knees. They were filthy. Their feet and legs were caked with mud that had dried in spots and turned ashy-white against their black skins. They were naked to the waist, and each wore a dirty pair of faded, patched trousers rolled to his knees. Dirt and mud stuck to the long, curled tufts of their hair like sickly, coffee-brown frosting on a molasses cake. But the woman who stood next to them wailing languorously as though with each cry all her breath would leave her body, was spotless. That is, except for her feet which, like the men's, were plastered with mud. Her hair was covered with a freshly starched white handkerchief and she wore a clean white pinafore over a clean, long white dress. She had carefully hooked the hem of her skirts to her belted waist, but otherwise she seemed oblivious to the dirt and to the men. She just stood there wailing painfully, rhythmically, to the beat of their drums, a long repetitious chant.

Inside, in the master bedroom of the de Balboa house, Emilia Heathrow sat on the bed near her pregnant daughter. She had brought with her candles and herbs and vials of holy oils and odious liquids, but they lay on the floor next to her feet, untouched.

She was speaking softly to her daughter now, her hand making gentle smooth circles over Marina's swollen belly.

"You have to believe, Marina, in the spirit that guides our people. You cannot forget. It is my duty to make you remember. I lay sick like you once."

Marina, her eyes shut, groaned softly.

"Yes, even as you are now. And nobody could save me until I believed in the spirit. Believe Marina. For the life of your child, believe."

The baby turned in Marina's belly and stuck its feet against her right side. She reached to touch the spot where she felt it move, but Emilia had shifted her hand so that when the palm of Marina's hand approached her stomach, it fell instead on the back of Emilia's hand. In that instant the blood of three generations pulsated together in a single, unifying rhythm. Emilia's, still warm from the brilliant light of the African continent, the birthplace of her mother, Emilia's blood flowing against the life that she herself had borne, sending quivering vibrations through her daughter and on down to the unborn child. Marina let her hand rest quietly on her mother's while Emilia repeated to her the lesson the old Ibo had taught her, the chastisement he had given her for her rejection of the old ways, the faith of her ancestors.

"Remember the place where you came from, Marina. We were brought here to this island. Remember the spirits we prayed to. Believe in them, Marina."

Marina tried to speak but Emilia silenced her. "Feel," she said. "Feel. Don't question. Feel. Let our ancestors speak to you."

Marina squeezed her eyelids together harder and harder, tighter and tighter until tiny teardrops trickled through her eyelashes. She felt her energy begin to drain out of her, down the sides of her face, her neck, past her shoulders. It circled her heart and stopped, but she felt the pressure of her mother's hand on her womb, pressing down on her, and she released it. Now her body felt infinitely light. The energy flowed past her thighs, through her legs. Out. The pain, the once unbearable tenderness around her swollen joints, her fingers, her wrists, her ankles, the violent headaches were outside of her. She could see her body lying still on the bed. And she felt no pain. Emilia smiled at her, and Marina's energy returned momentarily, allowing her to part her lips. Her eyes opened. She spoke. "Yes, yes." She affirmed what she felt. "Yes, yes." But she did not understand.

And Emilia got up from the bed, picked up her candles, herbs, oils and liquids and began her work.

When he turned into the dirt track that led to his house, Antonio saw the drummers first. Then he saw the wailing woman. His heart froze. He was too late, he thought, to save Marina. Glentower edged closer behind him and tapped his shoulder.

"Is this the place?" he asked, trying to control his nervousness. He looked foolish in his khaki colonial uniform—khaki stiff, wide-brimmed hat, brown oxfords and tall khaki socks covered with mud, knobby knees gleaming under his wide Bermuda shorts.

Antonio nodded but kept his eyes on the drummers. "Yes, here." He turned and looked for the Warao, who had stayed behind Glentower during the trip from Port-of-Spain, but the Warao had disappeared softly into the bush. He approached the drummers and the woman began to wail more loudly. Alma! It was Alma who was there in his house. Who had let her in? His mother? Where was she?

"Who the hell are you? Who sent you here?"

The wailing woman came between him and the drummers. "Emilia," she said. "Emilia." She pointed toward the house.

Antonio felt Glentower's hand tap his shoulder again. The doctor's voice shook. "What's going on here, old boy?"

Antonio pushed him away. The doctor lurched toward one of the drummers and kicked away his drum from between his knees. The drummer bent down, picked up his drum and began to beat it again as though nothing had happened.

"Leave! Leave, I say!" Antonio shouted. "Get away from here!"

The drumming intensified. Emilia! Emilia had brought her obeah to his house. Anger and revulsion rushed to Antonio's head. He raced to the house, Glentower staying close beside him. On the front porch he saw his mother rocking listlessly on the cane rocking chair. She looked at him with dull eyes.

"They are all over the place. Emilia has them all over the place."

Glentower sucked in his breath, clutched his black leather doctor bag tightly to his chest and began to back away. Antonio shot him a quick warning glance.

"Is she dead?" he asked his mother.

"No. They are in there. Saving her."

Glentower cleared his throat. He could barely keep his hands from trembling. "Look, old boy. This is where I stop. This was not part of the bargain. No, old man." He started to turn away from the house.

From out of nowhere the Warao appeared and stood before the doctor. "Go!" the Warao growled, and pointed toward the door. The paint around his eyes made him fearsome.

Glentower hesitated.

"The land," Antonio threatened.

Glentower looked from Antonio to the Warao. His people had colonized these people he thought. From the east to the west of the hemisphere his tiny island had owned people like these, countries hundreds of times larger than this one. This Warao—a whole tribe of Waraos, Arawaks, and Caribs for that matter, had cowered beneath his people's awesome power. He bent down and pulled up his socks closer to his knees. When he straightened up, the arrogance he had awakened dispelled his fear. How could he be afraid of these people? How could he?

"Is she in there?" he asked, looking scornfully down his nose at Antonio. He didn't have to look far. It was a fleshy nose, short and stubby.

As sometimes the mind under pressure relieves itself by contemplating trivia, Antonio thought, for no apparent reason, how much better his own nose would have been suited to the doctor's white skin. He smiled at the folly of the idea, and Glentower, thinking that he was gloating over his triumph, said, "I don't have to do this, you know."

The Warao did not speak this time. He grabbed Glentower's arm and pulled him through the open front door.

When Antonio entered Marina's bedroom, he could barely see. Thick gray smoke dispensed from incense decanters in dark, round puffs had dispersed throughout the room, clouding his vision. Antonio had to blink several times and rub his eyes before he could distinguish the windows at the far end of the room. His eyes smarting from the smoke, he left his mother and Glentower at the doorway, rushed across the room and flung the windows open, letting in the damp air. The smoke did not clear so easily. It curled its way across the room, licking its tongue past Virginia and Glentower before it finally got thinner and a strange, sickly odor that the incense had masked became more intense. Antonio saw clearly what he had vaguely made out through the thick smoke: Two dozen or more lighted candles were placed on the floor around Marina's bed. Large brass incense decanters stood everywhere—on tables, chairs, the dresser top, the windowsills—belching puffs of smoke. Marina lay stretched out on the bed, her eyes closed, her body limp, pale and damp. Her mother sat by her with a basin full of herbs soaked in water that she had clearly been rubbing all over Marina's body.

Glentower spoke first, before Antonio could say a word. For while Antonio had seen Emilia, the candles, the decanters, Glentower's eyes had fastened themselves to one object in the room and only one—Marina.

"Is this an Englishwoman here?" he asked, scampering across the room on his thin legs. "Whatever is this? What's this Englishwoman doing here? You better explain quickly, de Balboa." He was at Marina's side, his fingers searching her wrist for a pulse before he had finished speaking.

Emilia reached over to the other side of the bed and grabbed his arm, digging her fingernails deep into his skin. Glentower drew back his freed hand as if to slap Emilia, but at that moment Marina turned on her side and caught his hand before it could descend on her mother. Her hold on Glentower was not a strong one. She could not prevent him from slapping Emilia, but her sudden spark of vitality startled him and indeed everyone in the room.

Antonio saw the fear in his wife's eyes and he wanted to reassure her, to tell her that he had brought Glentower to help her, but he thought of how little she trusted him. He spoke to Emilia instead. "He's a doctor. I brought him to help Marina."

"Doctor?" From the bed, Marina's voice came weakly, as if that effort to protect her mother had taken the last of her energy. She riveted her eyes on Antonio. "You brought a doctor here?"

"Yes." Antonio drew closer to her.

Emilia watched him warily.

"He came in this hurricane?"

"Yes, he did, Marina. He'll deliver your baby. You'll be fine. Don't worry. He'll take care of you." Antonio's words spilled out rapidly, but still he dared not touch Marina.

"How did you get him to come here?"

"Huh?"

"She asked, how did you get him to come here?" Emilia still kept her eyes on Antonio.

"The land? Did you give him the land?" Marina's head lay to one side of her pillow. "Did you give the land, Antonio?"

Antonio averted his head to avoid her eyes.

"What did you give him, Antonio?"

"Shh, Marina. He's here to help you. I brought him from Port-of-Spain."

"The pain." Marina grasped the sides of the bed. "The pain, the pain. My God!"

Emilia pushed past Antonio, shoving Glentower aside. Her back barring the men's view, she deftly reached into her blouse and pulled out a thin, short piece of bamboo, its center cleared of pulp and filled with a liquid. Quickly she bent over Marina, and before the men could see what she was doing, she put the bamboo to Marina's lips and emptied the liquid down her throat. Its effect was instantaneous. Marina's hands released the mattress and hung limply against her protruding belly. Her head fell against the pillow and her eyes drooped shut. Glentower became alarmed. He had not seen Emilia put the bamboo vial to Marina's lips, but the sudden change in Marina frightened him. By now he was convinced Marina was an Englishwoman seduced there, as he heard rumored before of other white women, by black blood and black magic. Obeah. He rushed to the other side of the bed. Swiftly he placed his finger beneath Marina's eyebrows. Gently, he raised her eyelids. There was no movement. Marina's eyes remained dull and lifeless, and when he removed his hand her eyelids fell limply over her eyes.

"She's asleep," said Emilia quietly. "You can leave now. We'll take care of her. Alma and I know what to do."

Blood rushed to Glentower's head. "Get out! How dare you bring an Englishwoman here? Smith didn't tell me this. Get out! You dog!" He turned to Antonio. "How did you get her to come here and lie with you?"

Virginia was the first to understand Glentower's mistake. "She's not an Englishwoman. There!" She pointed to Emilia. "That's her mother."

Glentower's face turned paper white. "Jesus! Jesus Christ! Jesus! Shit." How could he have been wrong? He stared at Marina. Yes, the nose, the high cheekbones. He should have noticed them. "Shit!" he repeated. "Shit, shit."

"Get out of here!" Emilia confronted him. "You get out of here. We don't need you."

"No. You'll stay!" Antonio stood before Glentower.

"She's my daughter."

"And my wife."

"I say you get him out of here." Emilia's body was tense. "No!"

"You don't know what you're playing with, Antonio."

"No, he stays, Mrs. Heathrow."

Emilia flung herself on Antonio, almost knocking him down. "You murderer! You evil son of a Portogee! You made my daughter like this. You! You!"

Glentower was prepared to go. His papers had been signed. He did not want to be involved. But Antonio pushed Emilia away and stood in front of him.

"Stay," he said firmly. "Stay. I will handle her."

Emilia reached for the back of Antonio's shoulders. He spun around and she began to strike him everywhere, anywhere where her balled fists could reach. On his chest, his arms, his shoulders. She was not a tall woman, an inch or two shorter than Antonio, but she was large. Not fat, but her heavy breasts and wide hips gave the illusion that she was stronger than she was. She seemed to dwarf Antonio, to be able to crush him if she wanted. But while she had weight on her side, Antonio had agility. He ducked her blows and got behind her. Swiftly he pulled her arms back and pinned them to her sides.

Glentower, who moments before had been prevented from leaving by Antonio, tried to escape during the scuffle but now Virginia blocked his way at the door. She didn't touch him. She didn't say a word. She just dared him with her eyes to leave, and Glentower wilted under her penetrating glare and flaring nostrils and followed her back to Marina's bed.

By this time Antonio had managed to pull the screaming Emilia close to the door. As he reached for the doorknob, Emilia struck out with her foot, backward against his leg, and Antonio stumbled and fell forward, releasing her. Before he could grab hold of Emilia again, the three drummers who were outside the house, entered the room. Antonio knew he was beaten, but he braced himself for a fight. Yet the men ignored him. One of them wrapped his arms around Emilia, stopping her from striking Antonio, another whispered something in her ear. Whatever he said to her seemed to have a calming effect for she quietly let the men lead her back to Marina's bed.

Only Virginia thought that Emilia brought the drummer's message to Marina. The others simply saw Emilia brush her lips past Marina's ear, make the sign of the cross on her forehead and then kiss her cheek. Immediately afterward Emilia left the room with the drummers. The wailing woman followed them out of the yard, down the dirt track, away from the house.

When they had all gone, Antonio got busy. He emptied the basins full of herbs and water through the window and blew out the candles. He shouted to Glentower to help him, and the doctor, motivated by greed and the promise of wealth, complied. Together they cleared the room of all that Emilia had put there: the vials of foul-smelling liquids, the incense censers, the prayer books.

Only Virginia did not move from where she was.

An odd feeling now coursed its way through her, a strange emotion, familiar and yet foreign—as if she had known it once, but forgotten, and yet as if she had never known it, never experienced it. She shook her head as if to throw off the sensation, but it did not leave. She had felt it steal upon her the moment that she had seen Emilia put the bamboo vial to Marina's lips. It was what caused her to remain silent, not to warn Antonio. It seized her again when she knew that Emilia had not merely kissed her daughter's ear, but had whispered something to her, something the drummer had probably told her to say. A disturbing feeling, at once comforting and irritating. It filled her with compassion for Emilia and shame for herself. But for what reason, shame? She had done nothing wrong. She had enabled Antonio to get the doctor for Emilia's daughter. Wasn't she entitled to gratitude? But the feeling urged her to remember more, to stretch her memory further back in time. She tried, yet she remembered nothing, except now, looking at Glentower, she found herself wondering for the first time in her life if an English doctor knew enough to deliver a baby, if his science was good enough, or any better than what Miss Victoria knew.

"Blood poisoning," Glentower yelled triumphantly, cutting across her thoughts. "Blood poisoning. That's what's wrong with her." His fingers probed Marina's swollen fingers and ankles. "Common here. The wrong food. All that dasheen and cassava. See? See? Look here. See, her face is all bloated. Look here—her neck and arms. Blood poisoning! That's what it is."

"Toxemia?" From her corner in the room, Virginia battled against a growing uneasiness with Glentower's presence.

Glentower raised his eyebrows, surprised. "You know what it means?"

"Surely it's not toxemia?" The odd sensation took a stronger hold on Virginia. Perhaps she should call back Emilia. She pushed away the feeling. Obeah, never obeah. Hadn't she argued with Marina for science? Yes, the doctor's science was better than Emilia's roots. Yes, yes, yes.

"That's what it is all right," Glentower answered Virginia. "Has she eaten anything lately? Could that woman—? Hrumph." He cleared his throat. "Her mother—did she give her anything strange to eat? Herbs? Roots? You know what I mean?"

"The edema began before she came." Virginia fought to get the words out of her mouth.

"But Mother, she could have given something to Marina before."

"How could she, Antonio?"

"She was here before. Remember? When you weren't here. I told you. She came to see Marina. You were in Port-of-Spain at Greyfriar's. Remember?"

"But she was not pregnant then—"

"And the listlessness? Does she sleep off and on?" Glentower interrupted them.

"Yes," Virginia replied.

"Mother!"

"Mr. de Balboa?"

"I have never seen her fall asleep as suddenly as she did a while ago," Antonio said quietly.

"Fainted," corrected the doctor. "She'll come to."

Marina moaned softly and tossed her head from side to side on the bed. She seemed to be trying to regain consciousness, fighting to bring herself back. Virginia left the corner where she had stayed, a voyeur, an outsider, doubting Glentower but doing nothing, and went to Marina. She squeezed the girl's hand, and Marina smiled weakly and then relapsed into the still, comalike sleep that she had fallen into when Emilia put the bamboo vial to her lips.

Glentower seemed undisturbed. He looked briefly at Marina and then turned to Antonio. "How long has she had this swelling?"

"Aren't you going to try to revive her?" Antonio asked.

"No, it's best she stays this way. When her body is ready, she'll come to. How long has she had the swelling?" he repeated impatiently.

"The edema?" Virginia disliked the man. Minutes before, when he thought that Marina was English, he had tried to revive her. Now it didn't matter to him that she lay unconscious. Yet strangely she too was not worried. She was certain that Emilia was working her obeah on Marina. The possibility was oddly comforting.

"For weeks now," she snapped at Glentower.

"And now you call me?"

"It wasn't that bad. The swelling was gradual. And the midwife, Miss Victoria . . ." Antonio could not understand his mother's behavior. She had written her secrets on paper so that he could bring a doctor to Marina, and now she acted as though she regretted that the doctor was here. It was her pride, he was certain. She was insulted by the doctor's refusal to treat her as an educated woman. Referring to toxemia as blood poisoning, edema as swelling, as if she would not understand the scientific terms. Still, Antonio thought, still she could control herself. Still, she could hold her anger until he saved Marina. "Miss Victoria gave Mother some orange peel—"

Glentower cut across his words. "Miss Victoria? A colored woman?" He clicked his tongue and placed his stethoscope on Marina's chest.

"Yes, a colored woman," Virginia replied firmly.

"You call her a midwife?" Glentower glanced sharply at Virginia and then pulled the stethoscope from his ears, opened his bag and took out a large pair of scissors.

"What are you doing?" Virginia walked around the bed toward Glentower.

He pushed her aside and took out some rolls of white bandages from his bag. "Has she been complaining of head-aches?" He directed his question pointedly at Antonio. "Red spots in front of her eyes?"

"Yes, yes," Antonio replied quietly, not knowing what to do, but feeling uneasy about the scissors and bandages. To deliver a baby? he thought.

"Midwife, eh?" The doctor took out a knife and the last roll of bandages from his bag. "Toxemia. We have no time to lose here, Mr. de Balboa. This woman's blood has been poisoned. How, I don't know, but we must drain out some of it or she will die."

Virginia lunged for the knife, but Antonio held her back. "No, Mother. Don't. He knows what he is doing."

She struggled against her son. "Make him go, Antonio," she said.

"He's the best. You said so yourself."

"The best for the colonies."

Glentower coughed. "You want me to leave, Mrs. de Balboa?"

"No. No. Please." Antonio forced his mother into a chair. "Please, Dr. Glentower."

Glentower rolled up his sleeves. "The child will die no matter what," he said without compassion. "But we can save the mother, your wife. Here." He pulled out another sharp shining instrument from his bag. "Tell your mother to boil this scalpel," he said, averting his eyes from Virginia, his voice becoming more authoritative. "Bring me some clean towels, some boiling water and an empty pan. And tell your mother not to touch the scalpel! Tell her to bring it back in the same water she boiled it in."

Antonio touched his mother lightly on the arm. "Go, Mother, please," he said gently to her. "Do it for me. I went through a lot of trouble to get him here. Trust me, Mother. Trust me. He'll save Marina. I know it."

For her son's sake, Virginia took the scalpel and went to the kitchen. When she and Antonio returned, Glentower had already stripped the blankets off Marina and had rolled up her nightdress, exposing her legs up to the knees.

"Come here," he called to Virginia, still avoiding her eyes. "Hold her foot here so that it is off the bed. Here, Mr. de Balboa. Put this pan right here. Here. Under her leg. Like this. Do it now." Glentower's commands echoed through the room. "I'm going to cut the vein here." He pointed to Marina's ankle. "Let some blood out. It will reduce the swelling." Sensing Antonio's reluctance, he added, "Don't worry, the child will come out when the swelling goes down, and everything will be fine. Here, Antonio, lift the pan closer to her leg."

Antonio did as he was told and motioned to his mother to do the same.

"There'll be a big splash at first," warned Glentower. "It'll be a mess. Hope you're not squeamish. Ready?"

With one hand Glentower held firmly on to Marina's leg just above her ankle and with the other, he deftly cut through the saphenous vein on her ankle. The blood gushed out like a flood from a broken dam.

Christ, thought Antonio wildly, I wonder if they do this to their own. He looked up at Glentower questioningly.

"It's okay. It's fine. Don't worry, old chap." For a moment Glentower seemed compassionate. "See? The swelling is going down. A little more blood and I'll close it up and all will be well. She'll feel weak but then some of the poison will have left her system and she'll make clean blood again. There. That's enough." He squeezed Marina's skin so that the bleeding stopped. The wide pan beneath Marina's foot now had about two cups of blood in it, but the swelling around the ankles seemed to have gone down. The doctor swiftly took the clean white bandages and skillfully wrapped Marina's ankle, cutting off the flow of blood.

Marina, who throughout the ordeal remained unconscious, began to move her lips for the first time, murmuring her mother's name. "Emilia. Emilia. Mother. Emilia."

"See?" said the doctor, gloating at Virginia in triumph. He snipped off the bandage with the scissors and replaced them and the remaining bandages in his bag.

But in that moment, precisely as he had closed his bag, Marina's body stiffened. The baby in her belly rolled over, sending ripples across her nightdress. Her legs and arms became rigid and her head jerked back spasmodically on the pillow.

"Quick! A spoon," yelled Glentower.

Before he could touch Marina, Virginia expertly threw her daughter-in-law's head backward and clamped down her tongue firmly with a long-handled spoon that was on the night table. As quickly as the spasm had rippled through Marina's body, it subsided.

Glentower reached past Virginia and brusquely grasped her wrist, pulling the spoon out of her hand. Coming between her and Marina, he said with clinical observation, "I was afraid of that. She's fitting."

"What do you mean?" Antonio asked nervously from the bottom of the bed. "I thought you said that she would be fine."

"If she did not fit," replied Glentower, wiping the scalpel with a towel.

"You didn't say 'if,' " Antonio was now shouting. "If? If? What if?"

Virginia glared at Glentower.

"Look, look here, old chap," Glentower stammered. "I did you a favor. I—I came here to help you. I—I—I did the best I could." He reached for his bag. "There is little I can do once they start fitting."

"They?" questioned Antonio.

"It's a seizure," Virginia said coldly to the doctor. "Not a fit. A seizure."

The doctor began again: "I can try to let some blood from the other ankle. It may help—"

"No!" screamed Antonio. "No! Leave us alone."

"Jesus," Glentower hissed. "Jesus, these colored people are all the same. Jeez."

"Get out!" yelled Antonio, his stomach turning at the sight of the red blood splashed over the sheets and swirling in the basin on the floor. Done for nothing. And Marina's face paler than ever.

"I could try one more time," Glentower said again, thinking of the deal he had made the day before. "The other ankle will do the trick."

"Get out!" Antonio screamed.

Marina groaned again.

"No more blood. No more blood, I tell you."

The Warao appeared.

"Did you hear my son?" Virginia's voice was commanding.

"I'm going. I'm going." Glentower backed out of the room.

"Take Dr. Glentower to the warden's house," Virginia said without emotion, addressing the Warao.

Glentower had reached the door and almost collided with the Warao. "No. No—I can find my way," he stuttered.

"Take him to Mr. Smith's. We don't need him anymore."

The Warao grabbed Glentower's arm. The doctor's eyes pleaded with Virginia. He did not want to go with the Warao, but Virginia's lips remained firmly shut. She turned her back to him and led the Warao, still holding firmly to his captive, to the front door.

Antonio gazed helplessly at Marina. She was quiet now, calm. She had begun to breathe more easily since Virginia had arrested her seizure. The bandage around her ankle had stopped the bleeding. Antonio moved to her side. Tenderly he pushed away the damp curls that had stuck to her forehead. He now began to regret every minute of his silence, his refusal to talk to her all those past weeks, to make love to her.

He regretted his unkindness, his cruelty. He felt trapped by his own folly and pride.

"God," he whispered hoarsely, calling on the God he was not sure existed. "God, I love her. Don't let her die. Don't let her die."

"Call back her mother, Son." Virginia's voice weaved in easily through his ear. "Bring Emilia back."

It was as if the God he had prayed to was speaking to him, answering his prayer.

"Get Emilia for her," she repeated.

He turned to face his mother. She looked serene. He had never seen her like that before. She seemed to have just woken up from a long sleep. As if the hours of agony over Marina's suffering had not been, as if the tension and anxiety that Dr. Glentower had caused had soothed her nerves and relaxed her muscles.

She put her hands lightly on his shoulders and pushed him gently away from the bed. Then she sat down and crooned to Marina as though talking to a baby. "Your mother will be here soon. Soon, Marina." She looked up and repeated to Antonio, "Go, find Emilia for her. Go, Son."

Antonio jerked his head abruptly to the side as someone would who wanted to pull himself out of a numbing sleep that was dragging him down. He stared at his mother, a question forming behind his wrinkled forehead.

"Hush, Son. Hush."

"Mother, she's dying. Don't you see? Look at her."

"No, Son, she will live. She's not dying. She's waiting for Emilia. Go, Antonio. Go get Emilia for her."

"Mother!"

"Shh, Antonio." Virginia reached over the bed and held Marina's hand in hers, her face glowing, her eyes tender. "Shhh! She is fine now. She's fine."

"Mother!"

Virginia did not seem to hear him. "She does not look it, does she, Antonio? Yet she is one of us. It's we, Antonio, who forget who we are. Dr. Glentower with all his English medicine couldn't help her." Her eyes looked far away. "I've seen women live in spite of this." A lost memory seemed to return to her.

"And women die like this," Antonio said, agitated.

"Yes, Sara—poor Sara."

At the mention of Sara, all the residual energy that had kept Antonio moving drained out of him. His knees turned to jelly and his legs almost collapsed under the weight of his body. He had not remembered Sara and how quickly she died. How quickly Marina too could die. He leaned against the wall. "But you told me, Mother—" he began hoarsely.

Virginia did not let him finish. "I told you wrong. I told you to let the doctor bathe Sara in the river. It will cut the fever, he said. But they could have helped her even then."

"Who?" Antonio asked, knowing the answer.

Virginia ignored the question. "We try to be one of them, Antonio, but we can't. I didn't know my real father and mother. 'Savages,' Mrs. Smith called them. 'You, you're going to be better,' she said. 'Education,' she said, 'it kills the savage beast.' She was, she said, 'going to use education in the same way the fishermen use their knives to gut the fish.' She was going to 'gut all the African in me.' "

"Please, Mother, not now," Antonio pleaded again.

But Virginia was wrapped up in her own world. Her eyes had turned inward in a glassy, vacant stare and the voice she spoke with seemed to come from deep within her, almost apart from her. "Your father felt the same way," she said. "He felt sorry for us. One day I saw him looking at some children playing. They were fishermen's children. They had just come from the beach—cleaning fish I suppose, because their legs and arms were covered with fish, blood and scales. They were naked. Probably their mothers had sent them to wash off, but they played instead. I saw de Balboa watching those naked, bloody, black bodies and I thought that he looked as though a fearful ghost had appeared before him. As if some vision in his past had come back to haunt him. No, it was not fear I saw. It was something other than— compassion? No, pity. The pity you feel for a dying dog. His eyes welled up with tears that flowed down his cheeks. I had never seen him cry before. He moved toward them, to touch them, I suppose, but it seemed as though he also wanted to help them, to save them. But the children ran away scream- ing with laughter, pointing their fingers at him, ridiculing him."

"Mother!" Antonio steadied himself against the wall. "Mother, no more. Not now."

"He meant to save you too, that year before he died when he finally accepted that you were his son. He wanted to save you from me and from them—to make you different from the rest of colored people."

"No!" Antonio had to make an effort not to shout.

"He felt sorry for all of us. That's the real reason why he married me. He felt sorry for me because my skin is black."

"Mother. Marina—Not now—"

"I—I used to love to braid my hair. You see it? You see it?" Virginia removed the bandana from her head. "But she hated it. And I believe that he did too . . ."

Life returned to Marina's eyes. She opened them and smiled at Virginia. "Yes, yes," Virginia whispered to her. "Antonio will bring her to you."

Antonio rushed to his wife's side, his heart racing joyfully. She was fine. His mother was right. She was fine. He reached over to her to touch her face, but the moment that Marina felt his breath, she pulled her shoulders from her pillow and, pushing him off with strength Antonio could not imagine she could have, she screamed as though tormented by a hundred devils, a bloodcurdling scream that seemed to be wrenched from the pit of her stomach.

"Leave her, Son. Go." Virginia guided Marina gently back onto the pillows. "Go." She brushed Marina's forehead until the girl closed her eyes and breathed calmly. "She will be fine, Antonio. Get Emilia for her. Emilia knows what to do. The baby will be fine."

Antonio stood up as if by a will not his own.

"Go, Antonio. She won't die. Go, Son."

Outside the house the wind moaned through trees already sagging under the driving rain, and it brought with it the earth smells of worms crushed against the rotted leaves and branches of last season's rains, of the slush of new foliage stripped from trees in the prime of their growth, of recent weeds carried in the tiny dirt streams the hurricane had created, of this year's tree sap turned sour by the mud-laden water. The rain that had begun in drizzles about an hour ago now poured again. The interminable rain. Antonio looked out at the sunless sky darkened by heavy clouds. An unspeakable possibility pressed against his brain. Perhaps she was right.

Virginia seemed not to know that he was still in the room. She began to sing to Marina in a soft, melodic voice. It was a song Antonio had never heard her sing before, though he had heard it often on warm June nights when the fishermen's wives left the suffocating heat of their homes, and cradling their babies in their arms, they swang in burlap hammocks strung between coconut trees, and sang against the cool breezes that promised the end of the dry season.

Hearing her song, he thought she seemed so sure, so certain, so positive that Marina would not die.

The irony struck him that she should be the one to want Emilia to come back. He saw her face vividly as it was on that day, that time before the dry season, when trembling with fear, she begged him to call the Christian priest to bless her house against obeah. Could she be the same person who now urged him to bring back Emilia and all she meant? The odious liquid concoctions, the dried-out roots, the fermenting herbs and leaves, the lighted candles, the pigs' bristles, the tufts of human hair, all the bits and parts of the human world, the animal world, the plant world all thrown together while the obeahman chanted mysterious incantations to the spirit world? Yet her song mesmerized him. He let her lullaby soothe him as it soothed Marina. He let himself begin to believe what she had told him. Perhaps Marina would not die. Perhaps Emilia would deliver her daughter's baby safely. He began to feel that Marina would survive. Without understanding why, he began to feel hope. He abandoned rational analysis. Emilia would save her daughter. He called to Virginia, but she did not answer him. She continued her song. He walked toward the door, paused for a moment, looked again at his mother and his wife. Perhaps he should tell his mother now, that the old man was dead. But her song drove him forward, and he walked out of the room.

It seemed to Antonio that they were expecting him. As he turned into the track leading to Alma's house where he knew he would find Emilia, he saw them in the front yard under an open bamboo shed, all five of them, Emilia, Alma, the two drummers and the wailing woman, their bodies fused into a huddle, necks and shoulders craned forward in a mass, watching for something or someone that was to come from far out in front of them. He was sure that Alma saw him first.

She stepped out of the huddle, turned her body in his direction and placed her hand above her eyes, focusing her vision.

He jumped behind a tree to hide from her, irritated at the same time by his childish fear. She was no more than the old woman with young hands and legs whom he saw every day selling chataigne from a smoke-blackened tin can. Yet when he saw her searching him out through the liquid-silver rain, his heart froze. The peace, the calm he brought with him through the rain from his house, left him entirely. Images he despised because they filled him with shame for the ignorance of his people flooded his imagination: women dressed in white; half-naked men jumping in frenzy to the wild beat of drums; their babbling cries, foaming mouths, stinking sweat, clothes torn to shreds, bodies writhing on the ground in the dirt, and blood, the blood of their wretched cock, their sacrifice. Images, filling him not only with revulsion but with fear too, for more than once he had witnessed them "catching the spirit," transformed into beings he could not recognize as human.

Alma plucked her clay pipe from her mouth, threw back her head and keened loudly against the wind, "Uh-lalalalalalalalala!" Her tongue moved rapidly against the roof of her mouth, her voice clashing against the thunderous thumping of the rain pouring down the edges of the plaited palm-leaf roof. "Uhlalalalalala!" Her chant, ancient and mysterious, pierced deep into Antonio's soul. Fear, naked fear bolted him to the ground. Nothing could console him, not even when he boldly reminded himself that she was an old woman, an old chataigne-selling woman.

She was next to him before he saw her again, the thick, black smoke from her clay pipe circling his nostrils and stinging his eyes to water. He thought through the fog of his fear that her face was kind and gentle, her eyes like the eyes of the eternal mother, comforting and soothing. He remembered through the fog of his fear what he had thought he'd forgotten. That not long ago he had embraced her when his wives died and he wanted an answer. He did not speak to her then. She came through the clouds of his sleeping, caressing his ears, whispering to him, eternal mother, eternal Alma. "The Warao speaks the truth," she said. "You marry her. Marry that Marina. She'll bear your babies. She won't die." And now that he saw her in full consciousness, eternal mother, in the flesh, not chataigne-selling Alma, not old woman Alma, but Alma of the spirit, of his dreams, why was he afraid of her?

"Steady now," Alma spoke to him and grabbed him firmly by the shoulders. "Steady now. Don't fall down."

The earth spun beneath him. He felt vomit fill his mouth.

"That's it. Throw up. Throw it up." Alma moved to his side and hit him hard on the back. "Throw it up."

After the nausea left him, he let her lead him to the shed. He was still afraid, but not of her, he thought now. Not of her. But of himself. Of the quiet acquiescence that centered itself in the pit of his belly, of the calm that enveloped him, of the childlike acceptance that had taken hold of him, as if a whole big part of him had abandoned all rational thought and had given itself up completely into Alma's hands. He felt no revulsion, therefore, when he saw the open grave yawning behind the drummers and Emilia. A tiny fraction of his being, the part that still held on stubbornly to scientific reasoning, took in the facts and rapidly assessed them. A fresh grave! They had removed the mounds of earth from around it. Why? Whose grave was it? Whose body was it to hold? He kept his eyes away from it, but in averting his eyes from the grave, the very thought he wished to avoid snaked its way into his consciousness: it was Marina's grave! Marina's! His body grew hot beneath his wet clothes, and steam rose from his open collar.

One of the drummers saw it and laughed, "You smokin', man. What happen? You 'fraid or what, man? Nothin' to be 'fraid now, man. You safe."

Safe? Panic seized Antonio again. This time because he feared for Marina's life. They had not huddled there under the shed to save Marina. They had come to bury her. He wrenched his arm from Alma's hand and stumbled, falling near the edge of the grave. For the first time he saw it was not empty. There was a man lying in it, still and silent, except for the gentle rising and falling of his chest. His eyes were covered with a piece of white cloth tied at the back of his head. Two small circles of melted candle wax were placed on the cloth over his eyelids. On his head was a crown of thorns, like the one placed on the head of Jesus at Galilee. A narrow strip of cloth covered his genitals. Except for that, he was naked. His sickly yellow skin, which they'd rubbed with oil, was completely exposed. Antonio's knees felt weak, but he forced himself to get up. The grave was not for Marina! Still, this was something he wanted no part of. He had heard those stories of men who had the power to let their souls leave their bodies—of men who could travel through space and time, whose spirits could destroy their enemies or bring fortune to their friends. Old wives' tales, he'd called them. A new wave of nausea mounted his throat, and his legs buckled beneath him. His body swayed forward and he would have fallen into the grave had not Alma caught him in time in her strong, wiry arms.

"Steady, steady, de Balboa man. You have work to do now. Work, you hear meh?"

Through the scornful laughter of the drummers, Antonio

heard Emilia's voice, a painful whisper at first and then rising to a high shriek, razor sharp.

"Murderer! Murderer! Murderer!" she shrieked. "You want to murder my child, my only child."

The drummers held Emilia away from him, but still she strained forward, her eyes blazing red, the flesh around them swollen and puffy, red rouge smeared over her cheeks and dripping down to the bottom of her chin where dirt had caked the talcum powder she had dusted over her body to the top of her neck. Her heavy body was stuffed into a bright orange organza dress that was filthy at the hem. Now Antonio could see what made Glentower despise her.

"Consort," he heard himself mutter under his breath. "Consort."

Alma felt the scorn in his voice, though she could not distinguish the word he had used, and she dropped her arms from around him and twisted his body to face hers. "You say what?" Her eyes burned his face.

Antonio floundered to find his voice. "I—I—" he stammered.

"Murderer!" Emilia screamed again.

This time it was Alma who restrained her. Taking her eyes off Antonio, she turned to Emilia. Her voice was gentle when she told her to be quiet, and Antonio saw the obeahwoman transformed again into the eternal mother, the eternal mother Alma embracing her daughter Emilia. "Shh, shh," she cooed. "Shh. Marina won't die. I promised you. Shh. Remember what I tell you. Shh." And then like a cat protecting her young, the eternal mother turned her claws on Antonio. "You tell us now, de Balboa, why you here. What you want from us?"

With all his heart, Antonio wished he had not come. He

wanted to walk away, but Alma's eyes kept him rooted to the spot where he stood. He felt his hands begin to shake and he locked them together to keep them still. "Emilia. Mrs. Heathrow." He tried to make his voice bold. Unafraid. "Her daughter wants her."

"But she tell me you put her out of your house, de Balboa."

"I—I—"

"You sorry now you put her out of your house, de Balboa?"

"I—"

"You sorry, de Balboa?"

Antonio's tongue wrapped itself around the word she wanted. "Sorry," he said.

"Yes, you sorry, de Balboa. You sorry because only Alma can help you now. Emilia and Alma. You believe me, de Balboa?"

Antonio could not help himself. His hands began to shake uncontrollably. His fingers, intertwined and locked against the backs of his hands, could do nothing to stop the tremors that rippled through them. Alma watched his hands, not unkindly.

"Why you 'fraid so, de Balboa man? No one harm you here. You we people." She looked at him with steady eyes. "We very own people, de Balboa man."

She paused as though she expected Antonio to answer her, to tell her she was right, but Antonio did not speak the words that traveled in his mind: No, I'm not one of your people. I'm not your very own people.

"We want nothing from you. What that doctor want? Tell me. What he want from you? Tell me, de Balboa."

"Land," Antonio barely heard his own voice.

"See, see? That doctor can't help Marina. He don't want

to help Marina. He want reward. You foolish to put Emilia out of your house. Anyways, even if the doctor want to help you, he can't." She kept her eyes on Antonio. Her words came slowly now. "You see you have evil in you, de Balboa. Your father spirit was cursed and he cursed you. All you touch is cursed." Alma brought her face close to Antonio's. Her voice was soothing. "He cursed you, de Balboa. Don't let him have more power over you. Stop him, de Balboa."

Yes, yes she was right. That, ultimately, was why he was here. The dead, lying Portogee Jesuit priest was cursed: "The sins of the father shall be visited on their sons." The dead, lying Portogee had cursed him too.

Alma saw the trembling leave his hands and she urged him on to believe her. "Your medicine can do nothing for Marina. You bring that doctor but he can do nothing for her. We have to correct your father's evil, de Balboa. You know. I know. Listen, listen to me, de Balboa.

"We need powerful help to break this evil. Jesus Christ heself. The body and blood of Jesus. Understand me, de Balboa? Understand me?"

Antonio turned to the grave as if to make one last grasp at retaining his reason. Perhaps the sight of the man lying in the grave would revolt him again and he could resist her. But Alma's words ensnared him.

"I know you understand me, de Balboa. You we people." Her voice caressed his ears. She followed his eyes to the grave and knew she had to force him to look at her again. "Leave Harris be, de Balboa. He have his work. Now you do yours to save your wife. Come, de Balboa. Look at me. At six o'clock, this evening the priest—"

The priest, the priest. The word pierced Antonio's consciousness. The priest, his father. He looked up at Alma.

"The priest is giving a special mass to stop the hurricane," she was saying, "in the selfsame church that didn't take your Portogee father when he died. You go there to that selfsame church that throw back your dead father body. You go to the mass and take Communion. You understand? The Body of Jesus Christ. You keep it in your mouth."

Antonio's eyes returned involuntarily to the grave, but now Alma took no chances. She grabbed his arm firmly and commanded him to look at her. The drummers, who were hovering in the background, came close to Antonio, their eyes warning him to look away from the grave.

"Good. Good," said Alma when Antonio locked his eyes on hers again. Her voice resumed its gentleness. "You take that Communion on your tongue and hold it in your mouth. Don't swallow it. You hearing me?"

Antonio heard her clearly. Every word. He nodded his head slowly, his mind resisting the meaning of what she said.

"Then you bring it to me. Whole. The whole Body of Jesus Christ."

Antonio kept nodding. He wouldn't think. He wouldn't allow himself to think.

"Good. Good. Now go."

His legs would not budge. Not a muscle twitched.

"Go!" she repeated.

His paralysis deepened. It was as if his body in complicity with his mind now shut itself off from the reality it faced. On one level, the level of his senses, he was aware of where he was. He could see colors, shapes, movement, but his perceptions were blurred and indistinguishable. He sensed the presence of the drummers closing in on him and then the women pressing him, pushing him out of the shed, their voices swarming through him, urging him, commanding him to go, but he could not move. His mind had erected a wall that refused to permit him to respond to their orders. And then Alma's cry penetrated his defenses. "Uhlalalalala!" Her ancient cry cut deep through that wall and startled him back to consciousness. He saw her clearly now, her head flung back, her mouth wide open. "Uhlalalala!" Yes, he understood what she had asked him to do. Yes, he knew what she wanted. He looked wildly around him. Bodies, eyes pressed against him. He could not escape. He stepped backward out of the shed and fell into a puddle of mud. They loomed over him, Alma, Emilia, the drummers, the wailing woman. "Go! Go! Go!" Their voices forced him to his feet and he ran as if tigers chased him, as if mad dogs foaming at the mouth with rabies howled after him. The rain whipped through his clothes plastering them to his body like fur on a drowning cat, his felt hat streamed water in his face, blinding him. His feet splashed through mud and water, his hands pushed away branches and vines that came in his way. He stumbled, tripped, fell again, picked himself up and ran.

No, he did not want to desecrate the Sacrament. No, he did not want to take the Host in his soul blackened by mortal sin from years of omission, his refusal to pray, his refusal to go to mass, to go to confession. Yes, he understood what she wanted him to do. He was to be her agent, her messenger, her partner in sacrilege against the Church. "Faith is not intellect. It is feeling so deep that one is not conscious of believing until it's too late." No, he did not want to take the Host in his mouth to Alma for her evil purposes. The Body and Blood of Christ? Christ squeezed into a tiny bread wafer? A logical impossibility. But once you believe, that's all there is to it. You believe, Antonio's head sang out. Faith never leaves you. Damn them! Damn them all with their catechisms and their religion. You can stomp on it, curse it, deny it, but it stays deep in your soul, saying Yes. And at that moment when the bells jingle, at that moment when the bread and wine are raised high, at that moment, the transfiguration, the transubstantiation. "Lord, I am not worthy that thou shouldst enter under my roof; say but the word and my soul shall be healed. Lord—Agnus Dei—Agnus Dei—Lamb of God."

The wind ripped off his felt hat and Antonio barely noticed it leave his head. His thoughts pounded to the beat of his feet against the soggy earth. Is that what you did, Vasco de Balboa? Father Vasco de Balboa? You turned your back on all this? A priest who converted the bread and wine? One of God's ministers who was privileged to touch His Body and His Blood. To share in His miracle?

Excommunicado! Excommunicado! Antonio covered his ears as though even now he could hear the priest's voice booming down the church. *Excommunicado!* He saw the priest leaning over his father's dead body lying on a sheet in a donkey cart outside the church. He heard again the scapular rip under those priestly hands as he tore it off Vasco de Balboa's neck. Alma was right. Father Goodings had refused the dead body. He had known that Vasco de Balboa was a Jesuit priest.

How the body stank then, though it was packed in ice. But it was the dry season, and the sun found the worms that crawled beneath his skin. The donkey had to be beaten to pull that stinking load to Port-of-Spain. The Portuguese will take him, Antonio's mother said. And they did, those Christians, the Portuguese in Port-of-Spain. They remembered him, their brother with them on the *William*, though he sat in a corner of the deck of the ship and brooded after they strung up that African on the mast to die. They made Vasco de Balboa a Presbyterian, dead man that he was, and converted his wife too, and they buried him in Greyfriar's Church on Frederick Street.

"**S**on? Son? Son?" The priest grabbed him by the shoulder and shook him. "Son! Son!" He slapped him hard on the face. "Son! Come out of the rain. Come out!"

Antonio saw the face of a young man growing old with anxiety.

"Come in! Come in!" The priest draped his arm across Antonio's shoulders and pushed him forward.

Antonio shivered against him. "I am here," he whispered.

"What, Son?" The priest bent his ear toward him.

"I'm here," repeated Antonio staring at the church door.

"Yes, yes. But out of the rain, Son. What is it? What is wrong? Can I help you?"

Antonio stood at the entrance of the church. The candlelit altar beckoned him. He saw with acute clarity the golden tabernacle gleaming at its center. "No. No, Father. I am fine. I am all right. It's the rain. I got soaked."

"Yes, but you needn't have come in the hurricane. It's no sin to—"

"You are saying mass today?" Antonio interrupted him nervously.

"Yes, but you needn't stay—"

"The mass is for the hurricane?" Antonio persisted.

"Yes, but—"

"Father Goodings? Is he here? Will he say the mass?"

"He left with the others when the hurricane came. Is something wrong? Can I help you?"

"No, it's just that I—I expected Father Goodings to say the mass."

"I'm sorry, Son."

Antonio looked at this pink-cheeked priest with innocent, childlike eyes who called him Son and whom he called Father. He thought: They have to take them when they are young, before they know how to think. How old was my father when they got him?

"I have to go," the priest said, spreading out his arms to indicate the four people who were kneeling in their pews.

Antonio nodded and watched him walk toward the altar.

The mass was quick, the priest having a private conversation with his god in Latin. Antonio did not follow his words, though he could. A confirmed child can recite by heart the Low Mass in Latin. His mind remained tormented by the sin he was about to commit and the sacrilege that Alma and Emilia were soon to consummate with the Host. He waited for the bells, for the moment. And it came.

"Corpus Christi . . ."

Antonio closed his eyes and stuck out his tongue, and the young priest placed the Host in his mouth. And shutting his lips tightly, careful not to swallow, Antonio got up from before the altar and walked steadily down the church aisle, out of the church door, down the muddy road and up to Alma's shack.

I t was one hour since Antonio had left Virginia with Marina. The young woman's condition had not changed. She groaned weakly from her bed, her belly forming a mournful, silent mound, refusing to ease her anguish. The spasms that had ripped through her body were no longer as violent as they had been when Glentower had bled her, yet they had returned, and with rhythmic regularity, her body twitched and jerked, sending small ripples across the bed sheets like tiny waves on a sea before a storm. Still, she seemed comforted by Virginia's presence next to her on the bed. When the pain seemed most intense, she would squeeze Virginia's hand, drawing her strength from Virginia's steadfast reassurances to her that she would be well soon, that the pain would pass away soon, that Antonio had gone to fetch Emilia for her. "Wait and see. Emilia will deliver that baby, and in two shakes you'll be up and walking." Marina would manage to smile, and Virginia would begin to sing to her once more the old lullabies of the fishermen's wives.

For the past fifteen minutes, however, Virginia had stopped singing altogether and was now making soothing clicking sounds with her tongue. Marina did not seem to notice the difference or to see the sudden rigidity in Virginia's back or hear the long pauses between her clicking sounds. She did not seem to realize that while Virginia held her hands, she was quite distracted by something else.

For some time, Virginia had been aware that someone was standing behind her in the open doorway. She knew that it was not Antonio, not only because the person had not spoken to her, but also because the shadow the person cast was too large for Antonio's frame. Yet she was not afraid. She had an uncanny feeling that the person was a sort of protective shield between Marina and her and the outside world. She felt a sense of anticipation of something strange about to occur, something that would not be harmful to either herself or Marina. That she had to wait until she was approached, or the person would disappear. But when at last she felt the person begin to walk toward her, her curiosity had grown so great that she turned around, risking the chance that no one would be there.

The woman did not surprise her. She was oddly familiar.

Large and dark brown with kind, cocoa-brown eyes, she was dressed in white—white bandana, white peasant blouse, white long cotton skirt—but her feet were bare. The minute she caught Virginia's eyes, she put her finger to her lips to silence her. Then gently removing Virginia's hand from Marina's, she pulled her up to her feet, forcing Virginia to face her. Before Virginia could say a word, the woman wrapped her tightly in her wide, generous arms and kissed her on both cheeks. Then she placed Virginia's head against her large breasts and rocked her back and forth, back and forth, as if Virginia were a small child, a baby, whispering to her in a sing-song voice, "There, there, dou dou. You'll be alright. You'll be alright, dou dou. You find yourself now. You see. You know who you are now. Don't worry, dou dou."

At first Virginia resisted the woman. She squirmed in her arms, struggling to be free, but the woman held her firmly but gently, and rocked her. Soon, without knowing why, except that she felt a great need to do so, Virginia began to cry. The more the woman sang to her, the more she cried. The more the woman embraced her, the more Virginia's tears flowed. Something seemed to melt in her, as if her insides had turned to liquid and she needed this woman to breathe life into her.

"I know. I know." The woman sang. "You sent for Emilia. You know now."

Virginia felt herself grow innocent like a little girl, a mere infant. "I had a mother once," she sniffed, wiping her nose against the back of her hand. "Her skin was white as those anthuriums you see near the river, growing in the shade."

"No, no, dou dou," the woman said gently, still rocking Virginia. "She was not your mother."

"She was white and she had cornrows on her head."

"No, no," the woman sang again. "Your mother was beautiful."

"She loved me."

"Your real mother loved you. They took you away from us when she died."

"Her skin was like cocoa," Virginia said. "She was beautiful."

"Yes. Yes."

"My other mother hated me."

"Yes, dou dou," the woman cooed.

"I was her experiment."

"Yes, yes."

"She hated my blackness. She said the doll took my white skin from me. It drank and drank until it became white and I became black." Virginia stopped crying. Her eyes sparkled with the memory.

The woman released her now and made her sit on the chair next to the bed. Marina groaned, and Virginia turned to reach for her, but the woman shook her head. "She alright," she said. "She don't need you now." Then as if she had not been interrupted, she continued, "Your mother birthed you black like herself. Your real mother, my sister."

"Sister?"

"Yes, dou dou."

"You knew my mother?"

"No."

"But you said—"

"Her sister? Yes and your sister. We have the same mother, you and I and your mother. Do you understand?"

Virginia let the woman's voice soothe her. A dark, troubled mist began to lift from her spirit. A deep sorrow began to drain from her soul.

"Africa," the woman said. "She is our mother. Africa. You understand me now?"

Virginia nodded her head.

"Go," the woman said gently. "Go, do what you should have done, my sister. You are not needed here anymore. Let Antonio free. Free yourself."

The woman turned her eyes away from Virginia and went toward the sick girl on the bed. Virginia called to her, but she did not answer. It was as if she no longer knew that Virginia was in the room.

The wind had snatched Virginia's red bandana off her head and sent it spinning in the pitch-black skies. It looked like a streak of blood dipping and darting through the rain, buoyed by the ferocious hurricane winds that had begun again. Her head was exposed, her cornrow braids framed her face. When the lightning cut jagged scars of electric light across the trees, she could see the muddied road in front of her strewn with galvanized roofing, broken glass and wooden planks ripped off of houses by the wind, along with branches of trees that had fallen in the first wave of the hurricane's fury. The rain was gentle compared to the wind that howled and screamed, echoing the crashes of thunder that fell to the ground like exploding cannonballs at regular intervals of three minutes. But Virginia was not afraid.

She walked through the hurricane, clinging to a tree when the wind tossed her off the road, sloshing kneehigh through swirling waters when the rain slashed through the skies and poured down in torrents. Some of the braids on her head became undone, and soon her hair was tangled, wild and knotty, pieces of twigs and leaves caught between the coarse strands. Her dress was torn and caked with mud and clung where it could against her body. Her arms and legs were scratched and bleeding from the pieces of debris that swirled everywhere, but she kept walking. "I must get there. God, let me get there! Please, God!" She gritted her teeth and bent forward against the wind, picking herself up when she tripped, determined to move ahead. For as far as she could see, there was no one. Even the wild animals had sought shelter. A drowned bird or two lay strewn along the road in spots where the swirling waters had subsided, and the wind rolled their bodies against each other in the mud. In the distance she saw an old donkey tethered against a tree where his owners had abandoned him, fleeing for their own lives. It was a sign Virginia felt, God's hand approving what she was going to do. Her years of loneliness, her miserable, tormented, wasted years of hating herself, of denying her origins, gave her strength to loosen the rope that tied the donkey.

Yes, she could see it all. The sickness that Hilda Smith had fed her. The hatred she had nourished. Yes, she thought, and all along it was myself she taught me to hate. My God, is it too late? Can I be saved?

"Go!" the woman who called her sister had said. "Go, free yourself. Do what you should have done."

You thought I wanted your husband, Hilda. You thought I was a filthy whore. You taught me to hate love. Sex. Yes, sex. You taught me to hate sex. It was he who wanted me, you fool. Your slimy husband. He touched me when I was a child, not yet eight. You knew it. I saw it in your eyes that you knew it. His white paws feeling me. And when I visited him on the day you died, to tell my father, my white daddy, how I hurt, how I hurt for him and for myself that my white mother was dead . . . And you were not cold in the grave.

Didn't they wonder when he sent Philip to England to bury you and he stayed here? He wanted to be with me. He wanted me even then. I thought he wanted to embrace me. Like a father embraces his daughter. I thought those days had gone when he touched me. Why, I was a married woman. I had a son as old as his. I let him put his arms around me. I felt his hardness on my leg. I felt it. But I loved you so. I said nothing. And then he put his white hand in my blouse and fondled my breast. I knew what he wanted. I knew, but I loved you. I couldn't let him know that I knew. Then he pushed me against his bed. Your bed. Did you know that, Hilda? From your grave, did you know that? Did you try to save me when he loosened my bloomers? When I struggled to escape? When he plunged himself deep into me—when I cried out and fought and bit and hit and couldn't escape?

You helped Antonio, didn't you, old man? You didn't show him the letter, did you, old man? Antonio will kill you yet. You better run, old man.

The donkey brayed and stomped its hooves when it saw Virginia. It had been waiting to be rescued and it was glad when Virginia mounted it.

He saw her when she turned the bend on the main road that branched off to the track that led to his house. There was a lull in the hurricane. The wind had died down suddenly and the rain had stopped. He had opened his door to look at the damage that the rain had done to his cabbage beds and then, seeing two of his bison wandering across his fields, he ran out to tether them before the rain returned again. And then he saw her, her hair wild and nappy, mud splashed across her face and dress, her body bent and bruised, her clothes torn, pulling a tired donkey behind her. And Ranjit ran toward her.

When Antonio returned to the shed in front of Alma's shack, the women and the drummers were ready. Emilia had changed her clothes, and Antonio barely recognized her. She looked regal. Like an African queen. Her hair was wrapped with a white cloth that spiraled upward in an inverted cone crowning her head. The lipstick and rouge were gone from her face. So too the powder. She wore a long white dress. A bride's dress, it seemed to Antonio. Tiny mother-of-pearl beads were worked through the lace at the neckline, at the sleeves and at the hem. She stood on a clean white sheet, or rather several layers of clean white sheets, for no trace of mud was near her. In front of her was the open grave. Alma, the wailing woman and the two drummers, their feet still caked with mud, sat on stools opposite Emilia, on the other side of the grave. Tied to a stake next to them, a red-necked cock glared frantically at the open spaces before it, screeching and squawking, straining every nerve and sinew in its body in an attempt to escape, digging its long, clawlike toenails into the soft mud.

Alma was the first one to acknowledge Antonio. She signaled to him from across the open grave, and Antonio moved toward her like a man in a hypnotic trance, unable to respond to anything except what the hypnotist commanded, passing near the frenzied cock without flinching a muscle. He felt numb now. Free, he tried to console himself. It was over. Done. He had committed the ultimate sin. Yes, he knew it. He had dirtied his soul. He was a part of them now. "We people," as Alma had said. He was no longer a spectator, a voyeur. From the moment the priest raised the Host over Antonio's outstretched tongue, he knew there was no undoing, no turning back. Still he had made one last desperate effort as the Host approached his tongue to recall the prayer of repentance he had used as a boy. To prepare his soul to receive the Savior: *"Lord, I am not worthy that thou shouldst enter under my roof; say but the word and my soul shall be healed. Lord—Lord—''* But the words dragged from his memory fell on unbelieving ears. Years of doubting made the words sound hollow and false. And yet he expected the Host to burn his tongue, to sizzle and curl steam around his mouth. He half-braced himself for the impact. Jesus Christ, angered by the insult to His Body. But there was no heat, no fire, no brimstone. Just the cold, thin wafer tasting like saltless bread, leaving him with a single thought—to keep it whole until he returned to Alma.

Now, standing before Alma, he waited for her to take it from him. He remained still, unfeeling, as she made the sign of the cross on his forehead, lips and chest. And when he saw her eyebrows raised in a question, he pointed to his breast pocket where he had put the Host, wrapped safely in his handkerchief. He saw Emilia, the wailing woman and the two drummers drop to their knees, then, when Alma lifted out the Host, he knelt too, as if it were the natural thing to do, the right thing to do. Yes, he was one of them now, he said to himself. Yes, he repeated, like a sick man finally accepting his disease. Yes, he had done the deed, blackened his soul. He had brought the Host to them. He could not deny it. How could he not say he was now one of them? *Our people.*

Alma smiled briefly and nodded her head in approval when she saw him kneel with the others. Then, turning her back on them all, she raised the Host above her head, clutching it carefully with the thumbs and forefingers of both hands. Antonio knew what would happen next before it occurred. He had witnessed that scene played over and over on the Sundays of his childhood, kneeling next to his mother in the hard wooden pews in the Catholic church, his eyes squeezed shut, his head bowed low, waiting for the bells at the Consecration of the mass as the priest raised the Host above his head. And each time they came, his conscience would begin again a futile struggle against his questioning mind, reminding him that this was the holiest, the most sacred part of the mass, that God Himself would enter the bread and wine at this moment. Did he raise his head and open his eyes then because he wanted to see the power of God? Because he thought that God would come in a flood of light to give him some sign of His greatness as He came down from heaven to become one with the bread? Or was it because he disbelieved that he could not, like the others, bow his head low when the acolyte jingled the bells at the Consecration? Because even at the age of twelve, before his father had poisoned his mind against the Church, he had doubted her most sacred of doctrines? And yet here he was in the shed of an obeahwoman playing the part of a believer in a mock mass that defied every rational thought that had crossed his mind since his Jesuit father had taught him scorn for the Church.

The drummers rang the brass bells and Antonio shut his eyes and let Alma's words awaken his memory.

"Domine Deus, Agnus Dei, Filius Patris: qui tollis peccata mundi . . ."

He struck his breast. *"Miserere nobis."* His voice joined the others. For the second, then third time the drummers rang the bells, and again Alma repeated the prayer and again

Antonio responded with the others, *"Miserere nobis."* The Jesuit's son has linked hands with the devil, he told himself with dismal finality. Like Faust, he had made his pact with Satan to gain his wife. He was Orpheus at the gates of Hell come to save his Eurydice. There was no turning back, no running away, no bargaining. He had already damned himself.

He steeled himself against the silence that followed, the sudden deafening sound of the wind growing still, of the rain stopping in midair. Could he have imagined it—the rush of warm air that circled past his ears, the long loud shrill of a whistle that penetrated his eardrums, the presence that brushed past his cheeks? He tried to convince himself that nothing had happened, that the rituals of Alma's mock mass had played tricks on him, but he knew that the others sensed it too, the presence focusing on him. When at last he dared to look up, he saw the Host inches before his face offered to him from Alma's outstretched hand.

He supposed that Alma wanted him to take the Host from her, but he could not break the lock his fingers had made with each other. And she must have thought that he would not take it, for she turned away abruptly from him. As she did so, he heard the silence go with her, the whistle fade, and the rain sound furiously on the roof of the shed.

Now the wailing woman began her dull, languishing chant and the drummers followed her rhythm, beating softly on their goatskin drums. Alma danced before them in a tight circle, the Host still held above her head. When she stopped, this time before Emilia, the wailing woman grew silent. Alma lowered the Host and offered it to Emilia, and in that instant, as Emilia took the Host from her hands, a loud blood-curdling scream, not coming from the shed where they were, pierced the air.

Like a flash of lightning Alma ran to where the frenzied cock still strained against the rope tied around its legs, and before it could utter a sound, she grabbed its naked neck and swung its body in a whirlwind above her head. Then, satisfied that its neck was broken, she untied the rope from its scaly legs and cut off its head with one swift clean stroke of her machete. Instantaneously she clamped its neck shut with her young fingers so that no blood escaped to the ground, and approaching Emilia, she dropped the cock on the white sheet that protected Emilia's feet from the mud. Hot blood spurted out of the cock's neck like a sprung oil well, spraying everywhere, on Emilia's white dress, on her clean shoes, turning most of the white sheet into a sea of red.

Emilia seemed to know what was required of her. She bent down, placed the Host that Alma had given her on the only spot on the sheet that had not been bloodied, and returning to where the cock lay, soaked her fingers in the thick pool of blood around his neck and brought her bloodied fingers to her mouth.

It was that single action, Emilia licking her fingers clean of the cock's blood, that yanked Antonio from his numbing sense of shock, his fatalistic acceptance of his own damnation. The logical impossibility—God becoming one with a wafer of bread—became for him the most rational possibility in that sea of madness that surrounded him. It was the Holy Ghost who had brushed past his ear; it was Jesus Christ, the Son of God, who was one with the Host; it was God the Father who was present everywhere. The blood, the cock, their pagan sacrifice, the wine of their mock mass. He covered his head with his hands. God! No! No!

Alma saw him turn from them and she rushed to him and pulled away his hands from his face.

"No!" she shouted, her voice strong and firm. Commanding. "No. You can't turn away now, de Balboa. You one of us now. It too late for you to go back. Watch, de Balboa. Watch." She dragged him to the edge of the grave and pointed toward Emilia, the drummers and the wailing woman who stood on the other side. "Watch now, de Balboa! Keep your hands from your face. Be a man, de Balboa. Pray with Emilia. Pray."

Antonio twisted his head away from her, but she dug her fingernails into his lower jaw and jerked his face toward Emilia. "Look, de Balboa! Look what she doing to save your wife."

Antonio could have closed his eyes, but her voice, like that of the seductive siren, lured him toward the horror that he knew would revolt him. With open eyes he wished could not see, he saw Emilia jump into the grave, taking the slain cock and the Host with her. He saw her place the beheaded cock on the naked chest of the man lying in the grave. He watched, his vision following her movements in perverse obedience to his eyes, as she brought the Host to the man's lips, chanting some words in a garble of Latin, patois, English and Ibo. Three times Antonio saw the man's body twitch spasmodically and each time afterward he saw Emilia dig her fingers into the sides of the man's mouth, trying to pry his lips apart. And finally, when it seemed that she would never succeed in forcing the Host down his throat, Antonio heard her call out to the man by his name. "Harris! Harris! Harris!" At first Antonio could barely discern the anxiety in her voice but when he saw her look in desperation toward Alma, he knew she was afraid. He felt Alma release him then and he turned in time to see her grab her machete and give it to Emilia.

A single thought crossed Antonio's mind at that moment:

Emilia was going to kill the man in the grave. He was to be their human sacrifice. Cold sweat drenched his back as he felt his impotence, his weakness. He had not even made the slightest gesture to help the man. Why? Because the drummers now stood close to him? Because Alma had warned him before she gave the machete to Emilia to stay exactly where he was? Because, for a brief second before Emilia turned to the man in the grave with the machete in her hand, she looked at him with such pure terror in her eyes that he felt more pity for her than for the man whom he thought was about to be sacrificed? And what was it he pitied? That she was afraid that her obeah had not worked in time to save Marina? Had he also hoped that the obeah would work? Did he not try to wrench the machete from her hand because, after all, after all he felt and all he knew, he would still go further to damn his soul, to be an accomplice in murder to save Marina and himself?

Yet he need not have tormented himself with this possibility, for the machete was not meant to slay the man. Emilia used it to slash open the belly of the cock. Folding her skirt upward to make a pouch, she caught the cock's guts, bloodied and blue and stinking with excrement that still remained in its tiny intestines. The air around her turned foul as if the shit of a thousand cocks lay spread there in her skirt, but Emilia did not seem to notice the stench. She emptied her skirt on the man's belly and squashed the entrails of the cock against his flesh, her fingers moving in large circles around his navel, her eyes bulging from their sockets, bloodshot red. Now she shouted the man's name again. "Harris! Harris!" She tore at the cloth wrapped around his eyes, breaking the circles of white candle wax that adhered to it into tiny, fragile fragments that glowed against the darkness of his face. The man's eyelashes fluttered and Emilia called to him again. "Harris! Harris! Come back, Harris!" She yanked the crown of thorns from his head. Violent tremors ripped through the man's body, but he did not open his eyes nor part his lips. From the edge of the grave Alma, the wailing woman and the drummers now joined Emilia. "Harris! Harris!"

Another long, painful scream reverberated through the trees and yet another longer and more painful than the one before it. For a second Antonio thought that the screams came from a woman, a woman whose voice he knew well. The blood drained from his face. Frantically he searched among the people near him under the shed and through the bushes and trees outside. No one, no one he could see could have made those sounds. Quickly he looked down in the grave just in time to see Emilia place the Host on her tongue and swallow it. She seemed transformed. Her face had grown calm and peaceful, the redness in her eyes vanished. He saw her grab Alma's outstretched hand and hoist herself out of the grave. Then she and Alma stood quietly near the others at the side of the grave, their arms raised above their heads, the palms of their hands stretched open so that their fingers remained spread out like fans above their wrists.

Once again, without warning, another scream wailed through the air. This time Antonio listened carefully. This time he would be certain. And when the scream ended in a breathless hiss as though the screamer had delivered some burden that had caused her pain, Antonio knew. Yes. It was Marina's voice that he had heard. Marina's! The undeniable reality of that fact, beyond any shadow of a doubt, caused him not to question its possibility. How could Marina's voice travel one mile from where she lay to where he now stood? He felt only an increasing sickness in his stomach, bred not only of fear, but of revulsion too for the people before him. And for Marina.

The others seemed to welcome the final scream, to be joyful when it came. Their bodies relaxed, their arms returned to their sides, their eyes sparkled. They laughed with each other. They seemed to forget Antonio's presence and even the man in the grave. They gathered their things swiftly and quietly, Emilia rolling up the bloody sheet in a bundle and tucking it under her arm, one of the drummers climbing down in the grave to remove the bloodied machete from Harris's side, the other drummer and the wailing woman picking up the drums, they followed Alma out of the shed, down the dirt track.

Antonio let them go without a word. He was relieved when they left and he could barely see their backs against the trees. He wanted no part of them, he told himself. He did not belong with them. But soon the reality of the present sunk into his consciousness. They had left him alone with the man they had called Harris. He panicked. Fruitlessly he screamed at them to return, to take Harris back with them. "Harris! Harris! You forgot Harris!" he shouted. "Take Harris with you!" But no one stopped, no one turned around. He looked around him, not knowing what to do. Harris's body, bloodied with the entrails of the cock, glared at him. Marina's screams rent through his memory.

"Harris! Harris!" he shouted. "Enough of this, man! Harris! Come, get out of here! They left you, man. Harris!" But Harris did not move. Antonio jumped into the grave and bent over him, tasting the stink of the cock's excrement on his tongue. He slapped the man's face again and again. "Harris! Harris! Harris!" Harris stayed still, his head lying limp on one side. Frightened, Antonio called him again,

"Harris!" And then almost as if in response, Harris's fingers trembled, his legs twitched, stretched out suddenly and then stiffened to a final rigidity.

Antonio sucked in his breath. A chilling numbness, an unfeeling sensation seized him. He put his ear on the man's chest, knowing he would hear no heartbeat, knowing the futility of his effort. Perhaps—perhaps—he kept saying to himself. Perhaps, perhaps . . . The man's head, which had lain limp to one side of his neck, rolled over to the center and tipped backward into the dirt, probably due to the same spasm that had stretched out his legs, but the movement, sudden as it was, threw open his closed eyelids, and his eyes, dull and glassy like the eyes of fish carted to the market on the ice wagon, locked themselves onto Antonio's. Dead! The man was dead. There was no denying it.

Now, as if the years compressed themselves into a single minute, now as if today he were there at the foot of the altar, the bishop laying his hands on his head, as if today were his Confirmation day, Antonio affirmed aloud the vows he had made that day before God, his mother, the bishop, the priest and the whole church. Yes. Yes, he would renounce Satan and all his works and pomps. Yes. Yes, he would believe in the one true, Catholic and Apostolic Church, in the one true God, the Father, the Son and the Holy Ghost, the infinite mystery of the Church. Yes. Yes. He would denounce obeah. He would not, he could not have any part in the lives of people who dealt with magic, the unexplainable. Yes. Yes. He would renounce them. Murder! They had murdered the man. Cold sweat poured from his temples and made needle-thin rivulets in the mud that had splashed on his face when Emilia had jumped into the grave. He stayed there kneeling next to the dead man, and remembered again his father's fatalistic taunt: "Once a Catholic, always a Catholic."

The cycle had gone full circle. The Jesuit who had rejected his Church had fathered a Catholic.

From the other side of the trees, up the path leading to the de Balboas' house, the scream that Antonio had recognized had long ended. A large, brown-skinned woman with cocoa-brown eyes now guided another bloody baby safely out of Marina's womb. Like his sister, the child cried the second his lungs sucked in air. He kicked his feet, stretched out his fingers and yelled.

The woman laid him on his mother's belly next to his sister, and before his umbilical cord was cut, and before he was washed, the boy felt his mother's warm kisses all over his tiny face. His sister had already been kissed.

It was late when Antonio finally returned to his house— almost ten o'clock. The night sky was dark as it usually is in the rainy season. The stars were vanquished by the clouds; not even the moon could break the darkness that enveloped the earth. Antonio found his way to his house, dodging the pools of water that had collected everywhere and the trunks of trees felled by the hurricane. He heard the cries of the babies the moment he reached his front yard, but he felt nothing, neither joy nor pain. Nothing at all. He climbed the wooden staircase, opened the door and entered his house.

He found the women in his bedroom. Marina called to him, "Antonio! Antonio! Come see them. Come see your son and your daughter."

He gazed blankly at her and said nothing.

"Come! Come!" Marina called to him, cuddling the babies closer to her. "Come! I'm not sick anymore. I'm all right. I forgive you Antonio. Come! I forgive you."

Antonio shifted his eyes around the room, searching. "My mother?" They were the only words that left his lips.

"Gone to Ranjit," the large woman answered quickly.

He seemed to accept her answer. A brief shadow of joy broke his gloom. She was safe. His mother had escaped from them. He looked at his twins, longing perhaps to touch them, his eyes lingering on them, and then as if it took every ounce of his strength, he twisted his body away from them and walked toward the clothes closet.

Marina thought that she saw tears in his eyes and she called him to her again. "Antonio come! Don't turn away."

He pulled a suitcase from the closet.

"What are you doing Antonio? Come here!" Marina repeated softly.

Antonio opened the suitcase, shut it again and then, throwing it back into the closet, he walked toward the door.

"Qui méler zéfs nans calenda ouôches?" Alma whispered in patois as Antonio passed her. He had not seen her sitting there near the entrance of the room. She touched his hand briefly and made him pause. "What right have eggs among rocks when they are dancing?" Her voice was kind and loving.

Antonio wrenched his hand away from hers.

For hours after Antonio left the house, Marina continued to hope that he would return, but early the next morning when she heard the whispered conversations about Harris's death, she knew she would have to go to him to bring him back to her.

She was not surprised that Harris was dead. The gentle woman with cocoa-brown eyes who had come to deliver her twins had told her, while her body was wreathed in pain, that Harris's spirit would soon bring her the Body of Christ and she would be well. Each time the contractions tore through her body, she grabbed onto the woman's words of hope like a drowning person, not caring how she was saved, but that she would be. Yet even then, even in her most desperate moments of pain, she knew that Harris was risking his life for her. She remembered too well that night when her mother took her to Alma's backyard to see her father, who had been long dead. Another man had died then in the attempt to conjure up her father's spirit. Tens of times in her head she repeated to the woman that she did not want Harris to risk his life for her. And each time before she would articulate those words, she'd convince herself that Harris was in no danger, that his spirit would hear Alma calling him back and he would be safe. And after all, had not Harris done this before? He had done it for her when he predicted her illness. It was what he did for many people. But soon the woman sensed Marina's discomfort and sought to console her. "Is not everybody can do what Harris do. Harris has the gift from God. Don't bother yourself, chile. Harris do it willing. He say God give him dis gift special so he could help people. He willing to help you, chile. Harris always say everybody have to die. Is only a matter when. And he say if he was to die dis way, is the best and the happiest way a man could die. So he willing, chile. He willing to help you."

How people change was all the reason Marina could find

for her present acceptance of Harris's death. She would never be the same, she knew, since her mother had caused her spirit to leave her body there, on the bed, as Dr. Glentower made ready to bleed her. At first there was only the first sting of the bitter liquid that her mother poured down the back of her throat, then buzzing, tingling sensation in the tips of her fingers and the soles of her feet, a sense of her insides pressing against her extremities, of her life slipping, oozing out of her. Dying? She thought that she might be dying. But she was not afraid, for she felt Emilia's breath warm and moist against the hairs of her nostrils. Then an incredible peace and calm washed through her being. No pain. She rose out of her body, a feather buoyed by her own breath.

Had Glentower not cut her ankle she would have remained there, hovering above her silent body, not wanting to return to the pain. Except sometimes for Virginia. To comfort her. But when the blood gushed from her ankle and her body weakened, her spirit lurched down toward it in a desperate effort to save her life. The pain returned, but there was the memory of euphoria, of drifting like a weightless cloud, of a freedom that could not be described in human terms. That was what had happened to Harris, she knew. He had journeyed too far from his body and then it was too late. He did not want to return even after he heard Emilia and the others call out to him.

Yet Marina knew that Antonio would see Harris's death differently—that he would call it murder.

"I must find him to talk to him," she pleaded with Emilia.

"No. Let him go. He has made his choice. And he'll never understand or forgive you."

"I could explain it to him. He wouldn't come back if he thinks we killed Harris."

"You don't need a man who don't love you."

"Didn't you see it in his eyes? The way he watched the babies? He didn't want to go."

"You asked him to stay and he left."

"But that was because he didn't understand."

"He never will."

"Neither will the police." Marina did not mean to hurt Emilia. She had made her peace with her. She wanted to shatter her complacency, perhaps. To suggest to her that she was not out of trouble, perhaps. What had she and Alma done with Harris's body? What if the police asked questions? But she saw in the way Emilia's shoulders sagged that she had ripped open the scab of her guilt.

"It was not meant to happen," Emilia said quietly. "Sometimes, sometimes, they forget their word and they don't come back. You were too young to understand the last time. I had to force you not to talk to the police."

"Mother—I didn't mean—"

"There be no police this time." Alma had entered the room. Her voice, sturdy and commanding, stopped Marina's quivering apology, "I seen to dat dis time. There be no police looking for Harris." She placed her arm around Emilia's shoulders and patted her lightly on the forearm. "I went to see Philip Smith and I explain it to him. Don't worry. 'There be no police dis time,' I told him. He pretend he don't understand. Harris, I say to him, Harris he died of natural causes. You write his death certificate now, I say. Philip turn his back to me. He have his money now to go to England. His blood money. Antonio give dat doctor—"

"His blood money?"

"No, Alma! Not yet! It's still too soon!" Emilia rushed between Alma and Marina, afraid of her daughter's question.

Marina stared at her mother. "What, Mother? Too soon for what?"

"Yes, Antonio give him he blood money already," Alma continued.

"What blood money? Mother? Alma?" Marina clutched Alma's arm, turning away from her mother. She did not want to see again the truth in Emilia's eyes. Blood money. It couldn't be true.

She had asked Antonio about the land before her mother brought her peace with her magical liquid. She had accused him of giving it to the doctor. He had not said it was true. Yet, he had not answered her!

"You know, Marina." Alma pinned her eyes on her. "No sense you lying to yourself. I tell your mother you know—"

"Know what?"

"You know what."

"He tried to save you." Emilia reached for her daughter's hand. It wasn't that she felt sorry for Antonio, but that she wanted to soften the blow, quiet Marina's rage. "To him it was the only way."

"The doctor?"

"It was the only way he would come. I could have told him—"

"My land too?" Marina grasped her throat in disbelief.

"Yours and his."

"My five acres?"

"Philip confess it all when I tell him what I had to tell him," said Alma.

"My five acres? My land too?"

Alma looked beyond her. "I warn Philip how he born. I tell him his mother pass she time for making baby and yet she 'ceive him in her womb. Like he know. He watch me white, white, white. His red hair falling all in he face make him look like the devil heself. He didn't deny me. He just start confessing. He say the doctor have papers Antonio sign for him that give him all you land. Yes, dou dou." Alma forced Marina to accept the truth. "And you five acres too."

Marina's mouth opened in a hollow yawn. Her words gurgled in her throat and remained there, stuck between her voice box and the back of her tongue. She could not speak.

"He say the doctor claim it because you en't die and you babies live. Even though he didn't have nothing to do wid it. But it his now. He give Philip blood money and he went home. Then I tell Philip is alright he confess, but he must sign Harris death certificate—say he die natural—and then he can go back to the modder-country or wherever."

21

For weeks, burning with revenge, Marina searched for Antonio. It was her land, her piece of the earth, and he had given it away. The land she had married for, joined forces with obeah for. Her anger rose like a terrible storm throughout the house. She felt betrayed and not only by Antonio, but by herself. She had allowed her emotions to get in her way. She had pitied Antonio when she saw the sadness and gloom in his face the night he left her. Childbirth had softened her toward him. The twins she held in her arms, part of him and part of her, had warmed the distance between them. But no longer. It was not Harris's death that had chased him away from her. It was cowardice! His lack of courage to face her with the truth! Yes, she knew it. She saw the cowardice in his eyes even through her pain. She had lied to herself. The truth? Had she wanted the truth she would have accepted it then when he refused to answer her. She would have asked Virginia to tell her how they paid that English doctor who bled her. What had she hoped? That it was his land alone he had given away? Did she feel safe because she had five acres with her name, Marina E. Heathrow, written on the deed? Had she forgotten the power that he had? That in Trinidad he needed no more than his manhood to dispose of her property as he wished?

Day and night Marina raved, cursing Antonio, cursing all men. Nothing could assuage her fury, even Alma's warnings that the African gods would spite her for her ingratitude if she didn't tend her twins. Was the land much to lose when she had her children? "Is not everybody who could carry twins and birth them alive. You tink is you one who make them live?" Alma's eyes cut deep through Marina's soul. "What obeah giveth, obeah can taketh away, chile."

Nor did Emilia's words move Marina, Emilia who had learned her lesson well.

"It's my fault I made you love land so," Emilia admitted, "but not more than your children. It's a test you get now, Marina. This is your test. Let it go. Make peace with yourself. Come and live with Telly and me. We'll help you."

"No!"

"And what will you do when the government takes back Antonio's house? It's not his. You know that. Come. Your children are your life now. You think I don't know what it is to lose land? You know I know, Marina.

"I put it all behind me and I raised you. You do the same for your children. At least you better off than I was. You have somewhere to go to. Put down your vengeance. Leave it behind you. It can kill you. You not the first or the last woman a man cheated and you not the first or the last woman a man left."

But Marina's anger could not be stilled. Strapping her babies to her bosom, she combed the village, in and out of every dirt track, up and down every road. Anyone—a child, old man, the blind, the mad—she begged for news of Antonio. She swallowed her anger and made the trip to Siparia alone, hoping to persuade Virginia to help her. But she had miscalculated the intensity of the happiness that Virginia now found with Ranjit. No, Virginia told her, she did not know where Antonio was. She had seen him once when he came to say goodbye to her, but she did not try to make him stay. There was someone else who now filled her life. Forget him. Make a life for yourself, Virginia said.

In the end, when the colonial government requested their house (Mr. de Balboa was no longer on their staff), Marina finally surrendered. There was nothing left for her to do but to return to her mother in Princes Town.

In October Marina received an envelope from Antonio postmarked from Port-of-Spain. It contained five twenty-pound notes and a short letter informing her of his intentions to support her and their children. It stated also that he would be sailing to London on the 15th of October, therefore it might be two months or more before she would receive any more money from him. He had instructed his mother to lend her what she needed until she heard from him again.

Still burning with the desire to avenge his betrayal of her, Marina went to Port-of-Spain on October 15th hoping to find Antonio as he boarded the ship in the harbor. She wanted to confront him with her anger, believing that, more than anything else, he wished to avoid that confrontation.

But she was stopped on the road to the harbor by a thick wall of black smoke belching from a roaring fire somewhere in the heart of the upper-class residential district of Port-of-Spain. "A doctor's house," the English policeman told the crowds that he turned away from Port-of-Spain. "A Dr. Glentower's house." Arson, he said it was. Lucky for the doctor, he and his wife escaped.

The Warao had seen it all from behind the large saman tree that stood in front of Dr. Glentower's colonial-style house. He had seen his friend's son by the faint light of the moon—a thief in the night. He had seen him pour the kerosene around Glentower's house.

He had seen him too six weeks before as he walked down the main road of Moruga, heading northward to Port-of-Spain. He saw then in the deep slouch of Antonio's shoulders and the hard lines around his mouth and eyes, the heaviness in his heart, the coldness in his spirit, and though the young man carried no luggage, the Warao knew that his friend's son would not be back. For a brief moment the Warao felt the same urgency to help him as he had done many times before. A man should not leave his wife and newborn babies, he thought. Yet he did nothing. He did not call out to the man. There is a time to do nothing, he said to himself. To let things run their course. But weeks later, the Warao still could not purge his mind of the image of the young man coldly deserting his wife on the day his babies were born. It troubled him to know that Antonio would abandon his children, making the same mistake that his father had made.

Unable to make peace with his conscience, the Warao

decided he would find Antonio and speak to him. He went directly to Glentower's house, driven by a dream his wife had had the night before. She saw the medicine man on fire, she said, burning and burning in flames that no one could put out. So when the Warao saw Antonio dousing the doctor's house with a liquid, he did not have to be told it was kerosene. Yet, again he did not stop his friend's son. Antonio was not a boy. But after the flames began to ravish the house, he went to where he saw his friend's son stooped behind the thorny bougainvillea bush and asked him why.

"Yesterday I begged him to give the five acres back to Marina," Antonio told the Warao. "It was not mine to give, I told him. Then too he had not helped her. But he laughed and called me a fool. Then he went to his room and brought back the papers I had signed. I was surprised to see he had kept them in the house. I thought he had already registered them. I took the chance again to appeal to his honesty. I said it would be a simple matter for us to change the papers now. We could just strike out the part where I gave him Marina's land. He could have the rest. But he laughed again and waved the papers in my face. Why should he give away his money to Marina? Those five acres would make her rich. I was too stupid, he said, to see that the oil was valuable. The land that I gave him would make him richer than I would ever know. I didn't care for the money. I knew how much Marina wanted the land. I asked him again. Monday, he said, Monday he will register the papers in the Red House. His wife had been sick so he didn't have a chance to register them yet. But he would on Monday. I tried to warn him then. I told him that Marina used obeah to get the five acres of land from me. I told him obeah saved Marina and the babies, not him. Then he became angry and threatened to call the police. There was nothing else I could do. I had to destroy the papers. I had to burn down his house."

That night the Warao helped Antonio sneak past the crowds circling Glentower's home so that he could safely board the ship bound for England.

"This will make you a partner in my crime," Antonio protested unconvincingly when the Warao pulled out a knife to shave off his mustache.

"One colored person from the other, they won't know. But the doctor would have the police looking for a Negro with a mustache," the Warao insisted.

"But you don't have to help me."

"I do no more for you than your father did for me."

"How many times I wanted to ask why you always came to protect me."

"Your father spoke my language."

"Surely that was not enough."

"You don't understand. He took the time to learn my language. He didn't ask me to speak his."

"No, I don't understand."

"He was my friend."

"And you'll risk going to prison for that?"

"There is more." The Warao took a deep breath. He stopped shaving Antonio. "He saved me once. A long time ago when the coast guards stopped my pirogue right out on the sea. I was going back to my village, but I was still in British waters between here and Venezuela, you see, and they could stop me if they wanted to. They had stopped us before, but just to warn us not to come back. But that day they were drunk and they wanted a Warao for their fun. I was with but two of my men and there were five of them. They had guns. They pulled us into their boat and began to abuse us with their sticks. They forced our mouths open and poured rum down our throats. Then they made us dance for them." The Warao hung his head low.

"You needn't tell me more," said Antonio, feeling the Warao's shame.

"Yes. I want to tell you what your father did so you'll understand. A fisherman saw what they were doing to us and he told the people in Moruga. Your father got the fishermen to take him in his boat to where we were. I think it was his white skin that saved us. Though maybe they were too drunk to fight him. He made them believe that he was sent by the warden to bring us back to Moruga. They didn't want to release us at first, but he gave them money. Then they let us go. If your father had not come, they would have killed us that night."

After the Warao saw the ship that carried Antonio steam out of the Port-of-Spain harbor, he went to where he had hidden his pirogue behind some rocks off a bay near Carenage and from there he rowed to his rain forest in Venezuela. It was over now, he knew. The time had passed for the friendships he once had in Trinidad. Things would never be the same. De Balboa was dead, Antonio was gone and Emilia would not need him again. And in time Glentower would have the police looking for him too. Yes, it was time now for him to leave Trinidad forever. It was time for him and his men to find new trading grounds. No more would the odor of their shark-oiled bodies offend the Trinidad air. He was not bitter. Yet he knew that before long he would be forgotten. Before the next generation would feel the urgent stirrings between their legs to breed another race, before hair would grow on the chin of the man-child, before breasts would bud on the impatient chest of the female child, the mothers and fathers would use his people's name to frighten their sons and daughters into civilization. They would look at the man-child dancing in the rain, his legs splashed with mud, his shirt off, his pants torn, and they would shout at him, "Come out of the rain, you hear me? You little Warahoon!" And they would smell the female child, oblivious of the new odors pressing out of her body, so eager to play that she forgets the pot soda—the deodorant—and they would say, "Come here, Mildred. Go wash yourself and put some pot soda under your arms. You stink like a Warahoon." And in time, when it would become fashionable, they would talk about the Caribs who lived in Trinidad and the Arawaks who were there before them, and they would talk with pride about the battles these Amerindians fought against the Spaniards and the French. And one will ask, "What did you say—the Warahoons? Who?" And one will answer, "That's what we call filthy, crude children."

But the Warao forgave them all. He knew the days of the great chiefs were over and he sought the compassion of the tall, majestic forest trees of Venczuela which remembered too well.

In December of the following year, the flower buds on the cocoa trees turned hard and dry on their dying stems and fell like tiny teardrops on the murky pools of oil that lay around the bases of their tree trunks. Up the sides of the hills, the poui, angered by the untimely death of the cocoa flowers, pushed out their carnival of colors from the tips of their leafless branches, heroically defying the decay in the valleys beneath them with the promise of a season of unparalleled beauty. Despair and hope. The vegetation, like the people, either succumbed to the sterility the oil engendered or readied themselves to do battle with the earth.

For many of the cocoa planters it was all over that December; all their hopes for draining the land free of the oil, all their prayers for hurricanes that would wash the oil from out of the earth. Marina was among the few who refused to despair. Learning by letter from Antonio that he had destroyed the proof of Glentower's claim to her land, and fueled by dreams, she never surrendered. She fought for her barren land in Tabaquite until Glentower, neither having papers to prove his purchase of the land from Antonio, nor being able to persuade Philip Smith to testify for him, finally was forced to give in to her.

Marina E. Heathrow had her land at last. It was what she had always wanted.

ABOUT THE AUTHOR

Trinidad-born, **Elizabeth Nunez-Harrell** is a tenured professor in the Humanities Department at Medgar Evers College, the City University of New York. Dr. Nunez-Harrell now makes her home in New York State.

A CELEBRATION OF
BLACK LITERATURE

 MANY CULTURES ONE WORLD

___LONG DISTANCE LIFE, Marita Golden
This is the moving saga of an African-American family, from the great
migration north to the urban nightmare of today.   37616/$10.00

___MUSE-ECHO BLUES, Xam Cartiér
This lyrical celebration of the spirit of African-American life and music by
the author of *Be-Bop, Re-Bop* takes place in San Francisco in the 1990s.
                                                          37762/$9.00

___NO MAN IN THE HOUSE, Cecil Foster
This is a moving and beautifully written coming-of-age story of an
impoverished young boy in Barbados during its 1963 bid for independence.
                                                 38067/$17.00 (hardcover)

___TREE OF LIFE, Maryse Condé
The author of *Segu* and *Children of Segu* returns to her native Guadeloupe
for a multigenerational story of one 20th-century West Indian family's
attempts to escape a life filled with poverty and racism.
                                                 36074/$18.00 (hardcover)

___WHEN ROCKS DANCE, Elizabeth Nunez-Harrell
A chronicle of the struggles between English traders, African slaves and
indigenous Amerindians in turn-of-the-century Trinidad.   38068/$10.00

Name_____

Address_____

City_____ State_____Zip_____

Please send me the BALLANTINE BOOKS I have checked above. I am
enclosing $_____. (Please add $3.00 for the first book and $.50 for
each additional book for postage and handling and include the appropriate
state sales tax.) Send check or money order (no cash or C.O.D.'s) to
Ballantine Mail Sales Dept. OW, (8-4), 201 E. 50th St., NY, NY 10022.

To order by phone, call 1-800-733-3000 and use your major credit card.

Prices and numbers are subject to change without notice.
Valid in the U.S. only.
All orders are subject to availability.
20   Allow at least 4 weeks for delivery.   7/92   TA-292